There was quite a crowd outside, reluctant to return home since hearing the fateful news. One or two were glancing up at the skies, as if already expecting to see enemy planes loaded with bombs to drop on Bootle. Tony and Dominic, both wearing their gas masks, were playing at being aeroplanes, arms outstretched as they swooped on each other. When everyone saw Francis Costello emerge in his uniform, they clustered around, shaking his hand and wishing him well. Annie Poulson, who had her arms around a sobbing Rosie Gregson, looked more angry than upset. Her lads were in Aldershot and she was probably wondering when she'd see them again. Sheila emerged clutching the new baby, Mary, and came across to say goodbye to Francis.

Francis reached for his wife with his free arm and, in a dramatic gesture, swung her towards him. He kissed her long and hard on the lips and everyone cheered.

'Tara, luv,' he said, releasing her.

Suddenly, Eileen felt it was all too much. She burst into tears.

'Don't worry, Sis, he'll be back.'

Maureen Lee was born in Bootle and now lives in Colchester, Essex. She has had numerous short stories published and a play staged. *Stepping Stones, Liverpool Annie, Dancing in the Dark, The Girl from Barefoot House, Laceys of Liverpool, The House by Princes Park, Lime Street Blues, Queen of the Mersey, The Old House on the Corner, The September Girls, Kitty and Her Sisters, The Leaving of Liverpool* and the three novels in the Pearl Street series, *Lights Out Liverpool, Put Out the Fires* and *Through the Storm* are all available in Orion paperback. Her novel *Dancing in the Dark* won the Parker Romantic Novel of the Year Award. Her latest novel in hardback, *Mother of Pearl*, is also available from Orion. Visit her website at www.maureenlee.co.uk.

Lights Out Liverpool

Maureen Lee

An Orion Paperback
First published in Great Britain
by Orion in 1995
This paperback edition published in 1996
by Orion Books Ltd,
Orion House, 5 Upper St Martin's Lane,
London WC2H 9EA

An Hachette Livre UK company

A CIP catalogue record for this book
is available from the British Library.

Typeset at The Spartan Press Ltd,
Lymington, Hants
Printed and bound in Great Britain by
Clays Ltd, St Ives plc

The Orion Publishing Group's policy is to use papers that
are natural, renewable and recyclable products and
made from wood grown in sustainable forests. The logging
and manufacturing processes are expected to conform to
the environmental regulations of the country of origin.

www.orionbooks.co.uk

For David, the first one

Acknowledgments

The following very kindly wrote to me following my letter in the Liverpool *Echo*, to tell me of their experiences during the Second World War. I shall always remain grateful that they were willing to share that extraordinary part of their lives with me.

Mrs V. Armstrong, Alf Blackburn, Tom Brady, Peter Carlin, Margaret Clansey, Jim Collins, Barbara Darlington, Allan Ferris, Cathy Hankin, Mrs E. Jackson, Mary Leatherbarrow, Ken Livesey, Robert McDougall, Mr R. J. McMillan, William Monaghan, Sonny Rafferty, Rita Rees, Roy Stancombe, Mr H. J. Sowden, George A. Turrell, Max Wilson, Mrs M. Wright.

The poem, THE GATE OF THE YEAR, was written by Miss Minnie Haskins in 1908.

Chapter 1

The home-made bunting crisscrossed the little street from roof to roof, fluttering gently in the soft breath of a perfect late summer day. Half a dozen trestle tables, covered with an assortment of best damask tablecloths, had been set down the centre and strewn with ringlets of bright paper streamers. The tables groaned under the weight of trifles and jellies, plates piled high with sandwiches, home-made sausage rolls and confectionery. Squares of bead-edged muslin protected the food from the wasps and bluebottles which buzzed greedily overhead.

Mary and Joey Flaherty and their three children were going to live in Canada, leaving Bootle forever for a new life in a new country, and throwing a street party on their final Saturday as a gesture of farewell.

The children, almost out of their minds with excitement and waiting impatiently to be called for the first sitting, filled in the time by darting to and fro in search of tar bubbles on the cobbled surface of the street, caused by the relentless heat of the noon sun which poured down out of a cloudless blue sky. When a bubble was found, there'd be a shrill yell of triumph – 'You wanna see the size o'*this* one!' – and it would be burst with an already blackened thumb.

The grown-ups, equally excited, hid their feelings behind wide smiles and a general air of enjoyment, though their happiness was tempered by the fearful knowledge of what was going on outside their little world. That madman Adolf Hitler seemed intent on taking over all of

1

Europe and gradually, unbelievably, Great Britain was being drawn into the war.

Only the other day, anyone listening to the wireless had been astounded to hear Members of Parliament being urgently recalled to Westminster. Stomachs churned as people sat there expecting to hear hostilities were about to break out any minute. Two days later, the Emergency Powers Act had been passed, giving the Government total control over the lives of its people. Then yesterday, the BBC had announced there would be special extra news bulletins in the morning and afternoon.

In the homes of Army, Navy and RAF reservists, official-looking envelopes containing their recall notices had begun to arrive, and the Territorial Army was mobilised. Already, thousands of young men not yet out of their teens had been called up and were waiting, ready to fight for their country if need be. People felt as if they were on a train heading for a precipice and there was nothing they could do to stop it.

But the residents of Pearl Street were determined not to let this spoil their party, perhaps the last street party they would hold for a long, long time. The women seemed to have taken an unspoken vow not to talk about it. They resolutely pushed to the back of their minds, for today at least, the hideous gas masks collected from the Town Hall, the freshly-built brick shelters to which they were supposed to go in the unimaginable event of an air raid, the impending blackout and food rationing, and the barrage balloon suspended above the bowling green next to Bootle Hospital which looked so pretty, like a silver flower floating in the sky, yet was there for such a grim purpose. In their best frocks and their Sunday pinnies, the women bustled in and out of their own and their neighbours' houses carrying yet more refreshments. Although the

2

Flahertys had provided the ingredients, Mary couldn't be expected to prepare food for twenty-nine children and over forty adults, not all on her own.

The men who didn't work on Saturdays, or didn't work at all, were less inhibited. Many had already become voluntary ARP wardens or joined the Auxiliary Fire Service, and several of the younger ones were expecting their call-up papers at any minute. They stood in little groups, some playing pitch and toss, and from time to time preventing children from other streets from entering, and war was their sole topic of conversation. Despite this, they too seemed to have been affected by the gladness of the day; laughing more than usual and snapping their fingers or tapping their feet as if to music. Although none could be persuaded into their best suits – if they had one – most wore a collar and tie despite the scorching heat. The men had already done their bit towards the party, having collected the borrowed tables from the Holy Rosary Church Hall and put them up. As far as they were concerned, the rest was women's work.

Most of the front doors were wide open and the old people sat on their steps, sunning themselves, mouths watering at the sight of the food, wishing the women would hurry up and feed the children so it would be their turn to sit down. In the doorway of his lodgings at Number 10, big Paddy O'Hara sat nursing his little dog, Spot, in his arms. Paddy, not old, but blind for more than half his life, was sensually aware of the clatter of the women's shoes on the pavement, their varying scents, the swish of their skirts as they buzzed to and fro.

'Ah, 'tis a fine day Joey picked for his do,' he said to no-one in particular.

'It is that, Paddy,' replied Eileen Costello, who caught his words as she emerged from Number 16 carrying two plates of tomato and meatpaste sandwiches. Slim and graceful in her best blue crepe de Chine dress, her long fair hair tied back with a white ribbon, Eileen felt conscious of the heady, electric atmosphere in the street, though she could never have described it. Everywhere just seemed more than usually alive. There was a swing in her step as she took the plates over to the table.

Her sister Sheila, who lived opposite, came up carrying Ryan, her youngest child aged ten months, on her hip. Her pretty dimpled face was covered in perspiration. 'I'm sweating like a cob, Sis.' She nodded towards the little flags rippling above them. 'I wish we could get a bit of that wind down here before I bake to death.'

The heat was palpable. The ruddy chimneys, the grey slate roofs turned silver by the dazzling light, and the neat cobbled ground, seemed to shimmer, actually seemed to move if you stared hard enough, and Pearl Street, a cul-de-sac, was indeed like an oven, hemmed in by red brick terraced houses, fifteen each side, and the blackened, pitted roof-high wall at one end which separated the street from the railway lines beyond. The trains, now electric, ran three an hour during the day; to Liverpool city centre one way and Southport the other.

'Here, let me take him.' Eileen reached for the rosy baby. He went to her willingly and immediately began to pull at her hair. 'Y'shouldn't be cartin' him around, not in your condition.' Sheila was heavily pregnant with her sixth child, which was due in ten days' time.

'Those jellies'll be melted if they don't eat them soon,' Sheila said, wiping her brow. 'I hope the kids hurry up, I'm starving hungry.'

A few yards away, Mary Flaherty suddenly clapped her hands and shouted, 'C'mon, you little buggers, sit down, and don't forget your paper 'ats.'

The muslin covers were hurriedly removed as the giggling children scrambled for their chairs like little maniacs. Their voices rose angrily, demanding to sit next to one person, refusing to sit next to another. Eileen, holding Ryan, watched her own son Tony, who was five, slip into a chair without any argument. He sat waiting, wearing an orange paper crown, his hands folded on his lap, looking like a little wise owl in his wire-rimmed glasses. Tony had been well drilled in good manners, though not by her. Whilst he sat quietly, twenty or more hands reached for a sandwich.

'STOP!' thundered Mary Flaherty, and the hands paused mid-air. 'We haven't said grace.'

Heads were meekly bowed whilst Mary muttered, 'For what we are about to receive, may the good Lord make us truly thankful. Amen.'

Tony searched for his mam amongst the crowd who were watching benignly as the children fell upon the food – it was rarely that they sat down to such a feast. Eileen caught her son's eye and gave a slight nod and he took a sandwich. 'Poor Tony,' she thought. 'He's like a little trained puppy compared to all the rest.'

Ellis Evans, stout and red-cheeked, wearing the stiff blue brocade frock she'd bought for her sister's wedding ten years ago, said in her Welsh sing-song voice, 'There's two chairs empty. Who's missing?'

The children were hurriedly counted. Only twenty-seven.

'The Tuttys aren't here . . .' Annie Poulson, Eileen's special friend, raised her fine arched eyebrows questioningly. 'What should we do? Oh, I suppose we'd better get them.'

Everyone nodded, albeit reluctantly. The presence of the Tutty children would slightly flaw their perfect jewel of a day.

'I'll go,' Eileen offered. The Tuttys lived next door to her, so she had more to do with them than most.

'Oh, Mam, I don't want them sitting next to me,' Myfanwy Evans whined. 'They stink something awful.'

There was an immediate general shuffling of seats so no child would be left with an empty chair beside them, which was of course impossible, whilst Eileen hurried down the street to Number 14.

Gladys Tutty opened the door to her knock.

'The party's started. There'll be nowt left for Freda and Dicky if they don't come soon.'

No-one was well off in Pearl Street, but people had their pride. No matter how poor they were, they kept their houses, inside and out, as clean as humanly possible. The Tuttys' house stood out like a sore thumb amidst its immaculate neighbours with its grimy, cracked and curtainless windows, its unscrubbed step. The front door, a mass of peeling brown paint, had a scabrous look.

Eileen stood there, still clutching Ryan, repelled as always by the sight that met her and the smell that wafted out from her neighbour's house. The bare boards in the little narrow hallway were broken and eaten away by rot, and the varnished anaglypta wallpaper was worn more off the wall than on, revealing round sores of filthy crumbling plaster. Every corner was caked with inch-thick hardened dirt.

And, to complete this picture of wretchedness and poverty, there was Gladys. Gladys, in the clothes she wore every day which Eileen had never once seen washed and hanging on the line to dry; a jersey thick with foodstains, fuzzy with sweat underneath the arms, and a long black cotton skirt. Gladys was the only woman in the street who still wore a black shawl when she went out. Her little

6

peaked face, grey, with the texture of rotting rubber, wore a look of utter hopelessness, as if the heart had gone out of her a long time ago.

'I got nothing to give,' she mumbled in her low expressionless voice.

'You don't have to, luv,' Eileen said cheerfully. 'It's all free and there's places already set for Freda and Dicky.' She was uncomfortably conscious of her smart best dress with its puffed sleeves and heartshaped neckline and her sparkling white sandals; of the happy healthy baby on her arm who was cooing as he tried to get his mouth around her pearl stud earring. Eileen felt a world away from this poor little drab woman in the doorway. She stepped back, in the hope of avoiding the stink of decay and unwashed clothes which seemed doubly strong on such a hot day, and turned to look at the women in the street, the children eating, as if to make sure her own world was still there, waiting for her quick return.

Two barefoot scraggy urchins emerged hand in hand from the back of the house and stood behind their mother: Freda and Dicky, their mean narrow faces scabbed and bruised. Freda's cotton frock, which might once have been pink, was now a grimy grey. Eileen knew that beneath the dress the ten-year-old girl wore no underclothes of any description. Dicky, three years younger, had on a pair of thick flannel shorts and a grubby vest.

Freda muttered, 'Wanna go to the party.'

Eileen sensed desperation in the girl's hoarse voice. 'In that case,' she said brightly, 'go and wash your face and hands and find your shoes, and I'll get a plate of butties ready for you.'

The door closed without a word and Eileen thankfully returned to the party, where the tables were rapidly being emptied. The jelly and custard stage had been reached, though plenty of sandwiches still remained. Her eyes searched for Tony. To her relief, he seemed to have forgotten his inhibitions and was devouring food with as much enthusiasm as the other children. She noticed two chairs standing vacant, close together, separated from the others by several feet. Kids could be very cruel, she thought. She stood Ryan on one of the chairs and gave him a fairy cake, then, holding him by the waist, one-handedly heaped two paper plates with food.

'They're coming, then?' Annie came across to help. Annie looked particularly smart today, in a flowered silk two piece that fitted her slight, delicate figure perfectly. Eileen was the only one who knew the suit had cost just seven and sixpence in Paddy's Market. Annie's equally delicate oval face was etched with rather more lines than one would expect to see on a woman of thirty-eight. That, and her rough red chapped hands, which no amount of Nivea cream could return to their original white, were the only indication of the hard life Annie had led since her husband had been killed on the railways a month before her twin lads were born. In the long process of bringing up her sons without assistance from anybody, Annie had gone out and scrubbed more floors and washed more clothes than the rest of the women in the street put together.

Eileen nodded. 'I told 'em to get washed. They both looked as if they'd been up the chimney.'

Annie gave a rueful smile. 'I don't envy the family that gets Freda and Dicky evacuated on them.'

Two women began to bustle around removing the empty pudding dishes, followed by another who placed a clean paper plate in front of each child.

Freda and Dicky Tutty came out, each wearing a pair of tattered Wellington boots. Neither looked as if they'd

8

been within a mile of soap and water. Eileen plucked Ryan out of the way and showed them where to sit. Then she glanced around, searching for her sister. Sheila was sitting on the doorstep, keeping an eye on her four older children, making sure they behaved properly at the table. She looked exhausted but happy, her hands resting on her vastly swollen belly. Eileen went over.

'You'd better take Ryan for a while, Sheil, while I help with the washing up. Shall I put his reins on and hook him on the gate?'

Sheila's husband, Calum, had built a slide-in gate which fitted in the doorway to keep the younger children safe inside.

'Do y'mind, Sis? I haven't got the energy to hold him and he'll scream blue murder if he's stuck inside.'

The reins were hanging over the gate and Eileen buckled them on to the reluctant baby and sat him on the pavement. He immediately began to crawl away, straining against the leather straps. Both women laughed.

Eileen looked down at her sister wonderingly. Sheila never ceased to amaze her. They'd never been close as children, having little in common. Whilst Eileen stayed in, her head buried in a book or listening to plays on the wireless, her flighty, featherbrained younger sister was out having a good time with a never-ending stream of boys. Until seven years ago, that is, when she'd met Calum Reilly and fallen deeply and madly in love. To Eileen's surprise, Sheila had settled down to married life with Calum as if it were the role she'd been waiting to play since she was born. Her sunny contented nature seemed to expand and grow in order to encompass her ever-increasing family within its loving sphere. It was only the last few weeks of each pregnancy that wore her down, the baby pushing and kicking inside her womb, heavy and debilitating.

'I wish our Cal was here,' Sheila said wistfully. 'He's coming home next Thursday, and y'know how much he loves a party.'

That was another thing, thought Eileen. It wasn't as if Sheila had her husband there for most of the time. Calum Reilly was in the Merchant Navy and away at least ten months of the year.

'Never mind, luv.' Eileen briefly stroked her sister's untidy brown curls. 'I'd better set to and help with the washing up, else I'll have people calling me names behind me back.'

She walked down the street to Mary Flaherty's and found half a dozen women crowded in the tiny, steaming back kitchen washing and drying dishes, and twice as many in the living room having a quick ciggie before starting work again.

'You lazy buggers,' she cried. 'And here was us thinking I was slacking off having a chat with our Sheila.'

'Did y'see the way them Tutty children ate at the table, Eileen?' demanded Agnes Donovan from Number 27. Aggie was a terrible gossip. No-one was safe from her vicious tongue and Eileen avoided the woman whenever she could. When Eileen shook her head, Aggie went on breathlessly, 'Like little animals they were, stuffing food in their mouths with both hands like they'd never eaten in their lives before. Greedy little buggers! I've never seen anything like it,' she finished in an aggrieved voice.

'I don't suppose they know any better, poor mites,' Eileen said reasonably, but Aggie persisted. If it wasn't the kids' fault, then it was their mam's.

'I'm surprised Gladys had the gall to let them out,' she complained. 'Mrs Crean wouldn't let her two mongol lads come because she doesn't trust their table manners.'

Eileen reckoned Phoebe Crean was probably keeping

Harry and Owen out of sight of gawpers like Agnes Donovan, who seemed to get enjoyment from other people's misfortunes. She ignored the woman and asked Mary Flaherty if there was anything she could do, 'Seeing as how all the available help seems to have gone on strike.'

'Once the kids have finished, you can clear the tables, Eileen,' Mary told her, smiling. 'Then give the cloths a shake and turn them over so they're fresh for us when we sit down to our grub in about half an hour, like. Our Joey's going to organise some games in the meantime.' As Eileen was leaving, Mary followed her into the hall. 'And oh, is your feller back yet with the ale?'

'Not yet,' Eileen replied. 'He doesn't finish work till two o'clock, then someone's giving him a lift back in a car and they're collecting it on the way.'

Mary squeezed her hand. 'He's a dead good sport, your Francis, Joey's really made up. We could never have afforded so much ale if Francis hadn't been able to get it half price.'

Outside, the children had become restless. Seemingly unaffected by the almost suffocating heat and satiated with food, they were hurling paper plates and streamers at each other. Some had already left their seats and were playing tick round and round the table.

Eileen yelled, 'Behave yourselves!' and ducked to dodge a plate meant for the child beside her. She noticed Sheila grinning at her from the doorstep and made a face back. The Tuttys, isolated from the others on their separate chairs, were still gorging themselves. 'And you two have had enough. You'll be sick if you eat any more.' They stared at her resentfully, their open mouths full of half-chewed bunloaf, as she began to clear the table. Joey Flaherty came up groaning, 'This is the bit I've been dreading. Come on, youse lot, fetch your seats down this end and put 'em in a circle, and we'll play musical chairs.'

'Best of luck, Joey,' Eileen smiled, shooing away a couple of cats who were about to jump on the table in search of scraps.

In Number 3, Mr Singerman shoved his parlour window up as far as it would go and began to play a brisk march on the piano. A minute or so later, the music stopped abruptly and Eileen noticed her Tony, hanging back as ever, was the first to be out. A good job Francis wasn't around to see him lose. Tony came up, looking tearful. 'I didn't like pushing anybody, Mam.'

'All right, luv, it's only a game,' she soothed. 'C'mon, take these into Mary's, then you can help us turn the cloths over.' In a while, there'd be more children out and he'd have someone to play with. She noticed Freda Tutty, Wellington boots flapping against her skinny legs, was dragging Dicky around the circle of chairs by the hand, an almost fanatical expression on her little pinched face. When the music stopped, Freda swung Dicky onto a chair and bagged the next one for herself by the simple expedient of removing the boy already on it with a vicious shove of her bony hip. The boy – it was Sheila's eldest, Dominic – caught his head on the neighbouring chair before landing on the ground. He stood up, blood pouring from a cut on his forehead, and began to yell. Sheila struggled wearily up from the step where she was sitting. Angry at his precious day being spoilt, Joey Flaherty gave Freda a sharp slap on the wrist. The girl stared at him mutinously, eyes full of hate, then dragged her brother down the entry beside the coalyard at the end of the street to go indoors by the back way.

There was a general sigh of relief. Eileen's own relief was mixed with a sense of guilt. Always, she felt as if she should do something about the Tuttys, but never knew what. When she and Francis had taken Number 16 after they got married, the sound of poor Gladys being used as a punchbag by Eddie, her now long-departed husband, had upset her terribly. But Francis had refused to let her tell the Bobbies. 'It's none of our business, Eileen. Anyway, the Bobbies won't do nowt. He's not breaking any laws.' Now it was Freda and Dicky's turn to take the beatings. Gladys had learnt a thing or two from Eddie.

Eileen assuaged her conscience a little by resolving to take a plate of butties and a glass of ale along to Number 14 later on, though Gladys'd far prefer a bottle of gin. Everyone knew the lengths Gladys would go to for a bottle of gin when her Public Assistance money ran out.

Suddenly a cheer went up from the men on the corner, and she glanced across. A black car had stopped at the end of the street. The driver was Rodney Smith, a young man with a cherubic face who worked as a rent collector for Bootle Council. As Eileen watched, a tall figure got out of the passenger seat, a handsome man with a fine head of black wavy hair who beamed at everyone in sight. Francis! He pulled down the boot and began to struggle with something inside. The waiting men went eagerly to help, and a few minutes later a large barrel was rolled down Pearl Street. The ale had arrived.

The day wore on. The vivid sun grew larger, turned from bright yellow to musky gold, as it made its slow and inevitable journey across the gently changing sky, and a line of shadow began to creep across the cobbles of Pearl Street, sharply separating the light from the dark, though the air grew no cooler. Indeed, by late afternoon it seemed more suffocating than ever. The grown-ups had long finished their meal, the tables had been cleared and the cloths removed so they wouldn't get drink spilt on them, though most of the men sat on the pavement with their backs against the walls of the houses. The younger children began to grow tired and tetchy. Many of the older ones had disappeared, having gone to other streets to find their friends. Brenda Mahon's little girls were pushing round the home-made dolls' pram that they were usually only allowed to bring outside on Sundays. Sheila had put Ryan to bed, leaving the window open in case he woke and began to cry. Her next youngest, Caitlin, had fallen asleep in her arms.

The King's Arms pub on the corner of the street opened its doors, and some customers brought their drink outside to join the party.

At six o'clock, Miss Brazier came wearily around the corner, home from her job in the Co-Op Haberdashery Department, where she sat all day in a glass cage at the receiving end of little metal cannisters containing cash which whizzed across the shop on wires stretching in every direction. Miss Brazier would unscrew the cannister, remove the money, and send it back with the change.

'We've plenty of butties left, Miss Brazier,' Mary Flaherty said generously. 'Would you like us to make you a cup of tea, like?'

'No, thank you,' Miss Brazier said stiffly, scarcely glancing in their direction. Head bent, she made her way to Number 12 and disappeared inside.

'Poor ould soul,' said Mary sympathetically. 'I bet she'd love to join us, y'know, but she can't bring herself to unbend.'

'She's not so old,' Eileen said. 'No more than thirty-five, I reckon.'

Like Miss Brazier, not everyone in Pearl Street had condescended to join in the festivities. The Harrisons, who owned the coalyard at the end of the street and lived in the house next door, hadn't deigned to come – Edna Harrison told someone she thought street parties were 'common'. Nor Alfie Robinson from 22, a solid Orange-man, who'd never spoken to Joey Flaherty since he'd discovered one of Joey's brothers was in the IRA. The Kellys weren't there, either, May and her brothers, Fin and Failey, who were Eileen's other neighbours. The Kellys went into town shoplifting on Saturdays and stayed till late doing a tour of the city pubs to sell the loot – if they hadn't been nicked first. The Kellys stole to order; give them the size and the colour and they'd pinch the goods from Marks & Spencer or C & A for half the ticket price.

A trickle of people began to arrive; George Ransome, a middle-aged bachelor with a dashing pencil thin moustache, who worked in Littlewoods Pools, appeared with two bottles of cream sherry. 'A little treat for the ladies,' he said with a wink, and there was a rush indoors for glasses. Then Dilys Evans, only fourteen, looking worn out from her new job as a chambermaid in the Adelphi Hotel in Liverpool.

Soon afterwards, Sheila whispered to her sister, 'I feel as if I'd like a lie down, Sis.'

Eileen nodded. 'I'll be in later and help you settle the kids.' Caitlin had woken up by then, and Sheila led the tiny girl indoors by the hand.

The sky dimmed, turned to mauve, as dusk began to fall and the great orange ball of the sun slowly dipped behind a ridge of roofs, leaving chimneys silhouetted, stark and black, against its fiery brilliance before it disappeared altogether. Then the stars came out; just one at first, then another, and almost within the blinking of an eye, overhead became a blanket of twinkling yellow lights. At long last the air began to freshen and turn cool and the lamplighter arrived, propping his ladder against the arms of the lamppost on the corner by the pub. The gas jet began to splutter and fizz and gave off an eerie glow.

'Be out of a job soon,' he said mournfully as he was about to leave. 'Once the bloody blackout comes.'

And still they sat, talking quietly now, unwilling to let the day go; as if the longer they stayed, the longer it would take tomorrow to come, because nobody in their right mind wanted what tomorrow might bring. Dancing had been planned for after dark, the polka and *Knees Up Mother Brown* and the *Gay Gordons* – Mr Singerman had been practising all week – but somehow no-one felt like dancing. Instead, they listened to the haunting sound of Paddy O'Hara on his harmonica, the music quivering like invisible birds in the yellow-hued night air.

The glitter of the day had gone. Reality had set in.

'When are you sailing, Joey?' someone shouted across the street.

'Next Sat'day, on the *Athenia*,' Joey replied.

'We're going steerage,' put in Mary hastily, as if worried folks might think they'd booked a first-class cabin.

'Looks like you're getting out just in time.'

Joey flushed angrily. 'We've been saving for years to go to Canada. Me brother Kevin's already in Ontario.'

'D'you know who's taking on the house, Joey?' asked Ellis Evans, who lived next door.

'No-one yet, luv,' Joey answered. 'The landlord's agent said he'll have a job renting out a house in Bootle, because – well, you know why.'

They knew only too well. When war broke out, Bootle, with its multiplicity of docks and being the nearest British port to the Americas, would be one of the prime targets for Hitler's bombs. There was a long silence as they contemplated the awfulness of this.

'It mightn't happen', Eileen said eventually in a small voice. 'There's still time.' The situation had been building up for years like a pot gradually simmering on a stove. Now, with Hitler about to invade Poland, the pot was threatening to boil over. Surely he wouldn't go ahead, she thought desperately, not when he knew what the consequences would be? Having guaranteed Polish independence, Great Britain and France would consider invasion as an act of war against themselves and be forced to retaliate.

Eileen was uncomfortably aware of Francis glaring in her direction. Her husband didn't like her drawing attention to herself in company. She was beginning to wish she hadn't spoken, when a figure appeared under the flickering gas lamp. Her dad!

'Jack! Jack Doyle.' Joey Flaherty jumped to his feet, his face wreathed in smiles. 'You should've come before, Jack. Sit down, mate.'

There was a genuine chorus of welcome from the assembled crowd, and Eileen felt a surge of pride. Jack Doyle was one of the best liked and most respected men in the whole of Bootle.

'It was a Pearl Street do,' he said stiffly. 'It wouldn't've been right when it weren't my street.'

He touched his daughter's shoulder lightly and Eileen looked up, expecting some sort of greeting. Instead, he asked gruffly, 'Where's our Sheila?'

'She was a bit tired, she went indoors a while ago.' As ever, she felt let down. 'I could be invisible as far as me dad's concerned,' she thought bitterly. She recalled the wedding photograph on the sideboard in the house in Garnet Street, her mam, dimpled and smiling, the spitting image of Sheila. Since Mam died so unexpectedly of breast cancer fourteen years ago, her father seemed to have transferred almost the entire weight of his affections onto her sister. Her younger brother, Sean, only two when Mam died, had managed to stake a small claim on his dad's heart, but Eileen felt as if she didn't exist at all, yet she loved him so much and yearned for recognition.

Her husband poured the newcomer a glass of ale and showed him to an empty chair at the far end of the table. Eileen noticed Francis whisper in the older man's ear. Her dad nodded and stood up.

'Francis has asked me to say a few words,' he said. Everyone immediately fell silent and turned to look at the tall charismatic figure of Jack Doyle, docker, unpaid official of the dockworkers' union and well known scourge of management since the day he'd begun working for them twenty-five years ago. 'First thing is to wish Joey and Mary and their little 'uns well in their new life.'

There was a murmur of agreement and shouts of 'Good luck, Joey, Mary.'

Jack Doyle continued. 'Now, the war. It's going to happen, no doubt about it, any day now. I've already fought in one world war and I was lucky. I came through unscathed, but I weren't happy about risking me life for a country that had given me nowt, that was owned lock, stock and barrel by the rich folk, who only wanted it protected and preserved for theirselves. It weren't *my* country, it were *theirs*! What thanks did the widders get after their men spilt every last drop of their blood in the trenches of the Somme? Those lions led by donkeys? None! Paddy O'Hara gave 'em his eyes. What did they give you back, Paddy?'

'A few measly bob a week in pension, Jack, and an empty belly most of the time,' Paddy shouted.

'That's right!' Jack Doyle's lip curled. 'But this war's

different, lads,' he went on. 'This time it ain't a way of getting rid of the unemployed – though don't forget there's a million and a half of them. If I were a younger man, I'd volunteer. They wouldn't need to call me up. In fact, I'd have joined the Territorials like my son-in-law, Francis.'

He beamed down at the younger man and laid an affectionate hand on his shoulder. There was a smattering of applause and Francis gave his charming, devil-may-care smile which Annie always said made him look even more like Clark Gable than ever. Eileen wondered for the hundredth time what on earth had come over her husband to make him join the Royal Tank Regiment. He had a good, well paid job and at thirty-six wouldn't be called up for a while yet, but as a Territorial he would be involved straight away. She suspected it might have something to do with his political aspirations. Francis was an elected member of Bootle Corporation and had Parliament in his sights. He didn't expect the war to last more than a few months, and a spell in the army would look good on his record.

'This time,' her dad was saying, 'you'll be fighting to preserve summat worthwhile, to keep the world free from fascism.' He nodded towards Mr Singerman. The old man nodded back, dark eyes full of pain. 'Jacob can tell you more about it than I can. He's heard nowt from his Ruth in Austria for more'n a year now. Yes, this time,' he continued, his voice rising as he gradually began to be possessed with the rage against inequality and injustice that Eileen knew so well, 'it's different, but it's still only a case of defending the bad against the worse.' He smiled sardonically. ''Course, while you're fighting, you'll be told how brave you are, how much you're needed, but once it's over, you'll have no more than you had before. In other words, nowt!'

He paused dramatically with the air of an accomplished orator, yet he'd never addressed more than a few hundred dockers in his entire life. The yellow street lamp sizzled on the corner, but apart from that, the silence was total. He held his audience in the palm of his hand. Word had gone round the pub that Jack Doyle was on his feet and everyone, including Mack, the landlord, had come out to listen. Eileen thought her father would have made a far better politician than Francis, who had to learn every word of a speech by heart.

'Have you seen that poster?' He looked at them quizzically and several people shook their heads. 'It's all over town. "Your courage, your cheerfulness, your resolution, will bring us victory." Not *our* courage, *our* cheerfulness, *our* resolution . . . No, it's up to us, the workers, like usual, to fight the toffs' battles for them. Some from Pearl Street have already gone to do their bit, like Annie's lads, only nineteen and called up last May, and little Rosie Gregson here, wed just six weeks ago and already said tara to her Charlie.'

Annie Poulson reached across the table and took Rosie's hand. The two women stared at each other for several seconds, the younger one making a determined and obvious effort not to cry.

'There's one thing I haven't touched on,' Jack Doyle continued, 'but I reckon I should, an' that's this Non-Aggression Pact Russia's signed with Germany. It stinks, friends. It stinks bad. I've never actually *been* a Communist, I've allus stuck with Labour, but I never thought our Soviet comrades would betray us like that. After all . . .'

Suddenly, the night air was rent with a shrill scream. Jack Doyle paused and looked up at the open window of Number 21 where the sound had come from. 'That's our Sheila!'

Eileen jumped to her feet and raced into her sister's house and up the stairs. Sheila was lying on the double bed in the front bedroom doubled up in agony. The red eiderdown beneath her was stained and wet. Eileen paused in the doorway, horrified, thinking the stain was blood.

Sheila laughed hysterically. 'Me water's broke, Sis. The baby's on its way, no mistaking it.'

'Jesus, Sis, we'll never get the midwife here in time!' Sheila always had her babies quick.

Half a dozen women had followed and were standing on the landing or the stairs demanding to know what was going on.

'Someone send for Mollie Keaney, quick. The baby's coming.' Eileen was even more hysterical than her sister. 'Put the kettle on for hot water. Christ Almighty, is there anyone here knows how to deliver a baby?'

'Get out'a the way, girl. You're bloody useless, you young uns. Nobody had a midwife in our day.'

Eileen was roughly shoved aside by two of the older women. She went downstairs, legs shaking, and found her dad waiting outside on the pavement, smoking a cigarette.

'It's the baby,' she explained and he nodded, no longer concerned.

'It'll be all right,' he said complacently. 'Our Sheila has babbies easier than peas pop out of a pod.'

They stood there, listening to the sounds coming out of the open window above their heads. Between the agonising screams of labour, Sheila laughed, then cried, then laughed again. The women's voices could be heard, gruffly telling her when to push and when to hold back.

The men, uninterested – after all, it was only another woman having another baby – had started to fold the tables up. Joey Flaherty was tipping the barrel to drain the last few drops of ale, and most of the women had gone inside to make a cup of tea, though a few still waited, eager to know what Sheila Reilly would have this time.

Jack Doyle said to his daughter, 'It's about time you had another babby or two, Eileen.'

Eileen didn't answer. Her dad went on, 'A fine man like Francis deserves a big family. And after all, you're getting on.'

'I'm only twenty-six,' Eileen said stiffly.

He'd used the same words, 'You're getting on,' when she was twenty and he'd urged her to marry Francis Costello. And she'd done it, married him to please her dad, though she could never understand the awe in which this totally decent man held her husband. Francis had charmed him, the way he charmed everybody.

The sound of a new baby's piercing, almost inhuman wail came from the upstairs window and Jack Doyle and his eldest daughter smiled at each other, sharing a rare moment of intimacy.

Agnes Donovan shouted, 'It's a bonny girl. Reckon she's a good seven and a half pounds,' and a cheer went up from those who waited.

Most of the men, including Francis, had disappeared, having gone to the Holy Rosary to return the tables. One by one, the front doors began to close as people went into their houses for the night.

Eileen's father said, 'Well, I'm off to wet the babby's head in the King's Arms. I'll see our Sheila later.'

He left, and suddenly, almost incredibly, Pearl Street was empty for the moment, except for Eileen Costello standing alone outside her sister's house.

She shivered, struck by the desolation compared to the scene that morning; the blank front doors, the empty pavements. There was something almost sinister about the way in which a single paper streamer rolled silently across the cobbles, and for a dreadful moment Eileen felt as if the entire day had been a dream and she was the only person left in the world. Then a burst of raucous laughter came from the King's Arms and inside Sheila's a woman yelled, 'D'you wanna cuppa tea, Eileen?' Tony appeared with his cousin, Dominic, each carrying a bag of chips. Eileen smiled, relieved.

'We met Mr Singerman,' Tony said. 'And he gave us a penny each. He said Dominic's got a new sister.'

'That's right. C'mon, let's go indoors and take a look at her.' She ushered them inside, her spirits lifting at the thought of the new life, though in a somewhat precarious world.

All in all, she thought with satisfaction, it was impossible to imagine a more perfect end to an almost perfect day.

Chapter 2

It was Sunday, sunny and fresh, with an invigorating tang in the air. The heavy overnight rain seemed to have washed away the sultry heaviness of the previous week.

The party in Pearl Street eight days before had become no more than a pleasant memory, though throughout the dark times ahead people would look back upon the day with increasing fondness, as if it symbolised a mythical period when there were no worries to speak of and the world seemed an entirely happier place in which to live.

In Number 16, Eileen Costello had been up since well before seven o'clock. She'd woken, steeped in misery and despair, with Francis snoring volubly at her side, thinking it was still the middle of the night because the room was in total darkness. It was several seconds before she remembered the thick grey blanket pinned over the window. The blackout! It had begun two days ago, much to everyone's irritation. ARP Wardens had already started patrolling the streets ordering people to, 'Put that light out,' even when the light was no more than a pinprick. Dai Evans had told the one who knocked on his door to complain about the thin streak showing between the black curtains Ellis had made for the parlour to, 'Bugger off, you nosy bastard,' and had been threatened with a fine.

Eileen lay there for a long time until, in the far distance, she heard the peal of the Holy Rosary church bells, which meant it was time for the first Mass, time to get up. She slid furtively out of bed so as not to disturb her husband,

and felt for her dressing gown. Once downstairs, she stumbled through the darkness towards the back kitchen where she removed her nightdress and washed herself from head to toe with a face flannel, scrubbing her body with unnecessary vigour as if to rid it of something unsavoury. That done, she gave a sigh of relief and slipped back into her nightclothes. She felt better, cleansed.

It was time for some light. The sunshine outside came as a welcome surprise when she took the blankets off the windows. She waved to Phoebe Crean who was drawing back her parlour curtains at the same time. Phoebe's windows, like most in the street, were by now crisscrossed with sticky tape to reduce the effect of shattering glass following an explosion. Eileen was determined not to tape her windows or make proper blackout curtains until the war had actually begun. To do otherwise seemed defeatist, as if admitting war was a foregone conclusion – and it wasn't, not yet, though before today was out they'd know the worst.

As she put the kettle on for tea, she wondered if millions of people all over the country were doing the same thing at the same time, and did they have the same sickly ominous feeling in their stomachs as she had?

While the kettle boiled, she went into the living room and turned the wireless on for the seven o'clock news and was met by the sound of crackling which soon gave way to some rather gloomy music. As she stood waiting for the announcer's voice, she was surprised to hear a soft knock on the front door and went to answer it.

Jacob Singerman was standing outside. His eighty-year-old face looked drawn and tired, though he was impeccably dressed as usual, in a frayed white shirt and his best brown suit. His shabby shoes were highly polished and his wispy grey hair still damp from his attempts to comb it flat.

'I saw your curtains coming down, Eileen,' he said, 'and I wondered if I could listen to the news on your wireless?' His deep voice, which still held traces of a Russian accent, trembled slightly.

'Of course you can, Mr Singerman. You must excuse me, still in me dressing gown. Come in, luv. It's just about to begin.'

'This is the seven o'clock news from the BBC, on Sunday, the third of September . . .'

The bulletin was starting as Eileen led the old man into the living room, where they sat and listened in grave silence. According to the newsreader, there'd still been no response from Hitler to the British demand that he withdraw his troops from Poland. The broadcast finished with the announcement that there would be another bulletin in an hour's time.

Eileen switched the set off and turned to Mr Singerman. His rheumy eyes behind his half-moon glasses were moist and full of fear.

'I've been awake all night,' he whispered. 'I prayed there'd be some good news this morning, but he won't turn back now. We're on the brink of catastrophe, Eileen. Any minute . . .'

She patted his shrivelled, parchment-coloured hand, feeling glad there was someone to comfort and take her mind off her own despair. 'I'll make you a cup of tea, luv.'

The kettle was boiling away in the back kitchen and the window had misted up with steam. As Eileen stirred the pot vigorously — Mr Singerman liked his tea strong — she decided Hitler must be stark raving mad. Two days ago, despite all the warnings, his troops had brazenly marched into Poland, an invading army, and seemed intent on staying there.

'I don't understand it,' she said, as she returned with the tea. 'Why do countries want to invade other countries? People should be left to get on with their own lives in their own way.'

Mr Singerman shrugged his stooped, narrow shoulders. 'It's something in a lot of men. It goes right back to the Romans, Alexander, Genghis Khan, Napoleon, the lust for power and territory. Now they have such terrible, dangerous weapons and each war seems more unspeakable and bloody than the one before. They called the last, 'the war to end all wars'. I should never have believed them.' His face crumpled. 'Oh, why did I let my Ruth go to Austria?' he wailed.

He seemed on the verge of tears, a sad, lonely old widower whose wife had died in childbirth at the age of forty while giving birth to their only daughter, Ruth. Eileen had never known Ruth, but the neighbours had told her the whole story. 'Oh, she was such a lovely girl, Eileen. Spoilt rotten, mind you, because Mr Singerman, he doted on her. He went without to pay for her piano lessons. Going to be a proper pianist, she was.'

For Ruth's twenty-first birthday, her doting father's gift was to spend his entire savings on a three-month holiday in Austria, where Ruth would stay with his brother. 'He only wanted to show her off, like, Eileen. Let everyone see what a lovely girl he had. You never saw anything like the clothes she had to go with.'

That was nineteen years ago, and Ruth had never returned. She'd fallen in love with a dentist and got married. Mr Singerman, retired by then from his tailor's shop due to failing eyesight, and eking out a living from the small rent he received from the former assistant who'd taken the business over, could never afford to visit her, though Ruth wrote, often, sending snapshots of the grandchildren he'd never seen, which were proudly displayed on the sideboard in his home. But for more than a year now, since Austria had been forcibly taken over by Germany, there'd been nothing. No letters, no more snapshots, just an awful silence.

'That was a long time ago, luv,' Eileen said softly. 'You couldn't possibly have known what was going to happen.'

There were rumours, terrible rumours, nothing that you read about in the papers, but Mr Singerman seemed to have heard them, about what Hitler was doing to the Jews. It wasn't only Ruth and her family who'd disappeared. He'd spoken of camps — what were they called, Eileen racked her brains — concentration camps, where Jews were put to die, along with Communists and mentally defective people like Phoebe Crean's two boys. Though Eileen found this difficult to believe. Nobody, not even Hitler, could be so wicked.

'I'd better be getting back. I'm holding you up.' He struggled to rise, but she put her hand on his sleeve, noting how thin, almost skeletal, his arm felt.

'Don't go, luv. Stay and have another cup of tea. I'll be making a bite to eat soon and they said there'd be more news at eight o'clock.'

He looked grateful. 'Are you sure you don't mind, Eileen?'

'I wouldn't ask if I minded, would I?' She managed a grin.

'You're very kind. This is the sort of day people shouldn't be alone.'

'You'll never be alone in Pearl Street, Mr Singerman,' Eileen chided. 'Anyroad, I expect Paddy O'Hara'll be along any minute wanting to know what the latest news is, along with one or two other folk who haven't got a wireless. I've felt a bit like the BBC meself during the last few days.'

'I'm surprised your Francis isn't down yet.' The old man had begun to look a little more cheerful.

'He's having a bit of a lie-in this morning,' she explained. 'He was out late last night with his mates.'

'That was a fine thing he did, Eileen, joining the Territorials. He's a fine man altogether, is Francis Costello.'

'Everyone says that, Mr Singerman,' Eileen said. Then she sighed. 'I'll just pour you another cup of tea, luv, then get dressed. There'll be lots of visitors today, and it's about time I made meself look respectable.'

'You look lovely, Eileen. You always do.'

'Why, thank you, Mr Singerman.'

She poured a cup for Tony as well and took it up to him, though Francis wouldn't approve if he knew. The room was bright with sunlight and Tony was already awake, his glasses on, reading a comic. Eileen hadn't bothered with blackout in his room. It had been daylight when Tony had gone to bed and she'd instructed him on no account to switch the light on if he woke during the night. 'Otherwise we'll have one of them ARP wardens banging on the door.'

'Has the war started yet?'

Her hand, outstretched to stroke his fine blond hair, stopped in mid-air. The question took her by surprise, the expression on his face even more so. He looked quite animated, as if he hoped her answer would be in the affirmative.

'No, it hasn't,' she said sharply. Instead of stroking his head, she shook his shoulder impatiently.

'We're going to beat bloody hell out of them Jerries, just like we did the last time,' he said complacently. 'I'm keeping me gun under me piller, just in case.' He produced a tin pistol. 'Gosh, Mam, it's awful exciting.'

'Don't swear,' she said automatically. 'And it isn't exciting one bit. If it happens, it'll be bloody terrible.'

He smiled at her cheekily. He could only be cheeky with his mam. 'Don't swear.'

She had to smile back. 'Come on, you little monkey. Drink the tea and get up. Mr Singerman's downstairs. Don't forget to bring your best jersey and trousers down. It's Sunday.'

'All right, Mam.'

Eileen crept into the front bedroom. Francis was still snoring. With the door ajar, there was enough light to see the clothes she'd left on the chair the night before. She scooped them up and took them out onto the landing where she quickly got dressed. Later on, when Francis was up, she'd change into her best blue crepe de Chine. In the meantime, the white blouse and fawn cotton skirt she'd worn yesterday would have to do.

Downstairs, Mr Singerman appeared to be dozing off in the chair. Eileen made her face up in the little spotted mirror over the sink in the back kitchen – a touch of rose-pink lipstick, a quick dab of face powder – and combed her long fair hair, tying it back neatly with a white ribbon. Her cheeks looked pale and she wished she had a bit of rouge to rub on them. Later on, she might go over to Sheila's and borrow some. She thought about her recent conversation with her son. His sudden enthusiasm for war had taken her aback. Tony was such a nervous little thing normally. Still, she supposed it was better than being frightened out of his wits.

He appeared, peeping modestly around the door to see if Mr Singerman was looking. When he saw the old man was asleep, he scampered through the living room into the back kitchen in his vest and underpants, clutching his outer clothes to his chest.

'Wash me quick, Mam, before he wakes up,' he pleaded, and Eileen swiftly rubbed him over with a flannel. He cleaned his own teeth, something he'd been doing since he started school last Easter, and as soon as he'd finished, he shot out to the lavatory at the bottom of the yard. 'I'm dying for a wee-wee, Mam.'

He was still there when the door to the back entry opened and the broad figure of Paddy O'Hara appeared, Spot at his heels.

Paddy O'Hara couldn't see with his eyes, but saw more with his mind than people with the most perfect sight, and one thing he could see was that 16 Pearl Street was not a happy house and Eileen Costello was not a happy woman.

Which puzzled him somewhat. She was lovely. Even if the neighbours hadn't confirmed it was the case, he would have known. He could tell by the swish of her long hair, the smoothness of her hands on his when she led him indoors, her soft, welcoming voice. He could sense her beauty, just as he could sense the sadness which he couldn't understand. After all, she was married to a good, generous man, free with his money, always the first to buy a round of drinks in the pub. Everybody liked Francis Costello, who was on the Corporation and had a responsible job in the offices of the Mersey Docks & Harbour Board. Not only that, Number 16 was the finest house in the street, the only one to have electricity, and Eileen had a modern gas stove to cook on, when every other woman had to use the big iron range in the living room.

Eileen had shown him the new fireplace which had been installed in place of the range. 'What colour is it?' he asked, running his fingers over the smooth cold tiles.

'Dark green,' she replied, sighing, and Paddy, trying to

remember what dark green looked like and thinking of wet winter grass, wondered at the same time why she should sigh instead of being over the moon as most women would.

'Must've cost a pretty packet,' he said shrewdly.

'Y'reckon?'

There'd been a tinge of irony in her words and Paddy, with his finely tuned senses, had understood immediately. The fireplace had cost nothing! It had probably been destined for one of those new houses the Corpy were building, and the gas stove had no doubt come the same way. And Francis had almost certainly got Corpy work-men in to do the work once he got the landlord's approval, including the electric wiring, as 'foreigners', and just given them a few bob for their trouble. Well, nowt wrong with that, except if you were Jack Doyle's daughter. Jack was as straight as a die. So Eileen disapproved, but it still didn't account for her all-consuming unhappiness.

He was about to knock on the back door when it was opened. He knew it was Eileen before she spoke, recognis-ing the sweet smell of her face powder and the lemon soap she used — and something else! He felt a pang of raw gut envy. Francis had made love to his wife during the night.

Eileen touched his face briefly as she always did and said, 'Hallo, Paddy,' in a tremulous voice, and he knew immediately there was something terribly wrong this morning and wondered, as always, what it could be. She gently took his arm and led him inside. 'Mr Singerman's here.'

'Top of the morning, Jacob. You're up early today,' Paddy said jovially as he went into the living room.

'Who can sleep, Paddy, with this hanging over us?' the old man replied gloomily, little realising he'd been dozing for nearly an hour. 'And the news is no better than it was last night.'

'Jesus, Mary and Joseph!' Paddy settled himself in a chair. He could hear Tony trying to persuade Spot to beg for a biscuit, though neither the little dog's appetite, nor his ability to beg, was what it used to be. Paddy resolutely refused to acknowledge the fact that one day soon Spot would die, because the loss of the dog he'd never seen, who'd been the best friend a man could ever have, was too horrendous to contemplate. Instead, he sat contentedly listening to the sounds in the kitchen. Any minute now a cup of tea would arrive. He liked being around Eileen Costello. If the truth were known, he was probably a bit in love with her, though that was something he'd keep to himself until the day he died.

The news at eight o'clock was still no better. Polish troops were bravely fighting back, but there was still no sign of Hitler withdrawing his army. There would be another bulletin in two hours' time.

'Hadn't you better get your Francis up, Eileen?' Paddy suggested. 'I mean, if the worst comes to the worst, isn't he supposed to report for duty, him being in the Territorials, like?'

'I think so,' Eileen said vaguely. 'There's plenty of time. He'll get up when he's ready.' She was aware Mr Singerman was looking at her strangely and Paddy was frowning, 'I'll take a cup of tea up if he doesn't stir soon,' she added, which seemed to satisfy them both. She kept praying her husband would appear of his own accord so she wouldn't have to go into that bedroom again with him in it.

She made more tea and several rounds of toast and marmalade, and just as they were finishing Dominic called for Tony to play. Eileen winced as the front door slammed and the house shook as the two departed.

'You're not having your Tony evacuated, then?'

'Oh, no, Mr Singerman,' she said quickly. 'P'raps it's selfish of us, but I couldn't bear to let him go. And our Sheila's staying – I mean, who'd take in a woman with six children, two of 'em only babies? – and what with me dad only just round the corner . . .'

'A lot of children went on Friday,' the old man sighed. 'Pearl Street seemed uncommonly quiet yesterday. I never thought I'd miss the sound of the children playing outside, but I did.'

'They'll be back, Jacob, don't you worry,' Paddy grinned. 'And you'll be able to have a good old moan again.'

The children had gone in charabancs to safer areas, away from Bootle and the expected air-raids. Freda and Dicky Tutty had left for Southport, and neither had taken a scrap of luggage with them.

To Eileen's relief, the slam of the front door appeared to have woken Francis. She heard the bed springs creak. He was getting up. Once he heard voices downstairs, he'd probably want some warm water to get washed in private.

She jumped to her feet. 'There's Francis now,' she said brightly. 'Now, if you don't mind, I'll just slip round to the Holy Rosary for the nine o'clock Mass and I'll take our Tony with us. I'll leave the front door open, case anybody else drops in to listen to the wireless. Y'can tell Francis there's a cup of tea in the pot when he comes down.'

If he wanted warm water he'd just have to whistle for it.

The church was unusually crowded. Eileen saw a lot of people who didn't normally attend Mass except at Christmas and Easter. There was a tension in the air and during prayers, instead of the usual coughs and the sound of people shuffling around trying to make themselves comfortable on the wooden kneelers, you could have heard a pin drop, as if the congregation were praying especially hard. Father Jordan's sermon was a plaintive call for common sense and reason.

'S'not much good asking *us* to be reasonable,' Eileen heard someone say when they were outside. 'No-one's asked *us* if we want a war or not. Fact, no-one ever asks *us* anything. We just get told what to do and we bloody well go and do it, even if it means going out and getting bloody killed!'

She smiled to herself. It sounded just like her dad.

Tony, chattering nineteen to the dozen, skipped along beside her as they walked home along Marsh Lane, which was crowded with people in their best clothes going to and from their various churches or out buying a newspaper. Everyone looked very grave, and one or two self-consciously carried their gas masks in cases over their shoulders. There was none of the normal lighthearted Sunday atmosphere, despite the fact it was such a lovely, sunny day; balmy and exceptionally warm for September. Apart from the newsagent's, the shops were closed and shuttered.

'Why doesn't grandad ever go to Mass, Mam?'

'Because he's an atheist, luv. You ask me that question nearly every Sunday.'

'Is me Uncle Sean an atheist, too?'

'I don't think Sean's ever given it much thought. He was only two when your grandma died, so he didn't have her example, not like your Auntie Sheila and me. Your grandad never cared if Sean went to Mass or not.'

'Me dad doesn't always go to Mass, either.' He frowned and his glasses slipped halfway down his little snub nose. 'Does that mean he'll go to hell if he dies in the war?'

Eileen's heart missed a beat. It was a while before she answered. 'Your dad only misses the times he doesn't feel so well on Sunday mornings. Then he goes to Benediction in the evening instead. And of course your dad won't be killed in the war, don't be silly.'

She bought the *News of the World* and a bar of Fry's chocolate cream for Tony. 'Eat that up quick, now, before we get home, otherwise your dad'll have a fit. You know he doesn't like you eating chocolate.'

'Why not, Mam?'

'I dunno, luv. You'd better ask him that.'

The chocolate disappeared as if by magic. Eileen stopped and wiped his sticky hands and mouth with her hankie. His little face contorted grotesquely as she rubbed furiously away and she felt a sudden ache of love. 'Oh, you're a little pet, Tony Costello,' she said, spontaneously kissing his forehead.

'*Mam!*' He looked around to see if anyone was watching. Being kissed by your mam in a public street could take some living down. Then he glanced at her keenly. He'd been meaning to ask her something ever since he woke up and was waiting for the right moment. Perhaps this was it. 'Why were you crying last night, Mam?'

'Was I crying, luv? I don't remember.'

She was lying, he could tell. He couldn't bear his mam being unhappy. He felt an unpleasant knot of something peculiar in his tummy.

'I must've had a bad dream,' she said.

When Eileen got home, her dad had arrived along with her brother Sean, and Agnes Donovan was in the back kitchen making a cup of tea. Paddy O'Hara and Mr Singerman were still there.

'You don't mind, do you, Eileen?' Aggie's little black eyes were darting around the kitchen, searching every corner. If there was something amiss, a dirty sink or a grubby teatowel, it would be all around the street by tomorrow. 'But I popped in to see what the latest news was and your dad was here, parched for a cuppa. Oh, it's lovely using this stove of yours, boils the kettle a treat it does.'

'You missed the ten o'clock bulletin,' her dad said sharply. He resented the fact his daughters continued to go to church, despite his stern lectures on the evils of Catholicism and religion being the opium of the people.

'What did it say?'

'Neville Chamberlain is speaking to the nation at quarter past eleven,' he replied cuttingly. His feelings for the Prime Minister bordered on loathing.

'Oh, Lord!' That sounded ominous. 'Where's Francis?'

Paddy O'Hara said, 'He's gone round to Park Street, Eileen, to find out what time he's expected to report in, like. Rodney Smith came while you were gone and took him in the car.'

The Territorial Army Headquarters were in Park Street.

'He looked dead smart in his uniform,' Jack Doyle said proudly, then his craggy features twisted sardonically. 'He's officer material is Francis, but there's no way he'll be promoted beyond sergeant. He don't talk enough like a toff.'

'Oh, come off it, Dad,' Eileen said impatiently. 'You're the last person who'd want an officer for a son-in-law,' and he had the grace to smile, slightly shamefaced.

'I'm going to join the Fleet Air Arm,' Sean said excitedly. He was a lovely dark gypsy of a boy, a throw-back to some wild Gaelic strain in the family.

Eileen shook his bare brown arm irritably. 'Shurrup, you! You're only sixteen. The war'll be well finished by the time you're old enough to fight. Everyone sez it'll be over by Christmas.' It was no good adding, 'That's if there *is* a war,' because it looked beyond doubt by now.

Mr Singerman opened his mouth to say something, but must have thought better of it. He stayed silent.

The Prime Minister's voice was strained and weary. He was seventy, and the events of the past weeks and months would have taxed the nerves of a man half his age.

'*I am speaking to you from the Cabinet Room at Number Ten Downing Street . . .*'

The Costellos' house was crowded. Few families in Pearl Street could afford a wireless. Neighbours were packed in the hall and on the stairs. Eileen sat on a hard chair which was jammed between Mr Singerman and the table. Francis was back. Despite the ill-fitting, clumsily-made clothes, he still managed to look debonair and even slightly rakish as he stood framed in the back kitchen doorway. Rodney Smith was beside him, his blond wavy hair stiff with Brylcreem.

. . . unless the British Government heard by eleven o'clock that Germany were prepared to withdraw their troops from Poland, a state of war would exist between us. I have to tell you now that no such undertaking has been received, and that consequently this country is at war with Germany . . .

There was a swift drawing in of breath from everybody there. One or two of the women moaned softly and several people made the sign of the cross. Somebody giggled nervously. Eileen noticed Jacob Singerman's gnarled yellow hands tighten so hard that the knuckles showed white.

. . . May God bless you all. May he defend the right, for it is evil things that we shall be fighting against – brute force, bad faith, injustice, oppression and persecution; and against them I am certain that the right will prevail.

The Prime Minister's voice faded away and was followed by the National Anthem. Nobody moved, maintaining a respectful silence – though Jack Doyle, who had no truck with nationalism wherever it came from, irritably lit a cigarette.

Calum Reilly, Sheila's husband, was the first to speak when the music finished. 'Well,' he said ruefully, 'that's that, then. I'd better go and tell the missus.' His normally warm good humoured face was troubled. A Merchant Seaman's job was already hazardous enough without the now predictable threat of attack from German U-boats and planes.

'Tell our Sheila I'll pop over to see her later on,' Eileen told him. Her sister would be sick with worry. Cal was going back to sea in the morning.

People began to disperse, looked dazed. Their country was in a state of war and it hadn't quite sunk in yet.

'Tara, Eileen. Tara Francis,' they shouted.

Eileen felt thankful that her dad and Sean were tactless enough to remain. She didn't want to see Francis off on her own. To her astonishment, he picked up his bulging kitbag and swung it over his shoulder. 'I'll be off now.'

'Already? I thought you weren't due to report in till half past twelve?'

'It's not so far off that now. Rodney and I'll stop off on the way for a bevy. Fancy one, Jack?'

'D'you want us to come with you?' Eileen felt bound to ask, feeling awkward and inadequate. Her husband was going off to fight in a war and it had all happened so suddenly that it had taken her unawares.

'No, luv, it's all right.' He kissed her cheek and she stiffened. 'They won't be sending us far, not yet.'

They went to the door. 'Don't forget to say goodbye to

Tony. He's out playing with Dominic in the street,' she called.

There was quite a crowd outside, reluctant to return home since hearing the fateful news. One or two were glancing up at the skies, as if already expecting to see enemy planes loaded with bombs to drop on Bootle. Tony and Dominic, both wearing their gas masks, were playing at being aeroplanes, arms outstretched as they swooped on each other. When everyone saw Francis Costello emerge in his uniform, they clustered around, shaking his hand and wishing him well. Annie Poulson, who had her arms around a sobbing Rosie Gregson, looked more angry than upset. Her lads were in Aldershot and she was probably wondering when she'd see them again. Sheila emerged clutching the new baby, Mary, and came across to say goodbye to Francis.

Francis reached for his wife with his free arm and, in a dramatic gesture, swung her towards him. He kissed her long and hard on the lips and everybody cheered.

'Tara, luv,' he said, releasing her.

Suddenly, Eileen felt as if it was all too much. She burst into tears.

'Don't worry, Sis, he'll be back.' Sean put his arm around her shoulder.

'Poor Eileen,' she heard someone say. 'How will she manage without him?'

Eileen fled back into the house. She heard someone follow and ran upstairs, pausing at the darkened bedroom door where the blackout was still in place.

'Eileen!'

It was Annie.

'I'm upstairs.'

'I've got a drop of whisky in the house, luv. Come and have a sup? It'll calm you down, like.'

'In a minute.' She heard Annie's footsteps on the stairs. At the top, Annie turned and the two women faced each other across the landing.

'We're all upset this mornin',' Annie said. 'Francis, he'll be all right, you'll see. He'll come back safe and sound.'

'I don't want him back!' She had to tell someone. She couldn't stand the thought of everyone feeling sorry for her when the last thing she wanted was pity because Francis had gone away.

'What?' Annie frowned, struggling to understand.

'I hate him,' Eileen said flatly. 'I'm glad he's gone. I hope he gets killed and never comes back.' She wanted to add, 'In other words, I'm glad there's going to be a war,' but how could you say that to a widow whose two sons, her only children, were going to fight in it? 'Come here a minute,' she said instead.

She went into the bedroom and jerked the blanket off the window. Drawing pins scattered over the linoleum-covered floor.

Annie gasped at the sight that met her. The bed was in a state of total disarray. There were sheets and blankets everywhere, spilling onto the floor, and the striped palliasse was mainly bare. The room stank of the green vomit which was splattered on the sheets and both pillows and in a pool on the floor. A man's suit, shirt and underclothes had been thrown carelessly in a corner.

Annie frowned again, but didn't speak, as if she was stuck for words.

'It happens nearly every Saturday night,' Eileen explained bitterly. 'He goes off with Rodney Smith to some club or other in town. When he comes home he can scarcely stand, he's so bloody drunk, and he's always in a terrible wild temper, then . . .' She paused, unable to continue. How could she tell her friend the disgusting things Francis did when he came to bed?

Annie thought she understood. She glanced shrewdly at Eileen's strained face. 'Does he get a bit rough with you, luv?'

'You could say that,' Eileen replied briefly. Once she'd tried to hide in the parlour when she heard Rodney Smith's car stop at the end of the street, but Francis had searched for her and . . .

'I would never have believed it,' Annie breathed. 'A fine man like Francis Costello!'

'I'm sick to death of hearing people say that,' Eileen said exasperatedly. 'Everyone thinks the sun shines out his arse, me dad in particular. I even did meself for a while, but we hadn't been married long before he showed his true colours.'

Annie took hold of her arm. 'Come on, luv, let's get out of here. I'll help you clear it up later. How about that whisky?'

'I'd sooner not go outside, Annie, not with everyone still there and feeling sorry for me. Anyroad, there's already a bottle of Johnnie Walker in the parlour. I'd prefer a cup of tea, instead. I'll close the front door on the way down, else I'll have the world and his wife back in again.'

'He began coming round to our house when I was about fifteen to ask me dad help him get on Bootle Corporation, like,' said Eileen. 'He had such a lovely way with him, a real Irish charmer, that me dad was really taken with him. We all were. He kept on coming, even after he'd won the seat, and after a while I got the feeling he was interested in me. I suppose I felt flattered – he was older than I was, ten years older, and the women were all wild about him.'

Annie smiled ruefully. 'I always said he looked a bit like Clark Gable, and he has the same sort of smile, a touch

42

devilish in its way.'

They were on the second cup of tea. Annie had urged her to 'Get it off your chest, luv. You'll feel the better for it.'

Eileen nodded. 'He has, too. When I was twenty, he asked us to marry him. I turned him down, I don't know why. Our Sheila was married by then, and I expect I was waiting to meet someone I'd feel about the same way she felt about Cal. Francis must've told me dad, because *he* started going on about me being left on the shelf and saying I was getting on. After a while, I realised he really fancied having Francis for a son-in-law. He never liked Calum Reilly.' In fact, her dad resented the man who'd taken his favourite daughter away from him.

'In the end, I said "yes", mainly to please me dad,' she said simply. She leaned back in the easy chair, remembering. It hadn't been a very difficult decision. She didn't feel as if she were making a sacrifice, because men like Francis Costello didn't grow on trees.

'Here, you've let your tea go cold.' Annie jumped to her feet. 'I'll fill it up for you.'

'We were fine for a while,' Eileen continued when Annie returned, the cup filled to the brim. 'Then gradually he began to turn against us. He became dead unreasonable, criticising every little thing I did, losing his temper if he found a speck of dust or if I'd run out of something he wanted. No matter what sort of meal was waiting on the table, he'd find something wrong with it. At first, I thought it was me own fault, but in the end I decided that, right down at heart, Francis wasn't nice at all, though he liked people to like him. He liked being popular and everyone saying what a fine chap he was, but I reckon he found it too much, having to be nice at home as well.'

'Oh, Eileen, you should have told us this before,' Annie said gently.

Eileen shrugged. 'It never crossed me mind to tell anybody.' Not until this morning, when Francis left and everyone expected her to be heartbroken. Anyroad, it was too embarrassing, and even now she hadn't told Annie the half of it. There was the way he treated Tony, picking on him all the time till the poor little lad didn't know whether he was coming or going, though she'd stood up to him over that. But standing up to Francis only brought more misery in its wake. When particularly irked, he'd squeeze her wrist or shoulder until tears came to her eyes with the pain. She knew he'd hit her if he thought he could get away with it, but the wife of a fine man like Francis Costello couldn't be seen with a bruised face or a black eye. After all, he had his reputation to consider.

Eileen sighed. 'I thought of leaving him more than once, but it would have killed me dad. I think Francis knew that . . .' She stopped, realising she'd been going on for nearly an hour about her troubles, yet here was Annie not saying a word about her own.

'Oh, Annie, luv, I feel terrible selfish. You've got ten times more to worry about than us, what with your boys already called up.'

Annie shook her head impatiently. 'Don't be silly, Eileen. We've all got to get things off our chest once in a while and I've never known you moan before. As for Terry and Joe, all I can do is pray to God they'll come to no harm, though the longer I live the more I begin to wonder if there's a God up there, the things that happen in the world. Sometimes, I wish us were a Catholic like you. Having a faith is like having a crutch to get you through life.'

'Don't worry, Annie,' Eileen said comfortingly. 'Your

lads'll be all right. You'll see.'

'That's what I just told Rosie Gregson about her Charlie. That's what the folks outside said about Francis. Not every man's going to come home safe and sound, Eileen,' Annie said cynically. 'Some of 'em are bound to die.'

Eileen didn't answer because there didn't seem much to say. In her heart she knew Annie was right. There couldn't be a war without someone's sons or husbands or fathers being killed.

'Oh, Lord, Annie, it doesn't bear thinking about.' She jumped to her feet. 'I know, let's have some whisky. I could really do with a sup or two right now.'

Vivien Waterford lay on a deckchair outside the open French windows of the drawing room, wearing her new striped bathing costume. A silk robe had recently been thrown around her white shoulders by her solicitous husband when he'd decided a slight chill had come to the soft evening air. Her usually tranquil face was creased in an unaccustomed frown as she stared down the garden.

'What on earth are we going to do with them, darling?'

Her husband, Clive, followed her worried gaze. Two ragged, filthy children were sitting on the stone bench beside the lily pond. There'd been ten waterlilies that morning. Now there were only eight, two having been plucked out and pulled to pieces by the boy, Dicky.

'Beats me,' he replied, shrugging. 'Send 'em back, I suppose.'

'But you can't send *children* back,' said Vivien reasonably. 'I mean, it's not as if they're a frock or something.'

Clive mumbled something unintelligible. He felt guilty. It was his fault they'd got these two ragamuffins. On Friday, he'd promised Vivien faithfully he would leave the office prompt at midday to collect their evacuees from the reception centre. Then something had come up and he'd completely forgotten. It wasn't until she'd telephoned at two o'clock, wondering why he hadn't arrived home, that he remembered and had gone racing down to the centre to find the respectable-looking children had long gone – apparently, two women had come to blows over a pair of sweet looking, nicely dressed sisters – and these two pathetic specimens of humanity with labels around their necks, who hadn't even brought a change of clothes with them, were the only ones remaining.

'But you can't keep 'em, either,' he said eventually. 'I mean, they're barely civilised.'

Both wet the bed. There was a pile of sheets waiting for Mrs Critchley to wash in the morning. They peed in the rose bushes because using an inside toilet seemed beyond their comprehension, and their table manners were non-existent. He and Vivien had watched, him appalled, she, for some strange reason, amused, as they stuffed food into their mouths as if they'd been told it was the last meal they were going to have on earth. The first night, the girl actually had the nerve to ask for a 'sup of gin' before going to bed.

'I don't want to get rid of them,' Vivien said. 'In fact, I quite like them, poor little black and blue mites. They're terribly brave. They haven't cried once. Hetty said her two have never stopped weeping and wailing since they arrived. I was merely wondering what to *do* with them, that's all. I offered to take them to the beach or the fairground, but Freda just gave me a filthy look and didn't answer. I mean, darling, now this frightful war's started, we might have them with us for months and months.'

Clive glanced at her in bewilderment. She liked them! His wife never ceased to surprise him. They'd been married for fifteen years, yet he felt as if he understood her no more now than he did the day of the wedding. Her white legs were crossed daintily at the ankles, the toenails of her little feet painted pink. He felt a surge of desire. If it wasn't for those bloody kids, he'd pick her featherlight form up, carry her into the house and make love to her on the tangerine linen settee in the lounge.

'I worry about how you'll cope when I'm at work,' he growled. On Friday night they'd tried to bath the children. You could actually see the lice crawling on their dirt-caked scalps. The girl had screamed blue murder at the sight of the water and accused them of trying to kill her. She'd refused to remove the grubby frock she'd arrived in and change into one of the pretty ones Vivien had hastily acquired from one of her friends. Clive had made sure they never had children of their own. Vivien was little more than a child herself.

Vivien gave her little tinkling laugh. 'Sweetheart, I'll manage, and I'll have Mrs Critchley to help, won't I?'

She smiled at him and his heart turned over. She wasn't a strong woman, a fact he'd conveyed to the Billeting Officer when he'd called to assess what room they had available for evacuees. 'My wife is virtually an invalid. She has a frightfully weak heart.'

The man had looked at him shrewdly. 'We're only asking that you house a couple of children, sir. After all, there's likely to be a war any minute. Everyone has to do their bit.'

At the time, Clive had felt uncomfortable, as if he were shirking his responsibilities. 'I've every intention of "doing my bit", as you put it, when the time comes,' he replied stiffly, though it would be a while before he, at forty-one, would be called up. 'All I'm worried about is my wife having to look after a crowd of strange children.

And it's not just her health, she's . . .'

Clive paused. The man looked at him superciliously, eyebrows raised, waiting for him to finish. Clive cursed him inwardly. Some minor civil servant or Town Hall clerk who'd suddenly found himself with a little power over people's lives and was milking the situation for all its worth. He'd been nearly going to say, 'She's not quite right in the head,' but thought better of it. Hardly anybody noticed. It was merely a case of retarded development. Vivien hadn't quite grown up, that's all. He wasn't going to tell this jumped-up Government Johnnie his private business.

'It doesn't matter,' he said with a shrug.

'It won't be a crowd of children, sir. Two, that's all. Shouldn't tax your wife's strength too greatly, should it?'

To Clive's surprise, it hadn't. Vivien had been an absolute brick since Freda and Dicky had arrived. She hadn't shouted at the boy for tearing the waterlilies to pieces, though he personally could have broken the kid's neck, nor when one of them smashed the Venetian glass vase that her mother had given her last Christmas. She seemed more sympathetic and amused than shocked. 'They didn't mean it, darling. They just don't know any better.'

'I'll just go and have another little chat with them.'

He watched her slender, diminutive figure as she strolled down the garden towards the children, then went indoors and switched on the wireless. The King was speaking to the nation at six o'clock. He stood to attention for the National Anthem which preceded His Majesty's speech and kept the sound on low, just in case one of those dratted kids did something to his Vivien, like throw her in the lily pond, for instance.

★

48

'Hello, there!'

Freda Tutty clutched Dicky's hand protectively and stared sullenly at the pretty lady. She would never have admitted it in a million years, but she quite liked her, mainly because she had the oddest, never-felt-before feeling that the pretty lady actually liked her back. She hadn't yelled at them, not once, or criticised, or looked at them contemptuously or held her nose, the way people usually did when they met the Tuttys. Despite this, Freda felt an enormous weight of unhappiness. She hated Southport and the big bright house they'd been brought to. The house made her feel dizzy, almost sick, with its high ceilings and tall windows and huge pieces of peculiar furniture. She felt safer in the garden, though that was frightening, too, surrounded by towering trees and full of prickly bushes and funny looking flowers. The first night she'd scarcely slept, all by herself in a strange-smelling bed, and longed for the familiar palliasse on the floor of the bedroom in Pearl Street. She missed her mam and the warm body of Dicky curled up beside her – he was in the next room in a bed all of his own – though after two nights she'd grown used to the bed and the smell seemed slightly more pleasant than the one at home.

The pretty lady didn't seem to mind that Freda hadn't responded. She dropped onto the grass and watched them, smiling. 'What do you fancy doing tomorrow?'

Freda supposed she'd better answer. 'Nothing,' she replied churlishly.

'But you did nothing yesterday and nothing today. We could go into town and buy some toys. You'd like a doll, wouldn't you? And I'm sure Dicky would love a train set.'

Dicky nodded his head vigorously. 'Wanna train set,' he said gruffly.

Freda pinched his arm. 'No, you don't.'

He winced, but insisted stubbornly, 'I do.'

'*You don't!*'

'I think he does,' said the pretty lady reasonably. 'And most girls love dolls. I did, when I was little.'

'I hate dolls.'

The pretty lady shrugged. 'It doesn't matter. I'll just take Dicky, then.'

Freda frowned at the notion of being separated from her brother. She'd give Dicky a good kicking when they got upstairs. He was nothing but a bloody traitor.

The pretty lady was examining her pink fingernails. Freda noticed her toenails were painted the same colour. She glanced down at her own grubby, scratched hands on which the nails were bitten to the quick.

'Would you like me to paint your nails?'

Freda looked up quickly. The pretty lady was watching her with interest. It was such a strange, unexpected question that it made Freda feel funny inside. Nobody had ever offered to do anything nice for her before – except perhaps Eileen Costello from next door, and even she usually had a condescending look on her face as if it was all beneath her – but this lady was talking to her as if she were an equal. She looked down at her hands again and then back to the pretty lady's, which were soft and white and no bigger than her own.

'Will you paint me toes, too?'

'If you want,' the lady said generously. 'You can choose which colour, I've loads of different bottles. Though you'll have to have a bath first . . .'

'You mean the thing with the water?'

'Yes. You can wash yourself and I'll shampoo your hair. I reckon it would look terribly pretty if it was clean. It's lovely and thick.'

'Pretty?' Freda put her hand up to her stringy, greasy

50

hair. Pretty! It seemed inconceivable that anything about her should be regarded as pretty. 'Will it look like yours?' The lady had blonde hair, almost white, which fell in waves halfway down her back.

'Not exactly. Mine's longer and a different colour. We'll just have to see, won't we? Oh, isn't this exciting!'

When Clive emerged from the lounge, his wife was leading the children upstairs. He watched, open-mouthed, until they disappeared onto the landing, and heard Vivien say, 'When you've finished, Freda, we'll bath Dicky between us, then we'll do your nails . . .'

Joey and Mary Flaherty stood arm in arm on the steerage deck of the *Athenia*, The Atlantic ocean stretched before them, a seemingly endless expanse of large, rocking grey-brown waves. Their three children were fast asleep in the cramped cabin below.

'I wonder how they took the news in Pearl Street?' Mary said wistfully. 'I feel mean, somehow, not being with all me old neighbours.'

The outbreak of war had been announced by the captain on the loudspeaker system that morning.

'Don't be silly, luv,' Joey said impatiently. He was worried. After working on the docks for nearly twenty years, he knew enough about ships to realise that instead of sailing straight ahead, the *Athenia*, which was about two hundred and fifty miles off the Irish coast, was taking a zig-zag westward course, though he hadn't mentioned this to Mary. The ship had also been blacked out and passengers had been ordered not to smoke on deck. The Captain must consider there was a threat of attack.

'I can't wait to get there,' Mary breathed, forgetting all about Pearl Street. The ship was docking in Montreal and Kevin, Joey's brother, would meet them in his truck and take them across to Ontario. A job was waiting for Joey in the car plant where Kevin worked and the wages were more than double those he earned in Bootle. There was even a house that went with the job, a white wooden bungalow which had a garden *with their very own trees!* Mary felt a bubble of happiness rise in her throat at the thought of the fine life ahead. She pressed her cheek against Joey's shoulder, almost overcome by it all.

'You don't know what you want, woman. You wanted to be in Bootle less than half a minute ago.'

Mary stared up at him in surprise. 'You're a grumpy ould sod tonight, Joey Flaherty. What's the matter?'

Joey had opened his mouth to reply when the torpedo hit the ship amidships. A muffled explosion came from below and the whole vessel rocked. There was, for the moment, dead silence. Then Mary screamed, 'The children! Joey, we've got to get the children!'

Chapter 3

On Monday morning, the first full day of war, Jacob Singerman woke up very early as usual. His arm reached out involuntarily for Rebecca, then he remembered his beloved wife had been gone for more than forty years.

'You old fool,' he whispered.

He got out of bed and dressed immediately. If he lay there he'd only think about Ruth. It was best to be busy, doing something. He still possessed his sewing skills, though his weak eyes felt strained if he did too much, and had offered to run up blackout curtains for several of the neighbours, including Eileen Costello once she bought the material, on the old sewing machine he kept in the parlour. He drew his own curtains back and for a startled moment thought someone had painted the outside of his window pitch black, because he could see nothing. He stood there feeling claustrophobic and shut in, as if he was completely alone down the darkest mine.

Such utter blackness! Not a wink of light to be seen anywhere. He stood for several minutes leaning on the window frame listening to the rapid beat of his heart, which appeared to be the only sound on earth. He'd be glad when somebody moved in next door. He missed the sounds of life, of the Flahertys' noisy laughter and occasional tearful rows. The widow on his other side was as quiet as a mouse. Slowly, as if they were approaching through a murky fog, he began to make out the shape of the houses opposite, saw where the roofs merged with the sombre sky. Then, even more slowly, the heavens began to lighten in the east and the smudged silhouettes of the chimney pots could just be seen.

He took a deep breath. As a young man, he'd always had too much imagination. Lately, it had been getting out of hand. For a moment there, he thought he'd died and gone to hell!

Freda Tutty lay in the sweet-smelling bed staring up with fascination at her outstretched hands with their bright red fingernails. Then she wriggled her feet out of the bed-clothes and regarded her matching toes. She remembered her hair and sat up, craning her head until she could see her reflection in the mirror on top of the little dressing table on the wall opposite. It had hurt, having it washed; the pretty lady – Vivien, as they'd been told to call her – had scrubbed and scrubbed really hard with her fingertips, but the result had been worth it. Freda's hair had dried into bouncing shoulder-length brown curls.

'It's more chestnut than brown,' Vivien said admir-ingly, 'and lovely and thick.'

Vivien had loaned her a nightdress, white cotton with a pattern of little sprigs of mauve forget-me-nots and a drawstring neck threaded with mauve ribbon. The night-dress was a bit too long, but this morning they were going shopping, ostensibly to buy a train set for Dicky and a doll for herself, but also to buy clothes. Freda didn't want a doll, but she was looking forward to the clothes. Last night, when they'd gone in search of a nightdress, Vivien had let her look through the wardrobe at all her pretty frocks. She even let Freda try a couple on.

'Isn't this just too exciting for words?' Vivien had trilled. 'It's like having a little sister,' which Freda thought a strange thing to say, because Vivien was old enough to be her mam.

Suddenly, the bedroom door was pushed open with such force that it banged against the wall and swung back, almost striking the woman who entered and stood glaring down at Freda. She wore a green overall and was very tall and stout with fleshy, sallow features sprinkled with several hairy warts. Her tight grey curls were covered with a thick hairnet. This, assumed Freda, must be the daily, Mrs Critchley.

'I suppose you've wet the bed again,' she said in a grating voice.

'No, I haven't,' Freda said, quickly recovering her composure and recognising an enemy straight away.

The woman came over, grabbed Freda's wrist and squeezed it hard. 'I didn't appreciate coming in this morning and finding half a dozen sheets waiting to be washed.'

Not at all intimidated, Freda countered, 'It's what you're paid for, isn't it? Now, gerroff me, or I'll tell Vivien.'

The woman released her grip and took a surprised step backwards. 'So, it's "Vivien", is it?' she hissed. 'Well, you may have fooled Mrs W, but you haven't fooled me, my girl.'

'I wouldn't waste me time, you're not worth it. Sod off.'

Looking shaken, the woman left with a face like thunder. Freda felt the bed to see if it was wet, but the bottom sheet was dry. It was a pity about Mrs Critchley, but she was used to people talking to her as if she were a piece of dirt. And she was talking shit, anyway, because Freda wasn't fooling anyone. Vivien was the first person to treat her like a human being and she liked her more than she'd liked anyone in her life before, even more than her mam, in a sort of way. She knew, instinctively, whose side Vivien would be on if Mrs Critchley made a fuss. Vivien would be on the side of her little sister.

'I don't want you to go, Cal. I never want you to go, but this time . . .' Sheila Reilly was trying very hard not to cry. It always upset Cal, seeing her in tears when he was about to leave, but it was hard to remain dry-eyed when she was in such utter despair. He might be killed, she might never see him again, and the thought of life without Cal was so achingly unbearable that she was convinced she would die if anything happened to him.

'I know, luv, I know.' Cal stroked her naked body and she felt him harden. They were in bed, wrapped in each other's arms. His ship, the *Midnight Star* was sailing that night for Freemantle with a cargo of carpets and he had to be on board by midday. In a few hours he would leave. They had little time left to themselves, perhaps only minutes. Although Mary, the baby, was fast asleep in her cot in the corner, Sheila could hear the boys talking to each other in the next room. Any minute now, they'd come barging in and leap on the bed demanding a last play with their dad, or Mary would wake up wanting her feed. Outside, there came the sharp clip–clop of hooves and the creak of wheels on the cobbled street as Nelson, the coal horse, set off on the first deliveries of the day. It must be getting late.

'Do it, Cal. Please do it,' she whispered urgently.

'Oh, Jesus, girl! D'you think I don't want to?' he replied hoarsely. It was all he thought about when he was at sea, making love to his Sheila.

'Go on, then,' she coaxed. He hadn't done it properly since he came home last Thursday.

'No! It's only just over a week since you had the baby.'

'That's never stopped you before.'

'Oh, Sheil!' He began to kiss her passionately and she touched him till he came. She knew darned well why he wouldn't make love, because he was worried she would have another baby. It had never mattered before, but it mattered now, because this time there was a far greater risk that he mightn't come back.

'Why don't you give up the Merchant Navy, Cal? Do something else?' She sat up and began to pull on her nightie. She knew it was a stupid question and wondered why she'd bothered asking it, but it seemed even more stupid to sail across dangerous waters with a hold full of carpets when there was a war on.

'I've been at sea since I was thirteen, Sheil,' he replied patiently. 'There's nowt else I'm fit for. And don't forget, if I weren't in the Navy, I'd be getting me call-up papers anyroad.'

She *had* forgotten. Whichever way you looked at it, she was going to lose him somehow. She couldn't win. At least in the Navy he had some rank after his name. Cal was a Third Officer, which wasn't nearly as grand as it sounded, but in the Army he'd be starting at the bottom as a private.

Sheila sighed as she slipped out of bed, drew the curtains back and picked up the baby. Best get her feed over with now. There were still Cal's shirts to iron. She opened her nightie and Mary began to suck eagerly at her breast. Cal got up and Sheila watched as he began to get dressed, feeling herself grow dizzy with love at the sight of his thick muscled arms, his brown shoulders. She resisted the urge to put Mary back in her cot and demand he make love to her, properly, straight away.

Anyroad, just then, the bedroom door opened and the children poured in, all five of them, even Ryan at a rapid crawl. Dominic or Niall must have picked him up out of his cot. Ryan, no longer the baby, had been relegated to the boys' room since Mary arrived.

Calum laughed and lifted up his youngest son until the tiny boy almost touched the ceiling and squealed in a mixture of terror and delight.

'Me too, Dad, me too,' the others shouted, jumping up and down.

'Shurrup, youse lot. You'll wake up the whole street,' Sheila yelled. She regarded her family with a mixture of love and fear, then glanced hopefully at the big portrait of the Sacred Heart over the fireplace. 'Please, dear Jesus,' she prayed silently, 'look after Cal for me and keep me children safe from bombs and gas and all the terrible things that can happen in a war.'

Across the road, Eileen Costello was sitting up in bed smoking a cigarette. She rarely smoked, but last night had found a full packet of Capstan in a drawer and smoked several whilst she listened to the wireless with Mr Singerman and Paddy O'Hara. A writer called J. B. Priestley had read the first part of his book, *Let the People Sing*. She couldn't wait for next Sunday to hear the second part. It somehow seemed appropriate that morning, waking up after the first refreshing night's sleep in years, to nip downstairs, make a cup of tea and bring it back to bed along with the packet of ciggies and yesterday's special edition of the Liverpool *Echo*. The paper, never normally published on a Sunday, contained the news that all theatres and cinemas had been closed and sporting fixtures cancelled. Her dad nearly had a fit when he learned there'd be no football match on Saturday. Everton were due to play Manchester United and he was really looking forward to it, along with nearly every other man in Liverpool.

Hitler's ears must have really burnt last night, the curses that were heaped upon his head.

Eileen took a long puff of her cigarette, blew the smoke slowly out and watched it disperse lazily upwards in wavy layers. It didn't seem right, being so happy. On the other hand, there was a feeling of relief that the uncertainty, the awful waiting, was over and the country knew where it stood. But Eileen knew that wasn't the real reason for her happiness. Francis had gone. She was alone in the bed.

She giggled, feeling slightly hysterical, and wondered if she was the only woman in the country who was glad to see the back of her husband. Now he'd gone, she'd get herself a job. He'd refused to let her work before, something she'd wanted to do since Tony started school last Easter. 'I'm not having folks think I don't earn enough to keep me family on me own,' he said. But it wasn't the money Eileen was thinking of – one good thing about Francis, in fact the *only* good thing, was he never kept her short of cash. He liked her and the house to look nice when people came to see him on Corporation business. He'd hand over a few quid, unasked, for her to buy a new frock or a pair of shoes, though he insisted on coming with her and picking out what *he* liked, rather than let her choose for herself. And she was even better off now than when Francis was home. The Mersey Docks & Harbour Board would continue to pay his wages, and she got an allowance from the Army. But Eileen wanted to work for different reasons, reasons she couldn't quite explain, even to herself; she just felt there should be more to a woman's life than cooking and cleaning. Annie felt the same. Even when her boys started work and there was no more need to go out scrubbing and cleaning, she'd got herself a part-time job in Woolworths and it wasn't just for the money. Now that Terry and Joe were away, Annie was considering looking for a full-time job.

The door opened and Tony came in, his gun tucked in the waist of his pyjamas and his gas mask over his shoulder.

Eileen smiled. 'You're well prepared. God help Hitler if he invades Number Sixteen Pearl Street.'

'I'll kill him if he does,' Tony said stoutly.

'I know you will, son. Come on, get in bed for a minute while I finish this ciggie.'

His face lit up as he climbed in beside her. 'Me dad would have a fit if he knew.'

'Well, what the eye don't see . . .' She put an arm around his shoulders. 'What shall we do today?'

He looked up at her, puzzled. 'What d'you mean, Mam?'

'Well, you'll be back at school next week. Let's do something exciting, like go into town.'

'Honest, Mam? Honest?' She could feel his body tense with excitement. 'Can we go on the tram?'

Eileen groaned. 'It's much quicker on the train, luv.'

'I know, but the tram's more . . . more . . .' He searched for the right word.

'More noisy, uncomfortable and takes ten times longer?' she suggested.

'More *interesting*.'

'Oh, I suppose so,' she said with pretend impatience. 'Now, let's see. After breakfast, I'll go over to Auntie Sheila's and say tara to Cal and then nip round to the Co-op and buy some blackout material. Mr Singerman's promised to run me curtains up on his machine. When all that's done, we'll catch the tram into town. If it weren't for bloody Hitler, we could've gone to the pictures. Shirley Temple was on at the Trocadero in *The Little Princess*. Instead, we'll go to Pets Corner in Lewis's – after we've had our dinner in Lyons.'

'Oh, *Mam*!' he sighed blissfully. 'We mustn't forget our gas masks.'

'We won't,' she said comfortably. 'What frock shall I wear? The blue one or the green?'

'I like the blue one best.'

'The blue one it is.' She stubbed the cigarette out in the saucer. 'Come on, then, Tony Costello! Get your skates on. We've got a lot to do today.'

The Co-op appeared to have had a run on blackout material. There was none left in stock. Eileen stood in the middle of the shop, wondering where to try next. She preferred using the Co-op whenever she could. Twenty yards of material at one and eleven a yard meant quite a lot of divi being added to her account. She noticed Miss Brazier, alone and aloof in her cage, and smiled in her direction. The woman smiled stiffly back. Poor ould sod, you could tell it was only shyness that prevented her from being friendly.

Eileen crossed over. It wouldn't do any harm to exchange a few words. 'They've run out of blackout. I suppose I'll have to try somewhere else.'

Miss Brazier nodded without speaking. Eileen turned to walk away, when she heard a noise. Miss Brazier was tapping on the glass with a coin. 'I shouldn't tell you this, Mrs Costello, because they've only got a small amount and they didn't want a riot, but if you hang on another ten or fifteen minutes, they'll be bringing out another couple of bolts of material that came in this morning.'

'Thanks very much. I'll just go and look at the wool. I want to knit our Tony a jumper.'

'I'd advise you not buy the crepe. It's got no give, the rib stretches after a single wearing.'

'Thanks again.' Close up, Eileen was surprised to notice that behind the ugly horn-rimmed glasses Miss Brazier's eyes were quite pretty; a lovely blue, almost violet, with long dark lashes. If only she would do something with her hair and not wear those awful clothes which looked as if they'd belonged to her mother. Emboldened by such an unexpected display of friendliness from a person who normally kept herself very much to herself, she said, 'Y'know, you're always welcome to come around our house for a cup of tea on your day off, like, Miss Brazier?'

'Thank you very much.' The tone was cold. Miss Brazier seemed to shrink into herself. Eileen had gone too far.

'And thank you – for telling me about the blackout and the wool,' Eileen said cheerfully. 'Well, it's been nice talking to you, Miss Brazier. Tara.'

Ten minutes later Eileen paid for her material. The money whizzed across the shop in the little metal cannister. She waited for her change, watching Miss Brazier remove the two pound notes, tear off the top half of the bill, and put a handful of coppers back. The woman didn't look up once. Eileen waved as she left, but Miss Brazier didn't wave back.

When Eileen got back to Pearl Street, some sort of commotion was going on. Several women were standing outside and one or two were crying.

'What's up?' she asked of nobody in particular.

'Eh, Eileen!' Agnes Donovan darted across and seized her arm, anxious to be the first to convey what was obviously bad news. 'You'll never guess what's happened. The *Athenia*'s been sunk.'

'Oh, no!' gasped Eileen, horrified. 'What about Mary and Joey and the kids?'

'No-one knows,' Aggie said ghoulishly. 'It was on the Harrisons' wireless. Over a hundred people were drowned. I expect it was one of them torpedoes.'

'Has anyone told our Sheila?'

'I told her meself a while back.'

'Cal only went back to sea this morning,' Eileen snapped. 'I wish you'd kept your big mouth shut for once, Aggie Donovan.' The woman must have been in her element, running round the street, knocking on doors, telling everyone.

'She had to know sometime,' Aggie replied in an aggrieved voice.

'Well, you should've left it to me or me dad to tell her.' Eileen turned on her heel towards her sister's house. Somehow, she'd never thought that war would touch them so quickly and so personally. She recalled the day of the party, what a celebration that had been. Someone had said, 'You're getting out just in time, Joey.' But the Flahertys hadn't got out quick enough. Still, maybe they were all safe and sound, but even so, it must have been a terrible experience and would put a blight on the new life they were so looking forward to.

Sheila's front door was open as usual, and Ryan and Caitlin were playing in the hall. As Eileen struggled over the gate, she was surprised to hear the sound of laughter coming from the parlour and recognised Annie's voice.

Eileen paused in the parlour doorway, blinking. 'What the hell are they?'

Two monstrous contraptions, each made out of a combination of rubber and canvas with a little grille at one end and connected to an attachment similar to a set of bellows, stood on the polished table.

'Baby gas masks! The District Nurse just brought them.' Sheila could scarcely speak for laughing.

'Gerraway! How do they work?' Eileen approached cautiously. 'They don't half look complicated.'

'They are. In case of an attack, I've to put Mary in one and Ryan in the other, like, then pump like bloody hell so they don't suffocate.' Tears were running down Sheila's red cheeks. 'Trouble is, I can only manage one at a time.'

'Not only that, Eileen, but she'll be wearing a gas mask herself.' Annie was doubled up in mirth. 'Never mind, Shiel, I'll shoot over if there's a gas attack and pump one for you.'

'That's if you're not already dead yourself,' gasped Sheila.

For some reason, this made them howl. 'It doesn't seem the least bit funny to me,' said Eileen, mystified.

Annie rubbed her eyes. 'I suppose, luv, it's just a case of if you don't laugh, you'll only cry.'

Then Eileen understood. Cal had gone, Annie's boys were gone, the *Athenia* had been sunk, and this was how her friend and her sister were coping with their grief, hiding it behind a display of unnatural high spirits over something which wasn't funny at all. In fact, when you thought about it, baby gas masks were anything but a laughing matter

It was probably the finest kitchen in the finest road in Calderstones, the most exclusive area of Liverpool. Twenty-five feet square, the floors were tiled with cream stone, each square engraved with a brown fleur de lys. The freshly washed floor, the twin cream enamel sinks, the double draining board, the silver taps, all sparkled in the sunshine which came streaming through the long narrow lattice window and the lace curtain lifted gently in the soft afternoon breeze. A large cream refrigerator hummed noisily, a comforting, welcome sound. In pride of place stood the Aga cooker. Also cream, it served the central heating system, and a few coals glowed behind the thick glass door. Over the years, several people had come especially to see the Aga, curious to know how it worked before they bought one for themselves, and Jessica Fleming would explain its marvels before finishing off, 'Of course, it was frightfully expensive.' People would leave, impressed, not just with the Aga, but with Jessica herself. At forty-three, she was a magnificent woman with a milky, almost dazzling complexion, unusual dark green eyes, and a startling head of red wavy hair. The hair was slightly more red than it had been in her youth, as nowadays Jessica used henna to disguise unwelcome streaks of grey.

Now, sitting in the corner referred to as 'the nook', with its gingham-covered table and teak chairs, Jessica regarded her lovely kitchen with a feeling of unmitigated rage. Soon it would no longer be hers. Any day now, she would have to leave Calderstones and the five-bedroomed detached mock-Tudor house would be sold to someone else. Some other woman would soon be sitting here delighting in the sight of the Aga and the cream refrigerator, because the house had been mortgaged to the hilt and the bank wanted their money back.

It had come as a total shock. She hadn't suspected a thing, but last night, when every other sane person in the country had been discussing the war, Arthur had confessed the company was on its last legs, he'd borrowed thousands. Everything had to go.

'Why didn't you tell me before?' she asked, dazed, and as yet uncomprehending of the full nature of their misfortune.

'I didn't want to worry you.'

'Worry me? And what's all this if it isn't worrying?

65

Maybe I could have done something about it.'

She had a better head for figures than he had, but had thought him capable enough. After all, you didn't need much of a feel for business to take over the running of a fully-fledged haulage company with several secure contracts and a dependable force of well paid drivers. Her father, who'd started the firm over thirty years ago with a single horse and cart and built it up until there were a dozen lorries, had scarcely any education at all. She stared at her husband with contempt. He was a good-looking man, perhaps more handsome now than when they married, though she'd always known he was weak.

'I want to see the books, Arthur,' she demanded angrily.

Jessica noticed his hands were shaking when he laid the books and a brown cardboard folder in front of her. She pored over the accounts for quite a while until she could make sense of things.

'Why is there such a large amount for petrol? It's nearly double last year's?'

'I don't know.' He looked vague.

'But it doesn't make sense,' she said impatiently, 'We've done less work, far less, yet used more petrol. Why, Arthur?'

'I think some of the drivers have been thieving, siphoning it off,' he replied eventually. His voice was subdued, ashamed.

'Our drivers would never rob us.' She was outraged. 'Most are my father's old friends.'

'For Chrissakes, Jess,' he said petulantly, 'they left ages ago. They're a different lot altogether now. After all, Bert's been dead over ten years.'

Jessica took a deep breath and returned to the accounts. 'Why have our insurance premiums leapt up? This is a colossal amount.'

He fidgeted with his Paisley silk tie. He was a conceited man, always concerned with his appearance. He had a penchant for silk; ties, shirts, underwear, and expensive hand-tailored suits. 'We had quite a lot of claims last year,' he said awkwardly. 'Stuff went missing off the lorries . . .'

'The drivers again?' she remarked sarcastically.

'I suppose it must have been.'

'You didn't consider sacking them?'

He squirmed in his seat, but didn't reply.

'Or fetching in the police?'

When he still remained silent, she demanded, 'Why not?' Then, in a harder voice, 'Why not, Arthur?'

Incredibly, he looked close to tears. 'To tell you the truth, I was scared. The drivers, they gang together, and they're a rough lot.'

'*You bloody fool!*' she spat. Had she known, she would have wiped the floor with the drivers, every last one of them.

He began to cry. Too angry to be moved, Jessica left him sobbing and took the papers into the kitchen where she went through the figures item by item. There were massive amounts for maintenance of the lorries, mystifyingly large sums spent on tyres, the wage bill had trebled to include overtime, yet there'd been scarcely any income for months. After an hour of patient study Jessica came to the inevitable conclusion that her husband's employees had been fleecing the company for years.

She opened the file. It was full of angry letters; from clients who'd had furniture moved, found an expensive item missing and refused to pay the bill, from customers cancelling regular contracts on account of 'pilfering' – on several occasions entire loads had gone missing – from creditors demanding payment, from the Income Tax –

Arthur had paid nothing for years. But the letters that made Jessica's heart turn cold were those from the bank. Arthur had borrowed against the house, more than it was worth, she felt convinced. He must have been subsidising the firm for a long time. The final letter was dated last week. If he didn't repay at least part of the debt within twenty-eight days, they would take legal action.

Jessica tried to stay calm as the full scale of their predicament became clear. By now, it was past midnight and her head was thumping viciously. They were penni-less. Worse than penniless, they were up to their ears in debt. She tried to do a few quick sums; the sale of the house would almost clear what was owing to the bank and if they got rid of the lorries and the car it would settle some of the creditors' demands. There was a time when Hennessy's Haulage and Removal Company would have fetched a tidy sum, but Jessica knew it would be a waste of time trying to sell the firm as a going concern now. Who would want it when they saw the books?

But even then, when everything had gone, they would still owe money, and there was nothing more shameful than owing money. Her father had never owed a penny in his life. How would they live, *where* would they live, with nothing coming in and a debt of more than four figures hanging over their heads?

It was then she remembered the properties in Bootle. Her father had bought them as an investment not long before he died. Twelve houses at nine and six rent a week came to . . . Her brain was too tired to work out such a simple sum. Whatever it was, it might keep the remaining creditors and the Income Tax people happy.

Jessica sighed. It was curious, but she almost felt a sense of relief. Anything, anything was better than declaring themselves bankrupt. Just the thought of it made her cringe with shame. Bankrupts had to make an announcement in the paper. She imagined the neighbours reading it, her friends from the bridge club, the choir, the WVS which she'd only joined recently as her contribution towards the war effort.

Arthur appeared in the doorway. 'I'm going to bed,' he muttered.

'I thought you'd already gone,' she said icily. He was swaying on his feet. 'I see you've been at the brandy.'

'I'm sorry.'

'Sorry you're drunk or sorry about all this . . . this mess?' She gestured towards the papers spread over the table.

'About everything,' he said in a small voice.

She took a deep breath. 'What's going to happen, Arthur? After we've sold the house and the company's gone, what do we do then?'

'I don't know.'

'I don't know, either. What will we live on? There won't be a bean left by the time the whole mess has been sorted out. And *where* will we live, come to that?' For a moment, she considered leaving him to clear the entire shambles up by himself. She could get a job, start afresh alone. It was no more than he deserved. Yet, deep down, Jessica knew she still loved him. He was weak and conceited, a coward who'd let her father's business go to rack and ruin, but despite that, she couldn't bring herself to walk out and leave him to cope on his own. He needed her and perhaps, in her own strange way, she needed him. Sadly, they'd never had the children they'd both so longed for. He was all she had. But he'd behaved badly and it would be a long time before things would be the same again.

He was mumbling something she couldn't understand.

'What did you say?'

'I said, I'll get a job, and one of the properties is empty. We could live in . . .' he paused nervously at the sight of her horrified expression.

'Live in Bootle!' She couldn't believe her ears. She said it again in order to convince herself the words had been spoken. 'Live in Bootle?'

'Why not?' he asked simply.

'Because me dad, I mean my father would turn in his grave.' Just the mere mention of the place and she'd slipped up on her grammar. 'You've never lived there, Arthur, you don't know what it's like.'

He shrugged. 'It would be rent free.'

'Which street is it?'

'Pearl Street.'

'Oh, no!' She remembered the wall at the end, right next to their house, the trains puffing clouds of smoke, covering the washing with black smuts; she recalled the little rooms, the narrow stairs, the poky windows with horror. Yet, in a way, it made sense. You couldn't get much further away from Calderstones than Bootle. It was way over the other side of Liverpool, where there was no chance of coming face to face with any of her old friends and neighbours. And there'd be no landlord coming round for the rent. She couldn't bear the thought of going back to a landlord.

'Someone might recognise me,' she whispered.

Arthur actually had the gall to sound impatient. 'Don't be silly, Jess. You were only a girl when you left. What was it, fifteen?'

'Fourteen.'

'No-one will know you after all this time. And say someone did? It wouldn't be the end of the world.'

It would be for me, she thought. The shame would kill

me. 'What about our furniture?' she asked weakly.

'We could sell it with the house, I suppose. Just keep a few pieces for the new one.'

'New!' she said bitterly. 'I was born in one of those "new" houses. Our refrigerator would never fit in the kitchen and we'd have to leave the Aga behind. Not only that, the lounge isn't much bigger than this nook, it wouldn't take the three-piece and what would I do with the dining room suite?' The oak table, when extended, was twelve feet long and there were eight chairs upholstered in red sculptured velvet, two of them carvers. Overcome, Jessica began to cry.

Arthur patted her shoulder awkwardly. 'I'm sorry, darling.'

'And so you bloody well should be,' she wailed. 'You've ruined my life. You've ruined everything. Go away.'

She went to bed eventually and slept in one of the spare bedrooms. Next morning, she had a bath and struggled into her tightest and most flattering rubber corselet which showed off her voluptuous figure to its best advantage. After much deliberation in front of her packed wardrobe, she chose a beige linen suit which had a matching Robin Hood style hat with a freckled feather, put the books and the file in an attaché case, and went to see the bank manager. There was no sign of Arthur. She had no idea whether he was still in bed or had gone out, and wasn't much interested.

At the bank, the manager tried to insist on Arthur's presence, but she told him if he wanted the bank's money back he had to talk to her. 'It's *my* house,' she said tartly, 'and *my* company. Both of them belonged to my father, which I'm sure you're well aware of. I know they'd been transferred into our joint names, but if you'd had any common sense you'd have informed me what was going on. Instead, you gave money, hand over fist, to my husband and I didn't know a thing about it. I bet if I'd tried to borrow, you wouldn't have given me, a woman, a penny without consulting my husband first.'

The manager had the grace to look uncomfortable. Perhaps it was guilt, but he ended up being quite helpful. After briefly perusing the contents of the attaché case, he advised that the most important thing to do was pay the Income Tax. In fact, if the deeds of the house were signed over to the bank, the manager would advance a further loan for this purpose, otherwise Arthur could end up in jail. The bank would settle the outstanding debts with the proceeds from the house and eventual sale of the lorries and agree to 'monies still outstanding' being repaid weekly from the rents of the properties in Bootle.

'How does that suit you, madam?' he asked pompously when he'd finished explaining.

Jessica felt as if she'd like to spit in his well shaven, talcum-powdered face. Her corselet was killing her, digging into the flesh at the top of her legs and, although she appreciated the advice, he'd dispensed it in a slow pedantic way as if she were a child – or as stupid as Arthur. 'Apart from the fact it doesn't leave us a penny to live on, it suits me fine,' she said acidly.

'Of course, once the house is ours – the legal proceedings should only take a few weeks – I must insist you leave immediately, otherwise we would be obliged to charge you rent, and in the interim, any borrowings are subject to interest, which is rather high at the moment.'

So, they wanted blood as well as flesh. Bestowing upon him a smile that could have killed, Jessica left.

Outside, she was about to hail a taxi to the firm's depot in Long Lane, when she remembered she'd better start being careful where money was concerned. She caught a tram instead and sat behind a woman with two children who both kept drawing chewing gum out of their mouths in long, wet sticky strings. Jessica stared at them. They knelt on the seat and stared insolently back. These were the sort of people she'd be mixing with now. Damn Arthur, she could strangle him.

She got off at Long Lane and walked around the corner to the depot. Ten lorries, all painted the familiar fawn colour, with 'Hennessy's Haulage and Removal' in maroon, stood in a row in the yard, which meant there were only two out on a job of work. A dozen or more men were lounging outside the little wooden office – she hadn't realised how ramshackle it had become – some playing pitch and toss, others bent over a folded newspaper. As Jessica approached, she saw it was open on the racing page.

She didn't recognise a single face and cursed herself for not having taken more interest in the firm. Her father had built it up by the sweat of his brow, working from early morning till late at night, and it had been ruined by this crowd of . . . of louts!

There were several wolf whistles when they saw her approaching and comments about her figure which she affected not to hear.

'Can I help you, Missus?' one of them asked with a leer. Jessica had no intention of beating around the bush. 'I'm Mrs Fleming, the boss's wife,' she announced brusquely. 'All of you, get off these premises immediately. You're sacked.' She wouldn't give them the satisfaction of knowing the company was to close.

There was the expected outrage, a chorus of swearwords and threats, but Jessica held her ground fearlessly. The more they swore, the stronger she became. She was no longer Jessica Fleming of Calderstones, but

Jessie Hennessy, whose dad had started off as a rag and bone merchant in Pearl Street, Bootle, though even Arthur didn't know *that*!

'What about our wages?' One of the men came up and thrust his face against hers. It was an effort not to recoil from the stench of his foul breath.

'You're not getting a penny.'

There was a howl of incredulous laughter. 'D'you really think you'll get away with that?'

'Yes, I do,' Jessica said calmly, 'because if you don't leave immediately, I'll call the police. I know all about the thieving that's been going on, and unlike my husband, you don't scare me a bit.'

'You know, you're askin' for it, Missus.'

She was suddenly surrounded by half a dozen men looking down at her threateningly. She glanced across at the road. There weren't all that many people about. Still, she'd gone this far, she couldn't back down now.

'If that's the way you want it, I'll call the police from the office here and now.' As she pushed her way through the crowd, a hand reached out and grabbed her arm. Jessica looked down at the hand scornfully, then up at the man's angry face. 'Brave, aren't you? I reckon a woman is just about your match.'

Suddenly, one of the men burst out laughing. 'I'll say this for you, Missus,' he said admiringly. 'You've got more guts in your little finger than the boss's got in his entire body. Come on, mates, let's do as she sez. I'm expecting me calling up papers soon, so's I would've been leaving, anyway.'

When Jessica arrived home, Mrs Blanchard had just finished mopping the kitchen floor.

'Had some visitors over the weekend did you, Missus? I

noticed the bed in one of the spare rooms needed making,' she remarked breathlessly when she came back in through the utility room after having emptied the bucket and wrung out the mop. Her old eyes sparkled in her deeply lined face. Mrs Blanchard never looked anything but completely happy.

'Yes, we did,' Jessica said absently. She'd just realised Mrs Blanchard would have to go. From now on, Jessica would have to mop her own floors, make her own bed, polish her own furniture. It was going to be awkward, sacking the woman, who'd been a good worker and very dependable in the long time she'd worked there, despite her advancing years.

'Here, come on, luv, sit down and I'll make you a cup of tea. You look all flustered,' Mrs Blanchard said solicitously. 'In fact, I wouldn't mind one meself, I've hardly stopped since I came in this morning.'

Jessica had never encouraged the habit that even some of her most well-bred friends adopted, of sitting down for a gossip and a cup of tea or coffee with the charwoman. She usually made herself scarce when Mrs Blanchard stopped for her break. This morning, however, she sat down in the nook and allowed herself to be waited on.

'Now, what d'you think about this flipping war? That bloody Hitler, he's got a lot to answer for.' Mrs Blanchard sat opposite and pushed a cup of tea in front of Jessica.

'What war?' Jessica nearly asked, but stopped just in time. She'd been so embroiled in her own desperate situation that she'd almost forgotten a war had been declared little more than twenty-four hours ago. 'It scarcely bears thinking about,' she said, then, in a rush: 'In fact, I wanted to talk to you about that, Mrs Blanchard. My husband and I have decided to move to America for the duration. Arthur has some relatives there.'

'Oh! Oh, well.' Mrs Blanchard shrugged cheerfully. 'You won't want me no more, then?'

'I'm afraid not,' Jessica said uncomfortably. There wasn't a trace of envy or resentment on the old woman's face. For the first time ever, she wondered why her cleaner was always so happy and vaguely regretted never having spared the time to find out. 'Of course, I'll give you a good reference – and money in lieu of notice.'

She went into the lounge where the spare cash was kept and counted out ten pound notes. It was a lot, but when you considered how much the drivers had done them out of, a tenner wasn't too much to give a loyal employee who'd never taken a penny she wasn't due in all the time she'd been there.

After Mrs Blanchard had gone, minus her job, but over the moon with her unexpected windfall, Jessica went upstairs and removed the corselet which had begun to feel like a straitjacket. She felt pleased with her off-the-cuff lie. It had been an inspiration, America. That's what she'd tell everybody. It would explain why the business was being sold, and going abroad for the duration seemed a superior thing to do. Thank goodness they hadn't had that £350 landscaped air-raid shelter built in the garden. Nearly everyone else in the road already had one installed. No wonder Arthur kept trying to dissuade her, to the extent that she'd nearly gone ahead and ordered it herself. Of course, he knew things she didn't!

Feeling fidgety and on edge, she made a cake to take her mind off things, otherwise she'd just mope around thinking about the lovely possessions that would be left behind. She beat the mixture in the bowl with unusual ferocity. From time to time, it took on the look of Arthur's face and she beat it even harder.

The cake in the oven, she sat in the nook and stared

around the kitchen. The more she stared, the more her rage began to mount. In a few weeks or months, all this would belong to another woman.

'Damn you, Arthur Fleming, for being a fool,' she whispered. 'You've cost me my house, my life, everything!'

She'd miss their social life; the supper dances, dinner with their friends, the bridge club, but most of all, she'd miss the choir. At the moment, they were rehearsing *The Messiah* for a special Christmas concert in Liverpool Town Hall. Jessica was the lead soprano. Even when there wasn't a solo part, she always stood in the middle of the front row; the star. That morning, one of the drivers had said she had guts, but Jessica knew she didn't have the guts to tell anyone how low she and Arthur were about to fall. No-one knew where Jessica really came from. She told people she'd been born in Woolton. She'd even, once, pointed out the actual house. Her current friends made judgements according to their own standards; the size of your house, the horsepower of your car, the labels in your clothes, the food you set on your table. Jessica Fleming would sooner tell a lie and disappear out of their lives altogether than confess she was going to live in Bootle.

Chapter 4

'Eh, Eileen, come and have a gander at the woman moving into Number Five.' Annie Poulson came rushing into Eileen's house through the back way. 'She looks as if she's dressed for a garden party at Buckingham Palace – and you should see her furniture!'

'Annie! You sound just like Aggie Donovan. You haven't been spying out the window, surely!'

'I have. As for Aggie, she's out brushing her step to get a better look. Come on, Eileen.'

Somewhat reluctantly, Eileen followed her friend into the parlour, where she was already peering through the net curtains. It was best to humour Annie at the moment. She'd been in a strange, excitable mood ever since Terry and Joe had been home on leave for a week prior to being sent to France with the British Expeditionary Force. Her lads had looked very young and embarrassed in their clumsy khaki uniforms, their once curly heads clipped so short they looked like convicts. They'd returned to Aldershot with enough canary cake and bunloaf to feed the entire British Army for weeks – not just off their mam; the entire street had contributed.

'Jesus! Look at that wardrobe! You could live in that quite easily. It'll never go up the stairs.'

Eileen joined Annie at the window. A large furniture van was parked at the end of the street, its nose against the wall. Two men were struggling to manoeuvre a massive pale oak wardrobe through the front door of Number five, the Flahertys' old house. Aggie Donovan was making a half-hearted pretence of brushing her step whilst watching avidly.

'Here's the woman now,' Annie said. 'Just look at her.'

The wardrobe had been squeezed inside and a striking red-haired woman came out and regarded the contents of the lorry worriedly. She wore a navy-blue tailored dress, three-quarter length white gloves and a picture hat.

'She's wondering how she'll fit it all in,' deduced Annie.

'What are you, a thought reader or something?' asked Eileen sarcastically. 'I like her hair, though. It's a lovely colour.'

'Hennaed,' declared Annie flatly. 'And her corsets are killing her. She can hardly bend down.'

'Annie!' Eileen burst out laughing. She left the window and sat in an armchair. 'What else can you tell from just looking? What's her name, for instance? Where does she come from?'

Annie didn't reply, but continued to watch the activity outside with interest. Suddenly she gasped. 'Well, bugger me, if it isn't Jessie Hennessy! I *thought* she looked familiar.'

'You don't mean to tell me someone like that comes from round here?' Eileen said, astonished.

'This very street!' Annie was almost jumping up and down with excitement. 'Her dad used to run a rag and bone merchant's where the coalyard is now. I knew Jessie at school, though she was near the top when I started. She was full of airs and graces, even then. She had a lovely voice, though. I can remember her singing *Silent Night* at a carol concert as clear as if it were yesterday. Not long after she left school, they moved to Walton Road. Bert Hennessy had started doing deliveries on his cart by then and began to make a bit of cash. I've never seen Jessie since.'

'You can't recognise her after all this time?'

Annie was too engrossed to answer. 'You should see the three-piece, green velvet!' she gasped. 'Though it'll never go in the parlour. They'll have to stand the sofa on its end.'

'I've got a green velvet three-piece,' said Eileen indignantly. 'I've never known you drool over *it* before.' She patted the arm affectionately.

'Yes, but your three-piece could sit on this three-piece's knee,' replied Annie disparagingly. Bored with watching, she came and sat in the other armchair and pulled a packet of cigarettes out of the pocket of her pinnie. 'Have a fag, Eileen?'

'Ta. I'm smoking meself to death, lately. I must cut down.' As Eileen lit her cigarette, she said sadly, 'It seems funny, seeing people like that move into the Flahertys'. I wonder what Mary would have thought?'

'She would have laughed over it as much as we did.'

Nothing had been heard of Joey Flaherty and the kids, they presumed they'd arrived in Canada by now, but Mary's name had been among the list of casualties off the *Athenia* which had been printed in the *Echo*.

'It's awful, isn't it, when you think about the way they skimped and saved for years to get away,' Eileen mused.

'It's bloody terrible, but there you are, that's war for you,' Annie said in a harsh voice.

The two women were silent for a while, thinking about their old friend. Then Eileen sighed. 'Oh, well! What else do you know about this Jessie Hennessy?'

'Not much. Shortly after they left, Bert started putting adverts in the *Echo* for the business. He had a couple of lorries by then, so I reckon it must have really taken off.

There was an announcement years later when Jessie got married, her name's Fleming now if I remember rightly, and she calls herself Jessica. I began seeing her picture at some posh do or other, the Lord Mayor's Ball, or singing in some concert. I sort of kept track of her, without meaning to. I read once she lived in Calderstones.'

'Something awful must have happened to make her move back here,' Eileen said seriously. 'Poor ould thing.'

'Honestly, Eileen, you'd cry for Hitler if he cut his rotten finger. You're too soft by a mile.'

'No, I'm not,' Eileen countered defensively. 'I just feel sorry for people, that's all.' After a pause, she said softly, 'Annie?'

'What, luv?'

'Don't tell anyone about that Jessie Hennessy, will you? Maybe no-one else in the street'll recognise her.'

'I wasn't going to,' said Annie. 'If she wants to keep it a secret, it's up to her. I've no intention of telling another soul.'

They began to discuss the morality of buying stocks of food in anticipation of rationing. Was it unpatriotic to hoard non-perishables? Ration books had already arrived, a brown one for Eileen, blue for Tony, and people were expected to register with a grocer. Eileen and her sister had registered with the Maypole in Marsh Lane so it would be simpler to buy each other's rations when the occasion arose.

'I couldn't get sugar anywhere the other day,' Eileen said. 'There's a real shortage already.'

'I don't suppose it'd hurt to put a few odds and ends away each week if you can afford it.'

'Though it's not really fair on those who can't. I bet me dad wouldn't approve if I told him.'

Annie giggled. 'I was in Veronica's the other day

getting meself a couple of vests for the winter, and she advised me to buy plenty of stockings and knicker elastic.'

Eileen wrinkled her nose. 'I don't know why you go there, Annie, when you can go to the Co-op. That Veronica makes me come out in goose pimples.'

There was a shuddering roar from outside and the houses trembled as the furniture van backed out of the street. Annie left, and as soon as the back door closed, Eileen set a tray with an embroidered cloth and china from the teaset that had been a wedding present from Sheila and Calum. She poured two cups of tea and took the tray over to Number 5 as a gesture of welcome to the new residents. They were probably parched for a cuppa and searching desperately for the kettle or the teapot. She knocked on the door and it was opened by a lean, harrassed man in his forties.

'I reckon you must be parched after all that hard work,' she said, smiling warmly. 'So's I've brought you a drink. You can bring the tray back later. I'm Eileen Costello from Number Sixteen.'

His answering smile transformed his fine, rather delicate features. He was actually quite good-looking in a refined way, a bit like Leslie Howard only darker. 'That's very kind of you, thanks. I'm Arthur Fleming, by the way.' His voice was pleasant and cultured, without any trace of Liverpool accent.

'Arthur!' The red-haired woman appeared in the hallway minus her hat and gloves. She took one glance at the tray and said, 'There's no need, thank you. I've already got the kettle on.'

'But . . .' her husband protested.

The woman ignored him. She came down the hall, pushed him to one side and said to Eileen, 'We're all sorted out, thank you,' and closed the door firmly in her face. Eileen was left on the pavement holding the tray, feeling rather foolish and hurt.

She walked back across the street, saw her dad coming towards her and grinned. 'I was expecting you, Dad. See, I've got a cup of tea all ready – in the best china, too!'

He regarded her with astonishment and she shrugged. 'I made it for the new people who've just moved into the Flahertys' old house, but *she* sent me away with a flea in me ear.'

'That,' said Arthur Fleming, 'was utterly despicable.'

Jessica was already feeling slightly ashamed. After all, these people were her inferiors. It was up to her to show how the middle class behaved, not slam the door in their faces. There was no way she would have taken the tray, she wanted no truck with Pearl Street, but she should have declined with more graciousness. Her shame only made her feel even more irritable with Arthur. How dare he criticise?

'I've no intention of having anything to do with the neighbours,' she said angrily.

'That's stupid, Jess. We'll be living cheek by jowl from now on. You can't just ignore them.'

'I can and I will,' Jessica declared. 'Another thing, Arthur. I don't want people knowing we own property, else the tenants will be round by the minute demanding we get things fixed. The agent can collect the money, as before. His name is on the rent book, not ours.' It was worth the ten per cent fee to remain anonymous.

'Suit yourself' Arthur shrugged. 'Well, seeing as the kettle's on, I'll make that cup of tea.'

'I can't find the kettle,' Jessica said flatly. 'And even if I could, there's no stove. We'll have to buy one.' She thought about her Aga and could have spat.

'No stove!' Arthur frowned. 'I think this is a stove.' He nodded towards the blackleaded range. Mary Flaherty had left it gleaming, but by now there was a thin layer of dust.

'You *think!*' Jessica was so full of choking anger that the words came out in a scream. 'The trouble with you, Arthur Fleming, is you've never been poor. You've never even been in a house like this before. You *think* this is a stove! Well, you're right, it is. I cooked my father's meals on a stove like that in the house opposite when me mam, I mean, when my mother died and I looked after him. That stove is older than I am and I've no intention of using it. It can come out and I'll have a nice modern fireplace installed and buy a proper stove, one of those electric ones, for the kitchen.'

To her intense irritation, Arthur actually grinned. 'It looks quite an efficient system to me. I reckon it works the same way as an Aga, but you do what you want, though I don't know what you'll use for money.'

'I'll sell my musquash.'

'That's not a bad idea. You'd look pretty stupid going shopping around here in a fifty-guinea fur coat.'

She glared at him. To her surprise and indignation, over the last month, once Arthur had got over the initial shock of losing the business and the finances had been sorted out, he'd become a different man altogether. Not only had he brightened up considerably, but he'd begun to make all sorts of flippant, unsympathetic comments like that. He didn't appear to be the least bit sorry for what had happened, and went round whistling, apparently full of the joys of spring and indifferent to the fact she only spoke to him when she had to. He started whistling now and rubbed his hands together in a businesslike fashion.

'Well,' he said cheerfully, 'I'd better start sorting this lot out. Some of the stuff will have to go in the boxroom. Pity about that tea, though. I could have really done with a cup.'

He went into the lounge, leaving Jessica in the chaos of the living room.

They'd brought too much furniture from Calderstones, even though the smallest items had been taken, such as the three-piece out of Jessica's little sitting room, and the table and chairs from the nook. Even so, everything was too large. In fact, they could scarcely move. They had to edge themselves sideways into every room.

Jessica stood staring out of the window at the tiny whitewashed yard. The walls were scrawled with coloured chalk and the door to the outside lavatory was hanging half off its hinges.

An outside lavatory! She'd forgotten. She closed her eyes in horror, imagining the hell of sitting out there in winter. When she opened her eyes again, the room seemed to have grown smaller and she felt panicky and closed in. The house wasn't big enough for hens to live in, let alone people. Everything seemed to be on top of her, there was no space to breathe, and she felt sure she was going to faint.

'Arthur,' she whispered plaintively, but he was too busy to hear and she was glad. He was the weak one, she the strong. She wished she had someone to talk to, though, a friend. It was ironic, she thought, all those hundreds of women she'd got to know over the years, yet there wasn't a single one she could confide in. Now she thought about it, they'd been more rivals than friends, always trying to go one better than the other, whether it be clothes or cars or dinner parties. Though

Jessie had been the first to get an Aga, she thought with satisfaction.

Arthur had begun to sing, '*I, yi-yi-yi-yi, I like you verry much. I, yi-yi-yi-yi-, I think you're grand,*' a song Jessica particularly hated, along with the woman who sang it, Carmen Miranda, who wore too much make-up and looked as common as muck in her tutti frutti headgear.

She sighed. It was dark in here. She went to put the light on but couldn't find the switch. Frowning, she glanced behind the door and in the hall, but there was no sign. Then she looked up at the ceiling, saw the gas mantle, and shrieked, 'Arthur! *There's no electricity!*' She had entirely forgotten!

Arthur appeared, grinning. 'In that case, you'd better get on to the landlord, hadn't you?'

Vivien had worked a minor miracle, Clive Waterton thought proudly as he sat in his office and his thoughts turned, as they so frequently did, to his wife. In the five weeks since they'd had them, their evacuees had been transformed into a respectable-looking pair of children. They'd put on weight and numerous visits to flat, silvery Southport beach or the sandhills at Birkdale during what had been an exceptionally fine September had given them a healthy tan and cleared away all their spots and sores and those terrible purple bruises. Their behaviour had improved enormously. At first, Vivien had played a little game at mealtimes.

'Whoever is the *last* to finish gets a little prize!' So the two of them sat there eating sedately, dragging the meal out.

'There!' Vivien would sing. 'Doesn't food taste so much nicer when it's eaten slowly?' Now, there was no need to offer a prize. Vivien had taught them how to use a knife and fork properly and they ate like any other well-mannered children, perhaps more so. It was a pity Mrs Critchley hadn't taken to them, but as long as she kept her opinions to herself, it didn't matter.

In the office, several colleagues had complained about the children who had been billetted on them. 'Bloody little savages. The house is like a jungle.'

'My two are fine,' Clive would declare smugly.

'You're lucky. We can't wait to see the back of ours.'

The boy, Dicky, remained a bit sullen, obviously missing his mother, but seemed happy enough to go along with his sister or play with his train set, but it was Freda who had altered out of all recognition, as if it had only needed a good wash and a few pretty clothes to reveal the real child underneath. She had a quick, intelligent brain and Vivien was teaching her to read. The two would sit crushed together in an armchair looking at fashion magazines and discussing clothes and make-up as if they were the same age and had known each other forever. Of course, Freda was far too old for her years and Vivien seemed to be getting younger by the day. Clive supposed they sort of met in the middle.

But Clive was worried. Several evacuees had already returned home. After all, they'd come to get away from air raids and there hadn't been a single one so far in the entire country. In fact, a curious calm seemed to have descended and the Americans had begun to refer to the war as 'phoney' – though the Americans hadn't been on the *Athenia*, or the *Courageous*, or all the other ships sunk by the Germans, Clive thought disdainfully. The Jerries even had the gall to bomb the *Royal Oak* at anchor in Scapa Flow, the British Naval Base up in the Orkneys. But apart from the bloody activity on the high seas, nothing had happened. According to someone from the office whose brother was in the Royal Warwickshires, the British Expeditionary Force was having a fine old time in France, going to nightclubs and being wined and dined by the French, at least the officers were. All that the Royal Air Force had been allowed to drop on Germany was leaflets telling them to give up. There'd been a joke going around the office the other day. Some young pilot had returned earlier than expected from his mission dropping leaflets and explained he tipped them out still wrapped in parcels. 'Good God, man,' his CO said anxiously, 'you might have killed someone!' The war itself seemed a bit of a joke so far and when a communication arrived last week telling Clive to collect their Identity Cards, it had come as a little shock as, along with most other people, he'd almost forgotten they were in a state of conflict. Of course, the blackout was a bit of a bind, but since the children had arrived, he and Vivien didn't go out much of a night, so it didn't inconvenience them as much as it did some.

The last thing he wanted was for the war to escalate, but nor did he want his evacuees removed. Vivien had never looked or been so well. She was full of energy, and it was an indication of her amazing achievement that he actually wished to *keep* the two filthy little urchins who'd come into their lives on the first day of September. Not for his own sake, he didn't give a damn if he never saw either of them again, but for Vivien's, and not so much the boy, either, but the girl. Vivien loved her and he had no doubt that the girl genuinely loved her back. Sometimes he felt almost jealous, slightly shut out, when the two of them sat giggling together, but that didn't matter. All that mattered was his Vivien was happy.

Francis Costello came home on leave, unannounced,

taking Eileen completely by surprise. To everyone's amusement, The Royal Tank Regiment had only gone as far as Crosby, no more than a few miles down the road, and most of the men had been sent home when it was discovered there were no sleeping facilities, but to Eileen's heartfelt relief, Francis had been despatched to Kettering on a typing course.

Somehow, Eileen guessed who it was immediately the key sounded in the front door and her heart sank. She went into the hall.

'Hallo, luv.' He kissed her on the cheek. He looked bronzed and fit in his uniform. When he removed his hat, she saw his hair had been cut very short, though you could still see the little crinkly waves.

'Hallo, Francis.' Having greeted him, she could think of little else to say and was relieved when another khaki-clad form came into the hall behind him. It was a young lad, no more than eighteen, with a bright open face and girlish flushed skin.

'This is Pete English.' Francis introduced them. 'He's got no home to go to, so I thought I'd bring him back with me.'

'I hope you don't mind, Mrs Costello?' Pete said in a cracked voice that sounded as if it hadn't yet broken. He had a broad Lancashire accent.

Before Eileen could open her mouth to say Pete was more than welcome, Francis said for her, 'Of course she don't mind. Y'can sleep in the parlour and there's plenty of food – I hope.' There was a slight threat in the last two words, as if he'd like to find fault with her the minute he came in.

'I'll have to pop out later and buy a bit more stewing steak for the scouse,' Eileen said stiffly. 'I wasn't expecting you, was I? I'll go and make a cup of tea.'

89

As she put the kettle on, she noticed her hands were shaking. Ever since Francis left, she'd been going over and over in her mind what to do when he came back. She'd sworn to herself she'd never sleep with him again. There was no way she'd put up with that indignity one more time. She'd discussed it with Annie, who didn't know the full facts, of course, and Annie had said she and Tony could always sleep in her house if she wanted. But that seemed a coward's way out, thought Eileen. She should stand up to Francis and tell him of her decision to his face.

'How's our Tony?' Francis shouted from the living room.

'He's fine,' she shouted back. 'He doesn't come home at dinner time no more, they give them a nice meal at school.'

'I bet he's missing his dad,' Francis called, then, in a quieter voice to Pete English: 'He's a nice little lad, you'll meet him later.'

'Oh, yes,' she lied. Tony may well think he was missing his dad, but he'd come out of himself lately and been far more lively and animated, a different boy altogether, as if freed from an awful weight of oppression. Eileen understood the feeling exactly.

'It was terrible about Mary Flaherty,' Francis shouted. 'Rodney Smith wrote and told me about it.' There was a hint of accusation in his voice and Eileen felt a mixture of guilt and resentment. She'd only written to him once, a stiff polite little letter, not at all the sort of letter any normal wife would send to a husband who was away at war. But then, she told herself, Francis wasn't a normal husband.

She went to the doorway. He was lounging in his chair as if he'd never been away, and Pete English was sitting awkwardly at the table.

'They said a special Mass for Mary in the Holy Rosary last Sunday,' she said. 'But y'should see the people who've moved into their house, Francis. They're terrible posh. The man's all right, he speaks to you ever so friendly and he's got no side at all, but the woman acts like she's queen o'the midden. Y'get a nod if you're lucky, but she can scarcely bear to look at you in case she catches something.' She spread the next-to-best blue damask cloth on the table, kept especially for visitors.

'How's your dad keeping?'

'He's fine,' she said, glad of the mundane conversation. 'He's begun conducting the war from Garnet Street. I'm not sure who he likes less, Chamberlain for doing nowt, or Hitler. You'll never believe this, Francis, but he's suddenly taken up with Winston Churchill. Reckons he should be Prime Minister.'

'*What?*' Francis was astounded. 'I thought he hated Churchill?'

'Oh, he does, in fact, he hates most politicians, even some of the Labour ones, but he hates fascism more. He reckons Churchill would make a far better war leader than Chamberlain.'

She returned to the kitchen; the kettle had started to boil. Francis shouted, 'I still think it'll be over by Christmas. It's all phoney, like they say in the papers. By this time next year, we'll have forgotten there's ever been a war.'

'I hope so, for everyone's sake,' she replied, though she wondered if it was so phoney, then why had Mary died, and why was poor Annie going out of her mind with worry and her sister Sheila too terrified to listen to the wireless or read a newspaper in case she learnt another ship had been sunk? Eileen listened eagerly to the latest bulletins on the wireless whenever she could, and read the *Daily Herald* from cover to cover every day. She felt convinced Hitler was playing a waiting game. Any minute now, he'd pounce somewhere else and another country would be swallowed up by the mighty German army. But it was wise not to say anything to Francis. As far as he and a lot of other men were concerned, women weren't supposed to have an opinion on the war.

'Come on, Pete,' she said as she carried in the teapot. 'You're allowed to speak, y'know. You won't get put in the guardhouse, or whatever it's called, just for saying a few words. How much sugar d'you take?'

The boy smiled weakly, 'One spoonful,' he whispered.

'How long are you home for, Francis?' Eileen asked casually, praying he only had a twenty-four-hour pass. He might even have to go back that day.

'Till Thursday,' he replied.

Three days, two nights! Her hands began to shake again as she poured the tea. 'And are you going back to Kettering?'

To her relief, he nodded. She'd been worried he was only returning to Crosby.

'You haven't noticed something,' he said boastfully.

'What's that?' She looked at him, but couldn't see any difference. Except for his hair, he looked exactly the same as the day he left.

'He's got a stripe,' Pete English said in his strange squeaky voice. 'He's a Lance Corporal.'

'Congratulations!' She tried to sound pleased. 'Actually, Francis, I've got a bit of news meself. I'm starting work in November.' It was best to tell him now while someone else was there; he wasn't likely to get so mad.

She regarded him nervously, biting her lip. He hated her taking decisions, doing anything of her own accord, and he'd refused to let her work before. He was staring at the cup in his hands, frowning, and she could tell he was angry. There was a dark look in the brown eyes that seemed to smile so warmly at everyone outside the house, but never on her, and never on Tony.

'What sort of job?' There was menace in his voice. If Pete English hadn't been there, she knew he would have done something to her, something painful.

'It's in a factory in Melling. I'll be working on a lathe, making parts for aeroplanes. The money's good.'

'And who's going to look after our Tony?'

'It's shift work, though the women aren't expected to do nights,' she explained. 'It's six in the morning until two o'clock in the afternoon, then two till ten at night. Annie's starting with me, but she's going to do the other shift to mine and look after Tony when I'm working. I felt bound to do something for the war effort, Francis,' she added virtuously. 'There's nowt much to do here with you away and Tony at school – and me dad thinks it's a good idea.'

Eileen got support from an unexpected quarter. Pete English said, 'Good on yer, Mrs Costello. Me sister's gone down south to work in a refugee hostel, that's why I've got nowhere to go, she gave up our rooms in Preston. She's earning twice what she did in her old job in a bakery, and having a good old time to boot.'

Francis gave a steely smile. 'Well, Eileen won't be having a good old time, will you, luv? She'll be working hard instead. Now, I think you'd best go and buy that stewing steak. I'm starving, and I'm sure Pete is, too.'

They had an audience whilst they ate their tea; her dad and Sean, Paddy O'Hara and Mr Singerman, Sheila and half the kids, and numerous other neighbours. Francis beamed at them, and when the meal was finished, he opened a bottle of whisky and regaled them with funny stories about life in the army. There was the chap in his billet who put his false teeth in a glass before he went to bed and someone had filled the glass with green ink and his teeth were discoloured for weeks.

Everyone screamed with laughter, except Eileen, who didn't think it particularly funny. In fact, it seemed rather cruel.

'The Sarge, he's a regular and a right ould martinet,' Francis continued. 'Everybody hates him, but one night, I saw him in the pub all by himself and looking dead lonely, like, so I did no more than go over and offer to buy him a drink and we're good mates now. Fact, that's probably why I got me stripe, 'cos Vince put in a good word.'

'That's just like you, Francis,' Jack Doyle said admiringly. 'Sounds like you and the army get on like a house on fire.'

'I've settled in better than most chaps,' Francis said modestly. 'As long as you do as you're told and keep your nose clean, it's a good life, though I miss me family something rotten.' He reached out and chucked Tony under the chin and sent a warm glowing smile in the direction of his wife. 'Don't I, luv?'

'Yes, Francis,' Eileen replied obediently.

'Now, who'd like another drop of whisky?' Francis asked.

Soon afterwards, the women went home, the men disappeared to the King's Arms and Eileen put Tony to bed.

'You'll have to sleep in your own room tonight, son.' He'd been sleeping with her for weeks on the clear understanding he was only there to protect her against enemy attack.

'I know, Mam.'

She gave him a kiss and an extra hard hug, then went downstairs and began to prepare a little speech for Francis. But to her surprise, he came back from the pub and announced he and Pete were going into town to a club. She presumed it was the same one he went to with Rodney Smith.

'But how will you get home?' she asked.

'There might be a train running,' he replied airily. 'If not, we'll get a taxi back.'

'A taxi? It'll take forever in the blackout.' Headlights had to be covered with cardboard with only a narrow slit of light left to see by. Cars crept along the road at five miles an hour, guided by the kerbs which had been painted white.

'Well, that's for me to worry about, not you,' he said irritably, so different from the way he'd been when people had been there.

As the night wore on, Eileen turned off the light, feeling safer without it, though she wasn't sure why. Earlier, she'd lit the fire – October had turned out to be wet and chilly – and kept poking the dying embers for a bit of ghostly illumination, enough to see the clock on the mantelpiece. When the fire eventually went out altogether, she drew the curtains back, but the moon only came out in patches, and she sat there, shivering out of a mixture of cold and fear. She turned the wireless on low and, with her ear close to the cloth grille, listened to the music of Henry Hall and his Orchestra. The news bulletin at midnight turned her blood cold. German planes had attacked the Firth of the Forth! They'd missed the bridge, and four planes had been shot down, but even so, it was ominous news, the first air-raid attack on the British Isles.

Soon after that, the Kellys next door came home, and the two brothers had one of their flaming rows. But May Kelly kept Fin and Failey firmly under her thumb, and Eileen waited for the inevitable reaction.

'Shut your gobs, the pair of yez,' May bawled, 'or you'll wake the neighbours up,' which usually roused anyone who'd managed to sleep through the fight.

It was half past one when Francis came home and Eileen could tell, from the muffled curses and occasional giggles when he showed Pete English into the parlour where she'd made a bed up on the settee, that he was drunk out of his mind. He came stumbling through the room where she was sitting and, with her eyes now used to the dark, she saw him reach for the light switch. Then he uttered an obscenity. Even in his drunken state he'd noticed the curtains were open which meant he couldn't turn on the light. Imagine, that great man, Francis Costello, fined for a blackout offence! He staggered through the back kitchen and down the yard to the lavatory. A few minutes later, he came back and went upstairs.

He hadn't noticed she was there!

Eileen, listening hard, heard the bedsprings creak and breathed a sigh of relief. He was so drunk, he'd probably go asleep without her. She took a deep breath, her heart was thumping wildly, and after a while felt herself begin to doze and gave in to a blessed feeling of relief. She was safe!

She would have screamed, but she couldn't. There was a hand over her mouth and another on the back of her neck. She felt herself being yanked roughly out of the chair and a voice hissed in her ear, 'What the hell d'you think you're doing down here? You're me wife, you bitch!'

Francis!

He turned her round and flung her down into the chair and held her there, her face buried in the cushion. She gagged for breath as he tore away her clothes and she prayed she would die or at least lose consciousness, but her prayers weren't answered.

When he'd finished and removed his heavy weight from on top of her, she began to cry quietly. He said nothing, but returned to bed and left her there, feeling dirty and utterly despairing. She stopped crying after a while in case the sound disturbed Tony, and dragged herself into the back kitchen where she washed her body from head to toe. Then she made a cup of tea and sat in the chair, smoking, her mind a blur of confusion. What was a woman supposed to do in this situation? Just go on for the rest of her life being treated like an animal? She could leave him, but where would she go? There was Tony to think of. She'd have no furniture, what they had now belonged to Francis, and the rent book was in his name. People looked down on women who left their husbands. No matter what the man did, no matter how badly he treated her, the woman was supposed to stay by his side, in her place, and put up with it. Dai Evans knocked Ellis around when he was in his cups, but Ellis appeared rather proud of the occasional black eye, as if it were some sort of trophy, and she was almost as big as Dai and gave as good as she got. It was Dai who'd been taken to hospital with a broken nose one Christmas Eve, not Ellis. But there was no way Eileen could stand up to Francis like that.

But that was the future; it was the night to come that

Eileen was most worried about. She wouldn't put up with it again, she couldn't, and she knew it was a waste of time talking to him. Anyroad, she never wanted to face Francis again. Of course, Annie would take her in, she'd offered, but she wouldn't feel safe in Annie's, only a few doors away. It would be the first place Francis would look if she wasn't here when he came home, and although Francis would never make a scene in public when he was sober, she wasn't sure how he'd behave in his drunken state. He might beat on Annie's door and demand Eileen come back – it had happened before in Pearl Street, some man being locked out and hammering to get in, waking the whole street up – and everyone would think that brave man Francis Costello was in the right. Home on leave, about to go and fight for his country, yet his wife refused to sleep with him!

It was six o'clock and she was freezing. Outside, the dark watery sky was streaked with silver threads and it looked as if it was going to be another chilly day. The cold wet weather had come as something of a shock after such a lovely balmy September.

Eileen stood up. Her legs, her entire body, felt stiff and aching. She'd better light a fire, though Tony wouldn't be up for a few hours yet and God knows what time Francis would show himself.

'Oh, Jaysus,' she whispered aloud. 'What am I going to do?'

As if in answer to her prayer, she thought of the one person in the world she had a right to call on for protection, though he would be the person most difficult to convince she was entitled to it. She would be safe with him, there was no way Francis would create a scene with Jack Doyle.

Impulsively, Eileen snatched her coat out of the hall and went to see her dad.

It was just light enough to see as she made her way round to Garnet Street through the damp, deserted streets. A light drizzle fell and the blacked out windows shone like blind, unseeing eyes. The lampposts stood dejectedly, unused and unwanted. Eileen felt as if she was walking through an alien, scarcely recognisable world. She was glad when she reached her dad's and, instead of drawing the key through the letter box on its string, she knocked on the door in case she startled him at this time of the morning.

He was up, which she'd expected. He had to be at work by half past seven and answered the door almost immediately.

'What's the matter?' he asked grumpily.

'I just wanted to talk to you a bit, that's all.'

'You'd better come in, then.'

She followed him into the living room where a cheerful fire burned in the grate. The room hadn't changed a jot since her mam had died fourteen years ago. There were the same crocheted covers on the seats and arms of the chairs where the upholstery had worn away, and a little rag rug on the hearth. The sideboard was full of framed photographs. In pride of place stood a photo of her parents' wedding. Her mam's sweet dimpled face smiled back at her. It could have been Sheila on her dad's arm, slightly younger, slightly slimmer. The wireless was on, it sounded like Sandy MacPherson at the organ. He was playing *The Blue Danube*.

Eileen regarded the room with affection. It held nothing but pleasant memories. They'd always been poor, but mam had done wonders with the cheapest cuts of meat, so they'd never gone hungry, never gone cold, and there'd always been clothes on their backs, even if they were secondhand. Jack Doyle might be a dangerous troublemaker, but even so, he hadn't suffered as much as other men had from the iniquitous system by which dockers were employed, standing outside the gates on a daily basis waiting to be picked for work. The employers, reckoning it would be best to have Jack where they could keep an eye on him, chose him regularly. Anyway, he was as strong as an ox and could work as hard as two ordinary men.

'D'you want a cup of tea? I was just about to make one,' he asked.

'I always want a cup of tea,' she answered, sinking into a chair, grateful for the warmth.

She watched his deliberate movements through the doorway of the scrupulously clean back kitchen; the precise way he put the cups on the saucers, poured the milk in the jug, put a clean spoon in the sugar basin. She knew he wouldn't pour the tea out there, but fetch it in the pot covered with the cosy mam had knitted and which she felt sure he must darn regularly. He'd never asked her or Sheila to do it, that would seem maudlin and sentimental, and she could have wept, imagining big Jack Doyle sat mending the tea cosy made by the wife he adored because he couldn't bear to throw it away.

He came in, puffing slightly, his muscled arms bulging under the rolled-up sleeves of his flannel working shirt.

'You're smoking too much, Dad,' she said sternly. 'You're out of breath carrying the teapot.'

'Look who's talking!' He sat down at the table and poured out two cups of tea.

'I only started proper a few weeks ago. You've been doing it since you was a nipper.'

'Smoking keeps the working class and the tobacco companies happy,' he said, grinning slightly. She knew he only said it to irk her and she rose to the bait immediately.

'Oh, Dad! D'you have to make a political point out of everything?'

'You'll never learn, Eileen. Everything *is* political. The capitalists run this country for their own profit. The more we smoke, the more they like it.' As if to prove his point, he lit two cigarettes and handed her one. 'Have you heard the news this morning?'

'No, what's happened? Did they bomb the Germans back after that raid on Scotland?'

'Not bloody likely!' he said savagely. 'They drop bombs on us, we drop paper on them. If we're going to fight the Jerries, it's about time we started on it. It's about time Neville Chamberlain threw in the towel and gave way to Churchill. He'd know how to run a war, the Tory git. Look at the way he ordered the police in during the Sydney Street Siege! If he can do that to his own people, think of what he could do to the Jerries.'

'Oh, Dad!'

'According to Lord Haw Haw, we're all on our knees begging to surrender.'

Lord Haw Haw was the nickname for William Joyce, a notorious traitor, who tried to undermine the British people by broadcasting terrible lies from Germany. 'You should be ashamed of yerself, Dad,' she chided. 'I won't have him on in our house. Y'know the Government said we weren't to listen to him.'

'I can't think of a better reason for doing something than the Government telling me not to.'

Eileen supposed she'd asked for that.

'Anyroad,' he went on, 'what do you want? I'll be

leaving for work soon. It must be something important at this time of the morning.'

'It is.' Now the moment had come, she couldn't think of how to put it. She sat staring down at her hands, aware her dad was waiting impatiently. 'Where's our Sean? He's not about to come down any minute, is he?'

'The lazy bugger won't stir till he's had a cup of tea in bed.'

Eileen took a deep breath. 'Dad, I want to stay here with you until Francis has gone back off leave – and bring Tony with me.'

'You what?'

'You heard what I said.'

'But why?' His mouth had fallen open and Eileen was shocked at how old he suddenly looked, as if her request and all that lay behind it had taken the wind out of him completely. Perhaps she should have led up to it a bit more tactfully. 'Why?' he repeated.

'I can't tell you, Dad. You'll just have to believe there's a good reason for it. This is the only place I'll feel safe.'

'Safe? What d'you mean, safe?'

He looked so dazed, she began to wish she hadn't come. She should have risked it with Annie. She stood up suddenly. 'It doesn't matter, Dad. I shouldn't have asked. I'll sort it out some other way, don't worry.'

'Sit down!' he barked, his old self in an instant. 'You're my girl, and if you're in trouble this is the first place you should come. It's just that, well, this has come as a bit of a bolt from the blue.' He poured himself another cup of tea, too distraught to offer one to her. 'What's he done, then?'

'I can't tell you, Dad, honest.'

His face reddened slightly and he began to fiddle with his cigarette. Staring at the wall somewhere above her, he said awkwardly, 'Sometimes, women aren't keen on a certain side of marriage, but a wife has a duty to her husband, even if . . .'

'It's not that,' Eileen interrupted.

'Oh!' He looked at her sharply. 'Has he hit you?'

'Not exactly, Dad, but he can be cruel when he likes.'

'Francis? Francis Costello?'

'Yes, Francis Costello.'

He frowned, 'Has he been cruel to Tony?' Sheila might be his favourite daughter, but Tony was the grandchild he loved most.

Eileen nodded.

'The bastard! I'll bloody kill him. If there's one thing I can't stand, it's a man who beats his wife and children.' He rose, fists clenched, ready to go round that very minute and knock the living daylights out of his son-in-law.

'Dad! Dad! I never said he beat us! It's something different altogether, but I can't tell you what. You'll just have to believe me. You know I'd never lie to you.'

'Christ!' He sat down again and put his elbows on the table and dropped his head into his rough working hands. For an awful moment, Eileen thought he was about to cry. Then, in a curiously childish gesture, he rubbed his eyes with his fists, looked up and nodded. 'I know, girl. You've always been straight with me. If you say he's a wrong 'un, then I believe you. All right then, luv, stay here till he's gone back. I've got to go to work now, but tonight I'd like a few words with Francis Costello!'

'No, Dad,' she pleaded. 'Just leave him be. It'll only upset you.'

'It'll upset him the most. He was counting on me to get him the nomination when Albert Findlay retires.' Albert Findlay was the Labour Member of Parliament for

Bootle. Now old and in failing health, he was expected to give up the seat before the next election. This was what Francis had been working so assiduously towards, inheriting the seat with the help of Jack Doyle who was a powerful force in the local Labour Party. 'Francis was like a son to me,' he said querulously.

'You've already got a son, Dad,' Eileen said in a hard voice. 'And our Sean's worth ten Francis Costellos, just take my word for it.'

The sound of snoring came from the front bedroom when Eileen went home to collect Tony. He looked surprised at being woken and told to get dressed at such an early hour, but said nothing. He'd heard his mam cry during the night and knew it was something his dad must have done, because it was the first time she'd cried for weeks. 'We're going to your grandad's for a day or so,' she told him, which he didn't mind a bit. He loved his grandad much more than he loved his dad.

'What happens when Dominic or Niall call for me for school?'

'You'll just have to call for them first, won't you.'

Jack Doyle had left for work by the time Eileen got back to the house in Garnet Street. Sean was down, gloomily eating a bowl of cornflakes.

'You're a lazy sod, our Sean, having me dad take you a cup of tea up every morning,' she said crossly. 'It's you who should be taking one to him.'

'I was late to bed last night,' he muttered.

'You're never anything else. I suppose you were out with your latest girlfriend.' Sean seemed to have a new girlfriend every week.

Sean ignored the gibe. 'I've joined the Civil Defence Messenger Service,' he announced grandly.

'And what's that when it's at home?' Eileen asked sharply.

'It means I have to deliver messages on me bike during air raids and they're gonna train me in fire-fighting and first aid.'

'Will they train me, too?' Tony asked excitedly.

Sean gave him a supercilious glance. 'Not likely. First of all, you haven't got a bike, and second, you're too young by a mile.'

Eileen laughed at her son's crestfallen face. 'Let's hope there won't be any air raids,' she said, forgetting, for the moment, there'd already been one the night before.

After Sean and Tony had left, she pottered around the house, though there was little to do. Dad kept the place like a palace. She began to prepare a stew with dumplings for tea, when she heard the key being drawn through the letter box and the front door opened. She should have removed the key! It might be Francis, though she doubted he'd have the gall to come round and make a fuss in Jack Doyle's house. She went into the hall, but it was only her sister, who jumped when she saw Eileen.

'You gave me the fright of me life. I thought the house'd be empty.' Sheila put a paper bag on the table. 'I've just brought round a few scones I made this morning for me dad,' she explained. 'What the hell are you doing here? I've been over looking for you twice this morning and Francis said you were out shopping each time. He wants his uniform pressing. It don't half look in a state. God knows what he's been up to in it.'

'We've had a row,' Eileen lied. 'Don't ask questions, Sis, please. And don't tell anybody, neither, particularly not Francis, but I'm staying with me dad till he goes back.'

'Okay, luv, if that's the way you want it,' Sheila said,

laughing, though, to her, the idea of not spending every conceivable moment with your husband when he was home on leave seemed incomprehensible. But then, not everyone was married to a man like Calum Reilly.

'D'you want a cup of tea?' asked Eileen.

'No, ta. I've got four of the kids with me. I'm going to the clinic for their orange juice and cod liver oil and to get our Mary weighed. If I leave them outside much longer, there'll be a riot.'

Eileen went with her to the door. The four youngest children had somehow been squeezed into the big black Marmet pram that had been secondhand when Sheila bought it for Dominic six years before. Caitlin and Siobhan's legs were hanging over the side.

'You're a hero, Sis, wheeling all that lot round to Strand Road. D'you want me to come with you?'

'No, it's all right. I can manage fine once I get going.' Sheila took a deep breath and began to push the pram away. 'I'll call in on me way back for that cuppa.'

When her dad came home from work on Thursday night, he and Eileen went round to Pearl Street together to make sure Francis had gone. The house was dark and empty. Her dad went upstairs to double check, and came down again, his face dark with anger.

'Does he always leave the bedroom in that state? It needs fumigating.'

'I'll clean it later,' she said easily, glad he'd seen it. 'Anyway, thanks, Dad, for everything. You can send our Tony back when you get home.'

'There's something I want to do before I go.' He went into the back kitchen.

'What's that?'

'I'm going to change the locks on both the doors.'

'But you can't do that!' she said, scandalised. 'It's Francis's house. The rent book's in his name.'

'I can and I will,' he said curtly. 'No man's going to lay his hands on my daughter. In the meantime, you've got to live somewhere, and I'm not having you coming round mine every time the bastard comes home. You get on me nerves. You're too intelligent for a woman. You think too much, not like our Sheila. She never bothers her head with politics. You must be the only woman in Bootle with a *Daily Express* war map on the wall.' Rarely for him, he was smiling broadly. He seemed to have got over the shock of discovering the sun didn't rise and set according to Francis Costello, and Eileen felt she'd grown closer to him over the last couple of days than she'd ever been before.

'I got the map for Tony,' she explained, though it was a fact that she pored over it daily, following Hitler's movements in Europe.

'Anyroad,' her dad said ruefully, 'I've got to make up to you a bit, haven't I? I know you only married him to please me. I'm sorry, luv, but he seemed too good a catch to miss at the time. Don't worry, though, I'll straighten him out for you. If he lays a finger on you again, it'll be over my dead body.'

'Oh, get away with you, Dad,' she said, embarrassed, and quite sure she didn't want Francis straightening out. She would prefer it if she never set eyes on him again. 'You only had me best interests at heart.'

He shook his head. 'No, I didn't, luv. I fancied having an MP for a son-in-law. I fancied going to Westminster with him now'n again and having a good old barney with that lot down there.'

It was Saturday night, almost eleven, and Mack, the

landlord of the King's Arms, was wearily washing the last of the glasses. There were still the tables to wipe down, the floor to sweep, and a layer of fresh sawdust to sprinkle ready for the morning. Only then would he allow himself to retire to his warm bed, which always seemed more welcome at the weekend. Usually the barmaid, Marie, helped clear up, but since the blackout, Mack sent her home with one of the customers to make sure she got home safely. There'd been a couple of lunatics taking advantage of the dark to attack women out late on their own.

Mack turned the wireless on for company. Although he was glad to see the back of everyone, nowadays, the bar seemed uncannily quiet when it was empty, what with the windows painted black and no lamp outside shining through as it used to.

When the war started seven weeks ago, the pubs had been ordered to close, but there'd been such a clamour from the drinking public, indignantly demanding to know how being denied a pint would help bring about victory, that the authorities had allowed them to re-open, though closing time had been changed to nine instead of the normal ten. Some pubs, and the King's Arms was one, took no notice of the earlier closing. It was easy, with windows and doors blacked out, to drop the catch and carry on drinking with the regulars. They left by the back way and Mack felt it was his contribution towards the war effort, keeping his hard-working – and non-working – customers happy and contented.

He hung the last glass on a hook over the bar and was rinsing a cloth in the soapy water to wipe down the tables, when the music on the wireless faded, and a news bulletin began. He listened idly. Little was happening on the war front of any real significance. Then a familiar name caught his ear, and he stood there, the sopping cloth dripping unnoticed onto his boots, fully attentive to the well modulated voice of the announcer.

'. . . *The* Midnight Star *was sailing back to Liverpool from the South-West coast of Africa when it was attacked and sunk by an enemy ship, the identity of which is not yet known. So far, there have been no reports of survivors . . .*'

The *Midnight Star*! Calum Reilly's ship.

'Jesus, Mary and Joseph'. Mack could scarcely stop himself from bursting into tears. He flung the cloth across the bar in a gesture of despair. It hit the wall and left a wet stain on the green paint before falling to the floor. Considering the war had scarcely started, Pearl Street was having far more than its fair share of tragedies. First Mary, now Calum, and him with a missus and six little nippers.

Mack dried his hands and went to fetch his coat. Sod the tables and the floor, he'd leave them, although he hated having to do them in the morning. He wasn't going to tell Sheila, it was up to her family to do that, but he'd best go round to Jack Doyle's straight away in case he hadn't heard the news, even if it meant knocking him up. Otherwise, that cow Aggie Donovan might get in first.

Chapter 5

It had just gone midnight, and Sheila Reilly was sitting up in bed feeding the baby when she heard the front door being opened. At first, she thought it could only be Cal at such an unearthly hour and felt her entire body tingle with excitement.

'Is that you, luv?' she called.

'It's Eileen. Can I come up?'

She could tell by the tone of her sister's voice there was something wrong. Perhaps Dad was ill. But a few seconds later, Dad followed Eileen into the bedroom. There was no need to ask why they'd come. Their faces, scared and sorrowful, said it all.

'Ah!' The anguished cry came from the very core of Sheila's being. She turned and buried her head in the pillow, and Mary, part of her mother at that moment, seemed to sense her distress. She squirmed in her arms and came off the breast with a little whimper, before re-attaching herself with a grip that was almost painful.

'What happened?' Sheila asked in a deep, gruff voice that seemed to belong to someone else.

'The *Midnight Star*'s been torpedoed, luv,' Dad explained. 'I reckon it was the *Graf Spee*.' The German pocket battleship was responsible for most of the carnage on the high seas.

'Are you sure?' Sheila demanded angrily. It might be just a rumour. Almost every day, fresh rumours spread around like wildfire and most turned out to be untrue.

Though even as she asked the question, she knew it was a foolish one. Dad and Eileen wouldn't look so grave if that was the case.

'Mack heard it on the eleven o'clock news,' Eileen said. 'Dad and I listened to the midnight bulletin, just to make sure.' She sat on the edge of the bed and patted her sister's arm somewhat clumsily. 'I'm sorry, Sheil.'

Sorry! Such a trite, meaningless little word, thought Sheila. You were sorry if you trod on someone's toe or spilt tea in the saucer. There should be another word to express what you felt when the dearest husband in the world had been taken away so cruelly. 'Thanks for telling me,' Sheila said politely. 'I'd like to be alone now, if you don't mind.'

'But, Sheil,' Eileen began, but Dad said gruffly, 'Leave her, if that's what she wants.' As they left the room, he looked back at his youngest daughter. 'I'll be thinking of you, girl.'

'I know, Dad.'

Sheila Reilly heard the front door close. As she transferred the baby to her other breast, she briefly laid her hand on the pillow where her husband's head had rested.

'Oh, Cal!' she whispered. She closed her eyes and concentrated hard and, after a while, could almost feel the pressure of his arm across her belly. He usually laid it there when she was feeding a child. The arm became heavier and heavier and Sheila sat there all night, long after Mary had gone to sleep, scared to move in case Cal's arm disappeared and she lost him forever.

Part-time Asistent Wanted.

Jessica Fleming stared at the badly spelt, badly written notice in the half-glazed door of the little shop. The window was full of flesh-pink brocade corsets, winceyette nightwear, lock-knit bloomers, and various other items of women's cheap underwear. In the centre stood two plaster casts of legs from the crotch down, each wearing a rather picked and tatty lisle stocking. The legs were set at an acute angle to each other, giving the display a crazy, deformed look. Jessica stepped back and glanced at the sign above. Below the single word VERONICA'S she read 'Ladies' & Children's Lingerie'.

Taking her courage in both hands, Jessica opened the shop door and went in. A bell jangled loudly and her nasal passages were stung by the overpowering smell of lavender. A cadaverous looking woman with jet-black hair permed to a frizz and unhealthy yellow skin appeared from the back making the sign of the cross, and the lavender smell became even stronger. This, Jessica assumed, was Veronica.

'I'd like to apply . . .' She paused, her courage failing, and tried to think of something she could buy as an excuse for entering. She'd sooner die than wear a pair of those corsets or one of those scratchy nightgowns – even if she could afford it. She'd always bought her underwear from George Henry Lee's or Bon Marché or, at a pinch, Marks & Spencer's. 'I'd like to see some handkerchieves, please.' Were handkerchieves lingerie?

Apparently they were. 'And what sort would modom like?' the woman asked in a hoarse, cloying voice. 'Plain or fancy?'

'Fancy, please.' Jessica had enough hankies to last two lifetimes, but it was a way of getting out of the shop without embarrassment.

'Lace trimmed or embroidered?'

'Lace trimmed. No, embroidered. It doesn't matter.'

Two walls of the shop were covered with glass-fronted drawers reaching almost to the ceiling. The woman pulled open a drawer and produced a selection of handkerchieves.

'How much are these?' Jessica pointed to some with an embroidered corner.

'Threepence each, best Irish linen.'

'I'll have four, please. No, two.'

'And what initial, modom?'

'I beg your pardon?'

'The ones modom has selected are initialled. What initial is modom – I presume they're for yourself?'

'Oh!'

'O?'

'I'm sorry, I mean J.'

As the woman sorted through the handkerchieves with her bony fingers, Jessica noticed the nails were long and filthy.

'Does modom live around here?'

'Sort of,' Jessica replied vaguely.

'That'll be sixpence, please.'

'Thank you.' As Jessica paid and the hankies were placed in a white paper bag with VERONICA printed on it in dark blue, her mind was racing. She needed a job desperately. The small amount she'd got for her musquash had made her blanch, less than a quarter of what she'd paid for it. She had her mind set on a proper stove and a new, modern fireplace and she was determined that the house be wired for electricity and a bath installed in the old washhouse in the yard. If she wanted these things, it looked as if she'd have to pay for them herself. Arthur, damn his eyes, had got a job as a lorry driver working for one of their old rivals, and no matter how much she screamed at him, he stubbornly insisted on keeping most of his wages for himself, giving her a measly twelve-and-six housekeeping. She couldn't believe it when he first told her about the job.

'A *lorry* driver!'

'I like driving,' he said simply. 'I always have.'

That was how they'd first met, when he was a student at Liverpool University studying archaeology and looking for part-time work to pay for a holiday in Greece. Her father had taken a shine to him and given him a job driving at weekends. Somehow, archaeology had been forgotten after he'd taken his degree. They'd married, and Arthur had become immersed in the business.

'It's degrading,' she spluttered.

He shrugged. 'It suits me.'

'Modom!' The paper bag was held out for her to take.

Jessica came down to earth. 'Thank you.' She took a deep breath. 'Are you Veronica?'

The woman gave a little nod accompanied by a grisly smile which revealed teeth yellower than her skin. 'I am, modom.'

'I see you require an assistant.' She had to work, and Ladies' Lingerie seemed more refined than most other shops.

'Aye, I do.'

Jessica noticed she was no longer 'modom'. 'What does the job entail?'

'Have you had any previous retail experience?'

'Well, no,' Jessica confessed, 'except as a customer. I love clothes, I always have.' She'd had no experience of working in any capacity. Once she'd left school, they'd moved to Walton and the business had started to expand, so there'd been no need to work. She'd continued looking after her father until she married Arthur.

'I can see that.' Veronica took in the pure wool camel coat, the pink silk blouse underneath, the expensive lizard-skin handbag. This woman would be an asset

114

behind the counter. 'The job entails, as you put it, working nine till one and all day Saturday. The pay is elevenpence an hour and there's two-and-a-half per cent commission on your sales.'

'How many hours does that come to?' Jessica asked faintly.

'Twenty-seven. If you have trouble working that out, you won't be much good in a shop.' Never had a woman changed so much in such a short time as had Veronica. Gone was the cloying smile, the simpering, syrupy voice. Instead, her little black eyes were hard and calculating. The woman was desperate for a job, she could tell. She would enjoy having the stuck-up bitch under her control.

'I wasn't sure if you had included the Saturday lunch hour,' Jessica said in excuse.

'I hadn't. There's no sick pay and no holiday money. If you don't come in, you don't get paid. I only need someone because me veins are starting to come up something awful if I'm on me feet too long. Some days, it's all go in here, customers in and out by the minute,' Veronica complained.

'When can I start?'

'I haven't said you can, yet, have I?' Veronica gave Jessica a hard glare. Then she shrugged, 'Oh, I suppose I could give you a trial. See how you get on, like. You can start on Monday.'

As Jessica trudged home, she tried to decide on her priorities. Which was most important: a new stove, a modern fireplace, electric wiring or a bath? The trouble was, she wanted each one as desperately as the other. Life without proper light was every bit as unbearable as having to bath in a tin tub in front of the fire – when Arthur was out, of course – and just looking at that ghastly black kitchen range made her feel depressed. She got herself filthy, cleaning the dratted thing with black lead. Perhaps she should get estimates for everything and make her mind up then. The money from her musquash was safely in a new Post Office account after the manager of the local bank had refused to let her start up an account without her husband's signature, as if Arthur's name was a guarantee of monetary prudence! Jessica cursed men in general and Arthur and bank managers in particular.

Her heart sank as she approached the corner of Pearl Street and she felt a wave of self-pity, remembering the tree-lined avenue in Calderstones, her lovely house, her Aga. She was no more used to Bootle now than the day she'd moved in. She got up early to brush the step and clean the windows so as not to encounter any neighbours . . .

Jessica turned the corner and stopped, appalled. A horse and cart emerged from the coalyard leaving a trail of steaming excrement down the centre of the cobbled street and a woman scurried out and began to shovel it into a bucket. Jessica vaguely remembered her father used to sell their manure to a man who had an allotment. She shuddered. She thought she'd left all that behind forever.

A little woman in a black shawl came rolling unsteadily down the street and disappeared into a house which looked as scruffy and unhygienic as the woman herself. Several children were kicking a football against the wall, on which goalposts had been roughly chalked. At least there was something to be grateful for, Jessica thought piteously. The steam trains which used to run beyond the wall had been replaced by electric ones, so the washing was free from smuts.

She was so immersed in her misery she was only vaguely aware of the tall figure approaching, and came down to earth when the figure bumped into her.

'Why don't you look where . . .' She stopped. It was a man with a white stick, a sickly looking little dog at his heels. 'I'm sorry,' she stammered. 'I was miles away. I didn't see you.'

'And I didn't see you, either,' Paddy O'Hara said cheerfully. He raised his cap politely. 'Mrs Fleming, isn't it?'

'How . . . how did you know?'

'I can tell by your voice, luv. Everyone sez you talk dead posh, like. And that scent you're using, it's not *Evening in Paris*, is it? I bet that cost a bob or two.'

'It did,' Jessica said briefly. She had no intention of gossiping on the pavement, though it was difficult to be rude to a blind man. 'Well, Mr . . .'

'Call me Paddy, Paddy O'Hara.'

'Well, Paddy, I'd better be getting home,' she said awkwardly. 'My hubby comes home early on Saturdays.'

'And I suppose Arthur likes his dinner on the table, eh?'

Mumbling something incomprehensible, Jessica fled.

Once inside the house, she stood in the tiny hallway and leaned against the front door, panting. So, Arthur was already on first name terms with the neighbours! To her utter disgust, he'd started using the pub on the corner and went most nights for a drink. To him, it was all a bit of an adventure. He'd never mixed with people like this before. His father had been in insurance, manager of his own department. Arthur came from a home that was utterly respectable, a nice roomy semi-detached in a small village just outside Chester where his mother had been a stalwart of the local church, the Women's Institute and the Conservative party. What would they say if they could see him now, Jessica wondered? Thank God they were dead, along with her own father.

Arthur came home from the pub with all sorts of bits of gossip, which, despite herself and despite the fact she still wasn't speaking to him, at least not properly, she sat and listened to avidly. The woman who'd lived in this house before them had died on the *Athenia* which made Jessica feel peculiar; she had expected the ghost of Mary Flaherty to pop up now and then and accuse her of not keeping the range clean or complaining about the fact her children's chalk marks had been obliterated when the backyard was covered with a fresh coat of whitewash. The man next door was a retired tailor, a widower, Jacob Singerman, who hadn't heard from his daughter in Austria for more than a year.

'Singerman! You mean we live next door to a Jew boy?'

'We live next door to a Jewish gentleman of eighty, Jess,' Arthur replied gently and Jessica felt herself blush. In fact, the piano music from next door had come as a pleasant surprise when they moved in; sad, classical pieces played with feeling and a certain amount of skill, so different from the sounds coming from the people on their other side, who screamed at each other late at night in Welsh. The man seemed to be having a feud with the ARP warden and there were frequent rows over whether a light was showing or not.

Sighing, Jessica climbed the narrow stairs to the rear bedroom where there was a single bed. She hadn't slept with Arthur since the night he'd revealed their world was about to fall apart. She hung her coat in the wardrobe and lay down on the dark-green silk coverlet. Arthur would just have to wait for his lunch when he came home.

Something else he'd said the other night came to her;

a man from along the street who was in the Merchant Navy was missing, presumed killed, his ship torpedoed by the German battleship *Graf Spee*. He'd left a wife and six small children, the youngest only eight weeks old.

'Six!' said Jessica contemptuously. 'Those Catholics, they breed like rabbits.

Arthur said nothing.

'Six.' Jessica repeated, this time in a softer voice with a touch of longing. 'Six children!'

'It would have been nice, wouldn't it, Jess?'

Nice! Lying on the bed, Jessica thought it would have been more than nice, it would have been heaven. Six children! She cursed fate for making her barren.

There were voices coming from the adjacent yard outside, and she got up and peeped through the lace curtain. There were two men in the yard, one partially hidden inside the washhouse, moving something around. The one outside was obviously Jacob Singerman, a stooped elderly figure with wispy grey hair.

'Will that do you, Jacob?'

'Thanks, Jack, that'll do fine. It's just that the roof's leaking and turning the boiler all rusty. I tried moving it myself, but it wouldn't budge.'

The other man emerged and regarded the roof critically. 'If I can get me hands on a couple of slates, Jacob, I'll fix it for you.'

Jack Doyle! Jessica's hand tightened on the curtain. She would have recognised him anywhere. He was as handsome and as striking now as he'd been thirty years ago when he'd been the bane of her father's life, coming round to the yard regularly in a towering rage to complain about the fact some old lady had been given tuppence for a precious family heirloom worth at least five pounds, perhaps ten.

'You bloody, capitalist filth,' he'd yell. 'You'd sell your own grandma if she'd fetch a good price.'

'Bugger off, you socialist scum,' her father would yell back. 'I didn't force her to sell it, did I?'

In the end, Jack usually got a few bob extra for the old lady and went off, only partially satisfied, while her father sat muttering all night, complaining, somewhat unfairly Jessica thought in retrospect, that he'd been robbed. After all, he *did* make an enormous profit on the stuff he bought, and it *was* a bit unfair to take advantage of poor people when they were hard up.

Jessica stood at the window feeling slightly astonished. She'd never looked at it that way before. In the old days, she'd always considered it was Jack Doyle who was being unreasonable, though it hadn't stopped her from falling head over heels in love with him. Not that Jack knew, and if he had, he wouldn't have cared. She was only fourteen and he was eight or nine years older and already courting. The fond, yearning memory of the tall fiery young man had gone with her to Walton and hadn't faded until she met Arthur, six years later.

The two men had disappeared into the house next door. Jessica sat in front of the dressing-table mirror, fluffing out her red hair, applying a fresh coat of lipstick. Her cheeks were pinker than usual, her eyes brighter. Seeing Jack Doyle had made her feel young again, made her relive feelings she hadn't had in a long, long time.

When Arthur came home, she ran downstairs, more cheerful than she'd been since they left Calderstones.

The foreman was a sour-faced man in his fifties. 'This,' he said sarcastically, 'is a capstan lathe.'

Eileen Costello nodded knowingly. The machine

looked like three motorbikes joined together, and very complicated. A long narrow piece of metal had been fed in sideways and protruded out several feet.

'Now, what you're making is distance pieces, three-quarter inch diameter with a half-inch hole.'

'Right,' said Eileen, nodding again. It was her first day at Dunnings, the aeroplane parts factory in Melling, and she was determined to do well. She'd been put in the workshop, a vast single-storey building with a metal roof. There were about twenty other women working on similar machines, all, like her, dressed in navy cotton drill overalls covered with a thick canvas apron and a white scarf tied turban-wise around their heads, which seemed to take away each woman's individuality. Eileen thought they looked like a flock of giant birds.

'To start the lathe, you pull this lever and turn the stop.' He reached under the machine, then pointed to a six-sided plate on top. 'See that? That's the capstan, and each point is a different tool which relates to the position of this handwheel.' He began to turn the wheel and the capstan shot along a ridge and back again. 'This is the bar feed which releases the collet, there's the centre drill, the plain drill, the reamer . . .'

Eileen felt herself begin to panic. She'd never remember all this. He droned on about cross sticks and more levers, chucks and variable speeds, until her mind became a blur.

'Now,' he said, 'set it up the way I told you, like, while I keep an eye on you.'

'I can't remember how to begin,' she confessed weakly.

The foreman closed his eyes, bit his lip and leaned on the machine without saying a word, clearly at the end of his patience. All that careful explanation and she hadn't taken in a word. Bloody women! They were useless with machinery.

Eileen watched him, feeling guilty. 'If you could just go through it again,' she pleaded.

'Eh, Alfie, sod off, and let me show her.' A jolly-looking girl of about twenty stopped the machine next to Eileen's with a deft flick of a lever and came over. The curls escaping from underneath her turban were dyed an unnatural shade of orange and her lips were painted vivid purple. 'You're bloody useless at explaining. I bet when you started work in the last century, you didn't get the hang of it in the first five minutes.' She turned to Eileen. 'Hallo, luv, I'm Doris.'

Alfie departed with a filthy look in Doris's direction. There was a cry of 'Good riddance' from the other girls in the workshop.

'I'm Eileen, and I'm sure I'll never understand how this thing works,' Eileen said pathetically.

'It's quite simple, really. By the end of the week, you'll find it as easy as shoving meat in a mincer.'

Doris managed to make the operation appear much less complicated. Eileen watched, fascinated, as the long strip of metal was separated into little pieces, each neatly drilled with a hole, and dropping into a container underneath the machine.

'Come on, Eileen, you have a go, but take it careful, like.'

'I'll take over now, Doris.' A tall willowy girl with a thick fringe falling into her eyes, who was on Eileen's other side, approached. 'I'm Pauline. We can't stop for long, else we lose pay. Did they tell you, you're on piecework? You're allowed two minutes each for these.'

'I'm terribly sorry,' Eileen stammered, full of

confusion. These helpful girls were losing money on her account.

'Well, don't be. Alfie couldn't learn a monkey to pee,' Pauline said scathingly. 'We always help the newies out. Next Monday, it might be you expected to lend a hand if someone starts.'

Eileen couldn't for the life of her imagine such a situation. 'What's that stuff?' A white liquid was spewing up around each finished piece of metal and covering the front of her canvas pinafore with a fine spray.

'That's the cooling liquid. It stops the metal from getting too hot. It don't half pong.'

'Is that what the smell is?'

'You need a good wash every night to get rid of it.'

With the help of the other girls, Eileen managed more or less to get the hang of the lathe, though her progress was painfully slow. When the tea trolley came round at eight o'clock, she sat on the little stool in front of the machine, never more grateful for a cup of tea and a cigarette. Another six hours to go, and she already felt exhausted. Not only that, she was suffocating in her heavy overalls and canvas pinafore; she could feel perspiration running down her armpits, and her neck felt clammy.

Doris noticed her predicament. 'You've got too many clothes on, haven't you?'

'It was cold out. I wore a thick jumper.'

Doris grinned and her purple mouth seemed to extend from ear to ear. She undid the top buttons of her overall to reveal a grubby white cotton bra. 'I've only got me bra and keks on, all of us have. When you go to the lavvy next, put your jumper and skirt in your locker, else you'll melt away to nothing in here.'

'I will,' said Eileen fervently. 'I'll go the minute I've

finished me tea and this ciggie.'

'Miss Thomas would've told you that, but she's not in yet this morning. She usually has a talk to the newies before they start work.'

'Who's Miss Thomas?'

'She's the women's overseer. I reckon she's still at the hospital with Ginnie Macauley from the Tool Shop. Ginnie keeled over on Friday night, and you'll never believe this, Eileen, but she had a bun in the oven and didn't know.'

'Jaysus! How could you not know?'

'Beats me.' Doris shrugged. 'She didn't, though, she just thought she was getting fat. Oh, here's Miss Thomas, now.' A petite middle-aged woman with crop-ped hair, wearing a too-large navy-blue pin-striped suit and sensible flat shoes, came into the workshop. 'How's Ginnie, Miss Thomas?' Doris yelled.

'She was delivered of a fine six-pound baby boy on Saturday afternoon,' Miss Thomas answered in a crisp, refined voice. 'She's not so well herself, though I think it's more shock than anything. I've sat with her two nights in a row, the poor lamb can't stop crying.'

'You're an angel, Miss Thomas, you really are,' another girl shouted.

'Get away with you, Beattie,' Miss Thomas said dis-missively. She came up to Eileen and smiled. 'You're Eileen Costello, aren't you? I'd like you to come into my office so we can have a little chat. I'm sorry I wasn't here first thing, but as you will have understood, I was otherwise engaged.'

The woman was about to leave when her eye fell on Pauline, and she said sharply, 'Tuck that fringe beneath your scarf immediately! You know it's against regula-tions.' Her tone changed. 'Come on, Eileen.'

Once they were in the spartan glass-fronted office with its bare wooden floor, Miss Thomas pointed to a chair in front of the scrupulously tidy desk, and instead of sitting behind the desk, she perched herself on its end. She wore no make-up or jewellery and her freckled face had a scrubbed fresh look. Despite the lack of concession to fashion, her animated expression and lively brown eyes somehow made her appear attractive.

'How are you getting on so far, Eileen?'

'Not so well,' Eileen confessed. 'Though I think I'm beginning to get the hang of it.'

'You will, eventually,' Miss Thomas said confidently. 'Now, I have to ask this. Did you bring your gas mask?'

'Well, no. I've only taken it out with me once. I can't imagine using it and it's such a nuisance to carry.'

'I agree, and so, it would seem, does everybody else. Well, I've done my duty and given you a reminder, so that's out of the way.' She smiled briskly. 'My real reason for seeing you is to stress, if you have any problems, please bring them to me. Any problems, of any sort. I blame myself for not having guessed about Ginnie Macauley, but if the girl herself didn't know, I don't suppose I could be expected to. Husband problems, boyfriend problems, health problems, I'm always here to listen.' She picked up a sheet of paper from the desk behind her; Eileen recognised the form she'd completed when she'd come with Annie for an interview several weeks ago. 'I see you have a little boy, Eileen. Do you have someone to take care of him while you're at work?'

'Of course I do,' Eileen said indignantly. As if she'd come out and leave Tony on his own! 'There's me friend, Annie, for one, she's starting work here this avvy. Annie'll be seeing him off to school any minute now. Then there's me sister, Sheila, and me neighbours. I'll never be short of someone to look after our Tony and I would never have left him if I were.'

Miss Thomas looked suitably contrite. 'I'm sorry, Eileen, but some women go out to work without giving a damn if their little ones are being properly looked after.'

'Well, I'm not one of them,' Eileen muttered. She didn't like the woman's patronising attitude. She wouldn't have dreamt of discussing 'husband problems' with a total stranger and resented the assumption that she would. And she wasn't Jack Doyle's daughter for nothing. She also resented being called Eileen, when she was supposed to address the woman as Miss Thomas.

Miss Thomas seemed to sense the slight antagonism. She sighed and moved to sit behind the desk. 'There's just a few more things. I keep a supply of sanitary towels in my office in case any of the girls are caught short with their periods, and I always have a plentiful stock of aspirin to save you going to First Aid.'

Eileen would have loved a couple of aspirin there and then, her head was thumping from the strain of the morning, but there was no way she would ask for them. She'd put a bottle of her own in her bag tonight – and a sanitary rag.

'I expect you've already noticed how hot it gets in the workshop?' Miss Thomas went on. 'The girls work in their bras and pants. I've been pleading with those on high for softer, finer overalls, so there wouldn't be a need for such extreme measures, but I've had no luck so far.' She smiled. 'I'm afraid management aren't very accommodating when I ask for special treatment for my girls.'

Eileen bristled inside. She'd no wish to be one of Miss Thomas's 'girls'. 'I was about to take me jumper and skirt off as soon as I'd drunk me tea,' she said, and Miss Thomas nodded approvingly.

'Finally,' she said, 'you'll have already been lectured on this by Alfie, but please ensure your hair is kept well back from your face with your bandana. Even a fringe like Pauline's is dangerous. If you bend over the machine and your hair gets caught!' She paused, shuddering. 'I can't understand why some girls put glamour before safety.'

'I'll be careful,' Eileen said politely.

'Well,' Miss Thomas smiled, 'I think that's it. I hope you enjoy working here, Eileen. There's a nice atmosphere, everybody's very friendly. You should settle down in no time.' Then, almost to herself, she went on, 'Though let's hope the pundits are right and this phoney war is over soon and there won't be a need for such a massive rearmament programme.'

'My sister doesn't think it's a phoney war,' Eileen said shortly. 'Not since she lost her husband last month on the *Midnight Star*.'

'Oh, dear! I'm so sorry,' Miss Thomas looked genuinely concerned. 'How is she taking it?'

'Everyone thinks she's taking it very well, but I know she isn't.' Eileen stood up. 'Well, thank you for the talk. I'd better be getting back to work.'

Work had already re-started when she returned to the workshop. As the morning wore on, the coarse seams of the overalls began to rub against her bare flesh until it felt sore and the slightest movement hurt. Although she'd worn her most comfortable shoes, her feet felt as if they'd swollen to twice their size.

A pretty Chinese girl came round and examined the work Eileen had done, and pronounced it satisfactory.

'That's Winnie Li, the Quality Inspector,' Doris shouted when the girl had gone. 'Isn't she lovely? She's had terrible trouble with her dad, because he wants her to work in his restaurant. Though you're not to call him

Hoo Flung Dung, else she'll be annoyed.'

Eileen smiled without answering. The other girls seemed able to keep quite a conversation going above the noise of the machines. Every now and then, one would burst into song and the others would join in. A favourite seemed to be *When They Begin the Beguine*, which they sang repeatedly, closely followed by *Roll Out The Barrel*, and *Little Sir Echo*. Whenever Alfie, the foreman, appeared, the girls would stop singing and there would be a deluge of insults, mainly directed at his sexual prowess. After Alfie had left, cringing with embarrassment, they'd begin singing again at exactly the point they'd left off. Eileen noticed the long piece of metal sticking out of the machine had been used up. She told Doris, who screamed, 'Billy!' and a weedy little man without a single hair on his head came along and inserted another.

'What'cha doing tonight, Queen?' he asked Eileen, winking.

'I don't know what you mean.'

'Fancy a date?' He winked again.

'No, I bloody don't,' she said weakly.

'Please yourself, Queen.' He left, not looking the least bit hurt.

'Did he ask you out?' asked Doris.

'Yes.'

'He asks all the newies out. If one of 'em said yes, he'd faint. In fact, we all would.'

It seemed strange to sit down to a big meal at half past ten in the morning. The canteen was even hotter than the factory; the gleaming silver counter where they queued for their steak and kidney pie, cabbage and mashed potatoes, was wreathed in steam and the women, serving behind in their green overalls and turbans, were red-faced and perspiring. The meal was good value at ninepence, and fourpence for the apple pie and custard.

Eileen carried her tray over to the table where Doris had promised to save her a place, and where half a dozen girls from the workshop already sat. Doris introduced them. 'You already know Pauline, and this is Carmel, Beattie, Theresa, Lil, Patsy . . .'

'How d'you do?' Eileen glanced down at the plate heaped with food. 'I'll never eat all this!'

'You'll get used to it,' Theresa said comfortably.

'Aye, I suppose I will.' It seemed impossible to believe that she would get used to the heat and the noise and the awful smell, the funny hours, the uncomfortable overalls and being on her feet for seven hours a day, but if the other girls could, then so would she. In fact, close up, some of the 'girls' looked quite old; Lil and Beattie were well into their forties, and Carmel, who appeared to be entirely toothless, was sixty if she was a day. She watched, fascinated, when the woman took a full set of false teeth out of her overall pocket and put them in before attacking the meal.

Eileen picked at her own meal until Doris offered to eat it for her and she handed it over gladly. 'Is it possible to go outside? I'm gasping for some fresh air. I'll be back in time for a cup of tea and a ciggie.'

Pauline pointed to double doors in the wall on the far side of the canteen. 'Go through there, then through another door, and you'll find yourself outside. We used to sit out during the summer, but it's too cold now.'

'The summer? You mean you were making aeroplane parts during the summer? I thought this factory only opened when the war began.'

'Oh, no,' she was assured. 'We've been here a good year.'

'So Chamberlain wasn't as unprepared as everyone

thinks,' Eileen remarked.

The women looked at her blankly. 'Well, I'll be off,' she said hastily.

'Don't forget your coat, otherwise you'll get pneumonia,' Doris shouted. 'You're stripped naked underneath them overalls.'

There was a chorus of whistles from the men on the next table and Eileen fled, her face red, to the cloakroom to get her coat from the locker.

She emerged from the factory through a side door and to her delight found herself on a soil path next to a little stream which gurgled along over a layer of moss-covered rocks and white pebbles. The water was beautifully clear. Eileen knelt on the damp grassy bank, removed her scarf and splashed her face, rubbing her chafed and aching neck with her wet hands. She took several deep breaths of bracing fresh air and glanced around. It was a nondescript sort of day, neither bright nor dull, the sky was a mishmash of hazy clouds with patches of anaemic blue here and there and little sign of the sun making an appearance. Despite this, it seemed extraordinarily bright, and the brownstone bridge which spanned the narrow stream about twenty feet away on her left and the cows grazing in the field opposite were sharply defined, as if they'd been picked out by a spotlight. Further down the bank, a man in a corduroy suit and a wide-brimmed hat was sat fishing, apparently oblivious to the fact he had company. The smells, compared to the smells inside the factory, were wholesome: damp earth, damp grass, wild flowers. It was such a peaceful scene Eileen felt it was obscene that, in the midst of such beauty and tranquillity, parts were being made for aeroplanes which would eventually carry bombs to drop on the innocent citizens of Germany.

She made up her mind to bring Tony out here next summer. He knew nothing about the countryside and until now had only seen cows at a distance, on their way into Southport on the train, never at such close quarters. When she'd come to Melling for the interview, she and Annie had walked down the High Street, marvelling at the fact that such a sleepy little village existed a mere twelve miles or so away from the thriving metropolis of Liverpool.

After splashing her face a second time, she went inside reluctantly. Two o'clock, finishing time, seemed an eternity away.

Somehow, the time passed, crawling by, and at five to two a hooter sounded, and the girls downed tools and made for the door.

'Leave the machine as it is,' Doris instructed. 'Someone else'll take over where you left off.'

Eileen quickly got changed, put her overalls in her locker, and left the factory by the main exit. A row of double decker buses, windows painted black, stood in the forecourt, hired specially to take the workers to various parts of Liverpool. Eileen assumed Annie had come on one but, looking around, could see no sign of her. As she made her way towards the bus for Seaforth, she felt as if her unsteady legs were about to give way. She climbed up to the dimly lit top deck so she could have a welcome cigarette. The atmosphere was full of smoke and several girls from the workshop were already on, including Pauline, all sitting on the long seat at the back. They shoved up to make room for her.

'What d'you think then, Eileen, about your first day at Dunnings?' one of them asked, grinning.

'I'm completely worn out,' she confessed. 'I've got aches in bones I didn't know I had.'

'It's because you're using muscles you don't usually use, pushing all them levers and things. You'll get used to it.'

'If I had a pound for every time someone's said that to me today, I'd be well off,' Eileen said dryly.

Once home, she slipped out of her shoes and sank into a chair, totally exhausted, convinced she would never get up again. She hadn't been there long when Sheila came in, using her key, carrying Mary.

'How d'you get on, Eil?'

'I'm dead, Sis,' Eileen said dramatically. 'Completely dead.'

A shadow fell over Sheila's face. 'Oh, Christ!' thought Eileen, 'what a tactless thing to say.' Her sister had taken the news about Calum with surprising calm, but inside, Eileen knew she was devastated.

'Shall I make you a cup of tea?' Sheila asked lightly. 'I can't stay more than a minute. Ryan's asleep and Brenda Mahon took Siobhan and Caitlin off me hands for a few hours. I'll have to collect them soon.' She wrinkled her nose. 'What's that smell?'

'Me! I'll have a good wash in a minute. I'd love a cup of tea, though, Sheil. I think I'm stuck in this chair forever.'

'Here you are then, take our Mary while I put the kettle on.'

'I haven't got the strength, I'll drop her,' Eileen threatened when the baby was thrust into her arms.

'No, you won't.'

Mary nuzzled at her breast. 'You won't get a feed off me, miss,' she said sternly, providing a none-too-clean finger.

'Don't you wish you'd had more kids, Sis?' Sheila shouted from the kitchen.

Eileen looked down at the tiny face of her niece, the

little mouth sucking on her finger. 'Yes, I do,' she shouted back. Then, in a soft voice to herself, she added, 'Not that there's much chance of that with Francis.'

But somehow Sheila heard. She appeared in the doorway, her normally tranquil brow puckered in a frown. 'What d'you mean, Eileen?'

'Oh, nothing,' Eileen said dismissively.

'Come off it, Sis,' Sheila persisted. 'What did you mean, there's not much chance with Francis?'

Eileen took a deep breath. She would never reveal the real reason, of course, but the question of her future with Francis had occupied her mind almost every waking minute since he returned to Kettering a few weeks ago. Without him, the house was a different place altogether. She hadn't felt so relaxed and contented in years, and Tony was blossoming, becoming more assertive without his dad nagging at him over the least little thing. The decision had come to her like a blinding flash of light when she was in bed one night, and it was his absence that caused her to take it, but she knew it was essential to her and Tony's future happiness that they never live with Francis again. She'd felt somewhat nervous the following morning, knowing the furore it would cause when people found out. Apart from the brief conversation with her dad, she hadn't discussed it with anyone so far, not even Annie. Now the subject had come up with Sheila, more by accident than design. People had to find out sometime, and she wondered what her sister's reaction would be.

'I'm not having Francis back,' she said bluntly. 'In fact, Dad's already changed the locks on both the doors.'

'But you can't do that, our Eileen! He's your husband!'

Eileen was taken aback by how shocked her sister looked, and felt slightly annoyed. 'You don't know what he's like, Sis. It's not you that's had to live with him for the last six years.'

Sheila shook her head emphatically. 'It doesn't matter what he's like. You took him for better or for worse. You can't go back on your wedding vows.'

'Dad doesn't seem to mind,' Eileen said stiffly, which was not strictly true. Her dad only thought Francis needed 'straightening out' before he was allowed back. She began to wish she'd kept her mouth shut. Sheila had always been fervently religious, far more so than Eileen. Her house was stuffed with statues and holy pictures. The last thing Eileen wanted at the moment was a row, not with her brain so muggy with tiredness she could scarcely think straight.

'Well, he wouldn't, would he?' Sheila answered. 'Our dad doesn't think the way other people do.'

'Perhaps I take after him.'

'Aye perhaps you do.' Sheila could feel the hot fires of anger burning in her breast. She rarely lost her temper, but it seemed too unfair for words. Her Cal was missing, almost certainly dead. There'd been no time for a distress signal from the *Midnight Star* before the deadly torpedo struck, no reports of survivors having been picked up. Cal was dead, the most precious husband a woman could ever have, the only man she would ever love, gone forever, and she herself felt dead inside. It was an effort to get up each morning and see to the kids, to keep on living. Yet here was her sister talking about getting rid of Francis Costello, who may well have not turned out all he was cracked up to be, but even so, he and Eileen had been joined together in Holy Matrimony at a Nuptial Mass. They'd promised to stay together, 'till death do us part'. Breaking up with your husband, any husband, was against everything she believed in.

'What does Francis have to say about it?' she asked, trying to remain calm.

'I've no idea,' Eileen said tiredly. 'I wrote to him, but I haven't heard back yet.' The letter, sent soon after he'd returned, had taken days to write. She'd used an entire notepad, screwing up page after page until she got the wording more or less right. She'd told him she never wanted him back, but didn't say why, presuming he would know the reason only too well.

'That's nice, when he's about to fight for his country,' Sheila said hotly.

Eileen felt too weary to argue any longer. 'He's not going to do much damage with a typewriter. Anyway, Sis, you don't know the least thing about it. It's only since he went away that I found out what life could be like without him, not just for me, but for our Tony, too. When he came home on leave, I realised I wasn't prepared to take it any longer. It's easy for you to talk, your Cal's a different kettle of fish altogether. I mean, he was . . .' She stopped and stared at her sister in despair. 'I'm getting meself in a proper muddle.' She tried to smile. 'Talking of kettles, mine's been boiling away for ages. You've got me kitchen like a Turkish bath.'

Sheila made the tea, but didn't pour one for herself. 'I'll have to be getting back,' she said stiffly. 'The main reason I came was to say I've done pigs' trotters for tea and there's plenty enough for you and Tony. I thought you wouldn't feel up to getting a meal after your first day at work.'

'I don't. In fact, I was thinking of sending Tony to the chippy when he came home. Ta, Sheil. I'll be across later.'

After her sister had gone, Eileen determined not to rake over their argument. Right now, all that seemed to matter were her various aches and pains and enormous throbbing tiredness. She closed her eyes and imagined herself soaking in a bath of scented bubbles, the sort of thing you saw film stars do in the pictures. When she opened them again, to her surprise it was dark outside, and she panicked, thinking she'd fallen asleep and Tony was late home. Then she remembered that double summertime, which had been extended by five weeks until the middle of November, had ended the day before so the blackout had begun two hours earlier than usual. It was scarcely four o'clock, yet almost pitch black.

Eileen shuddered. She always felt a bit depressed when the winter closed in, but this year it seemed particularly heavy and oppressive, what with Cal and Mary dead, and the terrible carnage at sea where even neutral ships were being torpedoed. As if that wasn't enough, a few weeks ago, the Government had published a white paper on German concentration camps and poor Jacob Singerman, on the verge of tears, had brought the newspaper cutting across to show her, convinced there was little hope for his Ruth and the son-in-law and grandchildren he'd never met.

There'd been a moment of great hope at the beginning of November, though, when an attempt had been made on Adolf Hitler's life at a rally in Munich. Unfortunately, he'd left the rally early, before the planted bomb exploded, but the entire country, perhaps the entire world, had felt this might be a turning point and the people of Germany would rise up against the tyrant who was leading their great nation into a war which no sane person could possibly want. But nothing had happened, the phoney war continued, and Eileen could see no sign of it being over by Christmas as many people still predicted.

This wouldn't do! She got up somewhat unsteadily and

turned the wireless on, twiddling with the knob, looking for some cheerful music until she found Gracie Fields singing *Wish Me Luck As You Wave Me Goodbye*, then went into the back kitchen to get washed before Tony came home and wanted to know where the terrible smell came from.

'Goodnight, Miss Brazier. Do you think you'll be able to find your way home all right?'

'I'm sure I will, Mr Sanderson. Goodnight. I'll see you in the morning.'

The manager of the Co-op was only a few feet away, yet almost invisible, and she imagined him touching his hat courteously. She stood there, disorientated before she'd even taken a step, and felt for the Co-op window before making her way along the pavement, using the windows as a guide. With summertime ending yesterday, this was the first night the shop had closed in darkness. One of the girls had said there should be a full moon, but if so, there was no sign of it. The sky was like a heavy blanket of black, without even a cloud visible.

She collided with someone almost straight away, a woman, who said in a startled voice, 'Sorry, luv! Isn't this terrible? It's like walking through a bowl of ink.'

'Isn't it!' said Miss Brazier.

Everyone else seemed to have the same idea of using the windows as a guide. After several more collisions and 'Sorry, luvs' from both sides, she decided to venture, somewhat nervously, further out onto the pavement. Almost immediately, she bumped headlong into a man and almost fell before he grabbed her with both arms. 'Sorry, luv. Isn't this terrible?'

'It's awful,' she agreed. 'I think I'll bring me torch tomorrow.'

'They don't help much,' he said dismissively. 'You've got to have two thicknesses of tissue paper on the glass and you can only point it downwards. You're too busy concentrating on your feet to look where you're going. Well, goodnight, luv. I hope you get home safe and sound.'

'You, too,' said Miss Brazier, thinking it would be midnight before she arrived home at this rate. Some girls passed, giggling helplessly. A man cursed, 'Me toe! I stubbed it on the kerb. Bloody Hitler!'

'He won't need to bomb us,' someone said sarcastically. 'We'll all have bumped each other to death by then.'

'How the hell am I supposed to cross the road?' a woman asked. 'Does anyone know where the traffic lights are?'

It was a strange feeling, thought Miss Brazier, so many people, yet she couldn't see a thing. All that was visible were the little slits of headlights on the occasional car as it crawled by.

Her shoulder caught another somewhat sharply. 'Sorry, luv,' she said breathlessly. 'Isn't this terrible?'

It was a young woman, who laughed. 'Don't apologise, you must be about the fiftieth person I've bumped into. Have you got far to go?'

'Marsh Lane.'

'You poor ould thing. I'm nearly home. Goodnight, luv.'

'Goodnight.'

A spirit of camaraderie seemed to develop, a sense of adventure, as people struggled along, and there were more howls of laughter than complaints. Miss Brazier began to feel amost exhilarated.

'It won't be so bad once rationing comes in,' a man said cynically. 'We'll all be so thin, there'll be more room for us on the pavement.'

Miss Brazier found herself smiling broadly, though the smile vanished when she heard the lumbering sound of a tram coming directly towards her, headlights dimmed, windows painted black, and she leapt backwards. She must have walked right into the middle of Stanley Road which ran along the top without realising she'd stepped off the pavement. She turned, and walked right into a lamppost. There was a cracking sound as her glasses broke and fell off her nose and her hat fell off her head.

She cried aloud, frightened.

'Are you all right, luv? What's up?' A man's strong hand grasped her elbow.

'I've broke me glasses and lost me hat.' She felt around with her foot, located the glasses and bent down gingerly to pick them up. One of the lenses was completely shattered.

'I've got a torch. What colour is the hat?'

'Black.' For some reason, she giggled, and the man laughed.

'You couldn't have picked a worse colour to lose in the blackout, could you?'

She could see the narrow yellow beam of his torch searching the flags. 'It doesn't matter. It's me own fault for not using a hat pin and it was an old one, anyroad,' she said.

'Let's have a look at your face, make sure you haven't cut it.' The yellow light shone in her eyes and she blinked uncomfortably. 'No, you're all still in one piece, like. Which way are you going, luv?'

'Marsh Lane.'

'Well, link me arm and I'll go as far as the corner with you.'

Before she could say a word, her arm was tucked in his

and they began to stroll along Stanley Road together as if they'd known each other for years. It was an even stranger sensation than the blackout, linking arms with a man.

'What's your name, luv?' He had a nice voice, neither young nor old, but deep and slightly musical, with the faint suggestion of an Irish accent.

'Miss Brazier.'

'Miss? That's a funny name to call someone!' he chuckled.

'Sorry, it's Helen.' There'd been no-one to call her by her first name for so long that she'd almost forgotten what it was.

'Do your friends call you Nellie?'

'No . . . well, I haven't got many friends.'

'I'm Louis Murphy, known as Lou. And what d'you mean, Helen, you haven't got many friends, a fine-looking woman like you?'

She felt her cheeks burn and wondered what he looked like. She could tell he was tall, his voice came from somewhere above her head and his arm felt lean and wiry.

'I looked after me mother till she died when I was twenty-four,' she said simply. 'Since then, I've never known how to make friends.' She hadn't talked so openly to anyone in her life before, but it seemed easy to say these things in the dark to a total stranger she couldn't see. 'You'll never believe this,' she went on, gaining confidence, 'but I've spoken to more people coming up Strand Road tonight, then I've done since I began work in the Co-op when I left school.'

'You're just shy, that's all,' he said wisely. After a while, he began to tell her about himself. He worked in Burton's, the Gents' Outfitters, and lived with his sister, a widow with three young children. It came as a surprise when they reached the corner of Marsh Lane and she felt almost sorry he was going.

'Tell you what, Helen. I'll meet you on the corner of Stanley Road tomorrow night at the same time, eh?'

'If you like,' she said shyly, 'but how will we know each other in the dark?'

'I'll just keep on saying, "Helen, Helen, Helen" over and over again till you answer,' he laughed. He patted her arm. 'Don't worry, luv, we'll find each other somehow.'

Chapter 6

The lathe had turned into a giant mincing machine. A long strip of red meat was being fed through and chopped up into little cubes. The meat began to travel faster and faster until she lost control. Then the entire machine broke away from the floor and began to dance around the workshop with a horrendous clattering noise. The other girls shrieked with laughter as she chased after the machine and tried to catch it.

Eileen Costello woke up, the clattering sound still thumping in her head. It had all been a dream, a rather funny dream when you thought about it. She glanced over Tony's sleeping form at the clock beside the bed. Nearly half past seven. She gave a muffled shriek. 'I've slept in! I mustn't have heard the alarm.'

She was about to leap out and throw herself into her clothes when she remembered it was Saturday and she didn't have to go to work. She sank back onto the pillow, prepared to relish a welcome lie-in after her first exhausting week at work. It was several seconds before she realised that the banging from her silly dream still persisted. Someone was hammering on the door.

'Damn!' she muttered wearily. Who on earth could it be at this hour? Her heart turned over at the thought it might be Francis. Perhaps he'd tried to use his key and found it didn't fit. The banging increased. Whoever was there had begun to use their fists.

She climbed over Tony, slipped into her dressing gown

and crept downstairs. Peeping cautiously through the parlour curtains, she saw the black-shawled figure of Gladys Tutty outside in the pouring rain, beating on the front door with her fists like a madwoman.

'Damn!' she said again as she walked down the hall and opened the door to her neighbour.

'What's the matter, Gladys?' Eileen tried not to sound annoyed. Perhaps it was some sort of emergency.

'I want me kids back,' said Gladys hoarsely. She was soaking wet and swaying on her feet. Her matted hair stuck up wildly around her head like the tails of little animals, and rivulets of rain made white streaks on her filthy face. Eileen reckoned she'd probably been out all night drinking in the illegal den she frequented somewhere down the Dock Road. It was said by those who knew these things that Gladys would go outside with any man for a double gin.

'Well, I haven't got your kids, have I, Gladys?' Eileen said irritably, thinking about the warm bed she'd just vacated and to which she longed to return.

'I want them back!' Incredibly, the little woman looked on the verge of tears.

'You'll have to go and see the billeting people or something,' Eileen explained patiently. As if to prove how unreal the war was, how phoney, virtually all the children who'd been evacuated had come back weeks ago. Billy Templedown from Opal Street, who was only ten, had walked home from Southport on the railway line all by himself.

'The what?' Gladys's jaw dropped and she looked vacant.

'The billeting people, the ones who came to see you when Freda and Dicky were evacuated.' When Gladys looked no more enlightened, Eileen said reluctantly, 'Oh,

I suppose you'd better come in.' She hated having Gladys Tutty in her house, the smell persisted for days, but the poor woman was getting more soaked by the minute. As Gladys went down the hall, her too large men's boots squelched, squirting water all over the linoleum.

'D'know where Freda and Dicky are?' asked Eileen when Gladys was sitting down.

'Southport.'

'I know that much, Gladys. I meant have you got their address? Have you had a letter from them?' Even as she spoke, Eileen knew the last question was stupid. She couldn't for the life of her imagine Freda or Dicky writing a letter to their mam.

'I got a letter telling me the address where they were staying,' Gladys said vaguely. Then she added in a stubborn voice, 'I want me kids back. I want them back today. Everyone else's kids are back except mine.'

Which was, when you thought about it, and Eileen hadn't thought about it before, somewhat amazing. She would have expected anyone blessed with Freda and Dicky Tutty to have got rid of them at the very first opportunity. She wanted to ask Gladys *why* she wanted them back. Gladys paid no heed to her children. She fed them when she thought about it and then only with bread and dripping. During her frequent drinking bouts she often stayed out all night, and Freda and Dicky were left to their own devices in the cold, comfortless house. And when Gladys was there, the only acknowledgment the pair received was the occasional swipe or a good beating if their gin-starved mam was in a particularly foul mood. The Schoolie had long given up coming round to see why they weren't in school and the poor little mites were kept going by their own streetwise ability to stay alive and the goodwill of the neighbours who gave them food from time to time, though they were difficult kids to help. But, Eileen supposed, Gladys loved her children in her own peculiar way, every bit as much as she loved Tony.

'I want me kids back,' said Gladys, who'd begun to sound like a needle stuck on the turntable of a gramophone. Gladys could never have told anybody why she wanted her children. Deep within her muddled brain, she felt something was missing from her wretched life, that there was a curious emptiness she couldn't always put her finger on. Coming home that morning, she'd remembered. Freda and Dicky! They'd been gone for days, or was it months? How to get them back was quite beyond her, her mind couldn't begin to cope with the problem, but Eileen Costello would know. Eileen Costello seemed to know everything.

Eileen sighed. 'I'll tell you what, Gladys. Go and get that letter you mentioned and I'll write to the billeting people and ask them to send Freda and Dicky home.'

'I want them back today,' Gladys muttered. Rain was dripping from the ends of her shawl and the hem of her black skirt, making little puddles on the floor beneath the chair. The chair would be soaked, Eileen thought. She'd have to wash the cover and put the cushion in the airing cupboard to dry.

'But Gladys, there's nowt I can do about it,' she protested.

'This place, Southport. Is it far, like?'

'About fifteen miles, I reckon. You're not thinking of going, are you, Gladys?' The idea of Gladys catching a train and finding the address was ludicrous.

'You can fetch them for me.'

'*Me!*'

Gladys began to cry with hoarse, heartrending sobs

that shook her entire body. 'I want me kids back,' she moaned.

Eileen immediately felt terrible. The poor woman was obviously distraught, yet here she was, concerned only about her cushion covers getting wet and puddles on the lino. On the other hand, going to Southport to request the return of Freda and Dicky seemed a bit much to ask, though whoever had them would probably be only too glad to see the back of the pair – and they had to come home some time.

'I tell you what, Gladys, get me the address, and I'll go to Southport tomorrow and. . .' And what? Maybe Freda and Dicky wouldn't want to come back. 'And see what I can do,' she finished lamely.

'I want them back today.'

'Well, I'm sorry, but that's not possible,' Eileen said firmly, feeling irritated that she'd offered to do a good turn and it wasn't appreciated. 'I've got stacks of house-work to catch up on, I've been working all week, and I'm going out tonight with Annie Poulson to the pictures.'

The cinemas had been allowed to re-open in October. Eileen left Tony at home to listen to the wireless with Mr Singerman and Paddy O'Hara whilst she and Annie went to see *Love Affair* with Charles Boyer and Irene Dunne at the Palace in Marsh Lane. It was so sad and romantic they came out into the blackout in tears.

'I suppose it's nice to have a good cry now and then,' said Eileen tearfully as they made their way home down Marsh Lane.

'You're right, though I've no need to go to the pictures to have a cry nowadays,' Annie said, sniffing.

Eileen linked her arm. 'Sorry, luv. I'm forever putting me big foot in me mouth. I did the same thing with our Sheila the other day.'

Annie patted her hand in the dark. 'Don't take no notice of me, Eil. I'm being dead stupid. I've had a letter from our Terry and he and Joe are having a fine old time in France. Y'know, they drink wine over there the same way we drink water? Wine! Terry said it's cheaper than lemonade.'

'Honest? You don't say!'

'I suppose it's because if the war started proper like, and one of them got killed, I'd be so bloody angry I think I'd burst, 'cos it's all such a stupid waste, the whole thing. It's only men, the buggers, who start wars, never women. We just supply – what's it called – the cannon fodder, in order for them to play their silly games. Still, me lads are coming home on leave for Christmas, so I've got that to look forward to.'

They collided with another couple and, after laughing apologies on both sides, continued on their way more cautiously. 'Anyroad, I haven't had a chance to see you all week,' said Eileen. She'd been fast asleep by the time her friend got home at eleven o'clock. 'You haven't told me how you got on at Dunnings.' All she knew so far was that Annie had gone in the Assembly Shop.

'I hate it,' Annie said flatly. 'I'm learning to use a riveting gun and me bloody ears are still ringing from the noise and the other women are dead unfriendly, hardly one of 'em spoke to me all week. I've never been so glad to see Friday come in all me life before and I'm dreading Monday, I really am.'

Eileen felt uncomfortable. If Annie hadn't been looking after Tony, they would have started together and had each other for company – and they would have been on the early shift where the girls, in the Workshop at least, were as friendly and as helpful as could be. She said as much to her friend, but Annie only snorted. 'Don't be stupid, girl. If you stayed at home for Tony, it'd only mean one pair of hands less for the war effort, wouldn't it? Anyroad, how did you get on yourself?'

'Oh, all right,' Eileen replied, deciding not to enthuse too much, it might only make Annie feel worse, but by the end of the week, she'd firmly got the hang of the lathe, so much so that even the dour foreman, Alfie, had conceded she had an aptitude for it. She'd gradually got used to being on her feet for hours at a time, and with each day the time seemed to pass more quickly than the one before. By Friday, she was joining in the singing and the badinage, though still remained shocked at the lewd jokes the girls exchanged and the terrible foul language, directed mainly at Alfie and any other man who dared wander into the Workshop. 'I don't suppose you had an opportunity to go outside, being dark, like, did you, Annie, but it's dead peaceful out there. I went in the dinner time to splash me face in the stream and take a breather. There was a chap fishing every day, though he never noticed me. It'll be lovely in the summer.' She squeezed Annie's arm. 'Perhaps it won't be so bad next week, luv.'

'Oh, I'll get used to it. I've worked much harder than that in me day, and the fellers weren't so bad. One of them asked me out tonight.'

'Not a little man with a bald head who called you "Queen"? He asks everyone out.'

'No, thanks very much! This one wasn't bad looking at all. In fact, if I hadn't already promised to go the pictures, I might have said yes.'

'You wouldn't!' Eileen stopped dead, astonished. Annie had always been too wrapped up in her boys to show any interest in men.

148

'I would,' giggled Annie, adding indignantly, 'I don't know why you sound so surprised. You'd think I had a face like the back end of a bus or something. Come on.' She gave Eileen a tug and they began walking again.

'It's not that, Annie. For one thing, you've just been calling fellers everything for starting wars, and, oh, I dunno, I didn't think you could be bothered, that's all.'

'It's not *our* sort of fellers that start wars, it's the toffs, like your dad said,' Annie answered scathingly. 'As for being bothered, after Tom was killed, I couldn't have stood another man near me, not for a long time, but since me lads left and the war began, everything seems different somehow. I feel as if I should rush out and do things I wouldn't do ordinarily. D'you know what I mean, Eileen?'

Eileen paused before answering. 'I'm not sure,' she said eventually. 'When I thought about us all being killed in the air raids, I was sorry I might die without having been in love proper like our Sheila. It seems a terrible thing to miss, loving someone proper. Not that I ever will now,' she added wistfully. 'Not even if I live to be eighty. I'm stuck with Francis, even if we're not living together.'

'Don't be stupid, girl,' Annie said crossly. 'Have you never heard of divorce?'

'Divorce!' Eileen stopped again. 'Christ Almighty, Annie. I'd be the talk of Bootle! Anyroad, Catholics can't get divorced.' She laughed. 'Just imagine our Sheila's face if I said I was getting divorced! She nearly had a fit the other day when I told her I wasn't having Francis back.'

'It was just a suggestion, that's all.' Annie began to drag her along. 'Stop dawdling. If we hurry up, we'll just be in time to hear the last bit of *Band Waggon*. Y'know how much I love Arthur Askey.'

When they reached Pearl Street, Eileen said, 'Oh, by

the way, Annie, can I have that navy-blue coat you've been hiding for me since we went to Paddy's Market? I'd almost forgotten about it. I'm going to Southport tomorrow to fetch Freda and Dicky Tutty back and I thought I'd wear it.' Knowing Francis would never approve of her wearing something from Paddy's Market, she'd asked Annie to keep the coat until she could think up a convincing story to explain how it had been acquired. Now Francis had gone and there was no need to lie, she thought thankfully.

'Sooner you than me,' said Annie. 'I'd come with you, but I want to start on me Christmas puddings ready for when me lads come home.' She unlocked her front door. 'I'll get the coat for you now.'

'*Put that light out!*' a voice barked out of the blackness.

'What bloody light?' Annie barked back.

'The one shining out the door, Annie Poulson.'

Annie had left a dim gas light burning on the landing, which was faintly visible through the open doorway. 'Sod off, Nobby Geary,' she said sarcastically. 'I'm surprised you can't find something more useful to do with your time than going around bullying and badgering poor innocent women who are terrified of the blackout.'

'I'll come in and keep you company for a little while, Annie,' Nobby said in a leery voice. 'You wouldn't be terrified, not with me around.'

'No, and I wouldn't be innocent, either,' snapped Annie, closing the front door with a bang.

Next day, Eileen took particular pains with her appearance. The people who had the Tuttys might be posh, and she wanted to look her best. She made herself up carefully, brushed her hair till it shone and tucked it behind her pearl-studded ears. Standing in front of the wardrobe mirror, she experimented with the navy-blue crocheted beret Annie had given her for Christmas, together with a pair of matching gloves. Brenda Mahon made the sets for two shillings each if you supplied the wool. Satisfied that the angle was jaunty enough without being daring, Eileen secured the beret with a pearl hatpin and slipped into the fine serge coat. She'd forgotten how perfectly it fitted and smoothed her hands over her lean hips with a sigh of satisfaction. The full flared skirt came to just below the knee. The coat seemed little worn and had clearly been expensive. She decided she wouldn't be letting Bootle down when she turned up in Southport for the Tuttys, though wished she had a navy-blue handbag to match rather than the old black one which was getting very worn, and it was a pity she had to carry an umbrella, but the sky was heavy with grey clouds that promised rain.

'Don't you look smart!' Sheila said admiringly when Eileen called to say she was on her way. 'You look like Greta Garbo in that hat.'

Sheila was in the course of getting herself and the six small O'Briens dressed in their Sunday best for Mass. When Cal was away the two sisters usually went together, but today Eileen had been to church early, in the hope of getting to and from Southport before the blackout started.

She'd been worried relations with her sister would be soured after their conversation the previous week, but despite her deeply held beliefs, Sheila was too good-natured to let anything come between them and the subject of Francis hadn't been raised again.

'Keep an eye on Tony for me, Sheil. I won't be gone long – I hope.'

The names of all the stations on the way to Southport

had been removed in order to prevent spies from finding their way about. Eileen was glad she was going to the end of the line, else she would never have known where to get off! On most platforms, posters urged the public not to spread rumours; BE LIKE DAD, KEEP MUM, said one, and WALLS HAVE EARS, another.

Whenever Eileen had been to Southport in the past, it had been summer, when the place was sunny, warm and crowded, so it was strange to emerge from the station to find a grey, cold and almost deserted town and a poster demanding to know IS YOUR JOURNEY REALLY NECESSARY?

Clutching the letter Gladys had received from the Billeting Officer, she asked a woman perusing the train timetable the way to Sunhill Road.

'I'm afraid you've got a long walk ahead of you,' the woman said. 'The buses only go every two hours on a Sunday and one's just left. Unless you take a taxi. There's quite a chill in the wind today.'

'I'll walk,' Eileen said hastily. Hell could freeze over before she would consider the extravagance of a taxi.

'In that case, you go down Lord Street, turn right at the Golden Oak Café, then left . . .'

As Eileen walked along elegant Lord Street with its tree-lined reservation and exclusive shops which had been tastefully decorated for Christmas, she muttered the directions under her breath, but soon found herself distracted by the window displays. On previous occasions, she and Tony had made straight for the beach or the fairground: this was the first time she'd been alone with time to spare. Though she hadn't really got time to spare, she told herself sternly, she was supposed to be looking for Freda and Dicky Tutty. But the clothes were out of this world, as were the prices, she noticed ruefully. She stopped in front of a window full of exquisite lingerie that took her breath away. Wandering on, she heard the sound of carols being played and came to a soaring glassroofed arcade with two storeys of little old-fashioned shops on either side. She couldn't resist it. The Tuttys forgotten, she went inside, conscious of the sharp clatter of her heels on the intricately tiled floor. The sound seemed to echo upwards and upwards towards the pale pink and green arched roof. Eileen felt intrigued by the atmosphere which seemed to belong to another age altogether, a Victorian age when crinolined ladies came shopping in their carriages and shop assistants brought chairs, then showed them to the door, bowing respectfully. She strolled past the charming mullioned-windowed shops towards the music. At the wide curved end of the arcade she arrived at its source: a restaurant where, at the centre of a circle of crowded tables, two old ladies, one at a piano, the other on a violin, were playing *God Rest Ye Merrie Gentlemen* with gusto and obvious enjoyment. Eileen convinced herself there was time for a cup of tea. Hang the Tuttys for the moment. It might be ages before she came to Southport again and this was too fascinating to miss.

She found an empty table for two at the extreme edge of the circle, close to a twelve-foot-high Christmas tree decorated with coloured lights. After a while a waitress approached for her order.

'A pot of tea for one, please.'

'Anything else?' The girl looked at her, pencil poised.

'A buttered scone,' Eileen said recklessly. Most of the customers were eating, and after all, she'd got paid on Friday and had more money at her disposal than she'd ever had in her life before.

She leaned back in the chair and lit a cigarette, drinking

in the atmosphere and listening to the carols, feeling a million miles from Pearl Street.

'Penny for them!'

She came down to earth with a start. A young man, no more than eighteen, had sat in the empty chair and was smiling at her warmly.

'I beg your pardon?' she said stiffly.

'I said, penny for them. You looked as if you were miles away.'

'I was.' And I would have liked to stay there, she thought resentfully.

'You don't recognise me, do you?'

She frowned at him, unsure if he genuinely knew her or was just trying to pick her up – though it seemed unlikely he would try that with someone so much older than himself. She was forced to concede he was very prepossessing, with smooth olive skin and the loveliest eyes she'd ever seen, large and brown and liquid, with thick tangled lashes that most women would give their eye-teeth for. His hair was a tousled mop of black curls. He might have been considered handsome, had his nose not been too large and slightly crooked. His wide mouth twitched, as if he found her frowning stare amusing.

'No, I don't,' she said eventually, feeling at a disadvantage and not wanting to be rude, but not wanting to give him encouragement if this was just a complicated way of picking her up. 'You'd better give me a clue,' she added in a deliberately cold voice.

He laughed and the laugh, the way his eyes lit up and his mouth curled, was so infectious, that Eileen had trouble not laughing back. He said, in a slow, deep voice, 'Melling!'

'Oh,' she said in relief. 'You work at Dunnings. I've never noticed you. Mind you, it was me first week, and I

154

hardly noticed anyone much.'

He shook his head, clearly enjoying himself, and his enjoyment was so obvious Eileen began to smile. She looked at him again, but there was nothing familiar about his face.

The waitress arrived with her tea and scone. The young man said, 'Can I have a coffee and the biggest squashiest cream cake you've got?'

'I won't be a moment, sir.'

'Whew! It's hot in here.' He began to remove his heavy belted tweed overcoat. Underneath, he wore a baggy brown corduroy suit which Eileen recognised immediately.

'The fisherman!' she cried.

His face lit up like a beacon in a storm. 'Got it!' He thrust out a long brown hand. 'Nicolas Stephanopoulos, more commonly known as Nick Stephens. How do you do?'

She shook it. His grasp was firm and she winced. 'I'm Eileen Costello.'

'Ah!' he grinned. 'You're Oirish.'

'Me mam and dad both came from Northern Ireland, as well as me husband, but I've never been there meself.'

'My grandparents originated from Greece. I've never been there, either. Mother insisted on shortening the name after she got married. According to her, it was a frightful bore spelling Stephanopoulos out over the telephone when she wanted to order something from the grocer.'

'I reckon it must have been,' Eileen agreed sympathetically, though she'd never even been in a room with a telephone, let alone used one.

'Anyway,' he said dryly, 'she didn't use either name for long. As soon as my father died, she remarried. Both she and my stepfather did a quick exit to the States the minute war seemed imminent.'

'I expect you miss them.'

'Not really,' he replied, somewhat enigmatically.

Eileen decided to change the subject. 'What are you doing in Melling?' she asked. 'Are you just there for the fishing?'

'Of course not, I work in . . .' He stopped and his eyes twinkled. 'I'm sorry, was that a joke?'

'Obviously not a very funny one, but yes, it was. You'll never catch more than a tiddler in that stream. Anything bigger couldn't get its head under the water.'

'I'm afraid elements of Greek tragedy must still flow through my veins, despite the fact I'm as British as you are. I'm always the last person to catch onto a joke,' he said ruefully.

'I would never have guessed it. You look as if you find everything dead funny.'

'Only sometimes,' he answered, adding surprisingly: 'I have my dark side. Sometimes the world seems anything but funny, though you cheered me up somewhat last week. You looked so graceful with your ugly overalls and long fair hair, kneeling on the bank and dipping your face in the water like a mermaid.'

She felt embarrassed. It was such a lovely, unusual compliment and she reminded herself he was little more than a child, not much older than Sean, her brother. 'I didn't think you'd noticed me.' He hadn't acknowledged her presence once.

'I was watching you around the corner of my hat,' he said, grinning. 'Next week, I'll wave.'

'I won't be there next week,' she told him. 'I'm on the late shift.'

'I'll miss you,' he said shyly.

Their eyes met and, for some reason she couldn't define, Eileen felt slightly uncomfortable. 'You were about to tell me where you worked,' she prompted.

'The Royal Ordnance Factory at Kirkby. I'm on permanent night shift. I'm at my best during the midnight hours.'

The waitress arrived with his order and he bit into the cake enthusiastically, the way Tony would have done, and the cream spurted out onto his face. 'This is scrumptious!' he said between mouthfuls.

Eileen watched him indulgently like a mother. 'You're making a right old mess,' she remarked as she poured a second cup of tea.

'Aren't I just?' The cake finished, he wiped his mouth with the sleeve of his jacket and Eileen tut-tutted in disapproval. 'Haven't you got a hankie?'

· 'I have to wash the hankies. I can get the jacket dry cleaned, which is much easier.'

'You look after yourself then?'

'Yes. I rent a cottage in Melling, although I could have had a room in a hostel. I prefer being alone.'

He was a bundle of contradictions, thought Eileen. Cheerfully extrovert one minute, talking about his dark side and wanting to be alone the next.

'You don't come from round here?'

'No, London. I'm in a reserved occupation, much to my disgust. The entire laboratory was transferred to Kirkby.'

'Laboratory! What do you do?'

'I'm a scientist.'

Her jaw dropped. She'd never met a scientist before. 'You look awful young for that.'

'I'm twenty-four.'

Twenty-four! Eileen had no idea why this news should

157

affect her so deeply, but it did. Till then, she'd thought of him as an engaging boy with an attractive, almost irresistible personality. But knowing she was only two years his senior seemed to put him in a different light altogether. To her utter astonishment, there was a strange, pleasurable sensation in the pit of her stomach, as if butterflies had begun to flutter their wings wildly. It was something she'd never experienced before.

'Where is your husband?' he asked suddenly. 'I'm surprised he lets you out alone. If you were my wife, I wouldn't let you out of my sight.'

The butterflies went frantic. Eileen replied in what she hoped was a steady voice, 'Me husband's in the army.'

'Ah! That explains it.' His eyes met hers. 'And do you miss him?'

Eileen hesitated. 'Of course I do.' But even as she spoke she knew the hesitation had given her away. If she really had missed Francis, she would have answered immediately and with far more enthusiasm.

'I see.' He gave a little smile, and Eileen knew he saw too much. 'Do you have any children, Eileen?'

'I have a little boy, Tony. He's five. Lord! I'll have to go.' She glanced at the clock on the wall above his head, though she was too confused to take in the time. Once again, she became aware of the music and the fact they were in a crowded restaurant in an arcade in Southport, all of which she seemed to have forgotten whilst they'd been talking. She reached for the bill, but he grabbed it first.

'I'll get that,' he said despite her protests. To her dismay, he began putting on his overcoat. 'Where are you off to now?' he asked.

She explained about the Tuttys. 'I'm afraid I've forgotten the directions to Sunhill Road.'

'I've got a map outside. I'll give you a lift.'

Despite the fact a lift would be more than welcome, she would have preferred him to leave. In view of the pleasant sensation which still persisted in her stomach, it seemed wise to get rid of him as soon as possible. She decided, somewhat regretfully, that her visits to the little stream must stop until next summer, when the other girls would be with her. In the meantime, it was difficult to refuse his offer of a lift without being hurtful. 'Thank you,' she murmured.

It had begun to rain outside. She put her umbrella up and they walked without speaking past a line of cars parked alongside the pavement. 'Here she is,' he said eventually.

'She' turned out to be a motorbike and sidecar. Eileen couldn't help herself. She burst out laughing. 'I don't know why, but I wouldn't have expected you to have a car like ordinary people.'

'Are you suggesting I'm extraordinary?' He raised his eyebrows and began to strap on a leather helmet and a pair of goggles. She laughed again.

'In that hat you are. You look like Flash Gordon.'

'Well, you look like Greta Garbo in yours. Come on, get in. I take it you don't want to sit on the back?'

'No thanks.' Still laughing, she folded herself into the sidecar and he slid the roof across. It was like being inside a large bullet and she felt very close to the ground. Through the scratched perspex window, she saw Nick unfold a map and study it. He made the thumbs up sign, drew on a massive pair of leather gauntlets, and set off.

The journey seemed to take no time at all. Five minutes later, the motorbike drew up outside a pleasant detached house with a vast, lush garden full of mature trees and bushes. Eileen pulled the roof back and began to struggle out, whilst Nick dismounted and came around to help. She found herself being uplifted bodily by a pair of strong lean arms and placed on the pavement.

'There!' he said. 'I'd wait and take you home, but there isn't enough room for you and a couple of children.'

'You don't know where I live. It's miles away.'

His next words almost took her breath away. 'I'd take you if you lived on the other side of the moon,' he said simply.

She tried to make a joke. 'Well, being Flash Gordon, I suppose you know the moon well. Thank you for the lift, Nick. Tara.'

'Goodbye, Eileen. I'll see you a week tomorrow.'

She began to walk up the pebbled drive, still conscious of the pressure of his arms around her waist, and deliberately didn't turn and wave when the motorbike started up again. The feelings he evoked in her were strange and rather frightening – and dangerous! As far as she was concerned, that was the last time she'd have anything to do with Nick Stephens!

Eileen paused in front of the oak panelled, highly polished door to read Gladys's letter from the Billeting Officer. She'd forgotten the name of the people who'd taken Freda and Dicky in. *Mr & Mrs C. Waterton*, she read as she pressed the bell and heard it buzz deep inside the house.

After a while, a pretty girl of about ten, with curly, shoulder-length brown hair opened the door. She wore a red velvet dress with a lace collar, long white socks and patent leather shoes. She blinked when she saw Eileen, and regarded her unsmilingly and without speaking.

'Is your mother in, luv?'

The girl didn't answer, and Eileen was about to repeat

the question when a voice trilled, 'Who is it, darling?' and another girl came into the hall. This one wore a dress which was far too old for her, a trailing affair in fine patterned wool, and her wavy blonde hair was halfway down her back.

'I'm looking for Mrs Waterton,' Eileen explained.

'That's me.' As she came closer, Eileen saw the girl was older than she first appeared. In fact, she was not a girl at all, but a woman of at least forty. 'How can I help you?'

Although she'd rehearsed what she was going to say several times, now the time had come Eileen found herself stammering nervously, 'I'm, well, I'm a neighbour of Mrs Tutty, Mrs Gladys Tutty, and she'd, well, she'd like her children back.'

The woman gave a little tinkling laugh. 'I'm afraid that's just not possible.'

Eileen stood there, feeling nonplussed, and wondering what she was supposed to do next. The girl in the red dress was actually about to close the door in her face, when a man appeared, tall and balding, with a stern, unfriendly look on his thin features.

'I'm Clive Waterton and I've been expecting something like this. You'd better come in,' he said brusquely.

'Thank you.' She didn't like his autocratic manner. For all the trouble she had taken with her appearance, she felt over-conscious of her secondhand coat and her Liverpool accent as she followed him and his wife and the little girl into a high-ceilinged room full of bleached wooden furniture, the sort you saw in Hollywood films.

'Mrs Tutty has taken long enough to enquire about her children,' he said cuttingly when Eileen sat down. 'Other evacuees, who incidentally, went home weeks ago, had letters and visits right from the start.'

'I don't see what that's got to do with anything,' Eileen said reasonably. 'If Gladys wants her children back, then she should have them whether she came to see them or not.' The whole situation seemed profoundly mysterious. Why should people like this want to hold on to the Tuttys? And where were they, anyway?

That question was partly answered straight away.

'Freda, switch the percolator on, please. I'm sure Vivien would love a cup of coffee.'

With a triumphant glance at Eileen's startled face, the girl in the red dress left the room.

Freda!

As the door closed behind her, Mr Waterton said with a touch of irony, 'Surprised, eh? My wife has done wonders with the children, though quite frankly, the boy might not be averse to going home. I think he misses his mother. But the girl has changed out of all recognition and she and my wife are terribly fond of each other.'

'More than fond, Clive. Freda and I simply adore each other.' Mrs Waterton made a funny little gurgling sound. 'We're like sisters.'

With a sense of unease, Eileen realised the little girl–woman wasn't quite right in the head, and she didn't like the way her husband referred to Freda and Dicky as 'the girl' and 'the boy'. She reckoned *he* didn't give a damn about the children, but wanted them to stay, or at least wanted Freda to stay, in order to keep his dotty wife happy. Eileen felt she was in an impossible position. Gladys was expecting her to return with the kids, but what was she supposed to do if they didn't want to come?

'Perhaps we'd better ask Freda and Dicky what they want to do,' she suggested. 'I presume you don't want to keep them against their will. I'll go along with whatever they have to say. After all, I've no authority, have I? I'm just doing a favour for a neighbour.'

The door was flung open and a sunburnt little boy burst in. His eyes lit on Eileen joyfully. 'Our Freda said you were here. Have you come to take me back to me mam?'

'If that's what you want, Dicky?' It must be Dicky, though the neatly dressed, healthy-looking child bore no resemblance to the boy who'd left Pearl Street last September.

Clive Waterton shrugged carelessly. 'Well, you have your answer. Let's see what his sister has to say.'

'I want to stay with Vivien.' Freda stood in the doorway, ladylike and demure. She crossed over and sat on the arm of Mrs Waterton's chair.

'That's it, then.' Eileen got to her feet, anxious to get away. 'I'd better be going.' Lord knows what Gladys would have to say when she arrived back with only half her family. It all seemed very unsatisfactory, but she was at a loss to know what else she was supposed to do.

'But you must let me get Dicky's things together first,' Mrs Waterton trilled. 'He can't leave without his train set and his ration book and there's heaps and heaps of clothes. Let's find a little suitcase, shall we? Come on, Dicky.'

'You won't go without me?' The little boy looked anxiously at Eileen, before allowing himself to be led out of the room. Freda followed.

'Of course I won't, luv.'

Eileen was left alone with Mr Waterton. As soon as the door closed, he said coldly, 'I'm a solicitor. Tell Mrs Tutty that I'll go to court if there's any suggestion of removing the girl. Mrs Waterton has never been so happy as since she came.'

'You do whatever you please,' Eileen said, equally coldly. 'It's nowt to do with me, but I don't think Gladys is going to take this lying down, not for a moment.'

Eileen got back to Pearl Street just as it was beginning to grow dark. Tony was playing football with his cousins. The boys came running up to her, then stopped and stared curiously at the smartly dressed child at her side. Without a word of thanks, Dicky Tutty grabbed the suitcase and ran home down the back entry.

'Explain to your mam about Freda,' Eileen called after him. She went into her sister's in the hope of avoiding a rampaging Gladys demanding to know why Freda hadn't come. Today had been a day and a half, and she didn't feel in the mood for more drama just yet.

'You've been gone for hours,' remarked Sheila. She was nursing a fretful Ryan, who was cutting another tooth. Siobhan and Caitlin were playing house under the table, and the baby was fast asleep in her pram in the hall. 'I was expecting you back ages ago.'

'It was a long walk to and from the station,' Eileen explained as she put the kettle on for a welcome cup of tea. She decided to keep Nick Stephens a secret. She wouldn't be seeing him again, so there was little point in telling anyone. Instead, she described the strange set-up at the Watertons' and the remarkable transformation there'd been in Freda Tutty. 'I didn't recognise her, Sheil. She looked ever so pretty.'

'Freda, pretty?' Sheila said half-heartedly, as if she were trying to look surprised for the sake of politeness.

'She even talked different. And Dicky's changed, too.'

'He won't be changed for long,' Sheila said tiredly. 'Not now he's home again with Gladys.'

'I wonder what she'll do about Freda,' Eileen mused.

'If anyone asked me to make a decision, I wouldn't know what to say. I mean, is she better off with her mam, who isn't fit to be within a mile of children, or with that funny woman over in Southport who's one penny short of a shilling?'

When her sister didn't answer, Eileen asked in a soft voice, 'What's the matter, luv?'

'It's Cal's birthday today,' Sheila said sadly. 'No-one seems to have remembered, except me.'

'Oh, Sheil, I'm sorry!' Eileen cried. 'It's just that there's so many birthdays, and what with starting work and having to go to Southport, it slipped me mind altogether. . .'

'I don't suppose it matters – under the circumstances,' Sheila said wryly. 'But it's as if you've all forgotten he existed.'

'Oh, Sheil, as if we would!' Eileen wished with all her heart she could share her sister's grief, take some of the heavy load off her shoulders. 'Is there anything I can do, like?'

'There is something, Eileen. I asked Brenda Mahon to knit Cal a Fair Isle pullover for his birthday. I reckon it's well finished by now, but although I see Brenda every day, neither of us can bring ourselves to mention it. If I give you the money, will you collect it for me? Perhaps it'll do our Sean instead.' Sheila began to stroke Ryan's cheek with her little finger. 'He's the image of Cal, don't you think, Eileen? The other lads are more like our side of the family.'

'I suppose he is, luv.' Eileen nodded, though she was unable to see much likeness to Cal in the little boy.

'You know what I can't stop thinking about? It keeps me awake night after night. How did he die? Was he blown up or burnt alive? Or did he drown? He was a good swimmer, but there were no boats around to pick up any survivors. If only one or two had been saved to tell us what happened.'

'I don't know what to say, Sheil.' Eileen knelt in front of the chair and took both her sister and Ryan in her arms.

'He was studying for his Master's ticket, y'know, Eil,' Sheila said in a muffled voice. 'I used to listen to him reciting the Articles. I remember the sixth one in particular, "In fog, mist, falling snow, heavy rainstorms, all vessels must proceed at moderate speed." I always felt it should rhyme, like poetry.' She pulled away and made a brave attempt at a smile. 'I tell you what, though, Sis, a cup of tea wouldn't come amiss right now, and the kettle's about to boil any minute.'

Next morning, a letter with a Kettering postmark dropped on Eileen's mat, so she knew straight away it was from Francis, and her heart began to thump as she tore it open. She'd heard nothing since she'd written to him over a month ago.

To her amusement, the letter was neatly typed, as if he wanted to show off his new skill. It began, *My darling Eileen.* She skimmed through. He had seven days' leave at Christmas and wanted to return home and spend the holiday with his beloved wife and son. He loved her, he always had. Her behaviour during his leave and her subsequent letter had come as a total shock, so much so, it had taken all this time before he could bring himself to reply. He confessed himself heartbroken, but perplexed. What had he done? Most couples had their ups and downs and tolerance was needed – on both sides. *You never gave any sign you were unhappy,* he wrote. *If I'd thought you were, I would have wanted to put things right.*

The whole tone was grovelling, until she came to the last paragraph when he spoiled things by reminding her that it was *his* house, the rent book was in *his* name, and *his* money had paid for the furniture. Though he perished the thought, if she continued to refuse to have him back it was *she* who would have to leave. She would be without a roof over her head. *In which case, I would insist Tony stayed with his dad,* though Francis doubted if she would let things come to such a pretty pass.

Changing tone again, he finished off, *May God bless you, my darling Eileen. Your loving Francis.*

'You bloody hypocrite!'

Eileen screwed the letter in a ball and flung it across the room, unsure whether to laugh or cry. Francis would never change. He only wanted to come home to get his political ambitions back on course, and might even behave himself over Christmas, or even on the next leave, but she knew once he was back for good he'd soon return to his old ways because he couldn't help himself. He was right on one thing, though. She'd never given any sign that she was unhappy, but had let things go from bad to worse until they'd become untenable because she was too frightened of what he'd do if she spoke out. It had taken the advent of a war to make her see it didn't have to be this way. She wasn't frightened now, except of his strength, and if he wanted his house back, he could have it. She'd find somewhere else. She was independent and earning a good wage of her own. Although she'd never known a respectable woman walk out on her husband before, there had to be a first time for everything . . .

As for Tony staying with him! She guffawed. If he thought that, he had another think coming.

In fact, she felt so incensed she got a writing pad out

there and then and wrote to Francis, telling him exactly where he stood.

'Goodnight, Miss Brazier. Do you think you'll be able to find your way home all right?'

He'd said the same thing every single night last week.

'I will, Mr Sanderson. There's a bit of a moon tonight. Goodnight, then. I'll see you in the morning.'

He touched his hat politely. He was a nice man, a widower in his forties, rather withdrawn, and she sometimes wondered if he was as lonely and shy as she was herself.

Tonight, she made her way along Stanley Road without difficulty, towards Lou, who would be waiting on the corner. Last week at work, people kept saying, 'What've you done to yourself, Miss Brazier? You look quite different.'

'Well, I broke me glasses in the blackout, that's all,' she'd reply. 'I was going to get them mended, but I find I don't seem to need them any more.'

'You look ten years younger,' someone had remarked.

But Miss Brazier knew it wasn't the lack of glasses that made her look different. It was something else, something deep inside that was impossible to describe. The glasses had merely been a shield to hide behind from the world, but now she didn't need a shield. She'd come alive for the first time in her life. Suddenly, she could talk to people. That night in the blackout had broken down her reservations once and for all. People, she realised, were quite nice if you were nice to them in return.

But it was Lou who'd wrought the greatest change. The minutes they'd been together, walking arm in arm along Strand Road, came to no more than an hour if added up, but Lou, whom she wouldn't recognise if they met in daylight, who was no more than a tall shadowy figure, said the most flattering things and made her feel young and feminine and, well, almost attractive.

'Good evening, Helen.'

She gave a start. She hadn't reached the corner yet. 'Is that you, Lou?'

'I thought I'd walk down a bit to meet you, seeing as the good Lord has seen fit to send us a nice big moon. Romantic, isn't it?' He began to croon, *'Moonlight becomes you . . .'*

She dug him in the ribs with her elbow. 'Get away with you! You're always kidding, Lou Murphy.'

He tucked her arm in his, 'You like it, though, don't you, Helen?'

Oh, yes she liked it! She liked everything about him; his joking good humour, the way he listened so sympathetically when she confessed how terribly empty her life was, something she'd never told anyone before; the way he squeezed her arm affectionately, as if he understood completely.

Tonight, in the light of the half moon, she saw him for the first time. His face was long and thin, with sharp cheekbones and round pale eyes. She thought him very good-looking, almost handsome. He had a bushy light-coloured moustache and she had to suppress the urge to reach up and touch it. He wore a wide trilby hat and a mackintosh with the collar turned up.

'And what d'you think you're staring at, Miss?' he enquired jokingly.

'The cat can look at the Queen,' she said archly. 'I didn't realise you had a moustache. I was wondering what colour it was.'

'Same colour as me hair.' He removed his hat. 'I don't suppose you can see proper, like, but it's ginger.'

'Ginger?'

'That's what they call me at work, Ginger Murphy.'

'I prefer Lou.'

'So do I. Helen and Lou. Lou and Helen. Go together well, don't they?'

She didn't answer because she felt suddenly breathless and dizzy. Helen and Lou!

'What did you do with yourself yesterday, Helen?' he asked.

'I went to church, but there never seems much to do on a Sunday,' she replied. She always ended up going to bed early, before the silence and sense of isolation swallowed her up.

'Don't you ever go to the pictures? I love a good picture, it really takes you out of yourself.'

'Mother always disapproved of the pictures. She thought they were sinful.'

He laughed disparagingly. 'Well, Mother's been dead a long time. It's what Helen wants that's important now. What would you say to you and me going to the pictures one night? Would you like that?'

'I'd love to,' she replied weakly.

'I'll see what's on, and we'll fix it later in the week.' He began to tell her about the mischief his sister's children had got up to over the weekend, and before she knew where she was, they'd reached the corner of Marsh Lane and it was time for him to go. To her surprise, he held on to her arm. 'How about offering me a cup of tea, Helen?'

'But won't your sister be expecting you?' she asked in a shaky voice. Her insides were in such a state of turmoil that she felt as if they were about to fall out onto the pavement. She should really refuse, after all, she scarcely knew him, but say he took offence and she never saw him again? She wasn't prepared to risk that happening.

'Me sister won't mind,' he said dismissively. 'She'll just stick me dinner in the oven till I get home.'

'In that case, I suppose so.'

'You don't sound very enthusiastic.' There was disappointment in his voice and she was worried he was hurt.

'I am, really I am,' she assured him. Then she laughed gaily. 'Mr Murphy, what would you say to a cup of tea, like?'

Then he confused her more than ever by lifting her gloved hand to his lips and kissing it. 'Why, Miss Brazier, how nice of you to ask. I accept without hesitation. In fact, wild horses wouldn't stop me.'

Chapter 7

Jessica Fleming had never in her entire life hated anyone as much as she hated Veronica. As she'd been taken on to prevent Veronica's veins from swelling any larger, Jessica had envisaged being left to her own devices once she'd got the hang of things. But instead of resting her purple legs in the flat above the shop, Veronica stayed downstairs, to spy on her constantly from the stockroom at the back, to criticise, to poke fun at her accent, and generally make life as uncomfortable as it was in her power to do. More often than not, as soon as Jessica had made a sale, Veronica would emerge to 'finish it off', as if her assistant couldn't finish it off herself. It was as if the woman was paying elevenpence an hour to have someone to torture.

And Veronica was a crook. Well, almost a crook. At the end of Jessica's first week, when she'd thought she'd earned quite a lot in commission, she'd found merely a few pence extra in her wages.

'I should have far more than this,' she protested.

'Did you put the money in the till?' sneered Veronica.

Jessica looked puzzled. 'What are you talking about?'

'When you'd sold the goods, who was it put the money in the till?'

'You did, but only after I'd made the sale.'

'It's whoever puts the money in the till that gets the commission.'

'But that's not fair!' Jessica said indignantly. 'I was wrapping things up and you came out and took it.'

172

'It's sod your luck, then, isn't it? You'll just have to be a bit quicker off the mark next time.'

Since then, there was a tussle whenever a sale was being completed, with Jessica trying to get the customer to pay before she put the goods in a bag, and Veronica emerging from her eyrie in the back like a great black eagle, ready to pluck the money out of the customer's hand before Jessica could get to it.

What made Veronica's behaviour all the more hypocritical, thought Jessica, smarting with a sense of real injustice, was that the bloody woman had a little font of holy water attached to the wall of the stockroom, and she came swooping out making the sign of the cross, as if expecting Old Nick himself had come in to buy a pair of knickers.

There'd been few customers this particular morning and Jessica stood behind the counter, feeling bored. If Veronica had been a different kind of person, she could have sat on one of the rickety chairs in the stockroom and chatted to pass the time, but there was no way she would share air space with that woman if she could avoid it, apart from which, you could hardly breathe, Veronica sprinkled herself so liberally with cheap lavender water. Even in one of her rare friendly moods, all she went on about were her three late husbands, all of whom had been considerably older than herself, describing their various deaths in gruesome and unpleasant detail. Jessica glanced at her watch and sighed. Another hour and a half to go.

'Not keeping you, am I?'

Jessica jumped. Veronica was watching from the back, her horrible black eyes gleaming spitefully.

'I was merely wondering what time it was,' Jessica said coldly.

'Idle hands make the devil's work.'

'What do you expect me to do? I can't sell things if there are no customers.'

'You could tidy up a few drawers, instead of standing there like a pill garlic.'

Jessica shrugged. 'All right. You've only got to ask.'

None of the drawers needed tidying, but Jessica dutifully began to straighten up the contents. It was better than doing nothing. If only she could get another job, but there was little else she could *do*! Once she'd earned enough to pay for the alterations, she'd leave and take up something more befitting a woman of her background, voluntary war work, for instance. If she stayed much longer, she'd end up a nervous wreck.

A customer entered and bought two liberty bodices for her daughter. Jessica managed to snatch the ten shilling note out of her hand just as Veronica reached for it. The customer gone, she made a note of the sale on a piece of paper beside the till with an air of quiet triumph.

There was no time for further hostilities, because almost immediately the door opened again and a stout, middle-aged woman entered, carrying two loaded shopping bags and perspiring profusely.

'I'd like to see your range of corselets, please.'

'What size, Madam?' Jessica enquired courteously.

'Mrs Bingham!' Veronica came leaping into the shop making the sign of the cross and bowing obsequiously. It seemed this customer, who was undoubtedly better dressed and better spoken than the usual clientele, merited her oiliest and most servile manner. 'I've got a new range in. Let me show you.'

Jessica shrank back, relieved. She hated selling corsets. Customers usually tried them on in the curtained alcove behind, and she was expected to go in once they had the garments on and help pull laces and fasten hooks, which made her flesh crawl.

Mrs Bingham chose three pairs of corselets to try on, and she and Veronica went into the back where they remained for nearly half an hour. In the meantime, Jessica sold two long-sleeved vests to a woman with rheumatism in her elbows, and a pair of rayon stockings to another. She was making a note of the sales on the paper beside the till when Veronica emerged and flung two pairs of corselets on the counter.

'Sort these out and put them away,' she snapped. 'She's having the pair she's got on now, the dearest ones.'

Nose wrinkling, Jessica picked gingerly at the laces of the violent pink brocade garments which had touched another woman's sweaty flesh. Veronica was grinning to herself and nodding her head repeatedly like a gaunt yellow donkey, waiting for the customer to get dressed.

'Mrs Bingham's husband is the Town Clerk,' she hissed boastfully. 'Her son went to university and got a degree. He's a teacher at a grammar school in Waterloo.' She nodded again, as if to say, 'There now!' and waited for Jessica's protestations of incredulity.

'So what, my husband's got a degree,' said Jessica.

'Y'what!' Veronica's mouth fell open, revealing scraps of food wedged between her teeth. Jessica winced delicately. 'What are you doing here, then?'

Jessica didn't reply. Instead, she wondered what *was* she doing there? Why was she re-lacing corselets off fat sweaty women when her husband had a degree? She hadn't thought about it before, but Arthur could get a job on the strength of his qualifications. There was no need to drive a lorry when he had a BA with Honours in Archaeology. He too could work in a grammar school. With so many teachers being called up, there was a shortage. Her heart began to dance. They could escape from Bootle. She could tell Veronica what to do with her job. She'd have a word with Arthur the minute he got home that night.

Mrs Bingham emerged, fully dressed. As she rooted in her capacious bag for her purse, she smiled at Jessica. 'That's a pretty pendant you're wearing. What is it, mother of pearl and marcasite?'

'Yes, but it wasn't very expensive. My husband bought it for me in Paris on our honeymoon.' All Jessica's good jewellery had been sold to help pay their debts.

'Paris!' Impressed, Mrs Bingham leaned across and examined the pendant closely. Then she handed Jessica a pound note. 'Nineteen and eleven, isn't it? Oh, I tell you what, to save going through this again in a few months' time, I'll take two pairs.'

Jessica took the second proffered note and rang up 39/10d on the till, crowing inwardly. A whole shilling in commission, and she hadn't lifted a finger!

'Paris, eh!' Mrs Bingham said thoughtfully. She regarded Jessica critically, taking in her fashionable, expensive clothes. The woman was obviously down on her luck, otherwise she wouldn't be working here, but even so, she was outstanding in her way, and someone who'd been to Paris would be quite a catch to show off to her friends – and she'd probably be grateful for some civilised company. 'Perhaps you and your hubby would like to come to dinner one evening?' she suggested.

'It's kind of you to ask,' murmured Jessica politely, sensing she was being patronised, 'but I'm afraid my hubby is far too busy at the moment. He has business meetings every night of the week.' Two years ago, the Lord Mayor of Liverpool himself had been sick in the downstairs toilet in Calderstones, so she was less than impressed with the wife of a mere Town Clerk.

'Well, never mind,' Mrs Bingham said, clearly disappointed. 'Maybe you could come one morning for coffee?'

'That would be lovely, but as you can see, I work mornings.' Jessica did her best to look apologetic.

'Y'can always take the morning off,' chipped in Veronica, anxious to please the wife of the Town Clerk, even if her assistant wasn't.

'I couldn't possibly leave you to cope on your own right before Christmas, not with your veins the way they are,' Jessica said virtuously. 'Perhaps after the holiday . . .'

She bestowed a brilliant smile upon the somewhat bemused Mrs Bingham, who left with the uneasy feeling that she'd just been heartily snubbed by a part-time shop assistant.

'Arthur,' Jess began the minute he set foot in the house. 'Why don't you get a job as a teacher?'

She was entirely devoid of guile, thought Arthur Fleming. Any other woman would have left it until he'd finished his meal, waiting for the right moment before broaching a particularly sensitive subject. But not Jess. She plunged in tactlessly, because she had no regard for other people's feelings. His, in particular.

He didn't answer, but hung his overcoat and scarf in the hall, knowing she was hanging on tenterhooks for his answer.

'Because I don't want to,' he replied eventually. He sat in front of the blazing fire and opened his copy of *The Times*, knowing full well she wouldn't be satisfied with his answer. The argument could go on all night, or at least until he went out to the King's Arms.

'But Arthur, I only thought about it today, teachers earn quite high salaries. Not so much as we were used to, of course, but far more than you get now. We could move to Crosby or Southport. We could possibly afford a car.'

'I'm quite happy where I am,' he said contentedly, pretending to read the paper. 'I like this house and I like my job. I like the folks in Bootle. They're friendly and unpretentious.' Although this was true, the contented air was put on. Inwardly, he was fuming. So, she'd 'only thought about it today!' In other words, she'd entirely forgotten he had a degree. Archaeology had been his passion as a boy and going to university the culmination of a lifelong dream. He'd visualised a life spent roaming the ancient sites of Greece and Italy and Egypt, earning his living from writing articles and books. Instead, he'd met glorious Jessica Hennessy, impetuous and totally selfish, who'd captured him, heart, body and soul – she still had him clutched somewhat painfully in her long white avaricious fingers – and, somehow, he'd ended up in charge of a transport company he was incapable of running. He had no head for business and had never claimed otherwise. He'd tried to tell her father that, and later, Jess herself. Neither was interested. It didn't cross their minds that he might want to do something else – archaeology, for instance! For twenty unhappy years, he'd tried to cope. It wasn't so bad whilst Bert Hennessy remained in charge. Arthur had merely done as he was told. Then Bert died and the old drivers, loyal to the firm, had carried him for a while, but most were near retirement age. They left, new drivers came, and Arthur was on his own. Failure became inevitable. Over all that time, Jessica had remained indifferent to his misery – no, not indifferent, Jess wasn't an unkind woman, 'unaware' described it better – too busy climbing up and up the social ladder to notice how much he despised her worthless aspirations.

'But Arthur . . .' she began again, accusing him of not giving two hoots for her happiness.

'Did you ever give two hoots for mine?'

She stared at him, nonplussed. 'I always assumed you were happy.'

'You never asked.'

'Well, no, but . . .' She paused.

'But what?' he demanded.

'You never said anything,' she finished lamely.

'I did, actually. It's just that you affected not to hear.'

'But what was there to be unhappy about, Arthur? We were well off. We could afford to buy anything we wanted.'

Arthur shrugged and didn't answer, wondering if she would ever understand that money wasn't everything. That being able to 'buy anything you wanted' wasn't the be-all and end-all of existence.

He watched his wife covertly over the newspaper. She was biting her lip and staring into the fire, as if she'd found their recent exchange perplexing. He could sense her frustration and sympathised. This was the first time *she* was reliant on *him* for financial support. He knew he was being awkward over the teaching, but didn't care. Perhaps it would make her understand how he'd felt all those years. Of course he could take up teaching! It was one of the first options he'd considered when the business went for a burton, along with any self-confidence he still had, but he didn't feel up to the responsibility, not yet. There'd be plenty of time for that in the future. For the moment, he liked driving a lorry and being told what to do and where to go and given a wage at the end of the week, without having to take a single decision of his own accord. It was the first time since he'd left university that he had a sense of self-respect and worth. He was happy! Of course, he would have liked Jess to be happy, too, but he couldn't change her personality, make her see that there were more important things to life than the acquisition of material goods.

He watched her still over the paper. He had to give it to her, she'd taken their reversal of fortune much better than he would have expected, revealing an unexpected strength of character. Another woman might have walked out and left him to clear the mess up on his own, but not Jess. She'd ranted and raved, called him weak – which, he conceded, he was when it came to business – but she'd stood by him and hadn't shed a single tear. She'd seen the bank manager, sorted out their finances, then gone out and got herself a job, determined to bring the house up to the standard she considered she deserved. Out of sheer perversity, he kept back most of his wages. Looking at her now, leaning with one elbow on the table, pouting slightly and plucking at her red curls, he felt a twinge of conscience and wondered if he should let her have more. She could no more help being selfish and insensitive than she could help looking like a model for one of Rembrandt's most glorious paintings. Perhaps if he approached it tactfully, he could offer something towards the alterations she so desired without letting her think she'd won a victory over him.

'To change the subject,' he said conversationally, 'I thought you were planning on getting a new stove?'

Of course, Jess spoiled things straight away by saying irritably, 'I thought men were supposed to take those sort of decisions.'

'That's news to me,' he replied, managing a grin. 'If I

remember rightly, you bought everything for our old house. I don't recall my opinion being called for.'

He'd come home and find a major new item of furniture or kitchen appliance, bought without any reference to him. Of course, it was her money, but he would have liked to have been asked for his views.

'You never showed any interest.'

'I might, if asked,' he said lightly. 'Anyway, about the stove . . . ?'

Her smooth white brow puckered in a frown. 'I'm in a bit of a quandary,' she explained passionately. 'I'd like the wiring done before I buy a stove because I want an electric one, but that means the whole house will need redecorating afterwards, and I want decent wallpaper this time, not that horrid distemper. And while it's being decorated, I may as well have a new fireplace put in at the same time, I haven't saved up enough yet,' she finished breathlessly.

It was obvious, from the intense way she spoke, that her mind was consumed with alterations to the house. The world might be at war, ships were being sunk, the daily news offered little hope for peace, but all Jess could think about was wallpaper and wiring and stoves. And it was all 'I'. 'I want', 'I need', never 'we'. Nevertheless, he felt sorry for her. 'How much have you got?' he asked.

'Just over twenty-five pounds, with the money off my musquash,' she answered, adding proudly, 'I earned over two shillings in commission today.'

'Good girl,' he said approvingly.

She looked at him sharply. 'Are you being funny, Arthur?'

'Of course not!' he assured her, though it *was* funny when you thought about it. A few months ago, she would have tipped a waiter two shillings without a second thought. 'Perhaps I could put a bit to it,' he offered. 'Say ten bob a week.'

'Ten shillings,' she corrected automatically.

'Ten shillings, then.'

'That would be awfully nice of you, Arthur.' She smiled at him for the first time in months.

Later on, she got out a notebook and began to do calculations, and he left for the King's Arms.

It was a strange thing, he thought, entering to a welcome chorus of 'Evening, Arthur, what are y'drinking?' but the poor were far more generous than the rich. He'd noticed straight away, how no-one tried to get out of paying when it was their turn for a round. The poor had their pride. Some would sit with a single pint all night, rather than be termed a scrounger. Even if pressed, they'd refuse a drink if they couldn't buy one back.

He ordered a pint of Guinness and Paddy O'Hara said, 'That'll put lead in your pencil, Arthur,' which, he thought, was the last thing he needed at the moment. Jess had slept in a separate room for months. There was no way he'd force her, but he missed her warm body desperately, though even in bed relations had grown colder over the years. He recalled the passionate love-making of their Paris honeymoon, the creamy voluptuous body yielding to his slightest touch, her little cries of ecstasy. It was a long time since they'd made love with such natural, unreserved pleasure. Instead, he got the impression she was merely doing her wifely duty, that's if she hadn't cried off with a headache first!

Going home, he wondered hopefully if the extra ten shillings might have patched things up a little and she'd be waiting for him in the double bed where she properly belonged, but when he got in, she was already fast asleep in the back bedroom.

'Perhaps I should have made it a pound,' he thought wryly.

Eileen Costello hated being on the afternoon shift. She saw hardly anything of Tony, just half an hour in the mornings before he went to school. After he'd gone, the time seemed to fly by and before she knew it, it was one o'clock and she was due to leave to catch the bus to Dunnings. When she got home, Tony was fast asleep – Annie waited until he dropped off before going home to bed herself. Eileen would listen to the wireless for a while or read a book, feeling the day had been most un-satisfactory. She was therefore relieved when the week drew to a close and she could look forward to the early shift again.

On Monday, the younger women compared notes on the various dances and parties they'd been to that week-end. Pauline and Doris had been to a dance at the Rialto, where they'd met a couple of French sailors.

'My chap kept saying, "wee", so I thought he had the runs or something,' Doris complained. 'I kept showing him where the men's lavvy was, but it turned out "wee" is French for "yes".'

There was a screech of laughter and Doris went on, 'Trouble was, later on, I said "wee" in the wrong place after he took me home. He had his hand up me skirt like a bleeding shot, and there was me, screaming, "Non, non, non", all over the street, till me dad came out and told him to bugger off back to France.'

'What happened with your one, Pauline?' Eileen asked, fascinated by their goings-on. She'd never been to a proper dance, and regretted having missed out on what seemed a uniquely enjoyable experience.

'Oh, he was all right,' Pauline sighed. 'He was satisfied

183

with a good old snog. I enjoyed meself, I suppose.'

'Why don't y'come with us one Saturday, Eileen?' Doris suggested. 'Since the war began, dances are really the gear. With all the servicemen around, there's always far more fellers than girls, and they're queuing up to ask for a dance and pleading to take you home.'

'I've got a husband in the army, Doris. I couldn't possibly let anyone take me home!' Eileen replied, pretending to be shocked. She'd given the girls no hint of her domestic situation.

'Get away with you, girl! While the cat's away, the mice do play, that's what they say, don't they? Have a good old time, Eileen, while he's gone,' Doris advised sagely. 'As long as you keep your hand on your halfpenny, you'll be all right.'

'I'll think about it,' laughed Eileen.

Later on, at lunchtime, one of the girls asked, 'Aren't you going outside today, Eileen?'

'It's too cold,' she said, and wondered if Nick Stephens would be there, waiting, in his corduroy suit and funny fisherman's hat. She'd thought about him a lot last week, but still stuck to the decision made that Sunday in Southport not to see him again. It wasn't just that the feelings she had were so disturbing and she was a married woman – at least a sort of married woman, who'd yet to work out in her muddled brain exactly what her position was, but Nick Stephens was a scientist from London, someone who ordered groceries over the telephone, and she couldn't for the life of her see what they had in common. It was nothing to do with class. No daughter of Jack Doyle would consider herself worth more, or less, than anybody else. Eileen Costello was as good as the Queen of England. Even so, there had to be a meeting point somewhere between two people, and there was none between her and Nick Stephens.

She didn't go out the following day, either, but thought about him, and wished there was a window she could peep through to see if he was there.

On Wednesday morning, during the tea break, something occurred which the girls talked about for days. The foreman came in, grinning from ear to ear for a change, and carrying a large bouquet of red roses wrapped in cellophane. He was greeted by a chorus of catcalls and Lil began to sing, *'Here Comes the Bride . . .'*

'Aye aye, Alfie! Getting married are you? Who's the lucky feller?'

'D'you want me to give you away, Alfie?'

'Bagsy me the first night, Alfie. I'll show you a thing or two.'

The foreman came up to Eileen and laid the flowers on her lathe. 'Someone left these for you at the front desk.'

'For me!' She knew immediately who'd sent them. There was no need to read the white card tucked inside the big red satin bow.

'Eileen's got a secret admirer!'

The girls crowded round, eyes shining with curiosity.

'Get away, youse lot,' Eileen said, embarrassed.

'Who are they from?'

Eileen plucked the card out of the bow, curious herself to know what it said. The message was written in a large untidy scrawl. *Where are you? N.*

'Who's "N"?' demanded Doris, reading over Eileen's shoulder.

'It's Neville. Neville Chamberlain's got a crush on Eileen Costello!'

Carmel was counting the roses. 'Two dozen. They must have cost a fortune. You're a dark horse, Eileen. C'mon, who sent them?'

'I'm not telling you.' If she so much as dropped a hint, the entire workshop would go out for a look after dinner. Despite their repeated demands, she flatly refused to reveal the identity of the sender.

Fortunately, no-one seemed to notice at dinner-time when she slipped away after a half-eaten meal.

Nick was sitting on the bank directly opposite the canteen door, waiting for her, his large dark eyes dancing with merriment. He was hatless, and his fishing rod was on the ground behind him.

Eileen sat on her side and regarded him thoughtfully. The fluttering sensation had returned to her stomach. 'You're a bloody idiot,' she said eventually.

'How about, "Thank you for the flowers, Nick"?' he prompted, grinning broadly.

'Thank you for the flowers, Nick. But you're still a bloody idiot. You've got the girls going wild in there, wondering who they're from. I'm a married woman, you know, and I've got me reputation to consider.'

In that case, why did she burst out laughing? He seemed to have a perverse, unnatural effect on her.

'I know you're a married woman, and you've got a little boy called Tony,' he said with mock gravity. 'I only sent the flowers because you didn't come out on Monday and Tuesday as promised. They were a reminder, that's all.'

'I didn't promise any such thing. Anyroad, why didn't you speak to me the other week when I came out every day?' she demanded.

'Because I was in a terrible black mood. That's why I come fishing, to calm myself down.'

'Are you in a terrible black mood now?'

'No.'

'Why not?'

'Because you're here.'

She laughed again. 'That's awful funny logic.'

'I'm an awful funny fellow.'

'You're that all right,' she said dryly. Suddenly, she shivered. She'd forgotten to bring her coat and had nothing on under the overalls except her bra and pants.

'What's the matter?' he asked, and the concern on his mobile, sensitive face sent her stomach haywire.

'I'm cold. I forgot me coat.'

'There's a pub around the corner. It's just opened. We could go and have a drink?'

'No, ta,' she said quickly. A lot of men from Dunnings went to the pub. If she was seen with Nick, it would be around the factory in a flash.

He must have sensed the reason for her prompt refusal. As if he'd read her thoughts, he said, 'Why are you so concerned about what other people think?'

Somewhat confused, she replied, 'Well, you have to be, don't you?' She shivered again and to her further confusion, Nick came leaping across the narrow stream, his boots splashing in the rippling water, and sat beside her. Removing his jacket, he placed it around her shoulders.

'There! Is that better?' he asked gently. His arm remained, heavy across her. The jacket felt warm from his body.

'You'll freeze to death yourself,' she protested. To her utter consternation, she felt close to tears. No man in the past had ever been so caring and considerate.

'This is stupid, anyroad,' she said helplessly.

'What's stupid?'

'Oh, God, I wish you'd stop asking me questions I can't answer,' she said impatiently. '*This* is stupid.' Eileen pointed to the jacket. 'Sending me flowers is stupid. Asking me to come out and see you is stupid. There's no point to it. No point at all.'

'You're right, there's no point to anything.'

She was taken aback by the sheer hopelessness in his voice. Still struggling to hold back her tears, she asked, 'What d'you mean?'

He laughed bitterly and removed his arm. 'You should know. It was you who made the observation first.'

'I meant there was no point to *us*, not . . . not to the world in general.' Eileen realised the words were inadequate, but somehow she didn't have the vocabulary to express her thoughts coherently. She looked at Nick, who was sitting, arms on knees, his head cupped in his long brown hands, staring gloomily at the water.

'What's the matter?' she whispered.

'What else? The bloody war, that's what's the matter.' He grabbed a tuft of grass and began to examine it closely, as if it held a vital secret. 'You know what I used to do?'

'You've never told me, have you?'

'No, I've never told you, have I?' he said in a tight voice. 'I was building an electronic brain . . .'

'A what?'

'An electronic brain, a machine that thinks. Of course, I wasn't the only one. There were a dozen of us working on it, and there were other people in other countries doing the same thing. It was so exciting, so worthwhile. We were going to transform the world; alter the way people communicate with each other in a way previously unthinkable. Everyone, everything would benefit; medicine, education, commerce . . .' He looked down at her, eyes shining with enthusiasm. Then his expression became contemptuous. His mouth twisted and his anger and bitterness were almost palpable. 'Do you know what

I'm doing now?'

'No,' said Eileen in a small voice.

'I'm making booby traps.'

'Booby traps! D'you mean for animals, like?'

'No, for people. Bombs disguised as toys, pens, torches, packets of cigarettes. Innocuous little items which will explode when picked up by some unsuspecting German, possibly a child.'

Eileen said in a horrified voice, 'I wouldn't have thought our side would sink so low. I can imagine Hitler doing things like that, but not the British.'

Nick smiled sardonically. 'Where war's concerned, both sides reach the lowest common denominator. They have no choice. I bet you there's a secret establishment somewhere in Britain where poison gas is being made.'

'Never!' she breathed.

He pulled a face. 'I told you, there's no choice. Whatever the enemy has, we must have the same, no matter how evil, in fact, the more evil the better. I suppose you could even say it was a good thing. It's a deterrent. The Germans won't drop gas on us if we can drop it on them.'

Eileen made a determined effort to be cheerful. 'Well, you never know, it might be over by Christmas.'

Nick shook his head. 'Haven't you heard today's news? Russia invaded Finland this morning.'

'Jesus, Mary and Joseph! I didn't know.'

'Anyway, Eileen Costello, there's the reason for my black moods. I wouldn't have minded being called up. In fact, I expected to be. I was in the University Air Squadron at Cambridge. I'm a qualified pilot. There's something honest and decent about fighting for your country.' He slapped his knees and, to her relief, smiled

189

broadly. 'I used to go fishing in the Thames with my grandfather when I was a child. We only went to get away from my parents who rowed incessantly. Fishing means peace. I never have a hook on the line. Who wants to kill poor innocent fish when you've spent the night constructing neat little contraptions which will kill poor innocent people?'

'I'm sorry, Nick. It must be terrible for you.' Impulsively, she laid her hand on his. He laid his other hand on top of hers. He felt cold. She'd better go back inside soon and let him have his coat back.

'You will keep coming out, won't you? Just to talk,' he said urgently. 'When I saw you, I longed to speak, but when the depression grips me, I feel as if my throat is locked tight. Nothing will come. That's why I was so glad when I saw you in Southport.'

'Of course I will,' she promised. There was concern in her voice as she added, 'You shouldn't let it get you down so much.'

'Is there something wrong with me?' He looked at her, bewildered, a little lost boy expression on his face that reminded her of Tony. 'None of the chaps at work let it get to them.'

'Perhaps it's them that aren't normal,' she suggested gently. 'Or perhaps they're hiding how they feel. I remember the first day I came out here, I thought how pretty it was, and how obscene that I was making parts for planes that would drop bombs on Germany.'

'Maybe your planes will drop my bombs!'

'Oh, come on,' she urged. 'Try and snap out of it. I'll have to go back in a minute.' She stood up. 'What are you going to do with yourself all afternoon?'

'Read a book. I'm in the middle of *War and Peace*. Then I'll go to bed about six and snatch a few hours' sleep. I don't need much.'

'Couldn't you read something a bit more cheerful?' Eileen had never heard of *War and Peace*, but it didn't sound the right sort of book for someone in his frame of mind.

'I'll read a P.G. Wodehouse, instead,' he grinned.

She hadn't heard of that, either, but wasn't going to admit it. 'That's a good idea,' she said wisely. 'Anyroad, I'd better be going.' She handed him his jacket. 'I'll see you tomorrow.'

'I'll be waiting.'

'Y'know, Eileen, I reckon you've got a feller tucked up your sleeve. You've been all starry-eyed ever since those flowers came,' Doris observed later that morning.

'You're talking through the back of your neck,' Eileen told her, trying valiantly to look miserable, but not managing.

'Look at you! Grinning like a bleeding Cheshire cat. Have you noticed, girls?' Doris yelled. 'This one here's in love. It's written all over her face.'

'Honest to God, you don't have any privacy in this place,' Eileen protested, feeling her face flush crimson as the women whistled their agreement.

Just before the hooter went to signal time to go home, she went round the workshop and solemnly handed a single rose to everyone. She couldn't possibly take them home. Sheila, Annie, everyone, would demand to know where they came from, and she wouldn't be able to brush them off the way she'd done the girls.

When Alfie came in, she tucked a rose in his buttonhole and the foreman winked. 'I was by the front desk when the flowers came,' he said. 'He seemed a nice enough young feller.'

'Thanks for not saying anything.' The more she got to know Alfie, the more she liked him. His taciturn manner hid a heart of gold. 'I'd give you a kiss, if I didn't think it would send tongues wagging.'

Alfie winked again. 'I wouldn't mind, not if it was you and me they were wagging over, luv.'

'Let's go upstairs, Helen. It's much more comfortable in bed.'

He already had his shirt and vest off. They were on the settee in the parlour and he stood up and went to the door. Helen Brazier followed reluctantly. She hated doing it in the bed she'd slept in with her mother, where she had the unpleasant sensation of being watched. Although she'd told Lou, he didn't seem to care.

He noticed her hanging back and said crossly: 'Your mother's dead, Helen. How many times do I have to keep telling you?' Lately, she'd got the impression she was getting on his nerves.

'I'm coming.'

The waning moon illuminated the bedroom enough for her to see Lou was already undressed by the time she arrived. He was lying on the brown cotton coverlet, his arms behind his neck. She shivered when she saw his rampant nakedness.

'You can't wait for it, can you?' he said softly.

She shivered again, imagining mother's eyes watching from the dark corners, scandalised at her daughter's shameful behaviour. She began to fumble with her blouse, already half undone, then her lockknit petticoat, her liberty bodice, the short sleeved vest . . .

'Why don't you buy yourself some decent under-clothes, Helen? They're real passionkillers, that lot. Did they belong to your mother, or something?'

'Well, yes.' It seemed a shame to throw them away. 'Waste not, want not,' Mother always said.

'You should get yourself something a bit more modern, like. Something with a bit of lace on.'

'Perhaps I will.' She'd do anything to keep him. She'd already started wearing make-up and combed her hair out of its rather old-fashioned bun, worried it was her appearance that had prevented Lou from taking her to the pictures as he'd promised.

'After all, I bet you can afford it. I reckon you've got a bob or two stashed away?'

'I don't need much to live on.' Just food, coal, the gas bill. She'd been putting a pound away each week, sometimes more, in the tin box in the sideboard ever since Mother died. She removed her knee-length bloomers, undid her suspenders and rolled her stockings down, unlaced her stays.

'Christ Almighty! Talk about a strip tease!' Lou said exasperatedly. His tone changed when she was as naked as he. 'Come here,' he said roughly, reaching for her, and she slipped eagerly into his arms. He began to touch her and her insides turned to liquid. She forgot about Mother, forgot about everything except the thrill, the sheer rapture and excitement of a man being inside her. She gave a little cry when they finished, coming together, and clapped her hand over her mouth, worried the neighbours might have heard.

'You're a proper good screw, y'know that, Helen?' Lou sat up and reached for cigarettes out of his trouser pocket.

Instead of feeling offended, the coarse words sent a delicious shiver down her spine. He began to stroke her full breasts with his free hand, as she lay exhausted beside him.

Oh, God! She'd been so easy. A virgin for thirty-four years, you'd think she would have needed some persuasion, but it had been only on his second visit that she'd capitulated to Lou's coaxing charm. Now, he met her every night and came back for what he jokingly referred to as, 'a cup of tea.' To her delight and consternation, he'd actually turned up one Sunday afternoon when it was still daylight, and she'd glanced frantically up and down the street to see if anyone was watching before letting him in.

She'd tried to be firm, as far as she could be firm with Lou, that he must only come when it was dark. He'd pretended to be offended. 'Are you ashamed of me?'

'Of course not!'

'How else are a courting couple supposed to meet?'

A courting couple!

'There's nowt wrong with a gentleman calling on his lady friend,' he went on. 'I could be just coming for me dinner. In fact, I wouldn't mind some grub. I don't know what me sister does with me wages, but there's never much to eat at home.'

She'd made him bacon and eggs and fried bread, and since then he always had a meal when he came.

He stubbed his cigarette out on the marble-topped wash stand and immediately reached for another.

'I bought you some ciggies today,' she said.

'What sort?'

'Capstan. That's what y'like, isn't it?'

'They'll do. I prefer Senior Service. How many did you get?'

'Twenty.'

'Thanks, luv.'

She'd already bought a hundred pack of Capstan for his Christmas present. She'd change them tomorrow for Senior Service.

He sighed. 'It's lovely and peaceful here. Such a nice change from home. Me sister's kids are a right handful. It wouldn't be so bad if they could go out and play.'

'Why can't they? she asked lazily.

'I told you, me sister's a terrible manager. They've only got one decent pair of shoes each and they've got to be kept for school. Once they're in, that's it for the night, and it's hell on earth, the noise they make, I can tell you. Anyway, luv,' he slapped her arm playfully, 'that's none of your worry, is it? Is there any grub lined up? I'm starving.'

She climbed off the bed and took her dressing gown from behind the door. The dressing gown had also belonged to Mother and was brown plaid trimmed with cord, sensible and mannish. She noticed Lou's nose wrinkle as she put it on and decided to take a look at what the Co-op had in stock on Monday. 'I did some lamb chops last night,' she said. 'I've only got to warm them up with a few 'taters.'

'Is there any mint sauce?'

'Y'can't have lamb without mint sauce, can you?'

'Me sister can. She's no idea how to make a decent meal. Not like you, Helen.'

She flushed at the compliment and went down to get the meal ready. When Lou appeared, she said, 'I hope you won't take offence, but I'd like to buy shoes for your sister's children.' She handed him five pound notes. 'There's enough for Wellingtons too, for when it's raining.'

Lou's long thin face darkened and Helen felt full of trepidation, worried she'd hurt his feelings. He groaned and said, 'I've no right to take your money, Helen, but I suppose I should put me niece and nephews before me own feelings. Thanks a lot. Now, all they need is a good warm coat each, and they'll be set up for the winter.'

Chapter 8

It was bad enough, people complained bitterly, that their country seemed to be suspended precariously between a state of limbo and a state of war, but to make matters worse, the weather during the winter of 1939 turned out to be the bleakest in living memory. For some reason no-one was able to understand, the press was forbidden to publish details, which only increased the contempt of the population for a government that seemed to think people were so stupid that they couldn't feel for themselves the sub-zero temperatures, or observe the thick, dense snow which fell day after day, week after week; a government which dropped paper on the enemy instead of bombs and dithered over sending troops to the aid of gallant little Finland when Russia invaded — to such a degree that Finland had surrendered before the troops left British soil, though many brave Finns continued fighting. Wiser heads thought despairingly that even to have considered taking on the might of Russia, as well as Germany, would have been an act of total madness.

Lack of reporting about the arctic weather only led to wilder and wilder rumours. It was said that in the countryside birds froze on the trees, and that elsewhere, old people and babies were found perished to death in their beds; that cars and buses travelled on rivers of solid ice which were safer and more passable than the roads.

Those who could afford it spent lavishly on fur-lined boots and thick coats, on extra blankets and tons and tons of coke or coal, which resulted in a shortage of fuel for those who could only buy one sack at a time. In Pearl Street, for the first time the Harrisons' coalyard was swept clean. There wasn't a single cob to be seen, and Nelson was left to munch his oats in idleness, since no deliveries could be made. In the shops, there was a shortage of hot-water bottles and portable electric fires sold out like hot cakes.

Being a cul-de-sac, there was scarcely any traffic, and the snow piled up in Pearl Street. The silvery drifts against the railway wall gradually got higher and higher. Whooping children emerged each morning to try and climb the wonderful white mountain at the end of their street, and were soaked to the skin before they left for school.

Eileen Costello found her dishes frozen to the draining board, and hastily lagged her pipes lest they freeze too. Although it was an extravagance, she sometimes lit a fire in the unused parlour to keep the house warm and stop the parlour from feeling like the North Pole, and un-earthed the chamber pot from the washhouse for use in the middle of the night. One morning, she opened her door to find a three-foot snowdrift, which stayed there, frozen solid, even without the door to prop it up.

The bus for Dunnings arrived late almost every day, particularly in the mornings, when it encountered fresh snowfalls, and the men would get out and attempt to clear the roads and create a fresh channel for the buses following behind. Although the heating system in the factory was quite efficient, the girls no longer removed their clothes, only too glad to feel warm, if sticky.

'Sweating's a luxury in this bleeding weather,' Doris declared.

Eileen met Nick on her morning shifts in December

and they walked along the bank, trampling through the smooth, virginal snow or sliding on the frozen stream like children.

'The girls think I'm completely mad, coming out like this,' she told him.

As Jessica Fleming trudged home from Veronica's, she thought longingly of her old house with its central heating, though had to concede that, once the fire was banked up, it was quite cheerful, even cosy, in Pearl Street. When she couldn't find a hot-water bottle to buy anywhere in the shops, Arthur advised her to heat bricks in the oven and wrap them in a cloth to take to bed. 'Someone in the King's Arms told me that.'

'Where the hell am I supposed to find bricks?' she asked sharply, and he brought two home the next day.

Paddy O'Hara, who'd come into his own in the blackout – after all, he had lived in his own blackout since 1918, so could make his way around as well as he'd ever done – suddenly found himself in slippery, alien territory bounded by unfamiliar walls of snow. After falling over several times and twice getting lost and having to ask strangers to take him home, he stayed in his lodgings, sinking further and further into a slough of despondency as he nursed Spot, who by now could scarcely walk.

'We're a pair of ould crocks, aren't we boy?' he said, stroking the dog's shivering body.

All Sheila Reilly could think of were the sailors dying in the icy seas of the South Atlantic, where the Battle of the River Plate took place in the middle of December. Cal had told her once that you didn't stand a chance after you landed in the water if it was below a certain temperature. It was the shock that did for you. Even if you were fished out immediately, it was too late. In the end, the British were triumphant, though scores of men on both sides were killed. The *Admiral Graf Spee*, which had cost the German government six million pounds, limped into the port of Montevideo like a wounded animal, and the captain, faced with capture of both crew and vessel, decided to scuttle the ship, then killed himself to preserve the honour of the German flag. Everyone in Pearl Street seemed to think Sheila should be elated. After all, it was the *Graf Spee* that had sunk the *Midnight Star*.

'Why should I be happy because some poor German women have lost their men?' she asked, puzzled.

But at least the country had something to crow over, even though the happenings had taken place thousands of miles away on the coast of South America, and the First Lord of the Admiralty, Winston Churchill, was given due credit for the victory. Once again people began to ask, 'Why isn't this man Prime Minister?'

On the Saturday before Christmas, Eileen Costello and Annie Poulson were sitting listening to *Garrison Theatre* and wrapping presents in crêpe paper. The decorations were already up and an artificial tree stood on the sideboard. Mr Singerman had taken Tony and Dominic to the Palace in Marsh Lane to see Will Hay in *Ask a Policeman*. Tony's model of the Maginot Line and his box of lead soldiers were safely hidden in Annie's house and would be put beside his bed on Christmas morning.

'It's nice to have a few bob in your pocket for presents,' Annie said smugly, wrapping a shaving kit in a leather case. She'd bought one each for Terry and Joe. 'When they were little, I never had two pennies to scratch me arse with, let alone for Christmas presents. Yesterday, I got three pounds, two and sixpence in me wages and I feel like a millionaire. There!' She patted the finished parcel. 'What shall I do now?'

'Wrap this cardy up for Mary. I bought clothes for our Sheila's kids. They won't like it much, but it'll help their mam out a bit.'

'How's she getting on for money, like?' asked Annie.

'She's getting Cal's pay for six months, two pounds, ten bob, a week, but not the extra danger money he used to get,' Eileen answered.

'What'll she do when the six months is up?'

Eileen shrugged. 'Go on Public Assistance, I suppose, though there's no way me dad'll see our Sheila and her kids go hungry – nor would I, come to that.'

'Y'know Rosie Gregson is up the spout?' said Annie conversationally.

'Never! I suppose that must have happened when Charlie came home on leave at the end of September.'

'I reckon,' Annie said. 'The thing is, though, the silly girl hadn't told a soul. She got the sack from Jacob's Biscuit Factory because she was so sick, she was off work for weeks. The poor lamb's got no family – she met Charlie in the orphanage – and I found her the other day near froze to death in her lodgings. I gave her a good ticking off for not telling me and took her over to our house for a warm and a good meal. She's been living on seventeen and six a week Army allowance, on top of the seven bob she gets off Charlie.'

'How's she supposed to buy things for a baby out of that?' Eileen asked indignantly.

'Christ knows! Rosie, bless her heart, is as thick as two short planks. It didn't cross her mind to do anything about it. I made her apply for more money off the Army. It's a terrible disgrace, y'know, Eil. Two bob a day a soldier gets fighting for his country – and half that's taken off for his family.'

'Don't I know it,' groaned Eileen. 'Me dad pins me ear

back over the same thing every time I see him. The woman next door to him has had to take in sewing to make ends meet. It's all right for some – Francis still gets his wages off the Mersey Docks and Harbour Board, not that I touch it, mind you – but most men and their families have to live on what they get off the Army, and they get nowt but a pittance.'

Annie shook her head in disgust. 'Two bob a day! I bet there's politicians who spend two bob a day on cigars. When y'think about it, Eil, there's something wrong somewhere. Two bob a day!'

Paddy O'Hara lay in his room listening to the woman crying next door. Miss Brazier had been sobbing her heart out for nearly two hours. She was normally a cold, reserved person, but he always sensed an edge of desperation in her voice, as if behind the frigid façade she longed to let go, drop her icy reserve, and at least pass the time of day like everybody else.

He wondered, vaguely, if he should go round and ask what was the matter, though the woman would probably die of shame if she thought someone was eavesdropping, albeit innocently, on her misery.

In his box on the floor beside the bed, Spot gave a little almost human groan.

'There, boy,' said Paddy, reaching down to stroke the furry body. His hand accidentally touched the lump on the little dog's belly, and it whimpered in pain.

'Sorry, boy!' Paddy whispered. He lifted the dog up carefully and put it under the clothes beside him. In his heart, he knew that very soon he'd have to get Spot put down. The vet had told him, quite brutally, there was nothing that could be done. 'You're lucky to have had him so long. What is it? Fifteen years? It's cruel, in a way, to let him go on living. After all, you can always get another dog.'

Miss Brazier was still crying. Apart from that, and Spot's heavy breathing, the street seemed to be gripped in an all-consuming silence. It was probably snowing again. Paddy tried to remember what snow looked like, what the world looked like when it was covered with a blanket of white. He lay there for a long time listening to the crying and the breathing, imagining flakes as big as tennis balls dropping remorselessly outside, when he heard a commotion. Doors slammed, there was banging, people began to shout. They were happy shouts, joyous. There must be some good news. Perhaps the war was over. He struggled cautiously out of bed so as not to disturb Spot and began to get dressed. If it was good news, there was no way he was going to miss it.

Eileen's parcels were all wrapped and piled neatly under the tree. Annie put hers to one side, ready to take home. Her lads were expected on Wednesday afternoon, though with the weather the way it was, trains could be hours, even days, late.

'They look so much more interesting and mysterious like that, don't they?' said Annie. 'Shall we have a cuppa after all that hard work?'

Eileen switched on the wireless. 'Shush a minute. Let's hear the news headlines.'

Annie disappeared into the kitchen as Big Ben boomed and a cultured voice announced, 'This is the nine o'clock news from the BBC, and this is Alvar Lidell reading it.'

Eileen listened idly, not expecting to hear much of interest. The news was still concerned with the Battle of the River Plate. Apparently the American Republics had made a formal protest to Britain, claiming their security zone had been violated. Churchill had replied to President Roosevelt that the zone was now free from German harassment. The Ministry of Information had just revealed that the thirty-two-strong crew of the recently sunk British ship *Streonshalh* had been released from the *Graf Spee* before it was scuttled. They'd been taken prisoner prior to their ship being blasted out of the water. . . The announcer's pleasant voice droned on. At first, the momentous words went over Eileen's head and she found herself glaring at the wireless, wishing she'd listened properly. What had the man just said?

Annie appeared in the doorway. She was clutching the teapot to her chest like a loved one, unable to contain her excitement.

'Did you hear what I just heard?'

'I think so. Oh, I'm sure so.' Eileen gave a shout of joy. 'I'm going to tell our Sheila!'

Eileen grabbed her coat and ran out into the snow in her bedroom slippers. She hammered with both fists on Sheila's door. Mr and Mrs Harrison came hurrying out of their house next to the coalyard and a crowd of men poured out of the King's Arms.

'Did you hear the news, Eileen? Did you hear the news?'

'I heard!'

Sheila opened the door and took a startled step backwards when it appeared the entire street had come to see her in the middle of a snow storm. 'What on earth . . ?' she began.

'Sheil!' Eileen leaped into the hall, grabbed her sister by the waist, and began to twirl her round. 'Cal's alive! The crew of the *Midnight Star* were taken prisoner by the *Graf Spee*, and put on another ship. He's not dead, Sheil. None of the crew are dead.'

'But where is he?' Sheila looked dazed.

'He's on a ship called the *Altmark*, luv,' someone shouted, 'along with men off some other British ships.'

'But don't worry, Sheila. The Royal Navy's out looking for it. Calum Reilly'll soon be home safe and sound.'

'You never know, he might even be back for Christmas.'

'Cal's not dead? Y'mean my Cal's not dead?' Sheila, still dazed, had only just begun to take the news in. She burst into tears.

'What's going on?' Paddy O'Hara shouted from across the street.

'Calum Reilly's safe and sound on the *Altmark*.'

'It's drinks on the house,' yelled Mack, the landlord. 'C'mon, Paddy, me boy. You look froze to death. A nice drop of whisky'll warm you up no end. We'll drink to Cal and Sheila – and to the Royal Navy. I'll send a couple of port and lemon's over in a minute, Sheila, so you can join in the toast. Let's hope they find that bloody ship soon. In the meantime, this is going to be one of the best Christmases we've ever had!'

It had been a genuine mistake. A woman had handed in a pound note, and instead of Jessica giving a ten-shilling note and coins in change, she'd apparently handed a pound note and coins back. Later in the day, after Jessica had gone home, the woman had come into the shop to return the ten shillings when she noticed the error.

'It's a good job there's honest folk in the world,' sniffed Veronica, 'else I would have been well down on me takings.' She carried on about it all morning.

'How many times do I have to say I'm sorry?' pleaded Jessica. 'You'd think I was trying to steal it, the way you go on.'

Veronica was still going on days later. She kept a zealous eye on Jessica every time the till was opened, and several times emerged to go over the calculations when a customer was purchasing several items which needed adding up. Jessica, who had kept her father's books when she was little more than a child and had a good head for figures, took exception to being watched over as if she was a criminal.

'I know you're only doing it to rile me,' she said one morning in between customers and almost at the end of her tether. 'I can't understand someone like you. You seem to take pleasure in getting under people's skin.'

It was only a few days off Christmas and the shop was busy. There'd even been a few bold men in, buying underwear as presents for their wives.

'You don't give me much choice, do you? If I don't keep a close eye, who knows what you might get up to.'

Jessica felt like hitting her employer with the drawer of outsize lockknit bloomers on the counter. She put the drawer away, slammed it shut and counted up to ten, slowly.

'Oh, a bit touchy are we today?' Veronica said rudely, before ambling into the back.

Jessica recognised the next customer; a pleasant-looking woman, almost refined, who had been in the shop before and lived across the road from her in Pearl Street.

'I'd like a brassiere, something with a bit of uplift.' She laughed, a deep, throaty sound. 'The girls where I work are always on about uplift, so I thought I'd go for a bit meself.'

'What size, Madam?'

'Thirty-two, I think. I haven't bought a brassiere in ages,' she said with a grin.

'Would Madam like me to measure her?'

'No, it's all right. If it don't fit, I can always change it, can't I?'

'Mrs Poulson!' Veronica emerged from the back. 'Are your lads home yet?'

'They're on their way. I'm expecting them tonight if the snow holds off a bit.'

'Mrs Poulson's twin boys are with the British Expeditionary Force in France,' Veronica announced grandly to Jessica.

'I expect you can't wait to see them,' Jessica said politely, producing the drawer of size 32 brassieres.

'You're dead right. I'm longing to get me hands on the pair of them and give them a good old cuddle. Have you got any children, Mrs Fleming?'

'No, I'm afraid. . . No, I haven't,' Jessica replied shortly.

Mrs Poulson had begun to examine the brassieres. 'This one looks quite a nice shape – and it's even got a rosebud in the middle! Not that anyone's likely to see it except meself. How much is it?'

'Two and ninepence.'

Taking the money out of her purse, Mrs Poulson chuckled. 'I'll give you the right amount this time, so there's no chance of a mistake with me change.'

'I'm so sorry about that, Mrs Poulson,' Veronica grovelled. 'Mrs Fleming has been extra careful ever since.'

The woman's eyes widened. 'But it was *you* who gave me the wrong change, Veronica. I never said it was Jessie who took me money.'

It was then that Jessica remembered. Mrs Poulson had come in last week to buy a nightdress, and Veronica, up to her usual tricks, had snatched the note out of her hand.

'Merry Christmas to the pair of you,' Mrs Poulson said

happily as she left.

There was dead silence in the shop for several seconds.

'Well?' said Jessica ominously.

'Well, what?' Veronica snapped.

'I think I'm entitled to an apology, don't you?'

Veronica didn't reply.

'Don't you?'

When Veronica remained mute, Jessica went storming into the back and stood in the middle of the stockroom, taking deep breaths and seething. That was it! She'd leave. She couldn't stand Veronica and her shop another single minute. It was degrading. She glanced around at the cardboard boxes of cheap underwear that she wouldn't be seen dead in.

'Muck!' she said in a loud voice. 'Absolute muck!'

The shop bell rang, but Jessica remained where she was. Veronica could see to the customer – to all the customers from now on.

With a sense of overwhelming relief, she realised she was free! It was so easy, she wondered why she hadn't done it before.

She put on her coat, picked up her bag and marched through the shop.

'And where d'you think *you're* going?' snapped her ex-employer.

'Home,' cried Jessica. 'I'm going home. Merry Christmas, Veronica.'

Jessica pulled out the flue on the fire which she'd left banked up that morning. Little blue and red flames immediately shot through the mixture of coal and coke and began to dance on the surface.

She felt darts of happiness shoot through her body and rubbed her hands together in a surge of joy. She hadn't felt so exhilarated since . . . since she first met Arthur! Yet she'd just given up her job, relinquished a regular wage. None of the wonderful, expensive things she'd bought in the past; the jewellery, the clothes, the furniture, not even the Aga, had made her feel so delighted with herself. To think she didn't have to subject herself to that ordeal again! It had only been eleven weeks, but it felt more like eleven years.

This called for a celebration. A drink! She'd get one in a minute, but in the meantime, she couldn't help it, she just had to *sing!* She hadn't sung a note since Calderstones, but now the urge couldn't be contained another single minute.

Jessica threw back her head and began to sing *Silent Night* in her glorious soprano voice. There was no audience, no-one to applaud, but she had never sung so well or with so much feeling. *'All is calm, All is bright . . .'* As she sang, she thought, 'I must join another choir. I didn't realise how much I've missed this . . . *Holy Infant, so tender and mild, Sleep in . . .'*

To her astonishment, she heard the sound of a piano next door. She was being accompanied! Somewhat stumblingly at first, but then, once the pianist got her rhythm, he played with as much enthusiasm as she sang.

'Sleep in heavenly peace.' She hit top C smoothly and effortlessly. *'Sleep in heavenly peace.'*

Jessica sang two more verses, then began *The First Noel*. In the various living rooms and back kitchens of Pearl Street, surprised people stopped what they were doing to listen to the pure angelic voice coming from Number 5. Despite the cold, a few even opened their doors a crack to hear better. Paddy O'Hara, opposite, wretched and miserable because he'd taken Spot to the vet that morning to be put down, felt strangely uplifted.

Unable to think of any more verses, Jessica sank back in the chair, exhausted. A few minutes later, there was a knock on the front door and she went to answer it. She knew who it would be and didn't mind a bit, not at the moment. As expected, Mr Singerman was standing outside. He was holding a bottle of sherry.

'I thought you'd like a drink to celebrate,' he smiled.

Jessica smiled back. 'Celebrate what?'

He shrugged. 'I've no idea. It's just that you sounded as if you were celebrating something.'

'I think I was. Come in. I'd love a drink. In fact, I was about to have one . . .'

'It's only cheap sherry. I always buy a bottle in case people drop in over Christmas.' His rather rheumy eyes grew round as he entered the living room. 'You have this place looking nice – and a full size carpet, too!'

'If I have a sherry, would you like something else? Whisky, rum, a liqueur? There's all sorts in the cocktail cabinet.'

'A cocktail cabinet! This I must see.'

She took him into the front room and his eyes grew even rounder when she opened the doors of the black lacquered cocktail cabinet and a painted glass tray slid out at the same time. The cut glass decanters gleamed, reflected in the mirrored back and sides. Assorted matching glasses were stacked neatly in holders on each side. Jessica noticed the brandy was at exactly the same level as when they had moved in. Arthur seemed satisfied with his pint at the King's Arms nowadays.

'That's a fine piece of furniture!' Mr Singerman gasped. He surveyed the row of bottles at the back. 'I think I'd like a liqueur. Benedictine would be a treat. I haven't had a liqueur since the day I got married.'

When they were both settled in front of the fire nursing

their drinks, he said, 'You know, you should do something with that voice. It's a crying shame to let such a
talent go to waste.'

'I used to be in a choir,' Jessica explained. 'But I haven't
felt much like singing lately.'

'I'm playing at a carol concert tomorrow night. Why
don't you come with me?'

'You mean and sing?'

He nodded eagerly. 'We make a good pair. I felt as if
you were urging me to play better. My old fingers
seemed to come to life.'

Jessica felt pleased at the compliment, so sincerely
expressed. 'I wouldn't need much persuading,' she said.

'Then you'll do it!' He looked genuinely glad.

'Yes,' she said simply. 'All of a sudden, I feel like
singing again.'

'You know, I'm always being asked to play at concerts, particularly since this damned war began. Troops
in transit like a hearty sing-song, and good pianists are
hard to come by.' He looked, for the moment, a trifle
self-important. A lonely old man, pleased to feel wanted
now and then. Jessica, who rarely noticed other people's
feelings, found herself blinking at this awareness.

'Music is a great release,' she said, somewhat grandly
and not quite sure what she meant, though Mr Singerman seemed to understand.

'It certainly is,' he concurred. They smiled at each
other. 'I know it sounds ridiculous,' he went on, 'Arthur
said you're from Calderstones and I've never been that
side of Liverpool, but I have a strong feeling I've seen you
before.'

'I used to live across the road next door to the coalyard,' Jessica replied. It hadn't escaped her notice that
Mrs Poulson had referred to her as 'Jessie.' *I never said it*

was Jessie who took me money,' she'd said. Mrs Poulson must have recognised her from way back, and if she knew, all sorts of other people would know, too. She'd only make herself look ridiculous by denying her roots.

Mr Singerman's face lit up. 'Bert Hennessy's daughter! You used to sing even then.'

'And your daughter was a pianist!' The memories flooded back. A lovely, dark-haired, serious looking child, a few years younger than herself, who never played out with the other children, but practised on the piano hour after hour. And Mr Singerman, already stooped and grey haired, a widower whose wife had died giving birth to her talented daughter. What was the girl's name? Jessica racked her brains. 'Ruth!' she said aloud.

'That's right, my Ruth. Has Arthur told you . . ?'

'Yes. I'm terribly sorry.' His deeply lined jaw trembled and she felt a surge of pity. Her words of comfort seemed so trite and meaningless. 'Terribly sorry,' she repeated. In order to cheer him up a bit, she said, 'I've always intended to take up some sort of war work. I'll go along with you to all these troop concerts, if you like. I read in the paper, they're going to start giving concerts in factories in the lunch hour. "Workers' Playtimes", they'll be called. We could do them, too.'

In the early hours of Christmas morning, the snow fell thick and fast, but had stopped when daylight came. Eileen Costello, lighting the fire in the parlour where they'd be eating dinner later on, glanced out of the window. The world seemed to have changed shape lately, become rounder, smoother, everything buried under a thick crust of white. A few men were outside with shovels, yet again clearing a space to walk on. She sniffed as the smell of a roasting chicken wafted into the room. She'd peel the potatoes in a minute ready to roast with the bird, then prepare the stuffing, start boiling the pudding . . .

Tony was making battle noises in the living room as his soldiers attacked the Maginot line. The sounds had been going on since half past four, when he'd woken up and found the presents beside the bed, including a tank off Annie. So different from previous Christmases, when Francis, for some reason she could never fathom, had forbidden Tony to get up and touch his presents until eight o'clock, then only let him play with them for certain periods of time. Thinking of Francis made her feel uneasy. He hadn't replied to her letter, and she kept expecting him just to turn up. After all, a man had a right to expect to spend Christmas with his family. People kept asking when he'd be home.

'I'm not quite sure,' she told them vaguely. 'There's just a chance he might not make it.' She brushed off their expressions of shocked sympathy, with, 'We'll just have to manage without him, won't we?'

Her dad and Sean were coming to dinner, along with Sheila and the kids and poor Paddy O'Hara, who was in a right old state having had Spot put down. She'd asked Mr Singerman, but to her surprise, he'd refused. Apparently, he'd already accepted an invitation to the Flemings'.

'I hope you don't mind, Eileen. Perhaps I could come over in the afternoon?' he'd said, anxious not to hurt her feelings.

'You know you're always welcome in this house, luv,' she told him. 'There'll be a few folks coming in to listen to the King's speech.'

As Eileen opened up the leaves at each end of the table, she decided it would be best to have two sittings; kids first, grown-ups second. She'd never get that lot around the table in one go. She spread the thick felt undercloth and covered it with the best white damask. After studying the table thoughtfully for a while, she removed the white cloth and replaced it with the pale blue second best. The kids could make all the mess they liked on that, she'd use the white one for the second sitting.

She was getting the best cutlery out of its box – a wedding present from her dad – when Annie came dancing in.

Annie turned sideways and posed. 'What d'think of me uplift?'

'You don't look any different,' Eileen said after a while.

'Christ Almighty, girl. I pay two and ninepence for a new brassiere and I don't look any different?'

'Well, you're not big enough, are you? You need to stuff yourself with cotton wool if you want any shape at all.'

'Thanks a lot! Just for that, I might not wish you a Merry Christmas.'

When Eileen merely grinned, Annie sighed dramatically. 'I've brought your Christmas present.' She handed over a little box and gave Eileen a hearty kiss on the cheek at the same time. 'Merry Christmas, luv.'

'And the same to you, Annie.'

'It couldn't be any merrier, not with our Terry and Joe home. I'm so bloody happy I could hug meself to death.'

'Earrings! Oh, they're lovely, Annie. Thanks very much. I'll put them on this minute.' Eileen clipped the pearl drops on her ears. 'What do they look like?'

'They look a treat, honest.'

'I've got your present under the tree.' She'd bought Annie a leather purse, as her old one had worn away to the lining in places.

'It's exactly what I wanted!' said Annie delightedly when she opened the gift. 'And there's a penny piece already in it!'

'That's so it'll never be empty.'

'Ta, luv. I'd better be getting home. I've never had to make a meal for six people before. I was working meself up into a right tizzy earlier on.'

'Six people, Annie?'

'Well, you know I asked Charlie and Rosie Gregson?'

'That makes five, with you and the lads.'

Annie's eyes sparkled wickedly. 'And there's Barney.'

'Who the hell's Barney?' Eileen demanded.

'Remember me telling you about this chap from Dunnings who asked me out the first week?'

'Yes, but you never said you'd accepted.'

'That's 'cos I didn't. The other girls – I told you they turned out all right in the end, didn't I?' When Eileen nodded, Annie went on, 'Well, anyway, they told me Barney Clegg – he's a bachelor, by the way – was a proper womaniser, out with a different girl every night and a string of broken hearts behind him. I quite fancied him meself, but I'd no intention of joining his harem. I've been playing hard to get, though quite frankly, I don't know what he sees in me.'

Eileen began to protest indignantly at this and Annie shushed her with, 'Come off it, Eil. I'll be thirty-nine next birthday and I don't exactly look like Lorretta Young, do I? Anyroad, when Barney was complaining he had nowhere to go on Christmas Day, I asked him to dinner. I told him if me lads liked the look of him, I'd go out to this dance he's been going on about on New Year's Eve.'

Eileen burst out laughing. 'Annie! You're the end, you

really are! I'll be round to have a dekko at this heartbreaker later on.'

After Annie had left, Eileen thought about Nick, who'd gone down to London to spend Christmas with friends. For someone who played such a minor role in her life, he seemed to occupy a major part of her thoughts. She wished she were in Annie's position, free to go out with whosoever she chose and wondered, if she were free, if he asked, what would she say? Without hesitation, she knew it would be 'yes'. Despite the differences in their backgrounds, they seemed to have an endless amount to talk about. With him, she seemed to run through a whole gamut of emotions. One minute he would make her feel feminine and desirable, a real woman for the first time in her life, despite her old coat, her clumsy overalls and headscarf. Then they would begin an argument, usually over some aspect of the war, and he appeared interested, even anxious to hear her views, unlike the men she'd met so far, who didn't seem to think women were entitled to an opinion about anything. At other times, when he fell into one of his black moods, she would tenderly chivvy him back into a good humour.

Eileen sighed and Tony looked up. 'What's the matter, Mam?'

'Nothing, luv. I was just worried the 'taters wouldn't be ready in time, that's all.'

The house had never felt so quiet and so empty. You could almost touch the silence and although it seemed silly, you could almost *hear* it, ticking away in the background.

Helen Brazier had got used to spending Christmas on her own since her mother died. It was just another lonely day among hundreds of other lonely days. But this year, without Lou, she felt her isolation even more keenly. She tried not to think about him, but once again, for the umpteenth time, she let herself live through that Saturday dinnertime when she'd seen him with his wife and children.

At first she'd assumed the woman was his sister, that the three children were his niece and nephews, though she couldn't help but feel surprised when she saw the harassed looking woman was heavily pregnant. Hadn't Lou said she was a widow? They were in Woolworths, which was packed to the gills with Christmas shoppers, struggling past the sweet counter and through the crowds towards her. Helen stopped and waited for them to reach her, intending only to catch Lou's eye and give a secret smile. She wouldn't introduce herself, he might not have mentioned her to his sister. Perhaps she could even manage to whisper a little message, 'I've got you another Christmas present.' A black enamelled cigarette lighter, which she intended having engraved with his initials, L.M. She'd ordered a bird from the Co-op butchery and there were two bottles of wine, one red, one white, in the larder ready for their Christmas dinner. And she'd bought clothes; frocks, silk stockings and lots of pretty, lace-trimmed underwear, and made an appointment for a Carmel wave on half day closing.

They were almost touching, yet he still hadn't noticed her. He had a shabbily dressed child on either side, holding his hands. Children could easily get lost in the crush. The woman shoved past dragging a crying child behind her, almost knocking Helen over. She looked almost slatternly, with uncombed hair and her coat buttoned at the top, the rest hanging open over her swollen belly revealing a flowered pinny underneath. Despite the icy weather, she had neither gloves nor scarf. A different type from Lou altogether, decided Helen. He was dressed smartly, as always, in his mackintosh with the turned-up collar and his hat tipped over his right eye.

'Eh, Dad, can I have a lolly?' The little boy was actually standing on Helen's foot. He tugged at the sleeve of Lou's mack. 'Can I have a lolly, Dad?'

'For Christ Almighty's sake, shurrup,' Lou snapped. 'How many times . . .' His eyes met Helen's. She may as well not have been there. His expression didn't alter as he continued, '. . . must I tell you to stop pestering me?'

They were gone. Swallowed up by the crowd, and Helen was left, being jostled to and fro, feeling as if she had been hit by a thunderbolt.

He was married! His sister was not his sister, but his wife. The children belonged to him.

Helen and Lou. Lou and Helen. The words chased each other around her brain. He'd been playing her for a fool all this time. And that wasn't all. There was the money she'd given him, nearly twenty pounds in all, for coats and shoes and Christmas presents for the children, for a new kettle, because his 'sister' had burned the bottom out of the old one, for all sorts of things.

Sitting in her house on Christmas Day with her freshly waved hair and in one of the new frocks which she'd worn mostly as a gesture of defiance, because she didn't expect to see anyone, Helen Brazier wondered where the money had gone. Not on the children, by the look of them. He'd probably spent it at the dog track he frequented. She wondered if he'd waited for her last Monday. She could actually imagine him having the brazen cheek to carry on as before, to pretend they'd never seen each other in Woolworths. Since then, she'd gone home the long way round in order to avoid him.

She could hear the cries of children outside in the street and went into the parlour to peep through the lace curtain, hungry for signs of life, an indication that she was not the only person alive in the world that day. The children were playing with their new toys, skipping ropes, whips and tops, one or two scooters, on the narrow strip of pavement cleared to make a pathway. It was strange to see lights on in most parlours. Probably people were getting the tables ready for their Christmas dinner. A woman ran across the street and knocked on a door. The door was opened and Helen heard the sound of laughter as the woman entered. She saw the old man opposite, Mr Singerman, spruced up in his best suit, shuffle along to the neighbouring house and be let in by a lovely tall red-haired woman wearing a royal blue dress. Two cats emerged out of the back entry and chased each other down the street. Listening hard, Helen could hear singing from the King's Arms. *'Bless em all, bless em all, The long and the short and the tall.'* Helen shivered in the cold parlour and returned to sit by the fire in the living room.

'Oh, Lou!' she whispered. 'Oh, someone!'

At first, she thought she'd imagined the knock on the door. When it sounded again, she began to tremble. Lou! Who else could it be? She didn't move. Despite the fact she ached for company, Lou Murphy would never set foot in her house again. Yet . . .

Against her will, she felt herself being drawn into the hallway. Answering would make all the difference to the day. She was standing behind the door, wrestling with her emotions, when the letter box rattled and someone called, 'Are you all right, Miss Brazier?'

She wasn't sure whether to be disappointed or relieved when she realised it wasn't Lou, but the blind man from next door, Paddy O'Hara. She wondered why he should care? Why he should think she was *not* all right? For a moment, she considered merely shouting back that she was fine, but he was a nice man, gentle and courteous and, after all, it was Christmas Day.

She opened the door and he touched his cap politely. It was the first time she'd seen him without his little white dog.

'Yes?' she asked. Oh, why did it have to come out sounding so abrupt, almost rude?

'I'm just on me way to the King's Arms. I thought I'd stop by and wish you a Merry Christmas, like.' There was a guarded look on his face. Helen realised he was expecting to be snubbed.

'And a Merry Christmas to you.' She swallowed. 'Thanks for asking.' She made to close the door as a signal the conversation was over, expecting him to tip his cap again and go away. But, of course, she'd forgotten, he couldn't see!

'Are you all right, luv?' He actually looked worried.

Helen tried to laugh. 'Why shouldn't I be?'

He made a funny little movement with his mouth. 'Well, the walls of these houses are terrible thin.'

He'd heard her crying! She felt as if she could die on the spot with shame. 'I had a bit of upsetting news. I'm all right now.'

'Mind you, it's a wonder I could hear. I've shed a tear or two meself the last few days. There's nowt wrong with a good cry when you need it. I had to have Spot, me best friend, put down. He had cancer of the stomach, according to the vet.'

She felt a sudden pang of compassion. A blind man losing his dog was a terrible thing. 'I'm awful sorry. I bet you miss him.'

'More than words can say,' he replied sadly.

She swallowed again. 'Look, would you like to come in for a drink? I've got some wine.'

'Wine! I wouldn't say no. Sounds more inviting, like, than a pint of brown ale.'

He began to tap the snow with his stick, feeling for the doorstep.

'Here,' she said, 'Let me give you a hand.' She reached out and helped him into the hall. Once inside, he removed his cap and tucked it into the pocket of his jacket. He towered above her. She'd never noticed before, but he was a fine-looking man, though rather gaunt, his face weathered ruddy by being outdoors so much, and with neatly cut fair hair. You would never have guessed he was blind, except his pale blue eyes never met yours, but were fixed on your mouth or chin, on where the voice came from.

'What d'you fancy?' she asked. 'Red or white?'

'Whew! Thank God that's over!'

Eileen flung herself into a chair. The table had been cleared and set again for tea, the dishes washed and dried and all the debris off Christmas crackers and presents tied in a neat parcel, as they'd been urged by the Government to save paper. Mary and Ryan were having their afternoon nap upstairs on Eileen's bed, whilst Caitlin and Siobhan argued over a hair slide out of a cracker. Tony and the older boys, fed up with being tripped over and moved from place to place, had gone over to the Reillys' house to play with their new toys in peace.

'I wonder what happened to Paddy?' Sheila mused.

'Well, Dad said he weren't in the King's Arms when he left, and I sent Tony along to the house, and he weren't there, either,' Eileen said worriedly. 'I hope he's all right.

What d'you think, Dad?'

Jack Doyle had fallen asleep in front of the fire. The sisters smiled at each other.

'Oh, well,' Eileen shrugged. 'There's nowt we can do about it, is there? D'you fancy a glass of sherry, Sheil? If you do, you'll have to get it yourself. I'm fair worn out. I've been on the go since half past seven this morning.'

'D'you want one?'

'Please!' As she took the drink, Eileen said, 'I wonder what we'll be doing next Christmas? They say rationing's likely to come in any minute. That's why everyone went mad and spent like there was no tomorrow if they had the cash to do it. Maybe we won't be able to buy chickens and puddings and presents next year. On the other hand, maybe the war'll be over . . .'

'I can't think that far ahead,' Sheila confessed. 'All I can think of is our Cal and when he's likely to be home.'

Winston Churchill had ordered the Navy to 'scrub and search' the South Atlantic for the *Altmark*. It was suspected that the ship was sailing under different names and different flags.

The two little girls were having a tug of war with the hair slide. It snapped in two and Siobhan fell back against her grandad.

Jack Doyle woke up. 'Has our gracious majesty been on yet?' he demanded. When told no, he groaned. 'I'd been hoping to sleep right through it.'

'Dad! You've got a gob on you like a bee's bum. You must be the most unpatriotic man who ever lived,' his eldest daughter said.

'You can be a republican and a patriot,' he answered tartly. 'Where's our Sean?'

'Gone. He's having tea at his girlfriend's.'

'The flighty bugger! There can't be a girl in Bootle he

hasn't been out with. Still, it won't do him no harm to sow his wild oats early.'

'Let's hope the girls' dads agree,' said Eileen. She got to her feet. 'I'm just popping along to Annie's for a minute to look at her feller.'

'Annie's got a feller?' Sheila looked surprised.

'Well, she's considering it.'

When Eileen went outside, Dilys and Myfanwy Evans were standing on their doorstep looking scared.

'What's the matter?' she shouted.

'It's our Dad. He hasn't been home for his dinner.'

Suddenly, Ellis and Dai Evans came crashing out of the King's Arms, locked in combat, followed by Mack and several customers trying to separate them.

'I'll kill you, man. May the good lord forgive me, but I'll kill you,' screamed Ellis.

The pair fell into the snow and began to wrestle as Eileen knocked on Annie's door.

Annie answered, all decked out in a silver filigree necklace and earrings, with a blue and red striped scarf draped around her neck.

'Just look, Eil! The boys brought me these from France. Feel the scarf? It's pure silk!'

'You lucky devil!' Eileen said, impressed. 'See what's going on out here! Ellis and Dai are having a grand ould fight.'

The Evanses had begun to drag each other home. Eileen and Annie watched until they went inside and slammed the door.

'They'll make it up in bed tonight. Ellis and Dai have what's called a stormy relationship.' Annie winked. 'Come and say hallo to Barney. The lads have gone to see some of their old mates, and Rosie and Charlie went home a while ago.'

Barney wasn't at all what Eileen had expected. She'd anticipated someone looking like Franchot Tone or Cary Grant. Instead, he was a little teddy bear of a man with a thatch of slightly receding brown hair and humorous tobacco-coloured eyes.

'Pleased to meet any friend of Annie's,' he said, when they were introduced.

'I'll get you a drop of sherry, Eil.' Annie left for the kitchen.

As soon as she'd gone, Barney clutched Eileen's arm. 'Does she talk about me much? D'you think she likes me?'

'I've no idea,' Eileen replied. When his face fell, she went on, determined to support Annie in her campaign of playing hard to get. 'In fact, your name only came up for the first time this morning.'

'Oh, no!' He looked distraught. 'I've never liked a woman before as much as I like Annie. I could tell, the minute I saw her standing there with that riveting gun, that she was the only one for me.'

'Really!' Eileen tried hard not to sound sarcastic. She was worried her best friend might fall for some worthless man who'd end up making her unhappy. She wasn't sure if she liked Barney Clegg or not.

'*Really!*' Barney said with all the sincerity he could muster.

Eileen could hear Annie on her way in with the sherry. She said quickly, 'Just make sure y'don't hurt her.'

She didn't stay long. 'I'm expecting a few folk round any minute to listen to the wireless.'

Mr Singerman was already making his way across the road when Eileen left Annie's, followed, much to her amazement, by the Flemings. Mrs Fleming looked like a film star, in a royal blue dress and a black fluffy mohair coat. Eileen would have given her eye teeth for a pair of those ankle-length, high-heeled boots.

Mr Singerman raised his bushy grey eyebrows. 'You don't mind, do you, Eileen? I told them they'd be welcome.'

'Of course I don't,' she said.

'We've got a wireless,' Mrs Fleming put in quickly. 'It's all in one with the gramophone, but without electricity . . .' She drew Eileen to one side. 'I'm sorry I was so rude the day we moved in. I was upset, but that's no excuse. I've brought a peace offering.' She handed Eileen a tiny drawstring paper bag.

Eileen opened the bag and drew out a bottle of Chanel scent. She gasped. 'Oh, my goodness! This must have cost the earth. Thank you, Mrs Fleming, but there was no need.'

'It's not new. I mean,' the woman said hastily, 'I've had it some time, but it's never been opened. And call me Jess, please.'

'Thank you, Jess,' Eileen said, feeling touched.

They went inside, where the wireless was already on and a boy's choir was singing *The Holly and the Ivy*. Brenda Mahon and Aggie Donovan were there, and Tony and the boys had returned with two headless soldiers, tired of fighting and anxious for something to eat.

Eileen drew her son onto her lap. 'In a minute,' she whispered. 'As soon as the King's finished.'

It was strange, almost uncanny, to think that millions of people all over the country were doing the exact same thing at the same time, sitting round the wireless to hear their King. She wondered if Nick were listening, and tried to visualise him sitting in his friends' house.

The National Anthem sounded particularly stirring.

225

For the first time, Eileen felt a sense of real pride in her country. She forgot her previous impatience with Chamberlain and his government. It was a brave thing that had been done, taking on Hitler and the might of the German Army, declaring war on Fascism and all it represented. She glanced at Mr Singerman. His head was bent and he had one hand over his eyes and she knew he was thinking of Ruth.

The King was speaking. She could tell from the tone of his gentle, stammering voice that he knew how his people felt. He shared their concerns and sympathised. He finished his speech with a poem. *'I said to the man who stood at the Gate of the Year, "Give me a light that I may tread safely into the unknown." And he replied, "Go out into the darkness and put your hand into the hand of God. That shall be to you better than light and safer than a known way".'*

Chapter 9

To her relief, Eileen was on the morning shift the week after Christmas, which meant she was home by early afternoon and could spend the rest of the day with Tony, who was on holiday from school.

On the first day back, the younger women were full of the wonderful time they'd had at their Christmas dances.

'I went home with a different feller every night,' Doris boasted. 'One of 'em even wanted to marry me.'

'Did 'ya say "yes"?' Carmel shouted across the workshop.

'Not bloody likely! While the war's on, I'm having far too good a time to stick to one feller. I'll think about getting hitched once it's over.'

Later on, Doris announced she was going straight into town from work to buy a frock for New Year's Eve in the sales. 'It's gotta have sequins on. I'm dying for a frock with sequins.'

'Where are you off to New Year's Eve?' Lil asked.

'St George's Hall. It's not just a dance, it's a ball. The tickets cost five bob each.'

'I'm going, too,' said Theresa. 'Me mam made a dress for me Christmas present.'

'Catch me paying five bleeding bob for a dance, even if it is a ball,' someone remarked.

'What are you doing on New Year's Eve, Eileen?' Pauline asked.

'Nothing special. I suppose I'll just go over to me sister's.'

'Why don't you come with us?'

'Oh, I'd want to see the New Year in with me family, particularly our Tony.'

'Well, y'can always leave early,' Doris put in. 'Though you'd miss the best part. It's lovely when everybody joins hands and sings *Auld Lang Syne* together.'

'I haven't got a dance frock,' said Eileen, though the idea appealed to her. Sheila wouldn't mind, and Dad would be over, anyroad, as soon as the King's Arms closed. 'I'll think about it,' she promised.

'Is there any news yet about that ship your brother-in-law's on?' Pauline asked.

'No. It seems to have disappeared off the high seas altogether.'

'Don't worry. The Navy'll find it soon enough.'

'Well if they don't, our Sheila's likely to hire a rowboat and go looking for it herself!' said Eileen.

After a hurried meal she went outside, more anxious than she liked to admit, to meet Nick again. She hadn't seen him for ten whole days.

She felt her whole body tingle as he came sliding along the frozen stream towards her, a tweed cap on his head and a red scarf wrapped twice around his neck, the ends floating out behind. 'You look like a Christmas card,' she exclaimed.

Nick drew to a halt and looked up at her unsmilingly. 'I've missed you badly,' he said. The message in his brown eyes made her heart turn over.

'Oh!' 'And I've missed you too,' she wanted to say. 'In fact, I hardly stopped thinking about you over Christmas.' But she could never say such things to him! Worried he might read an answering message in her own eyes, she glanced around at the white fields. 'I can't imagine it ever being green again.'

He gave a quirky little smile, as if he could read her mind. 'It will be. As sure as night follows day, it will be.'

'Did you have a nice Christmas?' Eileen asked conversationally, glad the disturbing moment was over.

'Somewhat lonesome, but okay,' he replied lightly.

'I thought you were going to stay with friends in London?'

'I changed my mind in view of the arctic weather.'

Eileen was immediately concerned. 'Y'don't mean you spent it all by yourself? I didn't realise.'

'And would you have done anything about it if you *had* realised?' He held out his hand and she helped him struggle up the snowy bank beside her. 'I mean, would I have been invited to Christmas dinner at Pearl Street if you'd known I was eating sausage and mash all on my own?'

'Sausage and mash! Oh, Nick!'

'So? Would I? Have been invited, that is?'

They began to stroll along the bank together. At their approach, several birds came fluttering out of the white bushes, disturbing the snow, which fell with a dull plopping sound.

'They're starving, poor little things,' Eileen said. 'I'll bring some breadcrumbs tomorrow.'

'I take it you've no intention of answering my question.' He took her arm and linked it in his.

'How could I have invited you?' she demanded. 'I'm not footloose and fancy free like you. I've got a family to consider. You're like a little child, the way you expect things to happen without any regard for the consequences. How d'you know me husband wasn't there over Christmas, anyroad?'

'Because last time we met, you said it was unlikely. Was he?'

'No,' she muttered.

He stopped and turned her towards him, holding her firmly by the arms. 'You don't love him, do you?'

She dropped her eyes. 'What makes you say that?'

'Because you wouldn't be here if you did,' he said reasonably. 'If I'd sent you an entire flower shop, you wouldn't have come if you loved him. Some women would, but not you, Eileen. You're not a flirt. You came because you like me, perhaps as much as I like you. I might even love you, I'm not sure.'

Eileen wriggled out of his grasp. 'Don't say those sort of things!'

'Why not, when they're true? Admit it, Eileen, you don't love your husband.'

'So what if I don't,' she cried. 'What difference does it make?'

'For Chrissakes, woman,' he exploded. 'There's a war on. By this time next year we might both be dead. You can't deny there's something between us, can you?'

She took a deep breath. 'No.'

'Then come out with me,' he demanded. 'Let me take you to dinner one night?'

Eileen shook her head vigorously. 'I can't.'

'Why not?'

'Because . . .' she paused.

'Because what?'

'Because . . .' She paused again, and struggled for the words. 'It's just not done. I'd have to lie to people.'

'You never know, it might be worth it,' he said with a sardonic laugh.

'I could never lie to me family,' she said adamantly.

'Oh, well. I suppose that's that, then. It's a waste of

time us seeing each other again.' He stuffed his hands in his pockets and began to walk swiftly ahead. Eileen ran to catch up.

'Nick! You're not being fair.'

To her utter relief, he turned on her, smiling. 'No, I'm not, am I? I'm being unreasonable. It's just that I missed you so much. Am I forgiven?'

She would have forgiven him anything. 'Of course you are.'

Later on, he confessed he hadn't had sausage and mash for Christmas dinner, but had gone to the hostel and enjoyed a magnificent spread with half a dozen workmates who'd remained behind. He hadn't listened to the King's speech, either. 'We were as drunk as lords by then.'

'You bloody liar,' she said indignantly. 'And here was me, feeling sorry for you.'

'That's why I said it. I love it when that concerned look comes into your eyes and you worry over me.'

Tony Costello was glad he was an only child. He'd hate to share his mam with five brothers and sisters like his cousin, Dominic. He also liked peace and quiet from time to time, something you never got at the Reillys'. After spending the whole morning in his auntie's house, the noise began to get on his nerves. As soon as he'd eaten his dinner, he told his Auntie Sheila he was going home. Mam would be back from work soon, and in the meantime, he felt like doing a picture with the paints he'd got off his grandad for Christmas.

'Have you got a key, luv?' Auntie Sheila asked.

'It's in me pocket.' For some reason, grandad had changed the locks and there was no longer a key hanging from the letterbox inside the door.

Once home, he filled an egg cup with water and set the paintbox on the table, along with his big drawing pad. He'd already done five paintings since Christmas. He pursed his mouth, adjusted his wire-rimmed glasses, and glanced around the room, wondering what to paint this time. He decided on the vase of paper flowers on the sideboard. Mam said when he'd finished the book, she'd choose the best one and put it in a frame in the parlour.

The picture was almost finished when he heard a knock on the door and went to answer it, hoping it wasn't Dominic wanting to come in and play.

He wasn't quite sure what to think when he found his dad standing outside on the pavement.

'It seems me key won't fit the lock any more,' his dad said curtly as he pushed past into the hall. Tony followed nervously. He never seemed able to do the right thing as far as his dad was concerned. Apparently he'd done the wrong thing straight away, because, after throwing his kit bag on the floor, Dad nodded at the painting and said contemptuously, 'What the hell's this?'

'It's for me mam,' Tony explained in a small voice.

'You should've spread a newspaper out. You've got paint on the cloth, see!' His long, nicotine-stained finger seemed to quiver as he pointed to the spots.

'I'm sorry.'

'So you bloody should be. And it's cissy, a lad painting flowers.' He folded the sheet in two and stamped on it with his fist. Tony realised the wet picture would be ruined. 'Can't you paint something to do with the war, like a tank?'

Tony bit his lip. 'Annie gave me a tank for Christmas. I'll paint that, if you like.'

When his dad nodded, Tony ran upstairs to get the tank. Halfway down, dad shouted, 'Fetch me the Johnnie

Walker and a glass out the parlour.'

Tony had no idea what Johnnie Walker was, but felt too terrified to ask. But if he wanted a glass, it must be something to drink. He opened the best sideboard cupboard. There was only one bottle there and although he couldn't read yet, he recognised the initials on the label.

'Ta.' His dad was removing his overcoat when Tony went in. 'Does your mam usually leave you by yourself when she's at work?' he asked. He poured himself a drink, swallowed it quickly and poured another.

Tony shook his head. 'Annie looks after me, or me Auntie Sheila. I came home to do some painting.'

'Huh!' Dad said contemptuously. He rubbed his hands together. 'It's cold in here. Why didn't you pull the flue out on the fire?'

'I'm not allowed to touch it.'

'So, you could freeze to death, could you, and she doesn't give a damn?' He removed the fire guard and pulled out the flue, then turned impatiently on his son. 'Come on, then, get on with it!' When Tony gave him a puzzled look, he snapped, 'The painting!'

With trembling fingers, Tony began to mix the paints to get a khaki colour. He desperately wished he'd stayed with Dominic and prayed his mam would come home soon. He'd only make a hash of things with his dad watching over his shoulder. At one point, Dad leaned across and squeezed his arm so hard that the little boy felt tears come to his eyes.

'You've done that bit wrong!'

To his relief, after a while Dad seemed to lose interest and, taking off his jacket and shirt, went into the kitchen in his khaki vest and began to get washed.

At last, mam's key sounded in the door. She was

laughing as she spoke to someone outside.

'Thanks, Jess. I'd love to read them,' she called. Then, 'Tony, I'm home.'

She took her coat off in the hall and hung it up. He looked up at her beseechingly as she entered the room. Her face seemed to freeze when she saw his dad standing in the kitchen doorway. She came across, kissed Tony's cheek and said, 'Go on over to your Auntie Sheila's for a minute, luv.'

Tony leaped off the chair and was out of the house like a shot.

The slam of the front door seemed to reverberate through the house as Francis Costello stared at his wife. He couldn't understand her. He'd never cared much for women and had felt no inclination to get married until the suggestion had been made that he might get into parliament, and he realised a wife and family was a necessary appendage for a man in the public eye. He'd chosen Eileen Doyle, who was presentable and came from a good family. As far as he was concerned, she now belonged to him. He owned her, just as he owned his child, and the furniture in the house. That she should refuse to do his bidding was as incomprehensible as if one of his chairs refused to let him sit in it. At the same time, he felt confused. What was she complaining about? What had he done wrong? He didn't quite know how to deal with the situation.

'I see you've changed the lock on the door,' he said cuttingly.

'Both doors. It was me dad's idea,' Eileen replied.

His face darkened as he took in the implication of her words. His mentor, Jack Doyle, had turned against him.

'So, you told him,' he growled.

'Told him what, Francis?'

'Told him lies, that's what.'

She pushed past and began to fill the kettle with water. 'I didn't tell him half the truth,' she said. 'Now, if you don't mind, Francis, I'd like you to finish getting washed and go. If y'don't, then I'm off to me dad's with Tony. So, take your pick.'

'I'm staying. This is my house, and I'm staying.' The smouldering anger in Francis's head turned into a wrathful blaze.

'Please yourself. In that case, I'll pack a few things in a minute.'

The anger exploded. His head felt as if it was on fire. 'Oh, no you don't! You're my wife! You stay where I tell you to stay and you're staying here.'

'I'm sorry, Francis,' she said with a cool smile.

He knew he had to make her see sense once and for all, otherwise his entire world would collapse. He lifted the roller towel off the rung behind the kitchen door and put it in the sink, which was half full of water.

'What d'you think you're doing?' Eileen exclaimed.

Francis wrung the towel out, twisting and twisting until the coarse cloth became a thick rope. Then he turned on his wife and lashed out. The towel caught her around the neck and she screamed and fell against the wall. He lashed out again and again, first one way, then the other, until she slid, sobbing, down the wall onto the floor.

Staring down at her cowering form, Francis felt a sense of power, mixed with a throb of excitement. 'So, who's your husband, Eileen?'

'You are, Francis,' she said shakily.

He smiled. She'd learnt her lesson. 'And whose house is this?'

'It's yours.'

'Right then. And *my* wife's staying in *my* house, and that's all there is to it.'

He turned away. The matter was settled. There'd be no more whining from now on.

'But you won't be me husband for long, Francis. I'm getting a divorce. And as for the house, you can keep it. I'll find another one for me and our Tony.'

She was looking at him, eyes full of hate. Francis felt the sense of power, the excitement, ebb away, to be replaced with a rage greater and blacker than anything he'd felt before. The woman was stupid. She had to be taught an even harder lesson.

She was on all fours, trying to get back on her feet. He bent over and wrapped the towel around her neck and pulled. As he pulled and heard her choke, the excitement returned.

'You bloody bitch!' he snarled.

'Francis!'

He felt hands tugging at him, but scarcely noticed. The hands had no more strength than a bird. A woman, not Eileen, began to scream, but he still ignored it, too intent on punishing his wife to care. It wasn't until the scalding water touched his neck that he yelped in pain and let go.

Sheila Reilly was standing over him with a kettle of boiling water. She must have let herself in with a key.

'Get away from her!'

Francis stumbled blindly out of the kitchen and went upstairs. Sheila bent over her sister, who was lying on the floor, thankfully not dead, but panting hoarsely for breath.

'Eileen! Oh, luv! Are you all right?'

Eileen gave a little nod. 'Where is he?' she croaked.

'Upstairs.'

'I never want to see him again as long as I live.'

'You won't, luv, not if I've got anything to do with it. The minute you feel up to it, I'll help you over to our house.' Gently, she began to stroke Eileen's long fair hair. 'Oh, Sis,' she went on in a rush, 'I wish I'd come before. Tony said his dad was home, and I didn't give it a second thought. Then, all of a sudden, I got a funny feeling there was something wrong.'

'Thank God you came when you did.'

'Oh, Eil! I poured boiling water on him!'

'Well, it did the trick, didn't it?' Wincing painfully, Eileen sat up. Sheila helped her to her feet and into the living room, where she sank, groaning, into a chair.

'I never thought I was capable of such a thing!' Sheila said in an awed voice. 'But it seemed the only way to stop him. How d'you feel? Could you make your way across the road?'

'In a minute. I wish he weren't upstairs.' Unable to help herself, Eileen burst into tears. 'He nearly killed me!'

'Oh, Sis!' Sheila was in a dilemma. She'd left six small children at home, seven, if you included Tony, and she was worried about Ryan, who was crawling around, getting into everything. But how could she abandon Eileen in this state and with Francis still upstairs? To her relief, there was a knock on the door and she ran to open it. Jessica Fleming was outside, carrying an armful of magazines.

'Your sister said she'd like to. . .'

'Come in, quick, and look after our Eileen while I get someone to take care of me kids.' Sheila dragged the woman inside. 'I'll be as quick as I can.'

'Why?' asked Jessica in astonishment. 'What's the matter?'

'You'll see.'

Jessica went in, to find Eileen Costello with her blouse

undone, examining an assortment of angry weals on her body. Her neck was red raw. She looked up at the newcomer, eyes swollen with tears.

'What the hell's happened?' Jessica demanded in astonishment. 'Who did that?'

Eileen made a wry face. 'Me husband,' she whispered.

Jessica's jaw dropped. 'The bastard! Where is he?'

'Upstairs.'

'*Upstairs!* Have you called the police?'

'What's the point? A man has the right to do what he likes to his wife, so long as he don't kill her.'

Jessica Fleming lost her temper easily, but even she hadn't realised she was capable of such fury on behalf of someone she scarcely knew. It took her completely by surprise. To think a man could do this and get away with it! Her blood boiled.

'I'll kill him! I'll bloody kill him.' She picked the poker up off the hearth.

'Please don't!' Eileen grabbed her arm, wincing. 'I've had enough. I can't stand the thought of more trouble. And there's Tony to consider.'

Jessica flung the poker back. She noticed the khaki shirt and jacket on the chair, the overcoat, the kitbag, and collecting them together, threw the lot into the hall.

'Eh, you up there!' she screamed. 'Get these on, and be out of the house before I come up and smash your bloody face to a pulp! If you're not gone in five minutes, I'll fetch the Bobbies to you.'

To her surprise, when she went back, Eileen was actually grinning.

'You should have heard yourself. You sounded a right ould Mary Ellen.'

'I feel like a right ould Mary Ellen at the moment,' Jessica replied unashamedly.

They both stopped and listened to the sound of footsteps descending the stairs. Jessica stood by the fire, ready to take up the poker if the man came in. She saw a tall, handsome figure pass the door into the hall without a sideways glance at the waiting women. No-one spoke as Francis put on his clothes. A few minutes later the front door slammed.

'He's gone,' Jessica announced, unnecessarily. 'Good riddance to bad rubbish, as they say.'

Eileen sank back with a sigh of relief.

'How long has this been going on?' Jessica demanded.

'Since not long after we were married. Though he's never hurt me this bad before,' she added hastily.

Jessica said nothing. One of their old friends, a doctor, had told her once about the women who came into the Emergency Department of the hospital, with their broken bones and black eyes and bleeding faces, come by at the hands of violent, brutal husbands. The police were never called, charges were never pressed. The women were attended to and went back to their tormentors, to return to the hospital again and again for their wounds to be tended.

'I can't understand it,' the doctor said. 'I can only assume they're stupid. They must like being beaten black and blue.'

Jessica, who wouldn't have put up with it for five minutes, couldn't understand it, either. Yet Eileen Costello wasn't stupid. Jessica had a horrible feeling she might have overstepped the mark. Perhaps Eileen hadn't wanted her husband thrown out so unceremoniously. Perhaps this was just par for the course and in half an hour, if Jessica hadn't been there, everything would have been back to normal. She glanced at the woman; her eyes were closed, her breath came in little faint gasps, and her white face had a slightly blue tinge.

'Shall I send for the doctor?' she asked worriedly.

Eileen opened her eyes. 'No, ta. I already feel better than I did. I'm awful sorry you got involved,' she added apologetically. 'I bet this sort of thing doesn't happen round Calderstones.'

Jessica smiled. 'I'm afraid I completely lost my temper. I can't remember feeling so worked up before. I hope I did the right thing.'

'Well, you got rid of him in a hurry. Thanks.'

So, it was all right then! Jessica felt relieved. 'It's none of my business, but you're not going to sit back and let this happen again, are you?'

Eileen shook her head. 'He only tried to strangle me when I told him I wanted a divorce – though I haven't a clue how you go about getting one.'

'You need to see a solicitor,' Jessica advised.

'Yes, but in the meanwhile, there's nowt to stop him coming back whenever he likes. I daren't tell me dad what happened. He'd only track Francis down and kill him. It was him who changed the locks, though he'd no right. It's Francis's house, and by law, he can come and go as he pleases. I'll start looking for somewhere else. I'm earning enough money meself to pay the rent and buy a few odds and ends of furniture.'

Jessica glanced around the neat little room, noting the modern fireplace, the electric light. 'It seems a shame. You've got this place looking very nice.' If it had been one of her properties, the rent book would have been in Eileen's name by tomorrow!

'Would you like a cup of tea?' she asked.

'Please! Me throat's aching for one.' As Jessica went into the back kitchen, Eileen noticed the magazines she'd brought on the table. The top cover showed a model dripping with diamonds and wearing a glamorous satin ballgown with an off-the-shoulder neck trimmed with bunched organdie flowers. The woman was standing on a balcony, her lovely face silhouetted against a panoramic view of London by night. In one hand she casually held a fur coat, most of which was draped on the floor. The picture bore so little relation to her own life that Eileen gave a cracked, sardonic laugh.

'What's so funny?' Jessica called in surprise.

'I just remembered something. I was planning on going to a ball on New Year's Eve with some of the girls from work.'

Jessica appeared in the doorway. 'You can still go. It's days off yet.'

'I haven't got a frock. I can't try one on in a shop looking like this, can I? What would the assistant think?'

'I'll lend you one,' Jessica offered. She glanced at the magazine and smiled. 'It won't be as grand as that, but I've two wardrobes full of clothes. We're the same height. You can always tighten the belt or take it in a bit if it's too big around the waist.'

'I'm not sure if I'll be in the mood.' Eileen made a face. 'Dancing's the last thing I feel like at the moment.'

'It'll do you good,' Jessica said brightly. 'Take your mind off things.'

Despite Sheila's protests, Eileen went into work the following day, covering her still raw neck with a scarf — the last thing she wanted was curious comments from the girls. But by the time the tea trolley arrived, she was beginning to wish she'd heeded her sister's advice and stayed at home. The heat in the workshop was tremendous. Her neck and the weals on her body began to burn and she felt as if she'd been branded with hot irons. Reaching across the machine was such agony it was all she could do not to shout out loud in pain.

'Are you all right, Eileen?' Doris called, once work had recommenced. 'You don't look a hundred per cent today.'

Eileen didn't answer. The question had seemed to come from a long way away. She felt herself begin to sway and had enough sense to step back from the machine before sinking onto the floor. Someone shouted, 'Catch her, quick!' and Eileen remembered no more until she came to on a bed in a little white-painted room, with Sister Kean bending over her.

'You've certainly been in the wars!'

Sister Kean was a stocky, thickset woman with an abrupt manner and a faint black moustache, which was the subject of much hilarity in the workshop, where she was referred to as 'Hitler's sister'.

Eileen became aware her overalls and scarf had been removed and her blouse was undone. 'I had an accident,' she said defensively.

'You don't say! How are you feeling?'

'A bit dizzy, that's all.' She tried to sit up, but failed.

'Miss Thomas has gone to get you a cup of tea.'

Eileen groaned. Miss Thomas would be bound to want to know how she'd come by her injuries.

When she arrived, in the sensible flat shoes and navy striped suit she wore every day, Miss Thomas duly did. She sat on the edge of the bed and demanded in a shocked voice, 'Who did this to you, Eileen?'

Somewhat annoyed, Eileen nevertheless tried to be polite. 'I know you're only doing your job, but it's none of your business.'

'But perhaps there's something I can do to help?'

'What, exactly?' asked Eileen.

'I could inform you of your legal rights, for instance.'

'Really?' Eileen said sarcastically, with visions of telling Francis during the process of being strangled, 'You've no legal right to do this.'

Miss Thomas's earnest freckled face fell and Eileen felt uncomfortable, knowing she was being difficult – 'bolshie', as her dad would have said. Miss Thomas really cared about her charges. There was only one woman's overseer for the morning and afternoon shifts, and she always seemed to be there, no matter how early or late, except when she was seeing a girl in hospital, or sorting out a domestic problem. The trouble was, Eileen resented being one of the charges. She preferred to take care of her own affairs.

'Are you ready for this tea?' Thankfully, Miss Thomas appeared to have abandoned the interrogation.

'Yes, ta.'

'As soon as you feel up to it, I'll drive you home.'

'There's no need,' Eileen protested. 'I'll get back to work after dinner.'

'You'll do no such thing,' Miss Thomas said firmly. 'In fact, I don't want to see you here again until next Monday.'

'But. . .'

'No buts. You'll get sick pay, so you won't be out of pocket.'

Eileen, thinking of Tony on holiday all week, protested no more. Miss Thomas left, promising to come back in half an hour to take her home. Sister Kean brought Eileen's coat from the locker.

'D'you mind fetching Alfie?' Eileen asked the nurse. 'I'd like a word with him before I go.'

'Miss Thomas will tell Alfie all he needs to know,'

Sister Kean said abruptly.

'No, she won't. This is personal.'

'As you wish. I'll go and fetch him.'

The little black car chugged through the countryside, with Miss Thomas bent anxiously over the steering wheel, which was clutched tightly in her leather-gloved hands. She wore a mouldy fur coat that had seen many better days, and a battered felt hat, equally old.

'I hate driving in this weather,' she said.

The ditches each side of the narrow roads were piled high with snow. They passed Aintree Racecourse, an expanse of smooth, untrodden white.

'This is where they run the Grand National, isn't it?' Miss Thomas remarked. 'Have you ever been?'

Eileen shook her head. 'It's too cruel. Every year they shoot a couple of horses, but the horses didn't ask to run. They should shoot the jockeys, instead. That might make them realise how cruel it is.'

Miss Thomas looked at her in surprise. 'That's a very astute remark, Eileen.'

Eileen felt a sense of irritation. You'd think she was a child who'd said something unexpectedly intelligent. 'Why look so amazed? D'you think the working classes aren't capable of making astute remarks?' She didn't care if it sounded rude.

'I'm sorry. I was being patronising.' Miss Thomas looked flustered as she braked on a curve and the car skidded on the icy road. There was silence for a while. Then she said, 'You don't like me much, do you, Eileen? I could tell, right from the start.'

Eileen didn't answer straight away. 'It's not so much *you* I don't like,' she said eventually. 'It's your attitude. I can't understand why you think, because you're middle class, you can solve all the problems of us working classes. For all I know, you've problems of your own, but we never hear about them. Instead, we're made to feel we're the only ones who can't manage our money, or our men, or take care of our children.'

'It's the job I was employed to do,' Miss Thomas said defensively. She looked rather shaken by Eileen's attack. 'I'm there to look after the women's welfare.'

'Well, it's about time they trained working-class women to look after their own welfare.' Eileen hadn't dreamt she could be so vocal. 'All the charities, the Public Assistance boards, everywhere you turn for help, it's run by posh people who don't know what it's like to be dead poor and bring up half a dozen kids on thirty bob a week, at the same time as being beaten silly by your husband.'

'Is that what happened to you, Eileen?' Miss Thomas asked quickly.

Eileen could have bitten off her tongue. 'That's got nothing to do with it,' she said coldly.

'Because if so, violent husbands belong right across the social strata, from the very top to the very bottom.'

'Meaning I'm at the bottom, I suppose.'

'Oh, dear! I keep saying the wrong thing,' said Miss Thomas, flustered again. 'It's just that I knew a woman once whose husband was a highly respected lawyer with a title, a King's Counsel, well liked and popular with his friends. But with his wife, he was brutal beyond belief. He treated her like an animal. I won't go into all the things he did, you might not believe them, but he would make her sleep on the floor beside his bed or lock her in a cupboard for hours at a time. The servants pretended not to notice. When one little kitchen maid plucked up the courage to tell the police, they laughed in her face. "What? Sir Edward Matthews! Be off with you, girl, or we'll have you in for slander."'

'Why didn't she leave?' asked Eileen incredulously.

They'd come to the corner of a busy road where there was little snow to be seen, except on the roofs of the shops and in little dirty mounds in the gutter. Miss Thomas muttered, 'Isn't this filthy,' as she turned into the traffic, and the windscreen was immediately sprayed with dirt from a lorry in front.

'Why didn't she leave?' she repeated thoughtfully, almost to herself. 'She didn't leave because she had three daughters. She knew there was no way she would be allowed to have her girls.'

'Is she still there?' Eileen asked.

Miss Thomas shook her head. 'Five years ago, she realised she had the choice of leaving or losing her sanity. She left.'

'Without the children?'

'Without the children. They never realised what was going on and always preferred jovial daddy to their cowed, browbeaten mother. They're all in their teens now. She writes to them, but they don't reply. They think she just walked out on them, you see.' Miss Thomas gave a little nervous laugh. 'In the meantime, our heroine reverted to her maiden name, trained to be a social worker and went to work in London's East End to help other women who were being brutalised by their husbands. Then, when the war began, she got a job as the Women's Overseer in Dunnings.'

Eileen had already begun to suspect the truth. 'I think it's my turn to be sorry,' she said humbly.

'Just don't think we all do it to make ourselves feel virtuous, Eileen,' Miss Thomas said softly. 'Some of us genuinely want to help.' Suddenly, she smiled briskly and patted Eileen's knee. 'Now, I must confess I have no idea where I am. You'd better direct me from now on if you want to get home to Bootle.'

'What do I look like?' Eileen demanded.

'You look dead nice, Mam, honest,' Tony assured her.

'Are you positive you don't mind me going out on New Year's Eve, like? I mean, I'll stay home if you prefer.'

'No, Mam,' Tony said for the tenth time. 'Mr Singerman's going to teach me and Dominic and Niall how to play Monopoly. Auntie Sheila's lit the fire in the parlour, and Grandad's promised to bring lemonade when he comes.' He was very much looking forward to the evening ahead. He was being allowed to stay up as late as he liked – till midnight, if he could remain awake that long.

'Your Grandad won't approve of Monopoly. He'll say it's just learning you to be a capitalist.'

Tony had no idea what a capitalist was and didn't care. His mam had yet another look at her face in the mirror. She'd done her hair differently. It was pinned in a cushiony bump on top of her head. The posh lady, Mrs Fleming, from over the road, had loaned her a cream lace blouse with a high neck, the sort of blouse, he gathered from their conversation, that Queen Mary wore, and a brown velvet skirt. Mam looked a bit like a queen herself tonight, he thought proudly, though he couldn't help but wish she'd get a move on.

'If only I had a different coloured coat,' she said worriedly. 'Navy doesn't go with brown at all.'

Tony couldn't understand why she should care. Surely she'd take her coat off to dance?

'Well, I'll be off now,' she said, wrapping a thick scarf around her head, under her chin, and tying it at the back of her neck. She glanced in the mirror again. 'I look as if I'm going to see to the cows, or something, not to a dance that cost five bob a ticket. Where's me shoes?' She panicked for a moment, until Tony found the shoes in a paper bag on the chair and she tucked them under her arm. 'Come on, luv,' she said impatiently, ushering Tony towards the door, as if, he thought irritably, it was *him* that had been holding *her* up. 'I'll pop you over to your Auntie Sheila's on the way. I'm meeting one of the girls in the front carriage of the half past seven train, so I'd better get me skates on.'

On Wednesday last, Pauline, who lived in neighbouring Seaforth, had got off the Dunnings bus in Bootle to see how Eileen was, bringing with her a large box of chocolates from the women.

Eileen, touched, vowed to keep the round flowered box forever once the chocolates were eaten. 'It'll do for hankies or me jewellery.'

'Are you feeling better?' Pauline enquired.

'I feel fine,' she lied. Her neck still hurt and her body throbbed where the towel had struck her, but the pain was gradually fading.

'We all reckoned you were in the pudding club,' Pauline said with a sly smile.

Eileen laughed. 'Well, y'reckoned wrong. I'm not.'

'Doris got the message off Alfie saying you wanted to come on New Year's Eve. She's buying the tickets tomorrow, else we mightn't get in on the door. There's five of us going, including you. Even Winnie Li's dad's let her off for the night.'

'In that case, I'll give you my five bob now.'

'Us two can go together, Eileen. I'll meet you on the train.'

The girls gathered in Lyons restaurant, looking more like Eskimos, in their boots and scarves and fur gloves, than five women off to a ball at St George's Hall. After a coffee, they trudged along Lime Street through the slush and the blackout. In the weak light of a watery moon, Eileen could see the streets were full of people heavily wrapped up against the bitterly cold wind which came sweeping in from the River Mersey. Trams rolled noisily by, eerie blue sparks exploding from the overhead electric lines, and cars beeped their horns as they stopped and started along the busy road.

'I hope I meet someone with a car tonight,' said Doris. 'In fact, if some feller wants to dance, I'll ask if he's got a car first.'

'In that case, you'll be sitting out all night.'

'Have we reached St George's Hall yet? I'm sure we've passed it.'

After some argument, they managed to locate the entrance and made straight for the crowded Ladies to do their hair, adjust their make-up and change their shoes.

'Phew!' Eileen unwrapped her scarf and stuffed her gloves in her pocket.

'What'd'ya think of me frock?' Doris took off her coat and gave a little whirl to show off a black georgette creation, the bodice lavishly decorated with red and blue sequins. 'I got it dead cheap,' she boasted. ''Cos there's some sequins missing, though you'd never notice.'

'I noticed straight away,' said Pauline. 'There's no middle to that flower.'

'Oh, shurrup, spoilsport!'

'That's a lovely blouse, Eileen. It must have cost the

earth,' Theresa said admiringly.

'It's me neighbour's.' Jess had shown her a whole array of beautiful frocks, but Eileen's choice had been limited by the need to hide her neck, which still remained red and slightly sore.

She ducked under a woman's arm to examine herself in the mirror, powder her nose and apply another coat of lipstick. The earrings Annie had given her went well with the high-necked blouse and she had to concede she suited her hair smoothed back in a bun. In fact, she felt quite pleased with her appearance. You'd never guess the glowing woman in the mirror had been nearly strangled to death by her husband only a few short days ago. She shuddered, thinking about it. If it hadn't been for Sheila coming over when she did . . .

'Is everyone ready?'

They went out into the foyer and joined the queue for the cloakroom to leave their things. Eileen noticed a lot of people wearing evening dress and several men and a few women in uniform. There was a sparkle of excitement in the air, as if everyone had thrown off their immediate cares, forgotten the war, and were intent only on having a good time. Music could be heard, the orchestra was playing *Dancing in the Dark*.

Doris's eyes were everywhere, sizing up the men. 'I fancy that one over there! He's dead handsome. I wouldn't say no if he asked me to dance, car or no car.'

Eileen followed Doris's admiring gaze and saw Nick smiling at her across the foyer. She felt her heart skip a beat. So Alfie had passed on the second message!

Nick began to push through the crowds towards her. He wore an evening suit, which made him look sophisticated and less boyish than usual. His unruly curls had been brushed flat against his head.

'Christ! He's coming over!' Doris gasped. 'I think I'm going to wet me keks!'

'May I have the next dance?' Nick stopped in front of Eileen and gave a little bow.

'I think you're supposed to wait till you're inside,' Eileen muttered, embarrassed.

Doris's eyes narrowed jealously for a moment, then she gave a hoot of laughter. 'Go on, Eileen. We'll put your things in for you. That's a record, that is. It's the first time I've ever known anyone asked to dance before they got inside.'

Eileen's heart was pounding as Nick led her onto the dance floor. Although convinced he'd come, nevertheless she was slightly dazed to see him in the flesh.

'I can't dance,' she confessed as he drew her into his arms.

'Now she tells me!' he groaned, then, with his cheek against hers, he whispered, 'Neither can I. I was hoping you'd show me.'

'Me friend, Annie, has been trying to teach me all week.' Each lesson had ended with them doubled up in laughter. 'I think I've got the hang of the waltz and the foxtrot, but the quickstep's beyond me.'

'In that case,' said Nick, 'we'll sit the quicksteps out.'

Eileen let herself relax against him, little caring that the girls would be bound to notice her dancing cheek to cheek with a man who, as far as they were concerned, she'd only just met.

Neither spoke as they shuffled slowly around the ballroom, unsure what they were dancing. A few enthusiastic couples, anxious to show off their expertise before the floor became too crowded, bumped into them from time to time.

'I think that was Fred Astaire and Ginger Rogers,' Nick laughed, as another couple flashed by, missing them by inches.

The music finished and Nick led her to a corner where they sat down. 'Something's happened, hasn't it?' he said quietly. 'I knew that, as soon as I got your message.'

'What do you mean?' The response was automatic, because she knew exactly what he meant. Something *had* happened, and it wasn't just the beating she'd taken off Francis she was thinking of, but the certain knowledge that the marriage was irrevocably over. She would never have him back under any circumstances. In the heat of anger, she'd uttered the fateful word, 'divorce'. She didn't care what the church said or what the neighbours thought, she'd divorce him, even if it meant her name would be mud throughout the whole of Bootle. If necessary, she'd move away, out to Melling, where Tony would grow up surrounded by green fields and trees and flowers. Knowing this, knowing that one day, she wasn't sure how long it would take, she would be a single woman again, made her see Nick in a different light.

He hadn't answered her question, but was looking at her, his brown eyes glowing with an expression that only a fool would deny was love. Eileen felt her head begin to spin. What wonderful, previously undreamt of things might life have in store for her? Nick picked up her left hand and began to twist her wedding ring around her finger.

'You're different,' he murmured. 'Until tonight, you've always held me at a distance.'

'Things have changed since we last met,' she conceded. 'I'll tell you some time.'

The music began again, this time for the Gay Gordons. Nick made no attempt to ask her to dance. 'Are you better? The chap who brought the message said you were ill.'

'I'm fine. I wasn't really ill,' she said briefly.

'I kept thinking of you.' His eyes twinkled and she remembered that was the first thing that had attracted her the day they met in Southport. 'I said to myself, "Sickness is catching. O, were favours so, yours would I catch, fair Eileen, ere I go, my ear should catch your voice, my eye your eye. My tongue should catch your tongue's sweet melody".'

She laughed. 'That's pretty! Did you make it up?'

'No. It's Shakespeare. Didn't you do him at school?'

Eileen wanted the wooden floor to open up and swallow her. What a fool he'd think she was! And what a fool to think there could ever be anything between them when she was so ignorant she didn't even recognise Shakespeare!

'I left school when I was fourteen,' she muttered. 'We never did Shakespeare.'

'That's a shame,' he said sympathetically, and she glanced at him surreptitiously. He didn't seem the least bit shocked or disgusted. 'Perhaps we could go to the theatre next time there's one of his plays on?'

'Perhaps,' she said shortly.

He frowned. 'What's the matter?'

'You've just made me feel dead stupid,' she burst out. 'Fancy me thinking you'd made it up!'

'Oh, my dear girl!' He put his arm around her shoulders. 'You're anything but stupid. You're the wisest woman I've ever met. I can talk to you like I've never talked to anyone before. Just because you don't know everything written by a dead playwright doesn't make you stupid. Come here.'

She was close to tears of shame and embarrassment.

'As long as we could read and write and do a few sums, that's all the teachers cared.'

He cradled her in his arms. 'And that's all I care, too.'

'But it's not right!' she cried indignantly. 'Everyone has a right to a decent education. It should be the same for all children, rich or poor.'

She became aware that Nick was shaking and she pushed him away to find him convulsed with laughter. 'What's the matter?' she asked indignantly.

'This is a New Year's Eve ball. We're here to have a good time, and a good time seems to be what everyone is having.' He gestured towards the dancers stamping around the ballroom, twisting and turning to the Gay Gordons. 'Except Eileen Costello, upset because she doesn't know every single Shakespeare play off by heart, and ranting on about the lousy education system in the country.'

She felt her lips twitch. 'I'm sorry,' she said penitently.

'And so you should be!' He stood up, reaching for her. 'Come on, there's a bar somewhere. I think you need a drink.'

During the interval, Eileen tracked down the girls, feeling guilty for having deserted them, but they were happily surrounded by a crowd of foreign servicemen and claimed not to have noticed she wasn't there.

After she had introduced Nick, Doris gasped, 'Nick! So, *that's* who those flowers were from that day! You canny bugger, Eileen. Where've you been hiding him all this time?'

'I'll tell you Monday,' Eileen said hastily. 'C'mon, Nick. I think we're cramping this lot's style.'

As the evening wore on the ballroom became more and more packed, and it was a struggle to move on the crowded floor. Despite this, Eileen and Nick managed a passable waltz together. 'We should do this more often,' he suggested. 'A few more sessions and we could take it up professionally. We'll call ourselves Fred Stephens and Ginger Costello.'

'If you like,' she said contentedly, her head on his shoulder. They danced in silence for a while, then Eileen looked at him directly. 'It's funny, but I feel as if I've known you all my life.'

'We do get on well together, don't we?' He smiled down at her. 'Perhaps the gods on high marked us down for each other a long while ago.'

'Have you had many girlfriends?' She wondered, slightly jealous, if he got on with other women as well as he did with her.

'A few, but none like you. You're different from any other woman I've ever known.'

'I bet you told them that, too,' she said with a laugh.

'No!' He stopped dancing and they were immediately buffeted by other couples around them. 'There's something about you, Eileen Costello,' he said seriously. 'You're as innocent and unsullied as an angel.'

Before Eileen could digest this unusual compliment, Doris swirled by in the arms of a soldier with a face like a Greek god.

'Isn't my feller just like Gary Cooper?' she yelled. 'He's a Polish officer and he don't speak a word of English, but we get on fine. Don't forget I've got your cloakroom ticket if you're leaving early,' she shouted as she was waltzed away.

'You're leaving early?' Nick raised his eyebrows disappointedly. 'I was hoping to catch a balloon for you when they're released at midnight.' There were hundreds of them suspended from the ceiling in a net.

'I promised Tony I'd be back by then,' Eileen told him, disappointed herself, but firm in her resolve not to let Tony down.

'Just like Cinderella! In that case, can I take you home? I have a carriage waiting outside in the form of a motorbike and sidecar.'

'I'll get the train. I don't want to spoil your evening.' She trod on his toe and burst into giggles. 'If I haven't already spoilt it!'

'What point is there staying once you've gone?' He looked hurt, and the simple words made her head spin.

When half past eleven came, she found the girls and wished them a Happy New Year, then left with Nick to collect his bike from a nearby car park.

The drive to Bootle was unpleasant and claustrophobic along the unlit roads, with Nick scarcely visible on the bike beside her, and Eileen almost wished she'd taken up his joking offer to ride pillion. She felt relieved when they drew up outside the King's Arms. As she began to struggle out, Nick alighted and came round to help.

'Thank you,' she said politely. 'It's been a lovely evening.'

'Thank you, Mrs Costello. Likewise.'

She could sense him grinning down at her. 'Oh, I suppose you'd better come in.' She couldn't bear the idea of him driving through the countryside all by himself as New Year struck, though on the other hand, what on earth would Sheila and her dad think when she turned up with a strange man?

'I knew you'd ask,' he chuckled.

'You seem to know me better than I know meself,' she said dryly.

Sheila took their arrival with far more equanimity than

Eileen had expected. No matter how firmly you believed in the marriage vows, thought Sheila, it was a bit much to expect a woman to stay with a man who'd nearly killed her, particularly if the woman concerned happened to be your sister. In fact, she felt more than pleased to see Eileen looking so radiantly happy. She gave them the last of Jacob Singerman's sherry.

Jack Doyle merely grunted, 'Pleased to meet you,' when Nick was introduced.

'Where's Tony?' Eileen asked. The only child visible was Siobhan, playing with a doll in her favourite place underneath the table.

'Fast asleep in the parlour,' replied her sister. 'Mr Singerman went home a while ago. I think he was a bit upset and wanted to be by himself.'

'I'll go and see him tomorrow,' promised Eileen. She tugged Nick's sleeve. 'Come and meet Tony.'

They crept into the parlour. Tony was lying on the sofa covered with his grandad's overcoat, his glasses askew and sucking his thumb like a baby. Eileen leaned down, gently removed the glasses and kissed her son's pale cheek.

'I won't wake him,' she whispered.

'He's a lovely child,' said Nick seriously. 'Almost as lovely as his mother.' He pulled Eileen towards him and began to kiss her passionately. She felt his tongue wriggling against her lips, and for the briefest moment kept her mouth closed, her body stiff, then, unable to help herself, her body melted into his and she gave herself to him utterly.

'Eileen! It's almost midnight.'

Sheila's voice brought them down to earth.

'We'd better go in,' Eileen said shyly.

When they returned to the living room, she wondered

if she looked as bemused and dreamy as she felt, as they both sat and waited innocently for the clock to chime in the New Year.

When it did, Nick kissed her and Sheila modestly on the cheek and shook hands with her dad. Then he was despatched out of the back and ordered to collect a piece of coal on the way and return by the front door.

'A dark stranger bearing coal, you'll bring good luck,' Sheila told him, when he departed, somewhat mystified. Whilst they waited, she said wistfully, 'I wonder what Cal's doing right now?'

'I know exactly what Calum Reilly will be doing,' Eileen said, hugging her, 'thinking of you. He's probably never stopped since he was taken prisoner.'

'I can't *wait* for him to come back!'

'He'll be home to a hero's welcome,' Jack Doyle said gruffly. 'We'll put the flags out for our Cal.'

Eileen smiled, wondering what Calum would think when he found himself in favour and Francis no longer the object of her dad's stern affection. 'Talking of coming home, where's Nick? He's taking an awful long time.'

Nick turned up eventually, having knocked on next-door-but-one by mistake, where George Ransome was having a party, and several young ladies had captured him and refused to let him go. 'I've had two whiskies and a proposal of marriage,' he said, laughingly rubbing smears of bright red lipstick off his face. 'The people round here are very friendly.'

'Where's the coal?' demanded Sheila. 'I want to keep that piece on the mantelpiece beside Our Lady for luck.'

'I'd like to make a toast.' Jack Doyle stood, raising his glass. 'Here's to the year nineteen forty. May it bring Cal home safe and sound and good fortune to my family. But most of all, and I wish this more than I've ever wished anything in me life before, may it bring peace to this country of ours.'

Chapter 10

'But you *can't* take her!' Vivien Waterton stared with
horror at the tubby man in a black gabardine mackintosh
who was standing in the middle of the room twiddling his
bowler hat in his hands. She'd asked him to sit down, but
he'd taken no notice.

'I'm sorry, Madam, but I must. I have orders to return
Freda Tutty to her mother.'

'I don't want to go back to me mother!' Freda clung to
Vivien's arm. 'She doesn't want me. She doesn't care if
I'm there or not.'

'It would appear she does.' The man looked uncomfortable. He was sweating visibly in the over-heated room.
'We have a letter from Mrs Tutty requesting your return.'

'What d'yer mean, a letter?' snarled Freda. 'Me mam
can't write. She got the woman next door to do it.'

'That may be, but it makes no difference,' the man said
stubbornly. 'Now, if you'd like to pack a bag?'

'You've no right just to turn up without notice,' cried
Vivien, close to tears. 'Why didn't you let us know you
were coming?'

The man didn't answer, but proceeded to twiddle
further with his hat. This was the second case they'd had of
a couple refusing to return their evacuee. In the first, due
notice had been given that the child was to be removed on
a certain day, only to find when they turned up that the
boy had been whisked down south to relatives and had still
not been located. The Billeting Office had no intention of

making *that* mistake again. He felt sorry for the girl, though she looked a right little madam, and for the little, doll-like woman who wanted to keep her, but his main sympathy was with the mother, whom he had not yet met.

'I'd like to ring my husband.' The little woman reached for the telephone on the coffee table beside her. Clive wouldn't let them take Freda away. 'He'll come straight home.'

'I'm afraid I can't wait, Madam.'

'I won't let you take me. You'll have to drag me out,' the girl threatened.

'I hope that won't be necessary, Miss, but if so, I have a constable waiting outside in the car.'

'You can't do this! You can't!' Vivien leaped to her feet, catching her knee on the coffee table. There was a sharp crack as bone touched wood and she felt her heart thud crazily in her chest. As she reached down to rub her knee, she was overcome with dizziness and would have fallen if Freda hadn't flung her arms around her and begun to sob.

'Oh, God!' muttered the man, in agonies of embarrassment.

'This isn't the end, darling,' said Vivien, still dizzy, and unaccountably breathless. 'Clive will sort it out.'

'I don't want to leave, Vivien. I never want to leave.'

'I know, darling.' Vivien pushed the heaving form away. For the first time, staring at the strangely blurred little face convulsed with misery, she felt the stirrings of genuine, maternal love and with it came the realisation that Freda wasn't her little sister, a playmate, but a child who needed her protection. At that moment, Vivien grew up. 'Go with the man,' she whispered. 'It won't be for long.'

'Are you sure?'

'Quite sure. In fact, tell Mrs Critchley to pack only a few of your things.' She would have done it herself, but her head was whirling.

Ten minutes later, Vivien managed somehow to make her way to the door to wave goodbye to Freda. As soon as the car disappeared out of the drive, she turned to Mrs Critchley, who was standing gloating in the hall, 'Ring Mr Waterton and tell him what has happened, then call the doctor, I think . . .'

Before she could finish, Vivien collapsed onto the floor.

The man in the black mac didn't speak once on the drive back to Bootle, not even to the constable sitting at his side. In the back, Freda glowered at their red necks and wished they'd both drop dead and the car would crash and she'd escape back to Vivien. But her wish was in vain. Eventually, they drew up outside 14 Pearl Street.

The man looked in dismay at the filthy, curtainless windows of the house. He muttered, 'You stay there!' to Freda, as he got out and knocked on the door. He intended handing the girl over to her mother in person. Not until she was safely inside would he consider his job had been properly done.

To his further dismay, there was no answer to his knock. A woman stuck her head out of the upstairs window of a house opposite and shouted, 'She's not in.'

'Where is she?' he shouted back.

The woman shrugged. 'Pissed out of her mind somewhere, I reckon.'

The man stood there, flummoxed. What was he supposed to do? He couldn't very well take the girl back to Southport. He noticed an entry going down the side of the end house and walked down and round to the back of Number 14. The back door was open when he tried it and he shouted, 'Is anybody in?'

As expected, there was no reply. He went through the house. By God! It was *disgusting*! That poor kid, coming back to this! No wonder she hadn't wanted to leave. Almost retching from the smell, he opened the front door and beckoned to Freda. She climbed out of the car carrying her suitcase. No longer crying, her face was hard and expressionless.

'I haven't got time to wait until your mother comes,' he said abruptly. His conscience was pricking. He felt ashamed of the job he'd done that day. 'Get inside.'

Her head held high, the girl went into the house and the man slammed the door, then got into his car and reversed out of the street so fast that the tyres made a screeching sound as he backed around the corner.

Freda heard the car roar away as she entered the house in which she had spent her entire life until that wonderful day last September when she had been sent to live with Vivien. She shivered. It was almost as cold as the inside of Vivien's refrigerator. Wandering into the living room, she stared with mounting desperation at the thick dusty mould in the corners, the debris in the fireplace, the orange boxes used for chairs, the bare wooden table which held a few hard crusts of bread and a couple of filthy jam jars which were used as cups. Was she supposed to sit on one of those boxes in her best blue velvet coat? Sleep upstairs in that lousy smelling palliasse on the floor in her pretty nightdresses?

Where was Dicky? Perhaps he'd gone to school. They'd always gone more often in the winter than in summer, for warmth and a hot mid-morning drink.

Vivien had put Freda's name down for a little private school in Southport. She was supposed to start next Monday. She still might. Vivien had promised to come for her.

The back door opened and for a moment she thought it was Vivien come already. Perhaps she'd followed in a taxi?

But it was Mrs Costello who came into the house. She took a step back when she met Freda's look of loathing.

'Aggie Donovan said you were home. Are you all right?'

'What do you think?' Freda snarled.

'You'll soon settle back in,' Mrs Costello said, though she looked troubled. As well she might, the stupid woman, thought Freda.

'It's all your fault,' she spat. 'It was you who wrote the letter for me mam. Why couldn't you mind your own business?'

Eileen Costello sighed. Perhaps she should have refused, but Gladys was Freda's mam, with every right to insist on having her daughter back. Nevertheless, if Freda wanted to stay . . .

'I'm sorry,' she said lamely. 'If there's anything I can do?'

'You've already done enough,' snapped Freda.

The woman seemed reluctant to go. 'Would you like a cup of tea? I've got to leave for work soon, but there's time to put the kettle on.'

'You can keep your tea. I don't want anything off anyone.'

Freda went upstairs into the front bedroom, where she opened the window and sat on her suitcase waiting for Vivien. At the back of her mind, she visualised the scene;

264

Vivien would phone Clive, who'd come home immediately. They'd get in the car and drive straight to Bootle. In fact, they might arrive any minute. She leaned out of the window, watching anxiously.

She heard her mam come home, but made no attempt to go down and announce her return. It wasn't until Dicky found her hours later that Gladys realised Freda was back. She came up and regarded Freda blearily for several seconds. She had a feeling she hadn't seen her daughter for a long while, though couldn't remember why. Freda looked different. Where had she got those posh clothes from?

'Where've you been?' she asked.

'To the moon.'

Gladys's brain may well have been rotten with booze, but she recognised impudence when she heard it. She was also aware of the look of disgust on her daughter's strangely plump and rosy face. She lunged forward, fist raised ready to strike.

To her amazement, Freda stood up and caught the fist with surprising strength. 'Don't you *dare* lay a hand on me,' she hissed.

Gladys fell back in bewilderment. She stared at her daughter wordlessly, then stumbled down the stairs, muttering underneath her breath as she tried to take in what had just happened.

Dicky crept into the bedroom and sat on the floor beside his sister. He was glad she was back. There had been no-one to talk to whilst she'd been away. At school, the other pupils acted as if he was invisible except when they felt like beating someone up. No-one wanted to be a friend of Dicky Tutty's.

'Where's all your nice clothes gone?' asked Freda. The smartly dressed healthy-looking little boy might never have existed. Dicky was back in his rags, his face and his thin bare arms a mass of scabs and bruises.

'Me mam took them to the pawn shop.'

'I bet she took your train set, too.'

Dicky nodded. 'I'm glad you're home, Freda.' Freda would look after him at school and make sure he got fed from time to time. She was good at wheedling scraps from the fish and chip shop or the baker's, or pinching bars of chocolate out of Woolworths.

'I'm not staying,' Freda said sharply. 'I'm only waiting for Vivien to come and take me back.'

Dicky's face fell. He felt his whole body droop with misery. To his amazement, tears began to roll down his grubby cheeks. Neither of the children had cried much in the past. There seemed little point.

Freda regarded the tears coldly, then turned to look out of the window. But as she looked, she thought about her little brother. He'd scarcely crossed her mind the last few months, but seeing him now, such a scraggy little mass of bruised humanity, she felt a tightening of emotion in her throat. Poor Dicky!

'Have you missed me?' she demanded.

'Yes,' he sniffed.

'Perhaps, when I go back to Southport, you could come and see us every Sunday? Vivien wouldn't mind.'

He nodded eagerly. It was better than nothing. 'As long as I come back to me mam.'

'Are you hungry?'

He hunched his shoulders. 'I'm starving.'

'So'm I. If I give you some money, will you go and buy some food?'

'Chips?'

'No, they're bad for you. Vivien never made chips. Buy some apples.' Freda took her purse out of the grey lizardskin bag Vivien had bought for her eleventh birth-day.

'You've got money of your own!' gasped Dicky, impressed.

'Vivien put money in me new handbag,' Freda said boastfully, adding warningly, 'But don't tell our mam, or I'll bloody kill you.'

'I won't,' promised Dicky.

Freda wasn't sure how many days she sat by the window waiting for Vivien, leaving only to go to the lavatory at the bottom of the yard, her purse tucked safely in her pocket out of her mother's reach. She didn't even remove her clothes, but slept fully dressed, using the suitcase as a pillow, sending Dicky out for food. Gladys, aware her daughter must have money and thinking of all the gin it would buy, came up from time to time to demand it off her, sometimes wheedling, sometimes belligerent, but Freda adamantly refused.

'Sod off!' she said contemptuously. 'You're not getting a penny,' and Gladys would reel away, confused and shocked. She even went next door to complain to Mrs Costello, but her neighbour was impatient and refused to help. In fact, she seemed more concerned about Freda than Gladys. 'How's the poor little lamb settling in?' she asked.

One day, when Freda could stand it no longer, she went out to telephone Vivien, convinced something was wrong. If Vivien couldn't come, she would have written. Vivien would never, never let her down.

Freda could use a telephone, having frequently made calls on Vivien's behalf, though one with slots for coins was strange to her. She read the instructions carefully, put her pennies in the box, then, when Mrs Critchley gave the number, pressed the top button.

'I'd like to speak to Mrs Waterton,' she said in her most ladylike voice.

'Who's speaking?'

'A friend,' said Freda. She and Mrs Critchley had never got on and she had no intention of revealing who she was. The woman might well be awkward and refuse to fetch Vivien if she knew it was Freda calling.

'I'm afraid Mrs Waterton passed away from a heart attack last Monday. The funeral was yesterday.'

Freda felt as if her body had turned into a block of ice. She dropped the receiver and, as if from far away, heard it swing to and fro like a pendulum against the sides of the box. She began to wail and beat her fists on the glass.

At the other end of the line, Mrs Critchley listened to the almost inhuman cries. It was that girl, she'd suspected as much.

Clive Waterton came into the room. 'Who is it?' he asked listlessly.

The noise had ceased. The girl must have gone.

Mrs Critchley replaced the receiver. 'I think it was Freda,' she said expressionlessly. She'd always loathed the girl. But that noise! She must be heartbroken.

Freda!

Clive threw himself into a chair as Mrs Critchley left the room to get on with her work. The doctor reckoned Vivien must have died within an hour of Freda leaving and, at first, Clive felt nothing but hate for the girl. But in his heart of hearts he recognised it was unreasonable to blame Freda, who would have wanted to stay as much as Vivien wanted to keep her. He recalled the day she'd arrived with her brother. The pair had looked like something out of a Dickens novel. He'd never taken to either of them himself, and even now, although he tried, he couldn't raise the remotest feeling of affection for Freda. All his love had been centred on his lovely, diminutive wife. Vivien had been the only child he ever wanted. He clenched his fists and felt the nails bite into the palms of his hands. She'd gone! He would never see her again. No-one in the world would ever know how much he missed her.

Except, perhaps, Freda.

He knew that Vivien would want him to make sure she was all right. No, dammit, more than all right. He jumped to his feet. Vivien would want him to take care of her. To send her to school, raise her into womanhood, as she would have done herself. He went over to his desk and began to search through the papers, looking for Freda's address.

Eileen Costello's heart sank when she found Gladys Tutty outside her door yet again. 'What is it now, Gladys?'

'There's a man come, and I think he wants to buy our Freda!'

'What?'

'Come and have a word with him, Mrs Costello. I don't understand what he's on about.'

Dragging her pinny over her head, Eileen hurried next door.

Gladys must have had some vague notion that guests were taken into the parlour, for Eileen found Clive Waterton standing in the middle of the room where Gladys slept, because most nights climbing stairs was quite beyond her. The bed was a heap of tattered, grey blankets and there was no cover on the striped bolster, nor any sheets. The brass bedhead was as black as if it had been made that way. The man's nose was wrinkled, as well it might be, for the bed stank of urine and the stains were visible for all to see.

Clive Waterton had never believed until now that people lived this way. A conveyancing solicitor, he dealt with nice detached residences in their own grounds, or bungalows in Birkenhead or Formby. Occasionally, the deeds of smaller properties passed through his hands; neat little semi-detached homes in Southport. But these houses! They were no bigger than rabbit warrens. How on earth could people exist in such a confined space?

As for Gladys Tutty! The inside of her home was beyond belief, as was the woman herself. She stared at him drunkenly at first, though he noticed her eyes gleam when he mentioned money. He stood by the window, itching, convinced he'd been bitten by a flea or a bug of some sort, waiting for Mrs Tutty to return with her neighbour.

He recognised the woman when she came in. It was the one who'd turned up in Southport. She stared around the room for a moment, before shuddering slightly, as if she found the room as repellent as he did himself.

'Now, if you wouldn't mind explaining what you've come for?' she said pleasantly. 'Gladys seems to have got it in her head that you want to buy Freda.'

He shook his head irritably. 'I would like the girl to come back to Southport, but insist on Mrs Tutty signing a paper putting her into my care. If she does, then I am willing to pay a hundred pounds compensation.' He knew darned well the paper would never stand up in court, but was willing to take a risk on the women's ignorance.

'See, Mrs Costello, I told you!' Gladys shook Eileen's arm gleefully.

'You mean to say you go along with this, Gladys?' Eileen said, gaping.

Gladys frowned. All she could think of was the money. One hundred pounds! She hadn't understood about signing a paper. She'd take the money, then get Mrs Costello to write another letter and demand Freda back. 'I don't see what harm it would do,' she muttered. The expression on her neighbour's face made her feel slightly uneasy.

'Then I don't know why you bothered asking me in,' Eileen Costello said coldly. She felt as if she was taking part in a bizarre sort of pantomime.

'I have the paper here.' Clive Waterton drew a folded sheet out of the breast pocket of his black overcoat.

'Have you got the money?' Gladys asked eagerly.

He nodded. 'I went to the bank on the way.'

Gladys imagined a bag bursting with threepenny bits and sixpences and shillings, and hoped he hadn't left it in his car, where someone might pinch it.

'I take it your wife approves?' Eileen remembered the funny little woman who seemed to think the world of Freda.

Clive Waterton didn't answer immediately. 'She does,' he said eventually in clipped tones. Sensing the neighbour's disapproval, he was somewhat relieved when she shrugged and turned as if to leave.

Eileen was glad for Freda, glad she was going to where she wanted to be, but she found the idea of buying and selling a child totally repugnant.

'I don't suppose,' a voice said cuttingly, 'anybody thought of asking me what *I* want?'

Freda came into the room, still in her velvet coat, though looking creased and dishevelled. 'I don't want to go to Southport, not with Vivien dead,' she said, eyes blazing.

Eileen Costello looked at her sharply. 'What do you mean?'

'You heard. Vivien's dead.'

For once, Clive Waterton found himself disconcerted. He'd never dreamt the girl would refuse. 'It's what Vivien would have wanted,' he stammered.

Freda tossed her head proudly, 'Vivien would have wanted what was best for me. I want to stay and look after Dicky.'

'But, Freda . . .' Eileen began helplessly, it was getting beyond her, but Freda silenced her with a sharp, 'Shurrup!'

Now that Vivien had gone, the only person left to love was Dicky, Freda had concluded earlier. She'd no intention of slipping back into the old ways, of getting dirtier and dirtier, until she returned to being an object of contempt. Vivien had shown her she was pretty and clever, and Freda intended staying that way. She owed Vivien that much. Somehow, in some way, she vowed, she'd stay clean and go to school and make sure Dicky did, too. Now Clive had turned up, and she knew how it could be done.

'I want you to give me the money,' she said flatly to Clive.

Clive hadn't thought it possible, so soon after Vivien's death, but he almost laughed. The nerve of the girl!

'What for?'

With a disdainful glance around the room, Freda said, 'To clean this place up. To buy curtains and furniture and proper dishes and clothes for Dicky. To feed us, because it's no use expecting me mam to do it.' She glared at Gladys, then turned the glare on Clive, daring him to refuse.

He was looking at her, slightly puzzled. Eleven years

old, but she was tougher than old boots, he thought admiringly. He'd never noticed before, but she had more character in her little finger than most people had in their entire bodies.

'It's what Vivien would have wanted,' Freda added slyly.

Of course, she was right. 'Will it be safe? The money, I mean?'

'Of course it will,' Gladys said heartily. Gladys had been watching the proceedings, trying to fathom what was going on. One minute, it seemed Freda was leaving and a hundred pounds was within her grasp, next, Freda was staying and the money had slipped out of her fingers. Now it seemed as if she was going to get it after all.

Freda turned reluctantly to Eileen Costello. She hated asking for a favour. 'Will you look after the money for me?' She couldn't take it to school with her, and her mam would tear the house apart looking for it whilst she was gone.

'Of course I will, luv, for the time being, but you'd better start a Post Office account.'

'I will,' Freda said in a hard, determined voice. 'Don't worry, I will.'

On Saturday morning, Eileen Costello and Annie Poulson descended on Number 14 with buckets of hot water, scrubbing brushes, scouring powder and several pints of disinfectant. Freda would have liked to refuse their help, but she recognised the job would be done much quicker with a few extra pairs of hands. When Aggie Donovan saw what they were up to, she came too, if only because she liked to see the inside of other people's houses, particularly the Tuttys', where she clucked with disapproval at everything – though she was a good, thorough worker, and by midday, the walls and the ceilings had been cleaned, the skirtings, the floors and the stairs scrubbed, and the windows sparkled. The furniture had been piled in the yard for the rag and bone man to take, except for the double brass bedstead, which Aggie Donovan said would be a shame to throw away and could be brought up to look like new with a bit of Brasso.

At one o'clock, a van arrived with several rolls of patterned lino which Freda had bought the day before, and the women got to work laying it, to be joined by Dai Evans and Jack Doyle. Dicky was despatched for a box of tacks to keep the lino down in the corners.

'This won't last five minutes,' whispered Annie, cutting out a piece for round the fireplace. 'It's no better than cardboard. It must be the cheapest you can buy.'

'Shush!' Eileen pressed her arm. 'It's what Freda wants.'

'I'll never get the smell of disinfectant off before I meet Barney tonight,' Annie grumbled. 'He'll think he's out with a lavatory brush.'

'Are you going out with him again? I thought you were playing hard to get?'

'It'll only be the third time. I'm not exactly throwing meself at him, am I?' Annie said tartly.

It was just gone three when another van came with the furniture, all secondhand; a kitchen table and a set of wooden chairs, a couple of armchairs, a leatherette three-piece, an elaborately carved sideboard, a bedroom suite and a single bed. Freda had driven a hard bargain in the shop and bought the lot for almost half the asking price.

'Where are these to go, luv?' the delivery man asked, and Freda instructed him in which rooms to put the furniture.

Freda was in her element, though no-one would have guessed from her stern, unsmiling little face. She doubted if the Queen got more pleasure out of furnishing Buckingham Palace than she got that day. She just wished all these people would finish and go away. Once they'd gone, she'd light a fire in the living room, where the chimney had been swept early that morning, and sit in one of the new chairs and, later on, eat a proper meal off the table.

Poor Gladys hovered in the background, ignored whilst all this was going on. The neighbours who invaded her house that Saturday deferred only to Freda.

'Where d'you want this, luv?'

'Freda, which curtains do you fancy in the parlour over the blackout?'

The curtains, the dishes, the ornaments, had begun to arrive in the afternoon. Once the people in Pearl Street realised what was going on, that Number 14 was going through a transformation, they cleared out their boxrooms and their cupboards and came over with odds and ends of cutlery and crockery and faded, threadbare curtains, put away 'just in case'. Someone even bought a full size tin bath and a painting of reindeer standing gloomily in a forest.

Freda resented being the object of such charity; in fact, she hated it. She let Mrs Costello answer the door, take the stuff and say 'thank you'. On the other hand, she conceded privately, the more she was given, the less she'd need to spend and the longer she and Dicky would be able to live on Clive Waterton's hundred pounds. She never included her mam in her calculations.

The only person she vaguely liked was a new woman, Mrs Fleming, who'd come to live over the road, only because she reminded her a bit of Vivien. She was much taller and fatter, but she wore a pretty dress and her nails were painted red and she smelt of perfume, the way Vivien had always done. Mrs Fleming brought over a pair of beautiful curtains that even Freda had to admire. They were gold in one light and green in another. She also bought a little cherry-coloured rug for in front of the fire. Even so, Freda disappeared into the yard when she came so she wouldn't have to thank her.

By six o'clock, everyone had gone. Freda drew the faded cotton curtains across the black cardboard sheet pinned to the window, lit the fire in the range and moved the kettle on its hob over the flames. The gas mantle behind its cracked glass shade gave off a bright orange glow. It was the first time she could remember it being lit, only because it was the first time there was money in the meter. Gladys had used candles for illumination in the past.

'I'll make something to eat in a minute,' she said to Dicky. The pair sat stiff and upright in the armchairs. Dicky's legs scarcely touched the red rug on the floor.

'You can't cook,' exclaimed Dicky, then, frowning, 'Can you?'

Thinking of the miracles wrought by his sister over the last few days, if she'd announced she could fly he would have believed her.

'Of course, I can. I used to help Vivien make the meals at the weekend when Mrs Critchley wasn't there.'

Dicky sighed, reckoning he was going to hear about Vivien non-stop for the rest of his life. 'Couldn't we have chips from the chippy?' he asked longingly. He was starving, as usual, and chips were his favourite meal.

'Well,' Freda began reluctantly. 'Oh, I suppose so, just for once. Get a piece of cod as well, and we'll have half each.' She was worn out and, anyroad, there hadn't been time to get in much in the way of food.

'Shall I get some for me mam?'

'Where is she?' Freda glanced around the room, as if Gladys might be hiding in a corner or under the new table.

'I dunno. She went out ages ago.'

'There's not much point, then, is there?' Freda said disdainfully. 'She'll be in the pub by now. Here's a shilling for the fish and chips, and bring every penny of the change back safe, now.'

Dicky wouldn't have dared not to. As he was about to leave, Freda called him back. 'Where's the overcoat I bought the other day?' She'd got the tweed overcoat from the pawnshop. It was at least two sizes too big, but thick and warm. 'You're not to go out without your overcoat again,' she warned him sternly.

'No, Freda,' Dicky said meekly.

After Dicky had gone, Freda curled her legs underneath her and sat on them, the way Vivien used to do. She was pleased with what she'd achieved over the last few days. She'd created a home out of nothing. She forgot entirely that other people had helped. It was her achievement, no-one else's. From now on, Freda decided, smiling grimly, mam would be kept in line. If she thought she could hit Dicky again, she had another think coming, and she'd be made to use the toilet, not pee in the grid the way she usually did. Freda would buy a boiler and a mangle and show her how to do the washing. And another thing, mam could chuck away that smelly old shawl and wear a coat like the rest of the women in Pearl Street, if only because she let Freda down by looking so scruffy.

On Monday, she'd go back to school and study hard. She could read now, and do sums, and she'd teach Dicky to do the same.

The kettle began to boil. Freda reached out with her foot and pushed the hob away. She'd make the tea in a minute when Dicky came back. Next door, Mrs Costello switched her wireless on, and an orchestra began to play, *When they begin the beguine* . . . It was one of Vivien's favourites. In fact, she used to dance to it, swirling around the room like a little ballerina in one of her floating dresses. Freda had scarcely cried since she'd learnt Vivien was dead, only a few terrible minutes in the phone box. She cried now, sobbed her heart out, for the person who'd loved her so dearly. She cried quietly, though, for fear someone would hear. She wanted pity from nobody.

But when Dicky came home with the fish and chips, Freda was dry-eyed. That was the last time she'd cry for anybody, even Vivien.

With the new year the battle at sea continued, with ships sunk and terrible losses on both sides. On land, though, the conflict seemed to have reached stalemate. Nothing was happening and Jack Doyle remarked caustically, 'We'll win when the Fuhrer dies of old age,' but his eldest daughter felt there was something sinister in Hitler's apparent inactivity. 'He's plotting something,' she thought. 'He's too arrogant a man to start a war and then do nothing.' But at least the unexpected respite gave Britain the opportunity to arm herself.

Winston Churchill's speech, urging, *'Fill the armies, rule the air, pour out the munitions, strangle the U-Boats, sweep the mines, plough the land, build the ships, guard the streets, succour the wounded, uplift the downcast, and honour the brave . . .'* fell on deaf ears as far as the Government were concerned, though not amid the people who longed to have a crack at the tyrant. Chamberlain was universally loathed for his procrastination and ineptitude.

The country was sharply reminded they were at war when rationing came into force during the second week of January. Many people had already given up sugar in their tea, as it had been hard to get for months. Now, they were allowed twelve ounces a week, but at least it was available, along with four ounces each of bacon and butter. As margarine remained unrationed, the people of Pearl Street were not particularly bothered over the butter, which they used either not at all or only on Sundays. What bothered them more was the disappearance of onions from the shops. How could you make a decent stew without onions? Many were the curses heaped on Hitler's head when a man sat down to his tea of tripe and cabbage or cauliflower, instead of the much preferred traditional onions.

Eileen Costello offered most of her butter ration to Nick, who lived on sandwiches at home and declared he couldn't exist without it. 'You baby!' she declared fondly as they sat in the pub opposite Dunnings during the dinner hour. It seemed a waste of time hiding their friendship from the girls after New Year's Eve, though she winced at the suggestive remarks and coarse jokes flung to and fro across the workshop.

'We haven't done anything, I swear,' she protested vainly. They'd been out together once, to the pictures, where Nick merely put his arm around her and kissed her when he took her home. Eileen was slightly scared by her feelings for Nick, and not a little bewildered. She held herself at a discreet distance, not ready yet for anything deeper.

'Come off it, Eileen,' Doris hooted. She turned to the girls. 'You should see him! He could've had *my* keks off in the first five minutes.'

One day, Eileen decided to turn the tables on her tormentor. 'You're all talk, Doris,' she said scathingly. 'I bet five bob you're a virgin, and you'll still be one the day you get married.'

Doris pretended to look offended. 'How dare you call me a virgin! What a terrible thing to say. A woman with my experience!'

'Describe what a man's thingy looks like, and we might believe you,' Theresa screamed.

Doris began to describe a man's thingy in gory detail. 'It's about six inches long and covered in hairs . . .'

'No, it's not!'

Alfie came into the workshop just then, and Carmel shouted, 'Show Doris your thingy, Alfie. She's got the description all wrong,' and Alfie promptly turned tail and departed.

By now, Eileen was doubled up with laughter over the lathe. 'Youse lot!' she gasped. 'I'm really glad I came to work here. It's better than a finishing school.'

At two o'clock, when she got on the bus to go home, Pauline remarked, 'You look smart. Are you off to meet your feller?'

Eileen was wearing her navy-blue coat and beret, and had doused herself with Chanel scent to hide the unpleasant smell of the cooling liquid. 'I'm going with one of me neighbours to the Public Assistance,' she told Pauline. 'She's too scared to go by herself.'

At Annie's instigation, Rosie Gregson had applied for a supplementary allowance from the army, but the army didn't consider themselves obliged to pay until the child was born and Rosie had received a letter ordering her to attend the Public Assistance office at half past three that afternoon. As Annie would be working, she'd asked

Eileen to go along. Poor Rosie was petrified.

Rosie was waiting by North Park when Eileen alighted from the bus. She was a tall, almost unbearably thin girl with a long mournful face and pale grey eyes. Her four-month pregnancy was scarcely noticeable beneath her shabby coat.

'Rosie! Are they the best shoes you could find?' Eileen remarked, when she noticed the gaping holes between top and sole of the thin patent leather court shoes. They were entirely unsuitable for the arctic conditions which still persisted. In fact, there'd been a heavy snowfall the night before, and although the snow had vanished from the pavements, the surface was wet and slushy.

'They're the only ones I've got,' whispered Rosie. Her voice rarely rose above a whisper.

'What size do you take?'

'A six.'

'That's a pity. I take fives, otherwise I'd have given you a pair. I usually throw mine away before they reach that state.'

The office was situated in a large house in a wide pleasant road lined with bare trees. Eileen and Rosie were shown almost immediately into a high ceilinged room where three people sat behind a long table – two men and a woman in a tweed hat with a fox fur around her shoulders – a pile of papers in front of each. A chair had been placed in the middle of the room facing the table.

The man sitting at the centre of the three looked up. He was about fifty, his expansive form clothed in a black pin-striped suit.

'Mrs Gregson?'

Eileen pushed Rosie forward.

'I'm Mr Molyneux, Chairman of the panel. Please sit down.' He nodded curtly towards the chair, then turned to Eileen. 'And who are you?'

'A friend. I've come with her.'

'I can see that, but I'm not sure if I can allow you to stay. I think it might be preferable if you remained in the waiting room.'

Eileen's hackles rose immediately. 'Well, I think it would be preferable if I remained here. That's what you want, isn't it, Rosie?'

Rosie, hunched petrified in her chair, nodded weakly.

'Does the panel agree?' Mr Molyneux looked down at his colleagues. The woman glanced at the papers in front of her through a pair of lorgnettes, as if she expected to find her response printed there.

'I don't see that it would do any harm,' she said in a strangulated voice.

The other man looked like a tortoise with a high starched collar into which his entire head seemed to shrink. His chin emerged from the circle of white and he muttered in a squeaky voice, 'I have no objection.'

Eileen noticed a row of chairs lined up against the wall. She dragged one forward and plonked it firmly next to Rosie.

Mr Molyneux immediately took charge of the proceedings and began to question Rosie closely. How much rent did she pay? What did she spend on food? On clothes? On fuel?

Determined not to interrupt unless it became absolutely necessary, Eileen let the girl give her own stuttering replies. Even when the Chairman demanded to know what sort of soap she used and if she spent money on powder and lipstick, Eileen gritted her teeth and said nothing.

After a slight pause in the proceedings, the woman on the panel asked Rosie how long she'd been pregnant.

'Nearly four months,' the girl whispered.

'Mmm!' The woman raised her lorgnettes and studied her papers. 'Your husband, I take it, was home on leave in September?'

The insinuation was obvious. Eileen could hold her tongue no longer. The woman, who talked as if she had a plum in her gob, was suggesting someone else might have fathered Rosie's child.

'How dare you!' she gasped. 'What right have you got to say such a thing?'

Mr Molyneux gestured impatiently. 'Please let Mrs Gregson reply to the question.'

'No!' Eileen said fiercely to Rosie. 'Don't answer, luv. They wouldn't ask such a question if they had decent manners.' She turned on the woman and in an angry voice demanded, 'Would you like it if someone asked if you'd had it off with another man?'

'Please!' The Chairman raised his hands in an effort to calm the situation.

'As I see it,' said a squeaky voice and the little man, who had remained silent so far, popped his head out of his collar, 'Mrs Gregson is here because she cannot live on seventeen and sixpence a week, plus the seven shillings she gets off her husband, which is scarcely surprising. Once her baby is born, she will get a further five shillings off the army. I propose we allow her that five shillings in the meantime.' He smiled benignly on Rosie. 'Have you had your special green ration book, dear? There's extra rations for expectant mothers.'

Rosie nodded numbly, wondering what all the fuss had been about.

'I go along with that,' the Chairman said in a relieved voice. 'How about you, Mrs Woodhouse?'

The woman looked aggrieved. Sniffing audibly, she

adjusted her fur, and suggested Private Gregson contribute towards the five shillings, but even the Chairman looked perturbed at the idea. Before Eileen could open her mouth to express her outrage, he said reasonably, 'My dear lady, he is already left with a mere shilling a day.'

'Not much to pay a man willing to die for his country,' the other man remarked with squeaky sarcasm.

Rosie was told she would receive an official letter confirming the five-shilling allowance, and the two women left. As they walked down the path, Eileen had already begun a tirade against officialdom in general and the panel they'd just confronted in particular, when a squeaky voice shouted, 'I say!' and they turned to find the little man hurrying towards them. He thrust a pound note into Rosie's hand. 'Do me a favour, dear. Buy yourself a pair of stout shoes on the way home.'

'Oh, well,' Eileen said grudgingly. 'I suppose they're not all bad.'

It was snowing again when Jessica Fleming and Jacob Singerman arrived at St Catherine's Dock and found the troopship on which they were due to take part in a concert had already sailed.

'I'm terribly sorry.' Colin Evans, the concert organiser hurried towards them. 'Last minute orders from on high, I'm afraid. They were local men, the Royal Tank Regiment, on their way to Egypt, though they left a day earlier than expected.'

Jacob felt bitterly disappointed. He and Jess had ready an entire new repertoire of popular songs which they'd been rehearsing for days; *Wish Me Luck as You Wave Me Goodbye, The White Cliffs of Dover, There's a Boy Coming Home on Leave,* and as a finale, the song everybody loved, *We'll Meet Again*.

'Oh, well, never mind,' he sighed, 'though I was really looking forward to it.'

'We've another concert on Saturday,' Jessica said soothingly, thinking Eileen Costello would be relieved that Francis had left the country.

'Can I give you a lift home? It's the least I can do,' Colin offered, noticing the way the old man was shivering in his thin overcoat.

They both accepted gratefully. On the way, Colin told them that the Entertainments National Service Organisation, known as ENSA, was becoming more organised. The Government had begun to realise the importance of concerts to the morale of the troops and the workers, and was gradually taking the organisation under its control.

'There's even a suggestion entertainers won't be called up,' he chuckled.

'That's a worry off my mind,' Jacob remarked dryly.

'Pretty soon, I'll be in a position to send a car to collect you and take you home.'

After they'd been deposited outside the King's Arms, Jacob said, 'I think I'll have an early night. Sometimes, I forget I'm an old man who needs his rest.'

'We all forget that, Jacob,' Jessica said warmly. She'd become fond of Jacob Singerman over the last few weeks. Despite his apparent frailty, he had the energy of a man half his age. It was depression that laid him low from time to time, but never low enough not to turn out for one of the concerts which they took part in two or three times a week.

They said goodnight and Jessica went indoors. She sat listening to her neighbour as he pottered around in the kitchen, then heard him climb the stairs to bed. The Welsh people on the other side were quiet for a change, though there'd be the usual ructions later on when Dai came home drunk. Jessica decided to have a bath. Arthur was in the King's Arms and wouldn't be home until ten o'clock.

She spread a newspaper on the floor in front of the fire and fetched the long tin bath which was hanging on a hook in the yard. The bath was covered in snow and she gave it a thump. The snow fell off, but a rim of ice remained. As she began to fill the tub with pails of hot water from the kitchen, she sighed, remembering the blue and cream bathroom in Calderstones. Still, things hadn't turned out all that bad. In fact, she was having quite an enjoyable time, perhaps better than she would have had in the WVS with her old acquaintances, though she remained determined to get away from Bootle, no matter how long it took.

When the bath was full enough, she sprinkled in the last of her bath salts and wondered if she could afford more. Not that brand, for sure. Maybe they sold bath salts in Woolworths.

She folded a towel over the edge of the bath to rest her head on, removed her clothes and sank gratefully into the steaming water. She smiled, imagining what those old acquaintances would think if they could see Jessica Fleming lying in a tin bath in front of the fire in Pearl Street! What's more, she bathed only once a week nowadays, instead of daily. No wonder the poor were accused of being dirty, she thought indignantly, when they had to go through all this palaver to keep clean.

Jessica began to hum as she soaped her body, raising one long shapely white leg, then the other. An unexpected thought came to her as she washed her full, still firm breasts. *What a shame!*

What a shame that no-one touched them nowadays except herself!

She and Arthur still slept apart, and although she was happier nowadays, more content, she couldn't for the life of her imagine them coming together again, not in *that* way. Yet, the strange thing was, she found Arthur more attractive than she'd done for a long time. As if not wanting to stand out amongst his new friends, his 'mates' as he called them, he'd actually acquired a flat cap. Often, he went out without a collar and tie. His silk suits and shirts remained unworn in the wardrobe. And instead of Jessica feeling disgusted, Arthur actually became more desirable in her eyes. But even so, as she lay in bed at night, longing to go to him, to slip into his arms, something held her back. '*He* should come to *me*,' she told herself.

Arthur still surprised her. He'd actually offered to instal the electricity she so desired and Jack Doyle, who'd wired his own home, was helping. Jessica glanced at the wall beside the door where a little channel had been dug ready for the wiring. There was a newspaper on the sideboard, the *Daily Herald*, which Jack must have left behind that morning. Due to the appalling weather, the men had been laid off the docks and he'd come around, 'To get on with a bit,' as he put it, after Arthur left for work.

Jessica found herself even more disturbed by Jack than by Arthur. She couldn't take her eyes off the rippling muscles in his bulging arms as he chipped away at the wall. They said little to each other. Jack Doyle had always been a taciturn man, almost churlish. Even when she made him a cup of tea, he scarcely spoke. She wondered what he'd say if she told him she'd once been in love with him? Die of embarrassment, she thought with a little smile.

The water was beginning to cool, which was a shame, because she was enjoying daydreaming in front of the fire. She got to her feet, and was standing in the bath when the key sounded in the front door.

Arthur!

She glanced around for her dressing gown and realised she'd forgotten to bring it down. In a panic, she reached for the towel and knocked it in the water. She was about to grab the tablecloth, when she realised this was the chance she'd been waiting for, the chance to get Arthur back. He couldn't resist, surely he couldn't resist, if he found her naked and waiting. She could hardly breathe at the thought.

Jessica licked her lips and waited for the door to open.

When it did, it was Jack Doyle who came into the room.

She thought he might slam the door and run. Instead, he stood transfixed at the sight of her standing seductively in the bath.

'I thought you were out. Arthur lent me his key. I left me paper behind,' he said in a strangled voice. His eyes (oh, how she'd loved those blue eyes once!) gazed up and down her body, as if hypnotised by her beauty. His craggy, handsome face was impassive, but Jessica sensed there was a tremendous struggle going on within. He was a man of honour and integrity and she was the wife of a friend.

Jessica said nothing, but licked her lips again. Her insides felt as if they were on fire and all inhibitions fled. She didn't want him to leave. She wanted, more than anything she'd ever wanted in her life before, for Jack Doyle to stay.

She held out her hand, and with all her might, with

every fibre of her being, she willed him to come forward and take it, to take her.

And he did!

Chapter 11

'What the hell are y'smoking, Nobby?'

'Christ knows, Cal.' Nobby wrinkled his little gnome like face. 'Bit o'baccy, mainly tea leaves. I traded it for me breakfast.'

'Where did the paper come from? It's a funny colour.'

'Lavvy roll, mate,' Nobby grinned. 'Trouble is, it goes up in flames.'

Calum Reilly lay back in the sacking hammock which he'd made himself and slung up between two pipes in the flat of the *Altmark*. It was hard for him, a non-smoker, to understand the craving some men felt for a cigarette. One man insisted on smoking jute in his pipe, even though the acrid fumes sent him, and anyone unfortunate enough to be close, into paroxyms of coughing, and meant a day in solitary confinement on a diet of bread and water if he was discovered by their captors.

The flats were the areas between the decks, each containing a vast network of pipes of varying diameters, large and small. The men had managed to make themselves comfortable, on hammocks or pieces of carpet. There were no portholes in the flats, nor proper ventilation. Illumination was provided by low wattage electric bulbs.

Lately, Calum was beginning to wonder if they'd ever be found. His ship had been one of the first to have its crew taken prisoner by the *Graf Spee*. They'd stood on the deck of the German battleship and watched the *Midnight Star* blown to pieces before their very eyes. Not long afterwards, they'd been transferred to the *Altmark*. That was almost four months ago, Cal thought miserably, or sixteen weeks, 117 days. Once, a few weeks ago he'd worked out the hours.

They'd sailed like a ghost ship for what seemed like forever through the mountainous seas and mists of the South Atlantic. Now, despite the Jerries doing their utmost to keep their bearings a secret from the prisoners, the trapped men knew the ship was making its slow and tortuous way back to Germany. Once they reached that Godforsaken country, they'd be held prisoner for the duration of the war. At this very moment they were approaching Norway.

Was the Navy looking for them? If so, why hadn't they been found? Trouble was, the *Altmark* kept changing its name, which caused added worry. What if they were torpedoed by the Navy who didn't realise there were nearly three hundred British prisoners on board?

Cal sighed. At least Sheila knew he was safe. They'd heard on Christmas Eve that not only had the *Graf Spee* been scuttled by its captain, but the news had broken at home that the men off the *Midnight Star* and other ships were still alive.

Sheila! She was rarely out of his mind, his Sheila and his kids. Unlike some of the other men, Calum Reilly had taken no part in the plans to escape, which he regarded as foolhardy. Even if they got out of the flats, they were unarmed, and there was no way they could take over the ship. He was as brave as the next man when it came right down to it, but as long as it didn't mean acting like a coward, he considered his main aim was to stay alive for his wife and family. Besides, although conditions in the flats were appalling, damp and cold and vile-smelling with so many men living in close confinement, the Jerries had treated them surprisingly well. The food was basic, but adequate: they had even managed to provide a Christmas dinner, rabbit and tinned gooseberries and a bar of chocolate each. Of course, their captors weren't members of the German armed forces, but merchant seamen the same as themselves. Cal even recognised one he'd sailed with on a P & O ship several years ago. They nodded to each other, quite friendly, when they came face to face.

'Fancy a game of chess, Cal?' asked Nobby, who had just finished repairing his canvas shoes with twine.

'Not just now, mate.'

'What are you thinking about?'

'Me wife. Me kids. When will the Navy find us? That sort of thing.'

'Me, too.' Nobby laughed ruefully. 'S'funny thing, Cal, but although I can't wait to get away, I'll miss it in a way. Know what I mean?'

'I know, Nobby.' Cal reached down and squeezed Nobby's bony shoulder. The two had become firm friends since they'd come on board, Nobby arriving the week after Cal. After months of living, quite literally, on top of each other, you grew either to hate your companions or to love them. Cal knew it was unlikely he'd ever feel so close to other men again. They'd gone through a lot together, but had managed to retain their good humour and their friendship.

'Mind you, Nobby, I wouldn't shed a tear if I never saw a chessboard again.' He was utterly sick of it, as well as ludo and draughts, and it would be a long time before he would see a pack of cards and not think about the endless hours playing poker and blackjack in the flats of the *Altmark*.

'Land ahoy!'

The shout went through the flats like wildfire. The men emptying the latrine drums had seen land.

Cal looked at the calendar scratched on the bulwark beside him. 14 February, St Valentine's Day.

'It's Norway!'

The men had been forbidden to go on deck for several days. They knew the Jerries had good reason to keep their prisoners down below. Norway was a neutral country and didn't welcome ships from warring nations sailing through its waters. The Norwegian Naval Authorities would come on board as a matter of course, and if they suspected the *Altmark* was not the innocent supply ship she purported to be, they would insist on a thorough search. If so, the secret human cargo would assuredly be found.

As the *Altmark* proceeded at about eight knots, the prisoners reckoned the Norwegians might board any minute. All day long, they kept up a racket, banging the deckhead with iron bars, starting up a rowdy sing-song in order to make their presence known. But by the time dusk fell, nothing had happened, though most of the men, convinced rescue was at hand, had packed their few belongings, and those who still had a few precious cigarettes left smoked the lot, telling themselves there'd be plentiful supplies by tomorrow.

Night came. The men did their utmost to remain cheerful, though by now, the smell of unemptied latrine drums had become unbearable. Everyone was too excited to sleep and all night long there was a constant babble of conversation. Cal Reilly prayed, as he'd never prayed before, that they'd be rescued soon.

Next morning, the situation was the same. Somewhat subdued, the men began to curse the evil-smelling

293

drums, the stifling atmosphere. They felt unclean without a change of clothes nor a proper wash on deck for several days, and they were hungry. Ever since the welcome shout, 'Land ahoy!', they'd eaten nothing but dry biscuits washed down with water. Surely freedom wasn't to be denied when it had appeared so close? They listened intently for every sound, finding the most optimistic reasons for innocent, everyday movements. To add to their misery, the Jerries had turned out the lights, so they were in constant darkness.

That evening the Jerries kept the steam-winches going for a long time, making a terrible din. Thinking this was a way of disguising any noise the prisoners might make because the Norwegians were on board, the men set up a din of their own, stamping and shouting again, banging the deckhead with anything they could get their hands on, blowing the SOS code on their whistles. But it all appeared to be in vain.

'This is killing me,' groaned Nobby. It was now more than two days since Norway had been sighted. An air of hopelessness began to descend. They felt convinced the Norwegians had cleared the ship and allowed it to sail freely on to Germany.

'What's that!'

The men froze as the ship ground to a juddering halt with a loud crunching noise. The sound was so deafening that they stared around them, petrified, half expecting the sides to collapse and the sea outside to come pouring in.

'We've run into the ice!' someone said in relief.

Soon afterwards, they heard the steam jets at work, trying to free the trapped ship. The men tried to read what they could into this mishap. The German captain was an excellent seaman. Was he on the run? Had the ship been cornered? They listened intently, but there was no further activity. They sank back, disheartened, ready for a third sleepless night.

Suddenly, they were alerted by the sound of a shot being fired, then another. The men sat up, never more wide awake. There were a few excited whispered comments, but otherwise dead silence in the flat as the shots became more frequent, then louder, closer.

The suspense was almost unbearable. It seemed an eternity before bullets began to slam into the hatch door. The men listened, nerves at breaking point, to the noises behind the door. It sounded as if someone was trying to open it.

At last came the words they'd begun to think they'd never hear. A voice shouted, 'Are there any Englishmen down there?'

'We're all English,' came the joyful reply.

'Then come on up. The Navy's here.'

The Navy's here!

Those words were to echo around the world. They were repeated over the airwaves, in cinemas and newspapers, and in millions of homes. Calum Reilly knew he would never forget them as long as he lived. The prestige of the Navy soared, along with that of the First Lord of the Admiralty, Winston Churchill. Churchill got things done. He was a winner, the right man to be at the helm of a country fighting an evil fascist dictator.

Cal came home a hero to Pearl Street, where the bunting was hastily ironed and strung from the snow-covered roofs, along with a home-made banner painted with, 'Welcome Home, Cal.'

To everyone's surprise, Cal, leaner, paler, but otherwise fit and well, refused to say a bad word against his captors.

'They treated us fine,' he insisted, when a reporter from the *Bootle Times* came to interview him.

'Were you beaten or tortured?' the reporter asked.

Cal laughed. 'Of course not! The Jerries didn't lay a hand on us. They looked after us and fed us as well as they were able. It was only the last few days we went hungry. I shook hands with one of the *Altmark* crew before I left. We'd sailed on the same ship together once.'

Sheila Reilly was starry-eyed, clinging to her husband's hand as if determined never to let go, though she knew that in a few weeks' time Cal would be taken away from her again. He would be allocated to another ship and sent once more to risk his life on the high seas.

March came. As if in mitigation for the fearsome winter, God blessed the country with the balmiest of springs. Magically, almost overnight, every trace of snow disappeared, and in parks and gardens snowdrops and crocuses thrust their jubilant heads through the ground. The soil looked richer and blacker, the grass a vivid, almost unnatural green, as if renewed after so many months hidden under its winter blanket of white.

The clocks had gone back with a jump, two whole hours, which meant it was daylight when people made their way home from work and the blackout didn't seem to matter so much.

In Pearl Street, people wondered, some gleefully, others with sniffing disapproval, if Paddy O'Hara would continue calling on Miss Brazier now the nights were getting lighter.

It was the street's worst kept secret. Everyone knew Paddy came out of the front door of his lodgings, tapped his innocent way towards the King's Arms, then disappeared down the entry to go into the old maid's house by the back way. Hours later, he would appear in the pub just before closing time.

'You're late, Paddy,' Mack would say automatically.

'Had a bit of business to attend to, mate,' Paddy would explain.

The phrase became a joke in the pub. 'Well, I'll be off now,' various customers would say as they were leaving and looking forward to some activity between the sheets with their wives. 'I've got a bit of business to attend to.'

Mind you, nowadays few men would have turned down an invitation to a bit of business with Helen Brazier. Since Christmas, a transformation had taken place and a buxom, comely woman had taken the place of the bulkily clad, bespectacled spinster of old. Aggie Donovan claimed she looked no more than a tart, as she waltzed down the street, lipstick too bright and rouge too much, hair waved, earrings jangling. The men, though, envied Paddy. It was about time he got his end away.

Poor Paddy O'Hara was exhausted. He'd come to dread the light knock on the wall which meant Helen had his tea ready. Then, after tea . . . Paddy groaned. Helen was insatiable. Sometimes, he worried she'd knock a hole in the wall and he'd never have any peace.

Months ago, if someone had told him he'd be at the beck and call of such a passionate woman, it would have seemed like the answer to a prayer, the realisation of his ultimate fantasy, but the truth was, thought Paddy, grinning slightly, he'd sooner have a dog!

He'd never had a chance to mourn Spot, but had been swept up into Helen's welcoming, capacious bosom, and had scarcely lifted his head out since. But now the weather was fine and the streets were his again, he missed taking Spot for walks on Sunday afternoons and to the pub at night. He also missed the long hours spent chatting with his mates and calling on Eileen Costello to listen to her wireless.

Paddy wished Helen would let him go. He knew he could never bring himself to tell her. She was sensitive and easily hurt. He remembered the agonised sobbing coming through the thin walls, and couldn't have stood being the cause of similar distress.

He sighed. A woman in Opal Street had a litter of puppies to dispose of, a touch spaniel, so he understood, with a hint of sheepdog, though it might have been alsatian, the woman wasn't sure. There were three male puppies and Paddy would have liked one, but it didn't seem fair. He was scarcely in his room nowadays and hadn't the time to spare to train a dog.

Although Paddy's world remained as dark as ever, he understood the nights were getting lighter, which meant, he thought hopefully, that Helen's knock would come later and later. Like him, she wanted the affair kept a secret, but lately she'd been dropping hints and Paddy had a feeling she was hinting they should get married, which frightened him. He hadn't realised until now how much he treasured his freedom; freedom to get up when he liked, wander the streets with Spot at his heels, go for a drink.

There was a tap on the wall. Paddy sighed and went next door to do his duty.

Before going to work on the hated afternoon shift, Eileen Costello popped over to Jessica's to return a book she'd borrowed. Since Christmas, the two women had become friendly. Jessica opened the door in her dressing gown, looking wan and drawn.

'I'm not so well again this morning,' she explained.

'It's about time you went to see the doctor.' It was the third day in a row she'd been off colour.

'I will if I don't feel better soon. Would you like a cup of tea? I was just about to make one. For some reason, I've gone off coffee completely.' Jessica stood aside to let Eileen in.

'I wouldn't say no, though I'm in a rush as usual. I can't stop more than a few minutes, like.'

There was a fire burning in the new fireplace which Eileen's dad had helped Arthur Fleming instal.

'I like the colour of your tiles much better than mine, Jess,' Eileen remarked. The tiles were a sort of oyster colour, much more cheerful than her own dark green, but then it was Francis who'd chosen the fireplace, not her. She went into the kitchen and surveyed the electric stove with its peculiar solid metal rings, and watched with fascination as the electric kettle was plugged in. Suddenly, Jessica clapped her hand to her mouth. 'I think I'm going to be sick again.' She disappeared down the yard to the lavatory.

Eileen made the tea when the kettle boiled and was getting the cups ready when Jessica came back, her face grey, looking worse than ever.

'Come and sit down.' Eileen helped her to a chair. 'Perhaps you've got the flu or something.'

'It's something, all right. I've never felt so ill in all my life.'

'Perhaps you should go back to bed?' Eileen suggested.

Jessica shook her head. 'No, it'll pass. It usually does. By midday, I'll feel my old self. Anyway, Jacob and I have got a concert tonight.'

'Eileen smiled. 'If I didn't know any different, Jess, I'd say it was morning sickness.' Jessica had confided she couldn't have children.

'Morning sickness? What's that?' Jessica asked limply. She'd never heard of it before.

'I had it when I was expecting Tony. Quite a few women are sick in the morning when they first become pregnant.'

Pregnant!

After Eileen had let herself out, Jessica Fleming sat thunderstruck in the chair.

Pregnant!

Of course she was! As Eileen explained her own symptoms, Jessica realised hers were exactly the same. Even as the single word, 'pregnant' was spoken, Jessica knew with utter certainty it was the case. She'd missed two periods and had actually thought it the onset of the change of life. But now! She pulled up her nightdress and laid her hands flat on her stomach. There was a child curled up inside her, growing. It meant that all those years she'd thought she was barren, it had been Arthur's fault. There'd been just that one time with Jack Doyle and here she was, at forty-three, expecting a child. Since that night of ecstatic madness when all inhibitions had gone out of the window, they'd both acted as if nothing had happened; Jack churlish as ever, Jessica scrupulously polite. He was too honourable a man to conduct an affair, and she loved Arthur too much to be consistently un-faithful.

Jessica, still nauseous, was as yet unbothered as to how she would explain her condition to her husband. All that concerned her was the breathtaking, wondrous realisation that she was pregnant. A year ago, if she'd been offered the choice of giving up her house in Calderstones, her Aga, the car, her lovely clothes, in exchange for a child, Jessica wouldn't have hesitated.

She would have chosen the child.

And, in a way, that's how things had turned out. If she hadn't moved to Bootle, the miracle would never have occurred. All the upheaval, losing the business and the house, had been worth it, more than worth it, in the end.

Later on, when she felt better, she'd get dressed up to the nines and go into town and buy something from Henderson's or George Henry Lee's – a matinée jacket or a lacy bonnet. She didn't care if she met any of her old neighbours. Nothing mattered except that, at an age when most women became grandmothers, Jessica Fleming was expecting a baby of her own.

Nick's face was heavy and unsmiling when Eileen met him outside the factory at six o'clock. Since the weather had improved, they'd begun to meet during the afternoon dinner break.

'What's the matter'?' she asked warily.

'Nothing,' he said shortly. He didn't touch her and began to walk along the path beside the stream.

Eileen knew there was something seriously wrong as she followed a few feet behind. It was going to be a beautiful night, and she wished he was in a better mood so they could enjoy it together. Across the darkening green fields, the sun was slowly disappearing into the horizon, like a jelly melting, she thought to herself, and the sky was a rippling mass of vivid green and scarlet. The stream rippled busily along, washing the white stones even whiter as it frothed over them. She wondered where the stream ended up? Perhaps, one day, she and Nick might follow it.

'I've applied to join the Royal Air Force!' Nick stopped and began to kick at the grass like a sulky schoolboy. Pebbles landed in the water with a faint plopping sound.

'Oh, Nick!' Eileen cried, clutching his arm. Then, in a relieved voice, she said, 'They'll never take you.'

He looked down at her and said incredulously, 'So that's what you think! I'm not a fit person to fight for his country.'

'You know that's not what I meant,' she protested. 'You're doing too important a job already.'

'*You* might think it's important. *They* might think it's important. But I don't. It's a despicable job. It's sneaky and underhand and I hate it.'

'But, Nick . . .' she began.

He ignored the interruption. 'I loathe the very idea of war, but it's happening, and while it's happening I want to play a proper part, not stand around in a white coat fiddling with wires, but in a uniform like every other young man in the country.'

Eileen didn't bother to argue. It was no use telling him there were thousands of other young men who hadn't been called up because their trade or expertise was needed at home.

'What about us?' she asked in a small voice.

Nick laughed bitterly. 'What about us, Eileen?'

He was always doing that, turning her own question back on her.

'I would have thought you'd want to stay — for me,' she said hesitantly.

'Oh, you would, would you?' The sarcasm in his voice made Eileen flinch. 'Why? So we can walk along this blasted stream together for an hour every day? Have a drink in the pub? Go to the pictures once a week and say goodbye at your front door? Why should I want to stay for that?'

'I'm a married woman . . .'

Before she could finish, Nick broke in with a snort.

'I'm sick to death of hearing that. "I'm a married woman, Nick." So bloody what? You're not a *happily* married woman, at least I don't think so. I'm not trusted with your confidences. On New Year's Eve, you seemed different. You actually introduced me to your family, and I thought things were going to change, but they haven't. I've never seen your family since, and you're as hesitant and weak-willed as you ever were.'

'I'm not weak-willed,' she said indignantly.

'You're too weak-willed to make any sort of commitment.'

'What do you mean?' she asked, puzzled.

To her astonishment, he took her by the shoulders and shook her hard. 'Eileen. I'm in love with you. I want us to be married sometime in the future.'

'Married!' she said faintly.

He let her go, almost contemptuously, and turned away. He stood looking in the direction of the sun. At that moment, it vanished from the sky altogether. 'Has the thought of marriage never crossed your mind before?' he asked.

Eileen shoved her hands in her pockets. 'No. Well, yes. I'm not sure,' she stammered.

'You're making yourself very clear.'

'Don't be so sarcastic, Nick. You've no idea of my situation . . .'

He broke in again. 'Only because you won't tell me what your situation is. Every time I try to talk about your husband, you change the subject. You don't love him, but you won't tell me why. What sort of man is he, good or bad? Do you intend leaving him? If not, what are you doing here?' He kicked viciously at the grass. 'I feel as if we've had this conversation a dozen times before. You've no right to keep me in the dark, Eileen.'

'No, I haven't,' she conceded. She knew she was being unfair. For too long, she'd been stringing him along because it was nice, more than nice, to have someone like Nick in love with her whilst she held him at an appropriate distance. She bit her lip, suddenly nervous. It was time for a decision.

'You fell in love with the wrong person, Nick,' she began quietly.

But tonight Nick seemed determined never to let her finish a sentence. He caught her in his arms, murmuring hoarsely, 'No, no, no!' before pressing his lips against hers. She felt his tongue, hard and hungry, and opened her mouth to allow him to explore her own. They stood, so close, it was as if they were one person, on the banks of the little stream outside Dunnings, oblivious to everything except their own mounting passion.

'I love you! Dear God, Eileen, if you only knew how much I love you!' he groaned eventually. He clasped her face in both hands and she felt his thumbs heavy on her cheeks.

'And I love you.' She'd never said those words to anyone before. She said them again in a clear ringing voice. 'I love you, Nick.'

Eileen returned to work, exhilarated, convinced she would get little done for the remainder of the shift. The first person she saw was Miss Thomas going into her office. On impulse, Eileen followed, suddenly struck with an idea.

She knocked on the open glass door – it was never closed unless someone else was there – just as Miss Thomas sat down at her desk.

'Can I have a word with you?'

Miss Thomas gave her usual friendly smile. 'Of

course, Eileen. Come in and close the door.' She gestured towards the chair in front of the desk. 'How can I help?'

Eileen decided there was no point in beating about the bush. She plunged right in. 'I want to divorce me husband,' she said bluntly, 'and I've no idea how to go about it. I know you see a solicitor, but what happens then?'

For a moment, Miss Thomas looked stunned. 'Divorce?' Then she smiled, somewhat grimly. 'You're starting from the worst possible position.'

'In what way?'

'You're a woman! The odds are stacked against women when it comes to divorce. I don't know much about it, my husband specialised in criminal law, but I know men have everything on their side.'

'Oh!' Eileen felt suddenly deflated.

Miss Thomas didn't appear to notice her forlorn expression. She began to list further difficulties. Property and other possessions were always deemed to be the man's, even if the woman had contributed towards their purchase. And Eileen would need money. Solicitors didn't come cheap.

'I take it,' Miss Thomas said, 'that the grounds would be cruelty?' When Eileen nodded, she went on, 'In which case, I would be happy to appear as a witness. I can vouch for the injuries I saw.'

'Thank you,' Eileen whispered.

It was only then the woman behind the desk noticed Eileen's downcast face. 'I'm sorry, Eileen, to be such a Jeremiah, but from the woman's point of view, divorce is fraught with difficulties – I know only too well from my own experience. When I left, my husband told me not to bother trying. Cruelty is very difficult to prove. Judges are not only exclusively male, but very old-fashioned. They disapprove of women disposing of their husbands, no matter what the blighter has been up to. Some judges regard a wife as merely the property of the man, with him having the right to do whatsoever he pleases with her.'

As the total injustice of the situation sank in, Eileen began to boil with indignation. 'It's not bloody right!' she exclaimed.

'Women have always been second-class citizens,' Miss Thomas commented dryly. 'You never know, the war might go some way towards remedying the situation, we'll just have to see. But in the meantime, we've got a long fight on our hands, Eileen, if we are ever to expect equality with men.'

'Are you suggesting it's not worth trying − for a divorce, I mean?' Eileen asked.

'Oh, no!' Miss Thomas looked shocked. 'I was preparing you for the difficulties that lie ahead. We'll never win the fight, will we, if we give up before we've even started?'

'Well, thank you very much for the advice,' Eileen was about to leave when Miss Thomas said hesitantly, 'I don't wish to pry, but I've seen you outside with a young man. Is there a third party involved?'

'What do you mean?'

'To put it another way, are you having an affair? No!' she raised her hand, 'don't answer that, it's none of my business. It's just that if you could persuade your husband to divorce *you* on the grounds of your adultery, it might be the best option. It would be easier and cheaper, so long as you don't mind the damage to your reputation.'

'Eileen shrugged. 'Me reputation will be damaged, anyroad.' Divorce, particularly from such a fine man as Francis Costello, wouldn't go down well in Pearl Street, no matter what the reason. 'But what about Tony, me little boy? Francis threatened to take him off me.'

Miss Thomas pulled a face. 'I'd forgotten you had a child. If it's the woman who's been unfaithful, there's always the risk the man will get custody of the children.'

On Saturday night, instead of going to the pictures, Nick took Eileen out for a meal so they could talk. She relayed the gist of her conversation with Miss Thomas.

'It looks as though it'll be an uphill job, but I'm going to try,' she said determinedly. 'In fact, Miss Thomas found a solicitor in Bootle who specialises in divorce and made an appointment for me on Monday morning.'

Nick took both her hands across the table. 'Would you like me to come with you?'

Eileen shook her head. 'I think it would be best if I went by meself.'

'No matter what happens, darling, I want us to always be together. Promise me that.' His dark eyes smiled into hers.

'I promise,' she whispered.

Later on, when they were finishing dessert, Nick said, 'I was thinking of going down to London next week for Easter. Why don't you come with me?'

'London!' Eileen's first thought was for Tony, who'd been promised a visit to Pets Corner in Lewis's. She felt as if she was being torn in two, not wanting to let Tony down, but unwilling to hurt Nick by refusing his invitation.

Sensing her hesitation, and perhaps even the reason for it, Nick said, 'If you're thinking of Tony, bring him too.'

'You wouldn't mind?'

He laughed. 'For goodness' sake, woman. You've just promised we'll always be together. How can we be together without Tony? It's about time he got to know me if I'm going to be his stepfather. I'd like a relationship better than the one I had with mine. My stepfather would have preferred I didn't exist.'

'Jaysus! I hadn't thought about it that way.' For a moment, the problems of the future seemed insuperable. She almost wished Francis were still home and she was back in her life of drudgery and unhappiness; that she'd never met Nick and nothing had changed. She shook herself. It was stupid thinking in such a negative way.

'What's wrong?' Nick was always sensitive to the least alteration in her mood.

'Nothing. Francis crossed my mind, that's all.'

'Tell me about him?' Nick demanded. 'What's he like?'

Eileen didn't answer immediately. How much should she tell? After a pause, she decided he had a right to know everything, apart from the dark secret only she and Francis shared.

'He's charming,' she said eventually. 'Really charming – until you get to know him properly, and not many people do that. Only me and Tony knew what Francis was really like.' In an even voice, she told Nick how they'd met, that her dad had put pressure on her to marry him. 'Not that I minded too much,' she said. 'After all, like I said, he was really charming.' She explained how Francis had changed once they were married. 'There's a saying in Bootle, "outside angel, inside fiend", and that describes him perfectly.'

Nick's face grew dark as Eileen continued. 'Eventually, I told me dad, because . . . well, I needed somewhere safe to stay when Francis was home on leave last October. In fact, it was me dad who changed the locks on the doors to keep him out. That's one of the reasons why . . .' She paused.

'Why what?' Nick's eyes glittered angrily.

'Why Francis nearly killed me when he came home at Christmas,' Eileen finished simply.

'Killed you!' Nick exploded. Several people in the restaurant looked at them curiously. 'Christ! I could murder the man with my bare hands! Come and live with me in Melling! You'll be safe there. Francis must never come near you again.'

Eileen squeezed his hand. 'Don't worry,' she smiled. 'Francis is in Egypt. I reckon he won't be back to Pearl Street for a long time.'

After Nick paid the bill, they wandered arm and arm through the blacked out centre of Liverpool towards the car park where his motorbike had been left.

'Is there a particular reason you're going to London?' Eileen asked curiously. 'Or is it just a holiday, like?'

'Well, the fact is,' Nick replied, 'I've been in touch with a chap I was with at university, Ben Fulford, whose old man is a bigwig, a Wing Commander, in the RAF. I met him once and intend bearding him in his den and persuading him to use his influence to get me in.'

'Nick!' She stopped and stared at his blurred form, unable to believe her ears.

'What's wrong?' he asked, surprised at her anguished tone.

'How can you possibly think of leaving me?'

'My darling Eileen,' he said incredulously. 'There's a war on.'

'But you might be killed!'

'I might be killed anyway; two people have already died in explosions where I work.'

'That's different. Oh, how can you not see?' She could have cried with frustration. She thought, with everything that had happened between them over the last few days, he would have changed his mind about joining up. Men!

what was wrong with them? Why did they have this uncontrollable urge to fight? Even Tony, only five years old, strutted around with his gun in his shorts, ready to kill Germans on sight. 'Can't you ask to be transferred to something more, more . . .'

'Humane?' Nick suggested lightly.

'Well, yes.'

'Because it still wouldn't be what I want. I've told you, Eileen, I hate war as much as you do, but it's a matter of pride, pride in myself and pride in my country. Battle has been joined, as they say. That being the case, I want to be in the thick of things.'

'I don't understand,' groaned Eileen. 'I'll never understand.' He was prepared to risk his life, when he could stay safely at home in a reserved occupation. How could he possibly love her as he claimed?

Suddenly, Nick pushed her against the wall. He leaned against her, his hands on the bricks above her head. 'Don't you see, my dearest girl,' he whispered, 'that I want you to spend your life with the *real* me, not some silly boffin making boobytraps to blow up unsuspecting civilians? The real me wants to fight, wants you to be proud I'm playing my part. Don't you see, Eileen?'

She knew it was no use discussing the matter further. His mind was made up.

'I see,' she said shakily. But she didn't see at all. Instead, she prayed the RAF bigwig would refuse to help. Perhaps it was selfish, she didn't care, but she wanted Nick safe and sound in England.

The solicitor was a handsome middle-aged man with a wild shock of prematurely white hair. Head bent and cupped in his left hand, he made notes with a gold fountain pen as Eileen explained her case. She felt nervous and kept losing the thread of her tale, though he remained courteous throughout and corrected her with a smile when she contradicted herself from time to time.

'In what way was your husband violent?' he asked in his light, pleasant voice.

'He used to squeeze my arm or my shoulder really hard,' Eileen explained.

'Did he bruise the flesh?'

'No, but it went red.'

'And why did he squeeze your arm or your shoulder?' He smiled encouragingly.

'If he felt I hadn't dusted properly, or made him a dinner he didn't like – that sort of thing,' Eileen replied, wishing her voice would stop shaking.

'And did you? Not dust properly? Make him a dinner he didn't like?'

'Not deliberately. I can't remember,' she stammered.

'No matter.' He made a note. 'Now, about this incident at Christmas. You say the locks had been changed on the doors and he couldn't use his key?'

'That's right.'

'Had you apprised your husband of this fact beforehand?'

'No,' she replied, flustered. 'Perhaps I should've done. It didn't cross me mind.' She should have told him when she wrote that angry letter after he'd threatened to take Tony away, but was the solicitor hinting this omission excused Francis's behaviour? 'He nearly killed me,' she said. 'If me sister hadn't come in . . .'

The solicitor didn't wait for her to finish. 'Don't you think, Mrs Costello, that a soldier coming home on leave might be entitled to feel aggrieved when he finds his own house out of bounds?'

'Perhaps,' she conceded weakly, 'but he had no call to try and strangle me.' She realised with a shock that the man was definitely not on her side.

'I might be inclined to lose my own temper, if I came home and found my wife had unexpectedly changed the locks,' he went on.

'Only if there was no reason for it,' Eileen argued. 'With Francis, there was a good reason.'

'That's right. He'd squeezed your arm and your shoulder and made them red.' He made another note on his pad. 'Sexual relations? What were they like?'

Eileen blushed. 'Not very nice.'

'Not . . . very . . . nice.' He wrote the words down slowly. 'In what way were they not very nice?'

'He hurt me.'

'Every night?'

She looked down at her shoes, embarrassed. 'No. He . . . we only did it on Saturdays when he was drunk.'

'Did you ever refuse his attentions?'

'I tried to, but he didn't take any notice.' By now, Eileen knew she was wasting her time and wished she had the nerve to get up and leave. The solictor's response was almost predictable. He seemed to see things from Francis's side, not hers.

'In other words,' he said pleasantly, 'although you and your husband had sexual relations just once a week, you would have denied him the privilege completely if you could?'

'Only because he hurt me,' she said defensively.

'I see.' He smiled again. 'There is a saying, isn't there? "If rape is inevitable, just lie back and enjoy it." I think it's a matter of relaxation.'

'I don't know,' she whispered, praying the interview

or the consultation, whatever it was, would soon be over and she could escape. But it seemed there were still more questions to be asked.

'Did your husband keep you short of money?'

'Oh, no, he was generous with money, except that . . .' she paused.

'Except that what?'

'He insisted on choosing everything himself; the furniture, even my clothes. He always came with me and told me what to buy.'

'I always accompany my wife when she goes shopping for dresses,' the man said pleasantly.

'Do you always tell her what to buy?'

'Of course not, but she relies on my advice.'

Eileen didn't bother to respond. The solicitor picked up his notes, swung round in his swivel chair and began to study them, whilst she glanced about the office, for the first time taking in the faded carpet, the vast wooden desk with its leather top, the shelves and shelves of dusty leather-bound books.

Eventually, the man finished reading. He laid down the notes, leaned on the desk and looked directly at Eileen. The expression on his face told her all she needed to know. His words, when they came, were almost predictable.

'From what I have heard,' he said, in a voice that was no longer pleasant, 'I find no good reason why you should divorce your husband on the grounds of cruelty. What is more, I have a son in the Royal Tank Regiment, presently, like Mr Costello, in Egypt. There is no conceivable way in which I, or any member of this firm, would serve divorce papers on a man risking his life on foreign soil for his country.' He stood, saying dismissively, 'I'm afraid, Mrs Costello, that I can be of no assistance to you at this time. Or any other time, come to that.'

As Eileen went wordlessly towards the door, he said coldly, 'That will be one guinea. Pay my clerk if you wish. Otherwise, a bill will be sent.'

Eileen virtually ran home. The way he'd spoken to her! She felt like an insect that had crawled from beneath a stone. She blamed herself for not explaining things more clearly. On the other hand, the solicitor seemed determined not to see things her way. He made her feel a fool. She burst into her sister's house, close to tears.

There was a three-sided clothes maiden in front of the fireplace, full of nappies and bedding. It was Monday, washing day, and Sheila was in the kitchen dressed in a wrap-round pinny, her brown hair hidden underneath a scarf, rolling more sopping nappies through the mangle. The rack was half down, already packed with children's clothes, and the house was clouded with steam and smelt of soap and bleach and boiling washing. Siobhan had started school in January and Caitlin was playing with Ryan underneath the table. There was no sign of Mary, who was presumably asleep upstairs.

'Jaysus, Eil! What's the matter?' gasped Sheila when she saw her sister's face.

'That solicitor! He made me feel *this* big!' Eileen held her thumb and a finger an inch apart.

'It's no good then?'

'No bloody good at all. I'll tell you all about it in a minute when I've calmed down. Fancy stopping for a cuppa?'

'If you make it.'

As Eileen began to fill the kettle, Sheila said, 'You'll

never guess what happened this morning. Aggie Donovan came round and gave me most of her meat coupons.' Meat had been rationed the previous month.

'She never!'

'She said the kids needed meat more than she did.'

'Most people are nice, deep down,' said Eileen. 'Rosie Gregson always gets pushed to the front of the queue as soon as they see she's in the club.'

'I don't know what to do with these!' Sheila stared down at the bowl full of washing. 'The rack's full, the maiden's full. Where am I going to dry them?'

'I'll put them on my rack for you,' Eileen offered.

'Will you? Ta, Sis.'

'Though it's your own fault for having so many children. You need a private laundry all to yourself.'

'Well, actually . . .' Sheila stopped and looked at her sister, half smiling.

'Oh, Sheil! You're not up the stick again?'

'I'm a few days late.'

'For Chrissakes, girl! If you go on at this rate, you'll have twenty kids by the time you're forty.'

'I wouldn't mind,' Sheila said serenely, 'and neither would Cal. He'll be tickled pink when he finds out.'

Cal had gone back to sea on the freighter *Bird of Paradise*, which was sailing in a convoy to the United States to pick up a cargo of food. God willing, he would be home again in two weeks' time.

Eileen made the tea, and when they sat down she described in detail her encounter with the solicitor.

'When you put it into words, Francis doesn't sound so bad at all,' she said ruefully. 'I began to feel as if I was being dead unreasonable.'

'Perhaps I should have come with you, like. If I'd

told this solicitor what I saw, he might have believed you.'

'Huh!' Eileen snorted. 'He believed me all right, but seemed to think it was all me own fault. According to him, he might have done the same thing if his wife had changed the locks. Lords knows what Miss Thomas and Nick will have to say when I tell them what happened.'

In fact, Miss Thomas merely shook her head resignedly. 'It's no more than I would have expected. We'll just have to find someone more appropriate. I'll ask around, Eileen.'

Nick said airly, 'The man's an idiot. If it comes to it, we'll just have to get someone in London, the best man in his field – money's no object as far as this divorce is concerned. A good solicitor is always on the side of the client, even if the client is a thoroughly bad lot.'

'Thanks very much!' Eileen said indignantly.

He kissed her forehead. 'My dearest girl, you are the most adorable lot in the entire world.'

That night, Eileen had scarcely been home a few minutes when there was a tap on the back kitchen window, and she opened the door to find Annie outside.

'Come in,' she said stiffly. She felt slightly annoyed with her friend, whom she'd scarcely seen since the day they'd cleaned Freda Tutty's house. Every weekend, Annie's time was totally taken up with Barney Clegg. It had been a whirlwind romance. Eileen wondered if she'd come to say they were engaged, though Annie's pretty, delicate face was glum as she came into the house.

'He's ditched me,' she said immediately. 'Barney gave me me marching orders at work this morning.'

'I'm sorry, Annie.'

'You don't sound it,' Annie snapped.

'You knew before you went out with him he was a womaniser,' Eileen said reasonably. 'You said yourself he had a string of broken hearts behind him.'

'Yeh, but I thought it would be different with me. He made out he was madly in love.'

'I expect all the other broken hearts felt the same. Anyroad, I thought you intended playing hard to get?'

'Oh, you're full of sympathy, aren't you?' Annie said bitterly. 'You can't play hard to get forever.'

'I truly am sorry, Annie, but,' Eileen decided it was best to be completely honest, 'to tell the truth, I feel a bit hurt. One minute, it seemed we were the best of friends. Next, I hardly see you for months.'

Annie burst into tears. 'Oh, Eil! I'm at me wits' end worrying about Terry and Joe. I can hardly get them out of me mind for a minute when I'm stuck at home by meself. It was lovely going out with Barney. He took me to all sorts of places; North Wales and Chester and Southport. We even had best red salmon once for our tea. He was such a gentleman and couldn't do enough for me. I felt like a proper woman for the first time since Tom died. It took me mind off me lads for a while when I was with him.'

'Oh, Lord, Annie!'

'Then I went and slept with the beggar, and that was it! The chase was over. He'd caught me. Now he's after this new woman at work,' Annie sniffed.

'You slept with him!'

'Yeh! Ask me what it was like?' To Eileen's relief, there was a suspicion of a grin on Annie's face.

'What was it like?'

'It tickled all the time. I kept on wanting to giggle.'

The two women burst out laughing. Annie said, 'I'm sorry I neglected you, Eileen. Barney just swept me off me feet, but now I'm down to earth with a bump.'

'You're better off without him, luv,' Eileen said.

'That's what I keep telling meself,' Annie said wryly. 'But I take a bit of convincing. Anyroad, that's not why I'm here, though it did me good to get it off me chest. I came to tell you there's a rumour going round you're having an affair.'

'Jaysus!' gasped Eileen. 'Who told you that?'

'Ellis Evans heard it from Mrs Henderson who got it off you-know-who.'

'Aggie Donovan?'

'Who else? She's seen you coming back late on Saturday night with a feller in a motorbike and sidecar.'

'He usually leaves it parked around the corner.' Eileen wasn't sure whether to laugh or cry.

'You mean it's true? And there was I, insisting Aggie Donovan was off her rocker.'

'Some of it's true, but I'm not having an affair.'

'Who is the "he" you're not having an affair with?' Annie probed.

'Nick Stephens. I told you about him once.'

'It's coming along then!' said Annie delightedly.

'It's more than coming along,' Eileen said shyly. 'Once I divorce Francis, Nick and I are getting married.'

'Divorce! Oh, luv!' Annie clapped her hands together delightedly, seemingly back to her old self. 'To think what I've been missing, 'cos I was so wrapped up in that rotten Barney!'

'Me and Tony are going to London with him at Easter,' Eileen said, adding, 'As for the neighbours, I'll get Nick to park his bike further afield from now on, else I'll be the scarlet woman of Pearl Street if it becomes common knowledge I'm seeing another feller.'

Chapter 12

'Is that *really* where the King and Queen live?' Tony asked in an awed voice.

'Of course it is, luv.'

'Are they in right now?'

'Well, I'm not sure about that. They might have gone on their holidays for Easter, same as us.'

The three of them, Eileen, Tony and Nick, were standing at the gates of Buckingham Palace, where the windows glinted blankly in the late March sunshine. The guards, in their black busbies and red uniforms, stood motionless, one each side, staring unseeingly ahead.

'I wonder what they're thinking about,' Eileen whispered to Nick. 'It must be murder in those terrible hats.'

'That's probably what they're thinking,' said Nick. '"It's murder in this terrible hat". Or perhaps, "I wish the lovely lady with the long blonde hair belonged to me".'

'Oh, gerraway with you!' Eileen poked him in the ribs with her elbow.

Tony noticed them whispering together and grasped his mam's hand possessively. Eileen squeezed it warmly. There'd been a worrying atmosphere of jealousy between her son and Nick ever since they'd met early that Good Friday morning on Lime Street station. Both seemed to be vying for her attention. They spoke to each other rarely and then only with stiff politeness.

'Well, we've seen Buckingham Palace. Where are we off

to now?' she asked cheerfully.

'How about something to eat?' suggested Nick. 'Are you hungry, Tony?'

'Yes,' Tony answered briefly. 'Can I have an ice cream, Mam?'

'Not till you've had your tea.'

'He can have one for his afters,' said Nick. 'We'll go to Lyons Corner House. Then you can see Marble Arch.'

'Can we go on the underground train?' Tony asked, just as Nick raised his arm to hail a passing taxi.

'There'll be plenty of time tomorrow for the trains, luv. Gosh, isn't this exciting,' she said brightly, as they piled into the back of the big black cab. 'Wait till you tell your mates at school you had a ride in a London taxi!'

'I'd sooner have gone on the train,' Tony said sulkily.

Eileen sighed. It boded ill for the future if Tony and Nick didn't get on.

Conversation was forced throughout the meal. It wasn't until Nick spilt a dollop of ice cream on the lapel of his jacket that Tony stifled a giggle. Eileen wiped off the offending mess with her handkerchief.

'Lord knows when you get this suit cleaned. You never have it off your back,' she said sternly. It was the same corduroy one he had been wearing when she met him in Southport.

'What do you mean?' Nick said indignantly. 'I get both my suits cleaned regularly.'

'Both? D'you mean you've got two suits exactly the same?'

'No, they're different colours. One's browny-green and the other's greeny-brown.'

Tony giggled again. Nick turned on him. 'Is she always nagging you, too?'

Nodding solemnly, Tony said, 'She's got this thing

about being clean.'

'That's women all over!'

'Eh, youse two! Stop talking about me like I wasn't there,' Eileen said, delighted the atmosphere seemed to have lightened a little. She noticed Tony stifle a huge yawn. 'What time is it?' she asked Nick.

He glanced at his watch. 'Just gone six.'

'Perhaps we could make our way back to the hotel soon. I've no idea where we are. Is it very far away?'

'Piccadilly. We could walk down Park Lane, if you like?'

'That'd be nice. We might be back before the blackout. Come on, Tony, luv. Finish off your lemonade. It's not long off your bedtime.'

'But, Mam,' he groaned. 'He said it was only six o'clock.'

Eileen noticed he still couldn't bring himself to call Nick by name. 'We've got to get back yet,' she said briskly.

They strolled along Park Lane. On one side, the lush trees and grass of Hyde Park seemed to dim and fade before their eyes as dusk began to fall.

'There's an anti-aircraft battery somewhere behind those trees,' Nick said.

'Can we go and look at it?' Tony tugged at Eileen's hand.

But Eileen didn't hear. They'd reached the Dorchester and she was too busy gaping into the still brilliantly lit foyer, and at the top-hatted doormen opening the doors of long, sleek black cars for elegantly dressed women in fur coats and men in evening dress or uniform.

'See that chap?' Nick pointed to a tall, khaki-clad figure going into the hotel. 'He's a Brigadier General.'

A couple came walking towards them, arm in arm; a

plump young man in naval officer's uniform and a pretty girl in a mauve chiffon dress with a little white fur cape around her shoulders. The young man stopped dead when he saw Nick.

'Nick! Nicko Stephens! Is it really you?

'Hello, Perry.' Eileen sensed Nick wasn't too pleased at the encounter. He looked rather sour as his hand was vigorously shaken and his shoulder slapped. 'How are you?' he asked stiffly.

'Well – extraordinarily well, in fact,' Perry said jovially. 'Having a rattling good war so far, I can tell you. Got a forty-eight-hour pass and nipped up from Portsmouth in the old banger to see Belinda. Isn't she a poppet? Shake hands with my old chum, Nick, there's a darling.'

Belinda shook hands, pouting prettily. Eileen, feeling drab and very ordinary in her second-hand coat and the beret Brenda Mahon had made, shrank into the background. Nick would surely feel ashamed of her beside this beautifully dressed creature. Nick apparently did. He made no attempt to introduce her as Perry prattled on.

'I couldn't believe my ears when someone told me you were working in some Godforsaken place up north,' he said. 'I thought, it's not like Nicko to chicken out of the action.'

'I didn't have any choice in the matter,' Nick said shortly. It was only then he remembered Eileen and ushered her forward. 'This is Eileen Costello, my fiancée, and her son, Tony.'

'Fiancée, eh?' Perry's eyes raked Eileen up and down as they shook hands. 'Nicko could always pick 'em.'

Nick said, almost rudely, 'We're in a hurry to get back to the hotel. Tony's tired. Damn!' he swore as they walked away.

'What's the matter?' Eileen was reeling. He'd actually introduced her as his fiancée!

'I'm surprised he didn't hand me a white feather.'

He was silent for the rest of the way back. Tony skipped along beside Eileen. 'What's a fiancée?'

'It's a bit complicated to explain, luv. I'll tell you some other time.'

By the time they reached Green Park, London was in total darkness. Their small hotel, where they'd booked in that afternoon, was down a little street off Piccadilly. The drab, brownstone exterior was deceptive. Inside was the epitome of subdued luxury, with thick Persian carpets throughout the ground floor and comfortable chairs upholstered in maroon padded leather. The walls were full of gold-framed oil paintings. Tony was particularly enraptured by the little crystal wall lights, like miniature chandeliers, which cast a gentle glow on the dark brown walls.

As soon as they had pushed through the heavy curtain over the door, Nick said abruptly. 'I'm going to have a drink. I'll meet you in the bar when you're ready.'

'All right. Come on, luv.' Eileen began to lead Tony towards the stairs.

'Can we go up in the lift?'

'But we're only on the first floor, Tony.'

'Yes, but . . .' Her looked up at her pleadingly.

'Oh, I suppose so.'

He ran gleefully towards the old-fashioned iron lift which was standing waiting, and pulled back the metal folding door.

'Mind your fingers!' she shouted.

'Can I work the buttons?' he asked once they were inside.

'If you like.'

'Can we go up to the fifth floor and back down again?'

'For goodness sake, Tony!' she said, exasperated. Then, relenting, 'I don't suppose it'll do any harm. No-one seems to be waiting.'

The lift made its creaking, groaning progress up to the top floor. Tony watched, fascinated, as stairs gave way to more stairs. The lift stopped when they reached the top, and he looked up at his mam, starry-eyed, before pressing the button marked '1', and the lift began to grind its way down again.

'I'd like to be a lift maker when I grow up,' he said longingly.

'Well, we'll just have to see, won't we?'

When they reached their bedroom, Eileen found the blackout curtains had already been drawn, and the plush brown coverlet on the double bed turned down. Tony made a beeline for the bed and began to bounce up and down so enthusiastically that his glasses fell off.

'You'll have that bed right through the floor if you don't ease up a bit,' Eileen threatened. 'People downstairs will think a bomb's dropped.'

He stopped bouncing and immediately began to fiddle with the wireless on the bedside table. 'This is a much better one than ours. What's this, Mam?'

'It's a telephone.'

'Can I use it?'

'No, you can't.' Eileen switched on the cream-shaded lamps each side of the bed and turned the main light off. 'There! That looks cosier, doesn't it?' She glanced around the rather old-fashioned room, with its highly polished furniture, thick brown carpet and cream embossed walls, and gave a sigh of satisfaction. 'I like hotels. I wouldn't mind living here for the rest of me life.'

'I can walk round in me bare feet, see!' Tony had begun

to get undressed. 'And it doesn't feel the least bit cold. And Mam, the lav's only just outside the door. You don't have to go down the yard, like at home.'

'I wonder what Nick's room is like?' She opened the adjoining door. The adjacent room was exactly the same. Nick hadn't bothered to unpack. His small suitcase lay on the bed, unopened.

'He's got a cob on, hasn't he, Mam?'

Eileen came back and knelt down to help her son with his trouser buttons. 'I suppose he has, luv. But he'll get over it. He always does.'

'He won't be horrible to me, will he, like me dad was when he was in a bad temper?'

She hugged him fiercely. 'Of course not, luv. Nick's like a little boy sometimes. In certain ways, he hasn't grown up proper yet.'

Tony wasn't keen on his mam having another little boy, even if he was much taller than she was. 'I don't like him much,' he pouted, as he climbed into bed.

Eileen's heart sank. 'You will do, luv, eventually,' she replied with more confidence than she felt. She tucked the covers under his chin.

'Don't go till I'm asleep,' he pleaded.

'I won't. Anyroad, I want to change me frock and make me face up again.'

'What happens if there's an air raid and you're downstairs?' he asked nervously.

'That's not likely to happen, is it?' She removed her frock and began to run the water in the little cream sink in the corner. The water gushed forth in a cloud of steam. 'Jaysus! This is hot!'

'There was an air raid the other day,' Tony responded.

'That was hundreds of miles away up in Scotland,' she said sharply. On 17 March, St Patrick's Day, the

Germans had had another go at the naval base in the Orkneys. Several civilians living nearby had been killed. 'Anyroad, the RAF bombed the Germans back, didn't they? Perhaps that's put them off for good.'

'I bloody hope so,' said Tony.

'Don't swear!' She slapped his bottom through the bedclothes.

'That didn't hurt a bit,' he chortled.

'It wasn't meant to! Now, come on, Tony, go asleep. You're staying awake deliberately just to get up me nose.'

'There was silence from the bed as Eileen made her face up, then slipped into the strawberry pink moygashel suit she'd bought from C & A especially for London. It was very plain; the skirt straight with a kick pleat at the back, the short-sleeved top buttoning down the front. She pulled the stiff wide belt as tight as it would go. Finally, she pinned a bunch of white silk snowdrops to the lapel. She turned towards the bed.

'What do I look like?'

But, to her relief, Tony was fast asleep.

To her further relief, when she got downstairs, Nick seemed to have recovered his good humour. He waved to her from a table in the corner of the small but surprisingly crowded bar.

'I got you a gin and it,' he said when she reached him. His voice was slightly thick, as if he'd drunk too much, something which she'd never known him do before.

'Ta. Cheers!' She took a sip, then reached in her bag for her cigarettes. 'Are all these people staying here?' The hotel didn't look big enough for so many guests.

'No. This bar has become the place to meet if you're in the services,' he explained. He put his hand on his chest and murmured, 'Mea culpa, mea culpa, mea culpa.'

'What's that for?'

'Earlier. I'm sorry I went of the deep end, but I always loathed Perry Eccleston. He cheated his way through college. Seeing him in uniform was bad enough, but to have him suggest I dodged call-up made my blood boil over.'

'Never mind,' Eileen soothed. 'He was only showing off.'

'He's got good reason to show off. He's a Second Lieutenant in the Navy, I'm a Scientific Officer, grade something-or-other.' He sighed mournfully. 'I'm going to get another drink. How about you?'

'I've hardly touched this one yet.'

He got up and began to push his way through the crowd, and Eileen glanced around with interest. The air was thick with smoke and the buzz of conversation almost deafening. Nearly all the drinkers were in uniform, women as well as men. There were three WRENs at the next table, and it seemed odd to see women wearing collars and ties. She wondered if it felt uncomfortable and envied their air of self-assurance and sophistication. The bar seemed to be getting more crowded by the minute, as if it was definitely the place to be that night.

Two young soldiers paused at her table. 'Would you like some company, sweetheart?'

'I'm with someone,' she stammered.

'She's already spoken for!' Nick was back, grinning at the soldiers.

'I thought she would be, but there's no harm in trying,' one said wistfully.

Nick was about to sit down when a distinguished-looking middle-aged couple in evening dress entered the bar and paused at the doorway, as if searching for a table.

To Eileen's surprise, Nick said joyfully, 'That's the chap I've come to see. I won't be a minute.'

He hurried across and caught the man's arm just as the couple were about to be swallowed up in the crush. After a few seconds, the man's face broadened into a smile of recognition, and he shook Nick's hand and introduced the woman. They remained talking for quite a while, the older man nodding his head from time to time. Then Nick produced a piece of paper, wrote something on it and handed it over. They shook hands again and Nick returned to sit by Eileen, a satisfied look on his face.

'That was Ben Fulford's old man. Ben said he would be staying here. I gave him my address and he's going to do his best to get me out of Kirkby and into the Air Force. He reckons there'll be a shortage of pilots once the war gets going.'

Eileen glowered at him. 'That's what you'd like, isn't it? For the war to get going, so you men can play your silly games? Trouble is, you'll probably get killed in the process. But that doesn't matter; you'll be dead and gone and it's the women who are left behind to do the crying.'

'Will you cry for me?' he asked tenderly. He leaned across to kiss her cheek, but she turned her head away impatiently.

'You're drunk! Anyroad, it's a stupid question because you know damn well I'll cry for you.' She refused to look at him as she lit another cigarette and puffed on it angrily. 'I suppose I may as well go upstairs and pack me bags. You'll be wanting to leave, now you've sorted out your business.'

He didn't answer. Eileen continued to ignore him as she glared around the bar. The WRENs had been joined by two ATS girls and the five were involved in an animated conversation. At another table, half a dozen Air Force men were counting loudly, 'One two, three . . .' as one of their number downed a neat row of drinks, one after the other, each in a single gulp. When he reached six, he stared at his mates with glazed eyes, then gradually sank onto the floor, where he seemed to fall asleep. There was a burst of song from across the room: '*Bless 'em all, bless 'em all, the long and the short and the tall . . .*' One of the WRENs got up and demonstrated the Sailor's Hornpipe and someone shouted, 'Do it on the table, Admiral.' The WREN stuck out her tongue and sat down again.

If the war 'got going', Eileen wondered, how many of these young people would be alive this time next year? She felt strangely out of things. Her own contribution towards the war effort paled beside that of these youngsters in uniform. If it wasn't for Tony . . . Suddenly, she understood Nick's urge to be involved.

She turned to him. He was watching her solemnly, his hands folded primly on his lap, lips twitching. Unable to resist, as usual, Eileen burst out laughing. 'I said to Tony earlier, it's like having two little boys with the pair of you.'

'You didn't! Is that what you think of me?' He looked taken aback.

'Frankly, sometimes, yes,' she confessed.

'That's terrible! Let's go upstairs this very minute and I'll prove to you I'm anything but a little boy.'

Eileen had her drink halfway to her lips. At his words, she put the drink down and sat staring at the little cork mat on which the glass had been set. She'd been dreading this.

Or had she? She wasn't quite sure. She knew in her

heart of hearts it had to happen sometime, and once Nick had suggested London, that the sometime would be then. But her feelings were totally confused; one minute fearful, next a delightful anticipation.

'All right,' she said. The words seemed to come from some distance away, as if someone else had said them for her.

Nick put his arm around her shoulders. 'Are you sure?' His voice trembled.

'Yes,' she whispered, though she was anything but.

She stood up on legs so weak they nearly gave way and she stumbled. She felt Nick's hand on her elbow, where it stayed as he led her upstairs and into the blackness of his room.

'I'll just check on Tony.' She felt for the door. She'd left a lamp on, and saw her son hadn't moved.

Before Eileen had time to close the door, Nick's arms came round her roughly. He buried his head in her neck as he began to undo the buttons of her suit top. She felt his hands heavy on her shoulders, dragging the top away, pulling at the straps of her petticoat and bra, then his thumbs were rubbing her nipples, so hard that it hurt. She gasped in pain. Nick seemed to think the gasp was an echo of his own passion, because he lifted her up bodily and carried her to the bed.

'Oh, my darling, darling girl!' He was pulling at her skirt, her suspender belt and pants, until she was naked beneath him. Then he stood back from the bed and regarded her silently for several seconds, before beginning to remove his own clothes with startling rapidity. From the light falling through the partially open door, Eileen saw his tall, naked body, his limbs gleaming softly in the creamy glow. Then he lay beside her and began to kiss her passionately whilst his hands explored her intimately.

Eileen wasn't quite sure what did it. Perhaps it was the smell of alcohol on his breath or the wild, hot look in his dark eyes that reminded her of Francis.

'*No!*' She pushed him away. 'No!'

'What's the matter?' He removed his hands abruptly.

'I don't know.' She slipped off the bed, ran into her own room and closed the door behind her. She found her nightdress and put it on, then glanced around for her bag. She needed a cigarette desperately, but remembered the bag was in Nick's room. She'd just have to go without. She got herself a drink of water, instead, and sank, panting, into a chair.

Was it always like that, making love? Rough and hurtful, never gentle? Surely Cal didn't treat Sheila as if she was just a piece of flesh? Thoughts chased each other wildly through her head as she tried to understand. She loved Nick and if she wanted to be with him, perhaps she'd just have to get used to making love that way. But, could she?

There was a tap on the adjoining door and Nick said softly, 'Eileen. We've got to talk.'

'In a minute.'

She washed her face, then took a deep breath and went into his room. He was sitting on the bed in a red check dressing gown, smoking a cigarette. He patted the space next to him. 'Come and sit down. I promise not to touch you.'

She knew she could trust him. As she shut the door, she said, 'I didn't know you smoked.'

'I don't. This is one of yours.'

'Where's me bag? I'm gasping for one.' She propped a pillow up against the headboard and sat beside him.

'Take this. I can't stand it.'

'Ta.' She took a long puff. 'I wish I'd never begun

smoking. I don't seem to be able to live without them nowadays.'

'I wish you'd stop. They're bad for you.'

'I know,' she said conversationally. 'Me poor dad's getting terrible short of breath lately. He's smoked like a chimney all his life.'

'I liked your dad, and your sister. I'd like to meet them again sometime.'

Eileen didn't answer. After a while, Nick said, 'I'm sorry, Eileen. I was pissed out of my mind and I wanted you so much. Did I hurt you?'

'Yes,' she answered in a small voice.

'Can we try again? Not tonight,' he said quickly. 'Some other time?'

'I suppose so.'

'I love you. You know that, don't you?' He still made no attempt to touch her.

'I know, Nick,' she said gently. 'And I love you. We just got off on the wrong foot, that's all.'

'Stay with me tonight,' he said urgently. 'I won't lay a finger on you, I swear. I'll sleep on top of the covers, if you like.'

She laughed. 'There's no need for that.'

'So, you'll stay?'

'I'll stay.'

They sat in contented silence for a while, Eileen relieved that everything seemed all right between them again. She said, hesitantly, 'Nick?'

'Yes, darling?'

'Could we use the telephone and send down for a cup of tea?'

She couldn't sleep. Outside, the London traffic remained heavy, even into the early hours of the morning. Cars hooted continually and late night revellers laughed and sang as they went down nearby Piccadilly. Beside her, Nick slept peacefully, his back to her.

Edging up carefully so as not to disturb him, Eileen sat clutching her knees. Thin strips of light showed under the doors to Tony's room and the corridor, and gradually the objects in the room began to take shape; the big wardrobe, the tallboy and dressing table with their pretty little brass handles. Nick's shoulder and his left arm were out of the clothes and his smooth, satiny flesh gleamed dully. She held her breath, longing to reach out and stroke it. The nape of his neck, where his dark hair was clustered in little tight curls, seemed particularly appealing. She thought about before, when his hands had touched her, explored her, and shivered at the memory. Had it really been so bad? Why had she made him stop?

Heart racing, Eileen removed her nightdress and slid underneath the clothes. She kissed his neck. He turned so quickly she was convinced he must have been awake all the time.

'Darling!' He took her in his arms, and they lay entwined together for a long time. Then he began to touch her tentatively. 'Is this all right?' he whispered. 'Tell me the minute I do something wrong.'

He seemed to take forever, stroking, touching, kissing her trembling, responsive body.

'Now, Nick! Now!' she cried urgently, when she could stand his caresses no longer, and knew it was time for something more.

So *that*'s what it's like, she thought, when it was all over, and she lay beside him, exhausted.

'Did you like it? I didn't hurt, did I?' he asked anxiously.

'No, Nick. It was wonderful.' She sighed blissfully.

'Absolutely wonderful.'

'That's only the first of a million times,' he whispered.

'Mmm!' she mumbled.

'Are you going to sleep?'

'You've worn me out.'

'Eileen?'

She could scarcely raise the energy to answer. 'What?'

'Have I proved to you I'm not a little boy?'

Eileen didn't hear. She was asleep.

When she woke, Nick's side of the bed was empty. She stretched luxuriously, then remembered her son in the next room. He'd be worried if he woke up and she wasn't there. She found her nightdress tangled up in the bed-clothes and put it on before going next door. To her astonishment, the bed was empty and Tony's clothes had disappeared. Perhaps he and Nick had gone down to breakfast together, she thought hopefully.

She pulled the heavy curtains back and bright sunlight flooded the room. Outside, the traffic was nose to tail and she could see the shops in Piccadilly were open and quite a few people were already up and out.

Eileen dressed quickly in the blue crepe de Chine dress with the heart-shaped neckline that had been her best until she bought the moygashel suit. She hurried downstairs, but there was no sign of Nick or Tony in the half-empty dining room. Feeling worried, she went outside and stood looking up and down the street. To her relief, after a few minutes they appeared around the corner, Tony running in front with a small aeroplane in his hand, pretending to fly it, Nick's tall, curly-haired figure behind. His face lit up when he saw her waiting, and he began to hurry.

She'd never noticed before, but he had an odd sort of

ambling gait, slightly lopsided. It touched her, as nothing about him had ever done before, and she knew she would never love any man as much as she loved Nick. As they approached, Eileen had the strangest feeling, 'I'll remember this moment when I'm an old woman, my son and my lover coming to me in the London sunshine.'

She began to run. She scooped up her son, then, when Nick reached them, flung them both against him. He embraced them, laughing.

'I love you! I love you both so much I could die,' she cried.

But Tony was impatient with such a show of emotion. He struggled out of her arms. 'Look what Nick's bought me,' he said excitedly. 'It's a Spitfire. Once the war get's going properly, he's going to fly in one.'

Eileen groaned. 'Men!'

'We've got you a present, too, Mam. Show her, Nick. I helped pick it out.'

Nick produced a long velvet box from his pocket. 'I got fed up with you forever asking me the time.'

The box contained a gold watch with an expanding strap and a mother of pearl face. 'It's lovely!' Eileen breathed. 'I've always wanted a watch.'

'It's real gold, Mam!'

'Is it, luv?' She felt close to tears.

'Can we have breakfast now? I'm starving.' Tony began to drag her towards the hotel. 'Nick said we can have bacon and eggs and fried tomatoes and everything. A grilled mix.'

'A mixed grill, though it amounts to the same thing.' Nick ruffled Tony's silky fair hair. 'Come on, then. I'm starving, too.'

'Why are you suddenly such good friends?' Eileen whispered when they reached the dining room and Tony darted around choosing a table.

'I've no idea. It just seemed to happen. He came into the bedroom looking for you and wasn't at all shocked to find us together. When he saw you fast asleep, we both decided you were a lazy, idle woman and we'd go out without you. I remembered I was no longer a little boy, and behaved in a mature and fatherly fashion. In fact,' he finished complacently, 'I'm quite proud of myself.'

Eileen sighed rapturously as Nick helped her fasten the watch around her wrist. 'I'm so happy. This is going to be a perfect day. Nothing can possibly spoil it.'

And nothing did!

After breakfast, they wandered around the shops, where the prices were even higher than in Southport. Eileen steadfastly refused all Nick's offers to buy more presents. If he'd had his way, she'd have needed another suitcase to take things home.

'No,' she said adamantly, when he tried to persuade her to accept a Chinese silk dressing gown. 'You've already paid for the train and the hotel, if I let you pay for anything else, I'd feel like a kept woman.' She glanced down at the gold watch. 'Me watch is more than enough. Anyroad, I'd feel stupid wandering around the house in *that*!' She nodded at the dressing gown. 'Though it's very nice,' she added quickly, so as not to hurt his feelings.

She bought him a present, though; three pairs of socks because she'd noticed his current ones were thin on the heel.

'You haven't got a shred of romance in your body!' he cried as she handed him the gift.

'I didn't want to waste me money on a tie pin or a pair of cufflinks you'd only lose,' she said indignantly. 'Just thank your lucky stars you didn't get a box of hankies.'

Tony helped her choose little mementoes of London

337

for her family and friends; glass paperweights which shook into a snowstorm for Annie and Mr Singerman, a statue of Pope Pius XII for Sheila, rosary beads with an ivory crucifix for Paddy O'Hara, though she'd seen little of him since he'd taken up with Miss Brazier, and, finally, a tea caddy decorated with Beefeaters for her dad, because his old one was so bent the lid wouldn't close.

'I'd like to get a christening spoon for me friend, Jess,' she told Nick, so they went to Selfridges, the biggest shop Eileen had ever seen, stretching for an entire block along Oxford Street, and found a spoon on the silver counter. To Jess's unutterable and continuing delight, the doctor had confirmed she was pregnant and the baby was expected in September, though Eileen had promised to keep the information to herself. Not even Arthur knew he was going to become a father. Apparently, Jess was waiting for the right moment to tell him. 'It might come as a bit of a shock,' she said.

As Tony would be six in a week's time, she let him pick his birthday present. After a thorough search through the vast toy department, he eventually pounced on a box containing six little model aeroplanes, a hangar, and a dozen miniature figures in RAF uniform.

'Can I have this? *Please*, Mam!'

'If that's what you want, luv.'

'I'm going to join the Royal Air Force when I grow up, like Nick.'

'You were going to be a lift engineer last night,' she said tartly. 'You'll join the RAF over my dead body.'

Tony was too enraptured with his present to argue. 'Can I carry it?' he asked after they'd paid.

'You can carry it, you can look at it, but open it at your peril.' Eileen handed him the paper bag.

Nick shuddered. 'My God, Tony! What a terrible

woman your mam is! C'mon, son, there's a restaurant on the top floor. Let's have some ice cream and lemonade. I need a respite from all this relentless shopping.'

'I've nearly finished,' sang Eileen gaily. 'All that's left to buy is an Easter egg for Tony – and a present for meself.'

'What's that, Mam?'

'A navy-blue handbag. I'm sure everyone's looking at me using a black handbag with this coat.'

Nick and Tony looked at each other and raised their eyes to heaven. 'Women!' they said in unison.

After lunch, they went to the Natural History Museum. Tony regarded the rather sinister skeleton of a dinosaur with considerable nervousness. 'Did they really exist once?' he asked Nick.

'They certainly did!'

'Are they likely to come back again?'

'No, son. They're extinct. That means they've died out,' he explained in response to the little boy's puzzled look.

They spent nearly two hours in the museum, then strolled back to the hotel through Hyde Park, with Tony running ahead peeking in the bag from time to time at his present. The Anti-Tank Battery, complete with guns, looked out of place in its pretty green setting. Eileen shuddered at the constant reminders they were in a state of war. London seemed to be at the very hub. The sky was littered with silver barrage balloons and she noticed all the important buildings were protected by walls of sandbags. But then, she thought ruefully, if it hadn't been for the war, she would never have met Nick. She wouldn't be in London, strolling arm in arm through Hyde Park with this complex young man who had transported her to the very limits of joy the night before. She felt herself flush at the memory. She glanced up and caught his eye. Nick squeezed her arm.

'Happy?'

'I never thought it possible to be so happy,' she whispered.

'Me, neither.'

After they'd had tea, they went to see *The Wizard of Oz*. Eileen would have preferred *Gone With the Wind*, but Tony couldn't be expected to sit through a three-and-a-half-hour epic. They emerged, blinking, into the blacked out streets and sang *Somewhere Over the Rainbow* and *Follow the Yellow Brick Road* all the way down Piccadilly to the hotel.

Tony fell asleep as soon as his head touched the pillow. Eileen changed into her new suit and went down to meet Nick in the bar. This was to be their last night in London. Tomorrow, Sunday, they were going home. Nick had to work on Monday night and she was on the early shift the following day. The trains couldn't be trusted to get them home in a reasonable time if they left their return till Monday.

Someone was playing a piano downstairs, not in the crowded bar, as Eileen expected, but in the small dining room, where the tables had been pushed against the walls and the carpet rolled up. There were already several couples dancing. The only illumination came from the candles flickering on the tables and on the piano.

She found Nick had saved her a stool by the bar. 'There's no tables left,' he said. 'Shall we dance later?'

'I'd love to.' It would be a glorious end to a glorious day. She noticed the bar was full of servicemen and women again. Nick was glancing at them enviously. He couldn't wait to get in uniform, she thought painfully.

How could he think of leaving her so easily? She tried not to think what it would be like, on constant tenterhooks in case he was killed. Sheila already knew the feeling, and Annie, and thousands, if not millions of other wives and girlfriends and mothers. And fathers, too. Mr Singerman still grieved for his vanished Ruth.

'Penny for them!' Nick said.

'Oh, Nick!' They'd been his first words the day they'd met in Southport. She remembered how coldly she'd answered, trying to put him off. She'd thought him so young, yet now!

The pianist was playing *Beautiful Dreamer*, and Nick said, 'Dance with me.'

No-one was bothering to dance properly on the little patch of floor. The couples already there scarcely moved from the spot as they turned slowly in each other's arms. 'Come here!' Nick said gently, pulling Eileen towards him. She nestled her head in the space between his shoulder and his ear, which seemed to have been made especially for her. 'I love you more than life itself,' he whispered, his voice choking with emotion. 'When I die, your face will be the last thing my eyes will see, even if you're not there with me.'

'Don't talk about dying,' she whispered back. 'I can't bear it.'

The pianist finished *Beautiful Dreamer* with a flourish and began *We'll Meet Again*.

'I love this,' Eileen murmured. 'You should hear Jess sing it. It makes you want to weep.' She sang the words under her breath, '*We'll meet again . . .*'

Nick joined in in a rather tuneless baritone and suddenly everyone was singing: the dancers, the drinkers in the bar.

Nick grasped Eileen by the waist. She clung to his neck

as he began to whirl her around and around in the middle of the floor and she felt as if she might spin into oblivion, disappear altogether in a puff of smoke, then wake up and find herself in Pearl Street. This couldn't be happening. It was too unreal. No-one had a right to so much happiness.

When the last verse was reached, the tempo slowed slightly, the pianist put his foot on the loud pedal, voices rose, and it sounded as if the entire population of London had joined in. *WE'LL MEET AGAIN* . . .

There was a burst of laughter and applause when the song finished. Eileen and Nick skidded to a dizzy halt. The pianist said, Whew!' in a loud voice and reached for his drink off the piano top. The dancers returned to their tables.

'Let's go to bed,' said Nick.

'Yes, let's,' Eileen answered.

On Sunday morning, after they'd been to Mass at Westminster Cathedral, accompanied by Nick, a lapsed Catholic, they made their way to Euston Station.

'Let's hope going home is as easy as coming down,' said Nick. 'Though I think we were lucky.'

But there was to be no repeat of the fairly rapid, uninterrupted journey to London. Since the onset of the war, trains had become notoriously unpredictable and were usually packed to capacity, mainly with service-men, either going home or coming back off leave, or being transported to barracks en masse. The train they caught was already crowded. Eileen found a single seat and sat with Tony on her knee, their feet on their luggage, whilst Nick stood in the corridor making faces. They stopped and started all the way to Rugby, where everyone was told to change; their train had been commandeered by the army to take troops to Edinburgh. They hung around on Rugby Station for several hours, until another packed train took them as far as Crewe, where they changed again. It was almost midnight when they arrived, tired and hungry, at Lime Street Station, Liverpool.

'I'd swop my new handbag for a cup of tea,' Eileen said wearily. She refused Nick's offer of a taxi home. 'I think we might just catch the last train from Exchange Station. What about you?' He'd left his motorbike in Melling.

'I'll get a bus as far as I can, then walk the rest. A good long walk in the dark will do me good. I'll see you safely on the train.'

It seemed strange to walk through the near-deserted city centre after crowded, noisy London.

At Exchange Station, Nick gave Tony a hug, then kissed Eileen on the cheek. He said softly, 'We'll meet again?'

'Tuesday morning, outside Dunnings,' she confirmed.

She was unable to see the expression on his face in the dark station and was surprised when he pulled her against him and whispered in her ear, 'You're not going to push me to the fringes of your life again, are you, Eileen? Not after London?'

'Of course not! How could I? We'll work something out on Tuesday.'

'Till then!'

He was gone.

On the way home, Eileen said to Tony, 'I want you to keep a secret for me, luv.'

'A war secret?'

'Yes, I suppose it is, in a way. Don't tell anyone about Nick, will you?'

'Why should we have to keep Nick a secret?' He

looked surprised.

'Well, some people won't understand. The family know, and Jess and Annie, but I don't want the rest of the street knowing me private business till it suits me to tell them.'

'All right, Mam, but we won't have to keep him a secret forever, will we?'

'No, luv, not forever.'

Sheila was the first to call next morning.

'Did you have a nice time?' she asked, though the expression on her sister's radiant face answered the question for her. Any lingering doubts Sheila had about divorce fled. Everyone was entitled to love and be loved. Surely God would think that more important than sticking to a few words uttered at a marriage ceremony?

'It was the gear!' breathed Eileen. 'It seems awful funny to be back in Pearl Street after London. It was so noisy and full of life.'

'Give me Pearl Street, any day,' Sheila said contentedly. Apart from wanting Cal home, she had no wish to change her life one jot.

'What's been happening while I was gone?'

'Nothing much. Oh, Paddy O'Hara's got a puppy, Rover. He seems to have split up with Miss Brazier, though don't start feeling sorry for him. He's been grinning from ear to ear ever since.'

'I brought you a little present back from London.' Eileen presented her sister with the statue. 'I'll get your kids some Easter eggs later on. I should have got them before I went away, but it went out of me mind completely.'

'I'll put it on me mantelpiece straight away.' Sheila went off, delighted.

As soon as she'd gone, Eileen roused Tony. 'I'll make

your breakfast while you get dressed, but there's no grilled mix today. It's back to cornflakes, I'm afraid.'

'I don't mind. I'm dying to show Dominic me Spitfire.'

'While you're doing that, I'll pop round to Grandad's.'

She met Gladys Tutty on the way. Since Freda had returned from Southport, a new Gladys had begun to emerge from Number 14, with a scrubbed face and washed hair. She wore an old, but clean, black bouclé coat and proper shoes.

'Happy Easter, Gladys,' sang Eileen.

'Our Freda only sent me out for a new exercise book,' Gladys grumbled. 'That's all she ever does, bloody homework.'

'Well, you should be proud, Gladys, I hope Tony is as keen on homework when he gets a bit older.'

The woman went off, mumbling to herself, and Eileen smiled.

There was no sign of her dad when she let herself into the house in Garnet Street. Sean was pottering around, looking useless.

'Where is he?'

Her brother nodded towards the stairs. 'He's having a lie-in,' he said indignantly. 'He only made me get up and make a cup of tea.'

'Right thing, too. It's about time you took your turn.'

As she ran upstairs, Sean shouted, 'Tell him I'll leave home and get married if he makes me do it every morning like he said.'

Her dad was sitting smoking, propped against the pillows in the bed he'd shared with Mam, his striped winceyette pyjamas buttoned up to the neck. Several of yesterday's newspapers were spread over the green eiderdown.

'What's up with you?' she demanded.

'Nowt!' he growled. 'I just felt like a lie-in, that's all.'

'But you never lie in!'

'Well, I do now. I thought it'd do that lazy bugger downstairs good to wait on me for a change. Anyroad,' he offered her a cigarette and she shook her head, 'what have you been up to over the weekend?'

Eileen sat on the edge of the bed. 'You know darn well what I've been up to. I've been to London. In fact, I've brought you a present.' She handed him the tea caddy.

He gave it a cursory glance and said, 'Ta,' but didn't touch it.

Eileen put the caddy on the dressing table. She wasn't upset by his apparent rejection of the gift. He'd treasure it, as he treasured everything given him by his family.

'Did you go with Nick?' he asked gruffly.

'You know that, too,' she said. With Eileen's approval, her sister kept Dad up to date on her affairs. 'Do you mind?'

'Why should I mind?' he said, shrugging his massive shoulders. 'It's your life.' He picked up a paper and began to read.

Ah, but you didn't think so once, Eileen thought. Not when you persuaded me to marry Francis.

'You like Nick, don't you?' she asked cautiously.

He wrinkled his nose. 'I've only seen him the once. He seemed a reasonable enough feller. Bit poncey, but what more can you expect if he went to university like you said.'

'Oh, Dad!'

'Anyroad,' he turned a page, pretending to read, 'it don't matter if I like him or not, does it? According to our Sheila, you plan on getting wed once you're rid of Francis Costello.'

'Would that bother you?'

He put the paper down and stared at her accusingly. 'Why are you so keen on having my opinion? Course it wouldn't bother me.'

'Not even divorcing Francis?'

'I don't care if you shoot the bastard. Though again, according to Sheila, divorcing him won't be an easy matter.'

'No,' she confessed. 'The solicitor more or less told me to go and jump in the Mersey. Miss Thomas, a woman from work, is trying to find me another one.'

He lifted the paper and pretended to read again, his blue eyes moving to and fro over the print. 'I might be able to help you there,' he said casually.

'You!' she said astonished.

'I could write to Francis and promise to go through with the nomination as planned, as long as he made no objection to a divorce.'

'You'd do that! For me?' she gasped, even more astonished.

Her dad flung the paper down impatiently. 'For Chrissakes, girl,' he said angrily. 'You're my daughter. I'd lay down me life for you.'

'But,' she said, flustered, 'surely you wouldn't want Francis Costello for an MP, not after what you know about him?'

He smiled. 'He wouldn't be much worse than most. Anyroad, there's quite a few men want to fill Albert Findlay's shoes when he retires. I'm only promising to nominate Francis. I'm not promising he'll win.' He tapped his nose with his finger and said slyly, 'A few words in the right ears and Francis won't be any the wiser when he loses!'

'Oh, Dad!' She hugged him. 'Don't write the letter

yet, though. I'll see what the solicitor has to say.'

'Gerroff!' he muttered, pushing her away. Eileen felt a moment of hurt, because he welcomed the slightest gesture of affection from Sheila. 'Now leave me alone to read me papers in peace, and on your way out, tell our Sean I'd like another cup of tea.'

Chapter 13

When Arthur Fleming got home from work one evening just after Easter, Jess was sitting at the table reading a magazine. There was no sign of a meal, not even a cup of tea.

He nodded politely and said, 'Evening, Jess,' which was as far as any demonstration of affection went nowadays.

'Hallo, Arthur,' she replied absently.

He sat down, opened *The Times*, and decided not to comment on the lack of food and drink. Jess had been in the strangest mood lately. It was as if he'd lived with several different women over the last year. There was the greedy, grasping Jess of old, then the martyr bravely going out to work. After she'd given up her job, she'd changed. There'd been elements of the girl he'd married, as she'd gone round singing at the top of her voice. Lately, though, she seemed to be in a dream world all of her own. He would find her gazing abstractedly into the fire, as if she could see things invisible to him. Whatever those things were, they must have been pleasant, because she was forever smiling, if only to herself, like the cat that had got the best of the cream.

She was smiling now, as she sat with her chin in her hand, looking like a Botticelli angel with her red hair loose and rippling down her back. Her face seemed rather plump, thought Arthur, and it made her appear more youthful, almost girlish.

'How are you getting on in the ARP, Arthur?'

He jumped, the question was so unexpected. 'All right. They're a good crowd.' He'd joined just after Christmas when Jess and Jacob Singerman had started to give concerts for the troops, conscious of the fact that he himself was doing absolutely nothing towards the war effort.

'Are there any lady ARP wardens?' she asked innocently.

Alarm bells began to ring inside his head. What the hell was she driving at? 'A couple,' he answered, just as innocently.

'Then I expect the lipstick on your shirt belonged to one of them,' she said in a matter of fact voice.

'What shirt? What lipstick?' he spluttered.

'The red lipstick on the collar of your blue shirt. I scrubbed it off. It seemed silly to produce it, like evidence.'

'Now, look here, Jess,' he began heatedly, 'you're not to read things into this that don't exist.'

'Your blue shirt exists, Arthur,' she said calmly. 'The lipstick's gone now, but that existed for a while. Someone's been kissing you. Is that all you did, Arthur? Kiss?'

Oh, God! 'That's all, Jess, I swear,' he said with all the conviction he could muster, but he was no good at lying, never had been. One of the reasons the business had gone bust was because he was too honest for his own good.

'You're not telling the truth, dear. I can tell by your face. You're having an affair.'

There seemed little use denying it. 'Not a proper affair, Jess . . .'

'An improper one?' she suggested, smiling.

Her attitude made him feel uneasy. She was up to something. It seemed unnatural, this apparently calm, serene acceptance of the fact he'd been with another woman. Why didn't she scream and yell or throw him out of the house? Perhaps she was working up to a terrific rage and any minute now she'd chuck that vase of daffodils at his head. He almost hoped she would. It was no more than he deserved.

'I was lonely,' he said defensively. 'Mavis was . . .'

'Mavis? That's a pretty name,' she remarked.

'Her husband's been sent down to work at Plymouth Docks. She was lonely, too. And, and . . .'

'Frustrated?' suggested Jess.

'Well, since you mention it, yes,' he said bluntly.

'I know how Mavis felt.'

'Oh, do you now!' What a joke? She'd not come near his bed, not once, since they moved to Bootle.

There was silence for a good five minutes. He kept expecting Jess to explode and was ready to duck if the daffodils came his way, but her next remark took him even more by surprise.

'I've not been much of a wife to you, have I, Arthur?' She folded her arms on the table and stared at him thoughtfully.

'Well, I don't know about that, Jess,' he said uncomfortably, unsure whether the answer was yes or no.

She hardly seemed to notice he'd spoken. 'I think the worst thing was not being aware of how miserable you were at work. It wasn't until I worked for Veronica that I realised how important it was to be happy in your job. When I left, I felt as if I'd been liberated. Poor Arthur, you were in chains for nearly twenty years.'

'That's putting it a bit strong, Jess.' He felt worried that she'd begun to lose her mind.

'I'm sorry, Arthur, that I didn't notice. We should have got someone in to manage the business.'

'That's all right, Jess,' he muttered.

She seemed to forget he was there for a while, staring

dreamily into the fire, and Arthur wondered, of all the various Jesses he'd experienced lately, which did he prefer most? A bit of each, he decided eventually. This one was definitely too odd for him. He was more than a bit miffed that she'd accepted his hasty, not very pleasant affair so easily. Why wasn't she jealous? Surely, a husband was entitled to an angry reaction from his wife when he strayed off the straight and narrow? But she'd taken it all so calmly. Why?

'Arthur,' she said pleasantly, 'I'm pregnant.'

He stared at her, thunderstruck. It had been ages since they'd . . . He counted the months. Eight. Her face was plump, but that was all. She was definitely not eight months pregnant.

'Jess! You haven't . . .' He couldn't go on.

She nodded smilingly. 'I have, dear. I've had an affair, too.'

'Who with?'

'That, Arthur, I will never tell you. You can ask till your face is as blue as the shirt the lipstick was on, but I'll never, never tell you.'

'But how could you be unfaithful to me?' he demanded wildly.

'How could you be unfaithful to me, Arthur?'

'I told you, I was lonely and . . . and frustrated.'

'So was I.'

'You never said.'

'Neither did you.'

Arthur felt as if drums were beating a war chant in his head. Another man had touched his Jess! He wanted to kill him. 'I need a drink!'

He slammed his way into the front room and the glasses and bottles clinked together furiously as he pulled down the door of the cocktail cabinet. He poured himself a large glass of whisky and swallowed it neat.

'Arthur,' Jess had followed, 'don't be angry.'

'How can I not be angry when you've been with another man?' He flung the glass at the wall, where it shattered into a thousand pieces which fell like silver sparks onto the carpet.

'You've been with another woman, but let's not start all that again.'

'I'll never forgive you, Jess,' he said hoarsely. 'Never!'

She took his arm and led him gently to the settee. He sat down, still dazed, unable to believe what she'd just told him. To his surprise, she sat on his knee, but he left his arms stiff beside him. Somewhat unwillingly, he let her take his hand and place it on her stomach. 'There's a baby in here,' she whispered. 'And it'll be ours. You know how much I've always wanted a child, don't you, Arthur?'

A baby! He glanced down. There was a real, live child under his hand. With a shock that almost made him cry out loud, he realised the implication of her words. Some other man had given her a baby, which meant it was *his* fault she'd never conceived in the past, not hers! Yet she hadn't uttered a word of blame.

'Does he know, the father?'

She shook her head. 'No, and he never will. It's *our* baby. *You're* the father, dear.'

'Where did you meet him?'

Jess put her fingers over his lips. 'Don't ask questions. I don't want to know anything about Mavis.'

'At least you know her name,' he said sulkily.

'Oh, Arthur!' she chided. 'Don't be childish.'

'Do you love him?'

'No. Do you love Mavis?'

'Of course not! I told you, I felt lonely and she just

353

happened to be there . . .'

'It was the same for me,' said Jess.

Despite everything, his doubts, his jealousy, his fears, it was difficult to resist, with her lovely, curvaceous body tucked into his, putting his other arm around her.

'Say something nice to me,' she whispered. '*Please*, Arthur!'

He closed his eyes briefly. He knew that in the years to come, he would never stop wondering who the man was and what it had been like for her. Yet common sense told him it was time to forgive and forget. He had no choice, otherwise it meant losing Jess and he couldn't visualise life without her. She'd forgiven him, now it was his turn.

'I love you, Jess. I've never stopped loving you,' he said simply. Looking deep into her green eyes, he could tell she believed him. Her lips curved into a delicious smile as she cuddled even further into his arms, and he rubbed his hand over her belly. 'Is there really a baby in there?'

'Our baby, yes.'

'Do you think it will be a boy or a girl?'

'Who cares?'

'I'd quite like a son.' His heart quickened. He was going to be a father!

'But you won't be disappointed if it's a girl?'

'No, of course, not! I'd quite like a daughter, too.' Suddenly, it was too much. He wanted to weep. To his shame, he felt tears course down his cheeks. 'I'm sorry, Jess,' he sobbed.

Jess clasped his face fiercely. 'Don't be sorry, darling. Cry all you want and I'll cry with you. We've had a terrible year – no, a terrible twenty years. But let's forget the past. From this moment on, we'll start again, just you, me and our baby.'

★

It was Miss Thomas who broke the news. She came into the workshop during the tea break one morning in the second week of April and shouted, 'Can I have your attention a minute, girls.'

The women looked at her, wondering why she appeared so agitated and upset.

'What's the matter, Miss Thomas?' Carmel shouted.

'I'm afraid something quite awful has happened. As you know, we have a wireless in the staff room. It's just been announced that Hitler has invaded Norway and Denmark. Denmark has already fallen. God knows what will happen to the brave Norwegians. They're fighting back.'

She left. The stunned women struggled to digest the news.

'What does it mean, Eileen?' Doris asked nervously. Eileen was the acknowledged expert on all matters concerning the war.

'It means the phoney war is over,' Eileen said, thinking of Nick, 'and the proper one has begun.'

'But it was only a few days ago,' she said bitterly to Nick later on in his cottage, 'that Chamberlain said Hitler had "missed the bus". I thought that meant there'd be no war, that it'd just fade away.'

'I wish you wouldn't let yourself get so upset.' Nick tried to kiss her, but she avoided him.

'Upset! Who wouldn't be upset?' she cried angrily. 'How many people died in the fighting last night? Oh, it's such a bloody, stupid waste!'

'Personally, I think he, Hitler, has bitten off more than he can chew,' Nick said.

'I hope so, but if he has, even more lives will be lost proving it.'

Nick sighed. 'Eileen, the dinner hour is almost over and all you've done is rant and rave about the damn war. I desperately want to make love to you, but there's scarcely any time left.'

'I don't feel in the mood,' she said stubbornly.

'In that case, would you like a cup of tea?'

'Please.'

'I'm glad you're not in the War Cabinet,' he shouted from the back kitchen, 'otherwise I'd never get my hands on you at all.'

'I'm sorry,' she said penitently. Ever since they'd been to London, she hadn't bothered with dinner, but spent the entire hour in his home a short distance from Dunnings. His cottage was the sort you read about in novels. On its own down a path off the High Street, it had roses around the door and black beams crisscrossing the low, white ceilings. The two bedrooms and the single living room were sparsely furnished, but it had a simple charm all of its own. And it was theirs! The place where she and Nick made love.

Except today, she thought guiltily. She'd been cross that he didn't appear nearly as upset as she was. He might even be glad; glad, because now there was a greater chance he'd be called up.

'I suppose you're pleased,' she said crossly when he came in with the tea things. 'You'll be expecting to hear from your Air Force bigwig any minute now.'

His lovely sensitive face split into a wide smile. 'So, that's it! You're worried about me!'

'Not just you,' she confessed. 'Though you were the first person who passed through my mind when Miss Thomas broke the news.'

He knelt on the floor in front of the chair and put his arms around her waist. 'Can I have at least a kiss, if nothing else?'

'I suppose so.' She slipped off the chair into his arms. Immediately his lips touched hers, the magic began to work and her head swam. He twisted her around until she was on the rug beneath him.

'Nick! There's no time,' she protested, praying there would be.

'I can be quick when necessary,' he said, pushing at her skirt.

'What about the tea?'

'Damn the bloody tea!'

In the days that followed, it seemed that Nick was right and Hitler had indeed bitten off more than he could chew. The Royal Navy sank ten German destroyers off the coast of Norway and the British were cock-a-hoop, convinced they had the enemy on the run.

Gradually, though, as April progressed, and people stayed glued to their wirelesses, anxious for the latest bulletin, disillusionment set in. Victory, it seemed, was not to be theirs. British aircraft were shot out of the skies; the Navy, after their initial triumph, were driven back into the sea. Troops sent to help the Norwegians in their battle against the invaders found themselves attacked from the air by Luftwaffe planes and, to the dismay of the entire country, it was Britain who was on the run, as thousands of men were hurriedly evacuated back to their own country.

'It's the old, old story,' Jack Doyle railed in the King's Arms. 'Retreat and defeat!'

'Did you hear Lord Haw-Haw last night?' someone asked acidly. 'Going on and on about, "the British defeat in Norway".'

A serviceman from Ruby Street, one of those who'd

taken part in the fighting, came home injured and embittered, and described how the shells he'd been provided with were the wrong calibre for his gun.

For the first time, it dawned on everyone that there was a possibility they might lose the fight against Hitler. The idea of being invaded, of life thereafter spent under the heel of the Nazi jackboot, seemed a prospect so horrifying as barely to be contemplated.

Feeling against Chamberlain, who seemed content to sit back and let this appalling thing happen, turned from contempt to hatred. The newspapers led the attack. *Is this another case*, thundered one, *of lions being led by donkeys?*

At the beginning of May, a debate began in the House of Commons on a motion of confidence in the Government. After several days of heated argument, the vote was taken, and the Labour and Liberal opposition parties voted solidly against the motion. They were accompanied into the 'No' lobby, by thirty Conservative MPs. A further sixty abstained, to the accompaniment of shouts of 'rats' and 'quislings' from their fellow Tories.

Chamberlain had no alternative but to resign, and on 10 May, 1940, Winston Churchill became Prime Minister of Great Britain, and leader of a coalition government.

The country had found its soul!

Also on 10 May, Hitler invaded Holland and Belgium and began to proceed through the Maginot Line, previously thought impregnable, towards France.

It was, thought Eileen Costello, as if the entire country had taken a deep breath and been renewed. Despite the setbacks overseas, the effect of having a new leader was almost tangible. There seemed a spring in the step of people she saw in the street, and new hope in their faces. Even to *consider* defeat now seemed traitorous. She conceded sadly that, though the whole idea of war was sickening, there was no alternative. Britain and France couldn't just sit back and see Europe swallowed up by a dictator, nor not fight back when their own freedom was threatened. She remembered the words of the solicitor, 'When rape is inevitable . . .' Well, she had no intention of lying back and enjoying it, whether it be Francis or Hitler.

She went to work at Dunnings with renewed enthusiasm, as did all the girls. According to Alfie, output soared throughout the entire factory after Churchill came to power.

Miss Thomas called Eileen into her office one day. 'I've come across a solicitor who will treat your case sympathetically, Eileen. What time would be most convenient for me to make an appointment?'

Eileen shifted uneasily in the chair. 'Somehow, this doesn't seem the right moment to think about divorce.' It made her feel she was putting her own selfish affairs before the war effort. Even as they spoke, a terrible battle was being waged as the Germans fought the Allies for every inch of French soil – and it seemed as if the enemy were winning.

'I know exactly what you mean,' Miss Thomas said understandingly, 'but life must go on. We still have to eat and sleep and try to act as normally as possible. Who knows, it seems unlikely, but now Hitler is up against a proper army he might beat a hasty retreat, the war will be over, and your husband will be home again.'

Faced with the prospect of Francis Costello back in Bootle and still her husband, Eileen said reluctantly, 'I suppose you're right. Mornings would be best. Will you please make an appointment for the week after next, when I'll be on the late shift again?'

This time, Nick accompanied Eileen to see the solicitor. The new man had a far less pleasant manner than the first. His questions were clipped, almost rude. Yet when she finished, he said, 'You do indeed have grounds for divorce on the basis of cruelty, Mrs Costello. Your husband has behaved abominably. Nevertheless, I would advise against it at the present time. When the case eventually comes to court, you would lose a great deal of sympathy when it was shown the defendant was sued whilst engaged on the field of battle, no matter what the grounds.'

'What if he could be persuaded a divorce was in his best interests?' asked Nick.

The solicitor frowned. 'I don't understand?'

Nick turned to Eileen. 'Tell him about the letter your father offered to write.'

She explained Francis's political ambitions which needed the co-operation of Jack Doyle. 'That's why he married me, you see. One of the reasons he was so violent when he last came home, was he realised me dad knew all about him. But, if he got a letter promising to go ahead with the nomination as planned . . .' She left the sentence hanging in mid-air when she saw the solicitor give a little shudder.

'Thank God I don't vote Labour,' he said, allowing a smile at last. Then he slowly shook his head. 'A man, however stupid, who hopes to become a Member of Parliament, would hardly agree to being divorced for cruelty, would he?'

Eileen hadn't thought of that. 'I don't suppose so.'

'What if *he* could be persuaded to divorce *her*?'

suggested Nick.

'On what grounds?'

'Adultery.'

'And has adultery taken place?' The solicitor looked at them over his half-moon glasses.

'It has,' said Nick calmly. Eileen hung her head in embarrassment and envied his confident manner. Whilst she had felt unsure of herself throughout the interview, he had probed and queried, even argued from time to time, not the least inhibited by the fact the man was a solicitor. I suppose, she thought ruefully, that's what a good education does for you.

The solicitor tapped his teeth with his pen. 'I think that particular path holds out a great deal of hope,' he said thoughtfully. 'To sum up, a letter will be written to Mr Costello suggesting the political shenanigans continue, so long as he promises to divorce you on the grounds of your adultery.'

'And that I keep my little boy,' prompted Eileen.

The solicitor nodded. 'And that you keep the child,' he agreed. Then he added, somewhat grimly, 'I trust you are prepared for the public odium that will ensue?'

'I am,' said Eileen, just as grimly.

On the stairs outside the office, Nick and Eileen flung their arms around each other.

'This time next year we might be married!' Eileen crowed.

'Will your father definitely write the letter?' Nick asked anxiously.

'Of course, it was all his idea.'

'What happens if it all goes wrong? We'll still be together, won't we?'

'It won't go wrong,' she said confidently. 'Not if I know Francis. But even if it does, yes, Nick, we'll still be together. I'd sooner we were married, but if we can't be, then it's just too bad.'

It would mean leaving Pearl Street and her family, but nothing on earth would prevent her from spending the rest of her life with the man she loved.

When Eileen got home from Dunnings that night, she found Annie hunched in a chair listening to the wireless. It was all she seemed to do when she was home since Hitler had invaded France.

'Annie, luv,' she said gently, though she knew it was a waste of time, 'you've got to be up at half past four in the morning.'

'I can't sleep, even when I go to bed.' Annie's red-rimmed eyes seemed to have sunk back into her head. 'I'm waiting on the midnight bulletin.'

'What's happening?'

'Fighting, fighting and more bloody fighting,' Annie said despairingly. 'The Maginot Line might have been made of paper for all the good it did. The Jerries have got more troops and better equipment and our side don't stand a chance.'

'You still haven't heard from your lads?'

'How could I? They don't have postboxes in the middle of a battlefield.'

'I'll just pop up and look at Tony, then I'll make you a nice cup of tea.'

Tony was fast asleep, looking like an angel in the light of the candle flickering on the dressing table. How would *I* feel, wondered Eileen, if Tony had been called up? If Tony was, right at this very minute, at risk of being slaughtered by a German bayonet? She doubted if she could stay sane.

She went down and made a pot of tea, then listened to

Annie, reminiscing over her lads. It seemed to do her good, talking and remembering.

'You didn't know them when they was little, did you, Eil? Pair of little divils they were. Up to all sorts of mischief, particularly when I used to take them cleaning with me. There was one house I remember, the woman was awful fussy over her floors. As sure as eggs were eggs, the minute I mopped the kitchen, our Joe would run across it in his boots and leave a trail of marks. I'd pray it'd dry before the woman came home, else I'd have had to mop it all over again.'

'You did them proud, Annie. They couldn't have had a better mam than you.'

'They did me proud, too,' Annie said, glowing. 'The minute they started work, they made me stop cleaning. "It's time for a rest, Mam," they said. "Time to put your feet up for a change. It's our turn to earn the money now".'

'They're good lads,' murmured Eileen. 'The best.'

'Aye, the best,' agreed Annie, 'but it don't seem fair, does it, Eileen, to have them taken off me, just when they were about to become men? The struggle I had, raising them, filling their bellies, rooting through Paddy's Market for clothes for their backs. And all for what?'

'Oh, don't ask me, luv,' Eileen cried. 'I just think the whole world has gone mad. I met Rosie Gregson the other day. The baby's only eight weeks off, and who knows if Charlie will be alive to see it? Funnily enough, Rosie seems quite unconcerned. I don't think she quite understands what's going on.'

'They say ignorance is bliss. Perhaps I should stop living beside your bloody wireless,' Annie said wearily.

The twelve o'clock bulletin began just then, and they listened intently. The Germans had advanced even further into France. British and French troops were being driven back towards the coast, and heavy losses had been sustained on both sides.

That was all.

'They don't tell you much, do they?' Annie complained bitterly, as Eileen turned the set off.

'Well, they can't, can they, luv? I suppose the Germans are listening in. They don't want to give anything away.'

'It said in the paper that the Luftwaffe are machine-gunning refugees trying to escape the fighting. If they'll do that to innocent civilians, what on earth will they do to our boys?'

'Now that's enough, Annie,' Eileen said sternly. 'It's time you went home to bed and tried to catch up on a bit of sleep.'

After Annie had gone, she took the *Daily Herald* into the back kitchen and studied both it and the wall map pinned behind the door. It wasn't possible for the Allied troops to retreat much further. What would happen when they actually reached the English Channel? Would they be left to the mercy of an enemy who murdered refugees? Would Joe and Terry Poulson, and all the thousands of brave and innocent young men of the British Expeditionary Force, be massacred on the beaches of France?

As May drew towards its bitter end, an armada set sail. From the port of Harwich round to Weymouth, ferry craft, naval drifters and small coasters were commandeered by the Admiralty and, along with ships of the Royal Navy, sent to rescue the troops who were fighting a desperate rearguard action as they were driven back towards the coast and the French town of Dunkirk.

Although the Royal Air Force fought a desperate battle

in the skies to keep the Luftwaffe at bay, enemy planes got through and strafed the weary soldiers as they lay exhausted on the beaches. Amidst the carnage, even the rows of dead were machine-gunned and the badly injured, who'd been carried for miles by their mates, were casually finished off by bullets from the Stukas which buzzed like carrion overhead. Men who achieved the sanctuary of a rescue boat were still not safe, as the boats were bombed to smithereens with their precious human cargo on board, until the harbour of Dunkirk was blocked with the wrecks of British vessels.

It was then the ordinary citizens of Great Britain showed their true mettle. In response to a call from the BBC that there was an army urgently in need of rescue, off to sea went fire tenders and barges and Port of London tugs, cockle boats and drifters, pleasure boats and river cruisers and hundreds and hundreds of little boats that could carry no more than a handful of men, manned by the very young and the very old and all ages in between. They came from up river, from yachting harbours, from pleasure beaches and fishing ports, and set forth across the Channel, regardless of their own safety, to pluck the troops from under the noses of the enemy. Backwards and forwards they sailed, by day and by night, bringing the troops back to fight another day on other foreign soil. The little boats needed no navigational aids. They sailed towards the thunderous sounds of gunfire, of exploding shells and bombs, towards the black smoke spiralling into the sky above Dunkirk, where it seemed as if the entire town was ablaze.

By 4 June, nearly 340,000 English and French soldiers had been rescued, their tanks, weapons and equipment abandoned across the Channel. The Royal Air Force had lost an incalculable number of planes in the abortive campaign. Many thousands of men had lost their lives, and now only two British divisions remained behind to carry on the battle against Hitler, joining their French comrades on the new front along the Somme, where so many men had spilt their life blood during the Great War which was to end all wars.

Winston Churchill warned, 'Wars are not won by evacuation.' Nevertheless, in the eyes of the British people, Dunkirk was a triumphant victory snatched magically out of the jaws of defeat.

When it was all over and the men were back, Annie Poulson still had no idea whether her lads were alive or dead.

Dear Mam,

Seems a bit daft to begin this like usual with, 'hope this finds you as it leaves me', because my feet are swollen and full of blisters due to having no shoes for nearly a week. Also, I've got a bit of a bald patch where a bullett whistled past. It was a close shave, I can tell you.

Anyroad, you'll be pleased to know our Joe's okay and all in one piece. We got separatted on the shore, but I saw him land in Dover, though don't know where he got to after that.

You'd never believe the place I'm in, Mam. It's a big house on the side of a river and they've got a little motor boat which they keep moored at the bottom of the garden. The chap brought four of us over and two have gone next door. I've had a bath and it was pink, with a pink lav and sink. I lay there for so long, the woman had to come and knock on the door to make sure I was all right. I'd only fallen asleep!

When I said I wanted to write to you, they gave me this posh paper and the daughter, Sarah – she's a bit of all right, by the way – promised to go out and post it the minute I finish.

I don't know where to begin. Perhaps I shouldn't begin at all, but just write, 'Tara, your loving son, Terry', here and now and be done with it, but I'd like to put a few things down on paper, clear my mind, sort of thing.

You know how excitted me and Joe were when we were first called up a year ago. War seemed a bit of a game, particularly when it began and we were sent to France. We had a fine old time, I can tell you – well, you know, I've already said so loads of times. The officers can get you down, they seem to think they're the bees' knees, and full of airs and graces, or so I thought. I don't think that now.

We first saw action when the Jerries invaded Belgium. It was about that time we heard Churchill had become Prime Minister and we was all very excitted at the news.

We were transportted overnight by lorry into Belgium and the first thing we met were lines of refugees. The sight of women and children and old men pulling carts piled high with furniture gave us a fair old shock. Some of them tried to talk to us, but we'd been ordered not to talk back in case they were Fifth Columnists.

Believe it or not, we were heading for Waterloo, which if I remember right from school, was where Napoleon got his comeuppance. We could hear gunfire in the distance, and my stomach, which was empty because our rations hadn't put in an apearance, gave a funny turn. That night there was a heavy air-raid on Brussells and we could see the fires blazing away and German Stukkas dropped a few bombs on our positions, but luckily no-one was hurt.

Over the next few days, they kept moving us around, and to be quite honest, none of us knew whether we were advancing or retreatting. According to Sarge, it was 'sheer bloody kayoss'. (I hope I've spelt that right, and excuse the language, Mam, but that's what he said.) One minute we'd be digging a trench for a new position, next minute we'd be leaving. By now, the roads were even more full with refugees and I could have cried to see them straggling along the road looking so miserable. We even came across the body of an old man who seemed to have given up the ghost and collapsed in a ditch. Every now and then, we'd come to a little shrine where women were praying and I secretly made the sign of the cross and Joe did, too.

By now, we were terrible tired. The lorries had been commandered for other duties and we had to carry everything and it wasn't half hot, dead scorching, and we'd begun to feel a bit like the Wandering Jew, except there were more of us. There was no food, as the cook's lorry never seemed to catch up. Sarge told us we were nothing but a rabble and 'a pitifull sight to behold', as we tried to march along in formation, but we were past caring by then.

I remember thinking to myself, well, if this is war, you can keep it, but I hadn't seen the half of it yet.

One morning, we arrived at this little town which we all thought looked familiar. We'd only passed through it the other way a few days before!

'Cor, luv a bleeding duck!' says Micky Cohen (excuse the language again), 'the army's got us marching round in circles. Very soon, we'll dissappear up our own arses!' (He said that, too.)

Anyroad, we camped out in this farmhouse and an officer came in to tell us the Jerries were heavily concentratted across the river. Until then, nothing had seemed very real. It was almost like being in the pictures watching a film. But as the officer walked away across the farmyard, a shell landed right behind him, and I saw him with me own eyes explode to pieces. Oh, Mam, it was terrible! There was blood everywhere and bits of body and a mess pooring out of what was left of his poor head.

From then on, everything turned into a nightmare. The fighting went on all day and by the time it went dark, there were only thirty of us left out of a hundred and ten. There were bodies everywhere, some of them mates, and if they weren't dead, then they were badly injured. I've never felt so frightenned as I did that night. Sarge got a bullett in the chest, though he's a tough old nut and he was still concious when they carted him off on a stretcher, and he shouted, 'well, lads! You've had your baptism of fire with a vengance!'

You wouldn't think after that it could get worse, but it did. We'd been in France eight months, but it was only during the last eight days that I saw sights I never want to see again if I live to be a hundred.

I won't go into it too much, Mam, except to say, let's hope Hitler never get's as far as this countrey. I think that's what kept us going, imaginning our own people suffering in the same way as the French and the Belgiums, and doing our level best to stop it.

You know you always said not to bottle things up, that if a thing's upsetting, it's best to tell someone. 'A trouble shared is a trouble halved,' is how you put it. Well, something happened on the road back to Dunkirk, which I've GOT to get off my chest, because I can't stop thinking about it. I can't even bring myself to tell our Joe, and usually I can tell him anything. You're the only person in the world I can share this with, Mam, and I hope it doesn't make you too upset, like, reading it.

The Jerries had been shelling the refugees, and as we made our way down this little countrey lane, it seemed peculiar to see the hedges full of lovely pink blossom and wild flowers on the grass verge and crops growing in the fields, yet the ditches each side were litered with dead bodies. I said to the mate who was with me, (I'd lost our Joe by then), if it weren't for the bodies, how normal it all seemed. He said it wasn't normal at all, because there were no birds singing. I know it sounds awful, but we'd got used to bodies by then, though dead babies and little kids could still make you want to cry or puke, depending on how you felt at the time. Sometimes, the refugees were alive and badly injured and there was nothing you could do except give them water. We assumed the Red Cross took care of them. That's what we told ourselves, because it made us feel better about leaving them behind.

Anyroad, we passed this old woman who'd had her whole side blown off and she made a funny groaning noise, as if she was calling to us. She must have had what you call an 'iron constitution' to still be alive with only half a body. Me and me mate went over. She couldn't speak, yet both of us knew what she wanted. She wanted us to kill her! I'd already killed my share of Jerries by then, so I'd been 'blooded', as Sarge would have put it. But this was an old woman, and me mate and me just looked at each other and he said, 'Could you do it, Terry, because I don't think I can?'

So, Mam, I did no more than shoot the old woman through the head, and I thought to myself, war's not a game. War's deadly serious and don't let anybody tell you any different.

When we reached Dunkirk, it was bedlam on the shore. Remember you took us to New Brighton once when we were little and the shore was crammed with people? It was like that, except ten times as crowded and no-one was having a good time. It was a strange thing, but it was then I noticed the *Royal Daffodil* which had come all the way from Liverpool and had taken us across the Mersey that day.

I found our Joe and we spent three days in Dunkirk waiting to be rescued and it's three days I'd never want to live through again. Every now and then, some of the men would go wild and fight to get on the next boat, but most stayed calm.

Well, I'll finish now. I'm afraid there's a bit of bad news I've left to the end and that's the fact that Charlie Gregson's had it. He was standing right next to me when he got a piece of shrapnel in the back. The awful thing is, I felt glad it was him and not me, but that's the way you feel after a while. I leave it to you to tell Rosie, or wait till she get's an official letter.

Tara, your loving son,
Terry.

'Have you finished your letter?'

When the young woman, Sarah, the daughter of the house, went into the sun-drenched lounge, where the net curtains billowed gently in the soft breeze coming through the open window, and the scent of roses was heavy in the air from the bushes directly outside, she found one of the soldiers her father had rescued from the beach at Dunkirk sobbing uncontrollably.

'You poor thing!' she cried, and felt so affected by his distress that she impulsively reached out and cradled his head against her breast. He was only young, nineteen or twenty. She wondered what he'd think about the carnival atmosphere in Dover, where the bunting was out, flags were being waved and the band was playing *There'll Always be an England*, when she'd gone that morning.

'You're spoiling your letter,' she whispered, as she pushed the pad away. She noticed he'd written reams and reams in tight, crabbed script. The final page was splashed with tears and the ink had run.

'I can't send it,' he wept. 'I can't tell me mam those terrible things. I'll tear it up and start again.' His hands shook as he reached for the pad.

'Would you like me to write it for you? I'll just say you didn't have the time, you had to go right back to barracks or something, so she won't be worried.'

He sniffed and wiped his nose on the back of his hand. 'Would you mind? Just say me and our Joe are safe and sound. And, oh, you'd better tell her about Charlie.'

'She looked at him questioningly. 'About Charlie?'

'He's dead.'

'I'll do it straight away,' she said, wanting to weep. 'I've brought a stamp. If it catches the afternoon post, she'll get it in the morning.'

'Ta.'

'What's your surname?' She sat beside him at the table.

'Poulson.'

'Dear Mrs Poulson,' she said aloud as she wrote the words in her neat, rather childish handwriting. When the short letter was finished, she folded it into an envelope. 'Address?'

'Twenty-eight Pearl Street, Bootle, Liverpool Twenty.'

'Pearl Street! That sounds pretty. Is it?'

'Not exactly, but I'd sooner be there right now than anywhere in the world.'

'I bet you would!' To her relief, he was beginning to look a bit more cheerful. 'The local pub has sent a message. It's drinks on the house till closing time for you and your friends. If you like, I'll go with you and we can post the letter on the way.'

'I suppose I'd better find somewhere to report in, but I wouldn't say no to a pint of bitter first.'

'Neither would I.'

'You drink beer?' She looked too ladylike for beer, thought Terry.

'I'm training to be a nurse in London and we're often short of money. When we go for a drink, beer is all we can afford.'

Terry had forgotten for the moment that he'd thought her quite pretty when he first arrived. She had short straight brown hair pushed behind a red velvet band, and dark brown eyes. He could imagine she'd look good in a nurse's uniform.

'Shall we go then?' He stood up. The shoes her father had provided him with felt stiff and uncomfortable and his blisters throbbed. He'd be glad to return to a pair of Army boots.

'What about your letter, the first one?'

'Oh, yes.' He picked up the pad. He hadn't realised he'd written so many pages. He tore them out and hesitated before ripping them in two. He'd opened his heart to his mam and felt better for it.

'What's the matter?' Sarah asked.

'I don't know,' he answered puzzled. There was a strange reluctance to get rid of the letter without at least one other person reading it.

Sarah seemed to sense what he was feeling. 'Would you like me to read it?' she asked softly. 'Not now, some time later. Tonight, when you've gone.'

'I think I would. But promise to tear it up afterwards or burn it.'

'I promise, on my heart. I'll read it in bed.'

He handed her the letter, little caring that he would have shown his soul to a girl he would never meet again.

Chapter 14

There were no flags up in Pearl Street, no 'Welcome Home' banner for Annie's lads when they returned from Dunkirk, because how could you celebrate a homecoming when one young lad would never come home again?

Joe and Terry Poulson came home quietly and without a fuss. Their train arrived late one night, so it was dark when they slipped into their mam's house. Next day, the neighbours began to call in ones and twos, not wanting to overwhelm the young soldiers who'd gone away as boys and come back as men, and to bestow a tearful kiss or a hug, a warm handshake or slap on the shoulder.

'It's good to see you back, lads. You done us proud over there.'

Rosie Gregson flatly refused to believe her Charlie was dead, even when the official letter arrived confirming the news Annie had already gently broken to her. 'He's just missing,' she declared stubbornly. 'Or he's been taken prisoner. He'll come back, like Cal did, you'll see.'

'But Mam,' Terry Poulson said to Annie. 'He was standing right next to me when he got it. I saw him fall with me own eyes.' Not that he'd told Rosie that.

'I know, luv,' Annie said consolingly. 'Rosie just doesn't want to believe it, that's all. It'll sink in, eventually, poor lamb.'

Annie still couldn't get used to the expression in the eyes of both her sons. A look of horror, as if they were still seeing the terrible things they'd been witness to over the last few weeks.

'Come on, now, have another piece of bunloaf,' she urged.

It was all she could do, feed them and love them, until their leave was up and they were sent to fight somewhere else.

As two of Pearl Street's own returned from war, albeit temporarily, another was about to depart.

Eileen Costello had a visitor; a strange woman in ATS uniform, discreetly made up, with short crisp curls spurting out from under her khaki cap.

'I've come to say goodbye,' the woman said.

Eileen stared at her until recognition dawned. 'Miss Brazier!' she cried. 'Come in a minute.'

'I didn't want to just disappear,' Miss Brazier said when she was sitting down inside, 'and leave people wondering where I'd got to. Anyroad, I'd like you to keep an eye on the house for me, if you wouldn't mind. I've paid the rent in advance, like, else I wouldn't have a home to come back to when it's all over.'

'Of course I will,' Eileen promised. 'What made you join the ATS?' she asked, intrigued.

Miss Brazier took a packet of cigarettes out of her shoulder bag and offered them to Eileen.

'Not just now, ta. I'm trying to cut down.' Eileen watched the woman, impressed by the way she expertly lit the ciggie with a black enamelled lighter.

'Well, to put it bluntly,' she said with a girlish laugh, 'It was a case of getting wed or joining up. I've been going out with the manager of the Co-op, Bill Castleton, since Easter. A couple of weeks ago, he did no more than pop the question!' She fluttered her lightly mascara-ed lashes, 'Is there an ashtray, luv?'

Eileen quickly passed the visitor an ashtray, anxious for her to continue with her interesting tale.

'It's a funny thing,' Miss Brazier went on thoughtfully, 'I'd always wanted to be married. I suppose, if there hadn't been a war on, I would have jumped at the chance. Instead, I found meself telling Bill I'd think about it. I expect you think that was silly?' She looked at Eileen intently, as if genuinely interested in what the reply would be.

'Of course I don't!' Eileen shook her head vehemently. 'You can't be in love, else you would have snapped him up. There's more to life than getting married.' She thought about the WRENs she'd seen in London. 'Nowadays, there's all sorts of things women can do on their own.'

Miss Brazier nodded her head vigorously. 'That's what I thought,' she said. 'Anyroad, to cut a long story short, on half day closing, Bill took me into town to look at engagement rings. I reckon he thought a ring might tip the balance and I'd say yes, but the minute I saw the Recruiting Office in Renshaw Street, I knew exactly what I wanted to do. I promptly went in and joined up. Bill bought me a ring all the same, so I suppose I'm engaged in a sort of way.' She extended her hand. A diamond solitaire twinkled on the third finger. 'See!'

'It's very nice,' Eileen said admiringly.

'It's a bit small.' Miss Brazier regarded the ring disparagingly.

'Well, I suppose it's the thought that counts. I hope he wasn't too upset about you joining up.'

'He was a bit, but that can't be helped, can it?'

'I don't suppose so,' agreed Eileen. She couldn't wait to tell all this to Annie. It was like one of those romances out of the *Red Star* or *The Miracle* which the girls at work were forever reading. 'Anyroad, congratulations on both counts. You look dead smart in your uniform.'

'Why, thank you!' Miss Brazier said modestly. She looked down and brushed an imaginary spot off the jacket which strained slightly over her buxom, shapely breasts. 'I thought I'd have me hair cut at the same time. What do you think? she asked, removing her cap to reveal a Shirley Temple mop of curls.

'It takes years off,' Eileen said. 'You look like a young girl.'

'I feel like one. Well, I'd better be going.' Miss Brazier jumped to her feet. 'I'm off to Scotland in the morning, so there's a bit of packing to do.'

'Good luck!' Eileen said. 'Send us a card from time to time. I'd love to know how you're getting on.'

'I'll do that,' Miss Brazier promised. She paused at the door. 'You've been a good neighbour, Mrs Costello,' she said awkwardly. 'I wish I hadn't always been so stuck up.' For a moment, there was a glimpse of the old withdrawn Miss Brazier.

'You weren't stuck up, luv, just shy.' Eileen hesitated, then kissed the woman warmly on the cheek. 'Have a nice time in Scotland.'

The old Miss Brazier vanished and the new one cried, 'Oh, I will, don't worry. There's nearly a hundred men and only five women, so I think I'll enjoy meself.'

Eileen blinked as she closed the door. She had the strangest feeling Miss Brazier would enjoy herself very much.

She told Paddy O'Hara about her visitor when he came round later with Rover, watching his face closely for a reaction. There was none. Paddy felt only relief that Helen had gone, apparently forever. He still expected a knock on the wall, even now, after he'd thankfully been ditched months ago in favour of the manager of the Co-op.

'What's she like? I mean to look at?' he asked Eileen. He'd often wondered.

'Very attractive. She looked smart in her uniform.'

'I've had nowt much to do with her,' Paddy explained innocently, 'even though she lived next door.'

The subject of Miss Brazier was dropped as Eileen bent to stroke Rover's soft neck. 'He's a fine dog, Paddy. Going to be a big 'un, too. I can tell by his paws.'

Rover was a mixture of several breeds, with a fluffy golden body, long pointed nose and a tail like a flag. He wagged the tail in a frenzy as his neck was scratched.

'He'll never replace Spot,' Paddy said, 'but he's a good friend, all the same.' He asked casually, 'How's Francis?'

He was aware of a long pause before Eileen answered. A rumour had spread around the street that Eileen Costello was having an affair. He found this difficult to believe, but there was no hiding the fact that she was a much happier woman nowadays. Paddy was unable to work out whether this was due, somewhat inexplicably, to the fact Francis had left, or to the suspected affair.

'I haven't heard from Francis in a while,' Eileen said eventually. 'I expect the post's not what it should be, having to come all that way.'

Paddy knew quite a few men from the Royal Tank Regiment who were in Egypt and whose families heard from them regularly. Maybe the rumour had been passed on to Francis, which would explain why he hadn't written.

In fact, Eileen Costello was waiting anxiously to hear from Francis. It was several weeks since her dad had written the promised letter and sent it to the PO Box to re-direct to Alexandria where the Royal Tank Regiment was stationed. So far, neither he or Eileen had received a reply. After months of inactivity, it was only now, since the Italians had entered the war on the side of Germany, that an offensive had begun in North Africa. Not that Francis, office-bound and ensconced behind his type-writer, would be involved, but it might account for the delay. She tried to push the matter to the back of her mind. In view of the tragedy enveloping Europe, it would be sheer self-indulgence to do anything else.

17 June was referred to as 'Black Monday'. It was the day Marshall Petain petitioned for an amnesty, the day France fell.

The news was announced by Frank Phillips on the one o'clock bulletin from the BBC. By then, Eileen Costello had already left for work. When the crowded bus arrived at Dunnings, the laughing girls were silenced by the subdued expressions on the faces of those waiting to go home.

At first, the women thought there'd been an accident and someone had been hurt. 'What's happened?' Pauline asked.

'France has fallen,' someone shouted. 'That means we've had it! There's nowt between Britain and Hitler except a little strip of water. We'll be next, you'll see!'

Eileen felt an icy ball in her stomach. Suddenly, Annie grabbed her arm. 'Isn't it terrible, girl!' she cried. 'There's only us left to fight the battle from now on.'

'Jaysus!' Eileen whispered. 'Only us?'

Not even Gladys could raise a joke that afternoon, though later on she began to sing *We're gonna hang out the washing on the Siegfried Line,* and everyone thankfully joined in. It was a way of releasing the unbearable tension. A cartoon was pinned to the noticeboard showing a British soldier confronting a stormy sea and hordes of invading Germans, and saying, 'Very well, alone!'

Next day, Winston Churchill broadcast to the people. ' . . . *if the British Empire and its Commonwealth last for a thousand years, men will still say, "This was their finest hour".*'

The country began to prepare for an invasion: roads were blocked, signposts removed, milestones uprooted. Strikes were banned, Bank Holidays cancelled. Wrecked cars were strategically placed on corners and grass verges for use as barricades by troops if the enemy should dare to land. People were warned to keep an eye out for parachutists. Aliens were hurriedly rounded up, mainly Germans and Italians, and sent to internment camps; many of their shops and businesses were attacked. Church bells were silenced, except as a warning that the invasion had started, and every household received a leaflet entitled, IF THE INVADER COMES.

Britain collectively squared its shoulders and committed itself utterly to the war effort, whilst an even more implacable hatred built up against the enemy, Hitler.

And, a few days after Black Monday, Wing Commander Fulford having kept his promise, Nick Stephens heard he was being released from civilian duties and had been accepted in the RAF.

Nick met Eileen outside Dunnings with the news.

'When are you going?' she whispered as they walked to his cottage.

'Sunday.'

'*That* soon!' It was only three days away.

'They need every pilot they can lay their hands on. It's

going to be a war in the air from now on.' His dark eyes were serious, as if the enormity of what lay ahead had only just sunk in.

She wanted to cry, 'Please don't go! I can't live without you!' but knew she had to put on a brave face. It wasn't fair on Nick to collapse into tears in front of him.

'I'll miss you,' she said, trying to smile.

'I should hope so! I shall certainly miss you.'

As soon as they were inside the door, Nick took her in his arms and they made love, clinging to each other hungrily, knowing that their time together was limited.

'Why don't you and Tony come and stay on Saturday night?' he suggested, as they lay on the floor in front of the empty fireplace wrapped in each other's arms. 'It means we'll have a whole twenty-four hours together. Lord knows when we'll see each other again.'

Eileen needed no persuading. 'We'll come first thing Saturday morning,' she promised. 'Tony's dying to see you.'

Nick began to nibble at her ear. 'I hate being a secret. I want to come and see you openly, walk down Pearl Street with you on my arm.'

'Don't do that, Nick!' The nibbling was sending a delicious sensation through her entire body. It always did.

He looked down at her, smiling slyly, 'Why not?'

'You know damn well why not. Oh, God!' She could stand it no longer. She ran her hands down his body. He was ready for her again. 'Once more,' she pleaded. 'Just once more, then I'll have to go back to work.'

Saturday turned out to be a gloriously sunny day. The three of them did little, except go for walks, eat, and laze in Nick's big, wild, overgrown garden, where Tony found some ripe strawberries and made himself sick eating every single one.

In the evening, they strolled to the local pub and sat on a bench outside drinking home-brewed cider, whilst Tony had a lemonade.

'I understand you're off to give Adolf Hitler a good kick up the arse,' the landlord said to Nick when he came out to collect the glasses.

'I certainly hope so,' Nick said modestly.

'Well, give him a kick from me while you're at it.' The man glanced from Eileen to Tony, then back to Nick. 'So, this is your family, eh? You've never brought them before.'

'That's right,' said Nick. 'This is my family, and I think it's about time I took them home.'

'Good luck and take care!' Nick's hand was shaken fiercely. 'Give them Jerries hell.'

They went home and had a light supper and Tony went to bed without a word of complaint, as if he realised it was time for his mam and Nick to be alone. 'Let's go outside for a while,' Nick said. 'I think this is the longest day of the year.'

They sat on the striped deckchairs, chatting idly.

'I know nothing about you,' Eileen said sadly. She felt slightly tipsy, although she'd only had half a pint of cider. It must have been very strong.

'You know everything!' he protested indignantly.

'Only big things, like how you feel about religion and war and politics. I don't know the little things − your favourite colour, for instance.'

'I haven't got one. I haven't got a favourite anything, except woman, and you're it!'

'You need to live with someone to find out the little things.'

'Darling, you could have moved in with me months and months ago,' he said, 'then you'd know everything there is to know. How often I cut my nails, for instance, how much toothpaste I use, the funny way I tie my shoelaces, the . . .'

'Don't, Nick!' She put her hand on his arm. His shirt sleeves were rolled up and the flesh felt warm to the touch. He'd caught the sun during the day and he was browner than ever, a lovely deep bronze. She was conscious of the tiny hairs as she rubbed his arm with her thumb.

'If you do that for much longer,' he said seriously after a while, 'I shall drag you down onto the grass and make you pay.'

'In the open air!' she responded, pretending to be shocked.

'That's right. With all the neighbours looking on.'

In fact, the cottage was too isolated for the garden to be overlooked – and Tony was asleep in the front bedroom!

Eileen rubbed her thumb even harder. Nick stood up and dragged her from the chair and they fell together onto the rough lawn, laughing.

The grass felt cool underneath her body. She'd never thought that making love to Nick could have got better, but there was an added zest, an extra air of excitement to doing it in the open air.

When it was over, they stayed where they were, Eileen with her head in the crook of his arm, as dusk began to fall.

'It's uncanny,' she said. 'It's gone eleven, yet it's still light.' With the extra hours of daylight, it didn't get properly dark until midnight.

'I think we'd better go in,' said Nick, stretching. 'It'll get damp soon.'

'Have you got any cocoa?'

'There might be a tin around with a few lumps left at the bottom.'

'Oh, Nick! You're a terrible housewife!'

'I need looking after,' he said pathetically.

Eileen sat up. 'Give me your shirt?'

He looked at her incredulously. 'Are you going to wash it here and now?'

'No, I'm going to wear it. I'm not making cocoa with nothing on. And you can just put your trousers back on, too, else I won't put any sugar in yours.'

'You're a hard woman, Eileen Costello!' he said darkly. 'I shall miss being bossed around.'

It was the first reference all day to the fact he would soon be gone.

Eileen stared at him silently for several seconds, then leapt to her feet and ran into the house, fighting to hold back the tears. By the time Nick came in, she'd put the kettle on, found the tin of lumpy cocoa, and recovered her composure a little.

'What's happening to the cottage, Nick?' she asked with forced brightness. There seemed little reason for him, a southerner, to keep the place on whilst he was gone. His reply took her totally by surprise.

'Actually,' he said, 'I've bought it. I thought it would do for us once we're married. I know it's only small,' he added hastily, misreading her look of amazement, 'but we can have it extended at the side.'

'Oh, Nick!' She flung herself into his arms. 'Thank you,' she cried. 'I love it here – and so does Tony.'

'I assumed you wouldn't want to move too far from your family.'

'I don't. Sheila can bring her kids out. They'll love the garden, and Annie and Jess, once she has the baby. Me dad's always wanted to grow vegetables . . .'

'Hold on a minute!' Nick threw his arms up in despair. 'I bought it for you, for us, not the whole of Pearl Street!'

'You mustn't half be well off, to be able to buy a house,' she said in awe.

'It was only two hundred and fifty quid.'

'*Only!*' She began to press the lumps of cocoa into powder, then added the boiling water, milk and sugar. They carried the drinks into the living room.

'You've never asked, have you, Eileen, about money?' Nick said curiously. 'I mean, you've never wanted to know if I had any.'

'I still don't want to know,' Eileen said flatly.

Nick was bent over the cup, stirring it with a spoon. She realised he was deliberately avoiding her eyes.

'The reason I brought the subject up,' he said casually, 'is I do have a bit my father left me, and I made a will the other day, leaving everything I possess to you, including the cottage.'

Which only went to show, Eileen thought bleakly, that he acknowledged the possibility he might not come back. She wanted to yell at him, to scream that he could have stayed, he didn't *have* to go, and that it was *him* she wanted, not his house, not his money. Instead, she said politely, 'Thank you very much.'

'I'll give you a key. It may be useful to come here, when, if, the air raids start.' He gave a little laugh. 'I'd hate to come back and find you and Tony weren't here for me.'

Eileen pondered silently for a while, wondering what horrors might lie in store for her, for everyone through-out the country, throughout Europe. Why, right now, Hitler might have started to cross the English Channel. She closed her eyes and imagined big, dark ships forging through the water towards the south coast. She saw the decks packed with German soldiers wearing those sinister helmets, with the Nazi swastika on their sleeves.

'Switch the wireless on, quick,' she said, panicking. 'We'll just catch the midnight bulletin.' They'd deliberately not listened to the wireless all day.

But if the invasion had begun, the BBC didn't know about it.

'Let's go to bed,' Eileen said urgently. 'There's not much time left, and Nick . . .'

He reached for her. 'What, darling?'

'Tonight, don't take precautions . . .'

'Are you *mad*?' His mouth fell open in an expression of total shock, and she'd never known his voice so hard and incredulous.

'But, Nick,' she began, thinking he was worried how she'd manage on her own with a baby.

Before she could continue, he interrupted hoarsely, 'Do you seriously think I'd bring a child into the world at this moment in time? For Chrissakes, woman, if the Germans landed, I'd seriously think about killing you and Tony! To create a new life now would be sheer insanity.'

She hadn't realised he had such a terrible vision of the future. There was nothing of the little boy about him at the moment. You'd think he'd lived a hundred bitter years, the way he spoke.

'I'm sorry,' she whispered. A baby, Nick's baby, would be the best possible thing to remember him by if . . . Tears threatened again and she blinked them back.

'I'm sorry, too, for losing my rag.' As they went upstairs, Eileen first, he slid his hands under the shirt and pulled her back against him. 'There'll be plenty of time for children, Eileen, once it's all over.'

Eileen didn't bother to argue, but his last words were

at odds with those he'd uttered previously.

Once in bed, they made love feverishly, but Eileen couldn't get Nick's furious outburst out of her mind. It didn't seem possible, she thought, that they'd come through it all and live happily ever after.

She woke up with a jump when it was still dark. She'd been dreaming that the dark ships had landed, that the soldiers were running up the south coast beaches, bayonets poised, ready to strike . . .

After that, sleep refused to return, so she got up, put Nick's shirt on and went downstairs, where she made a cup of tea and pretended to read a book until a glimmer of light appeared round the edge of the blackout curtains and she went outside.

A strange white mist hung over the garden, seemingly solid, and suspended about three feet from the ground. She walked into it, intrigued, and when she turned back, the cottage had disappeared! The grass was soaking under her bare feet. There were plopping noises everywhere, and when she investigated, she found large drops of moisture falling from the trees and the bushes. They sparkled as they slid from leaf to leaf like a little waterfall of jewels. Eileen knelt and caught several drops in the palms of her hands and rubbed them on her face. It made her skin feel fresh and invigorated.

She walked further into the garden. There was nothing to be seen except the white mist which surrounded her on all sides. She had the same feeling she'd had before on many occasions in her life, even when she was a little girl, that she was the only person left on earth, but this time it wasn't unpleasant, but strangely comforting.

Suddenly, the mist lifted, simply disappeared, as if someone had waved a wand and ordered it to go. A little slice of brilliant sun appeared over the crumbling brick wall on her right, like a section of an orange. Gradually, as she watched, the slice grew bigger and she felt a welcome warmth on her face.

Then Nick called to her from the back door.

She stared at him, the man she loved, across the long untidy lawn, dotted with daisies and yellow dandelions. Roses had begun to uncurl their velvet leaves from within the tangle of shrubs and ivy clinging to the walls, and a tractor chugged in the distance. There were strange scents in the air; the earthy smell of soil, of flowers, grass, and things that she, from town, didn't recognise.

'Nick!'

She hurried towards him, wondering if this would be the last time she would run to her lover across the wet grass, the sun on her face? Perhaps they would never know another morning together.

'There's my girl.' He caught her in his arms. 'Have I ever told you how much I love you?'

'No, not once, but there's still time,' she cried.

But not much time. In another five hours, he would be gone.

Nick left on his motorbike at midday. He had to report in at an Air Force base near Ipswich by nine o'clock next morning. The journey would be hazardous without sign-posts to guide him.

'I've got my identity card handy, in case anyone thinks I'm a spy when I ask for directions,' he joked.

'Take care,' Eileen whispered.

'You, too.' He lifted Tony up and gave him a vigorous hug. 'Keep an eye on your mam for me, won't you, son?'

'Don't worry, I'll look after her,' Tony promised stoutly.

'Bye, love.' It was little more than a peck on the cheek

he gave her, but Eileen knew there were tears in his eyes he didn't want her to see.

He climbed on the bike, started it up, and, with a wave, was gone. Eileen watched until the bike rounded a bend, Nick still waving. She still watched, even when it had disappeared from sight and the sound of the engine had faded.

'Oh, well,' she said, sighing. 'That's it, then.'

'Are we going home, now, Mam?'

She came down to earth at the sound of her son's voice. 'Not just yet, luv. I'll tidy up a bit first.'

'Can I play outside?'

'If you like.' He trotted beside her as they went down the path. 'Do you like it here, Tony?'

'It's the gear. You can't half play football in the garden.'

'Would you like to live here all the time?' she asked cautiously. She was glad he was with her as they entered the house, which would have seemed so empty otherwise, without Nick.

'You mean sleep here every night?'

'That's right.'

He wrinkled his nose. 'I'm not sure. Would I still see Dominic and Grandad?'

'Not every day, like you do now, only at weekends.' She began to collect the dishes and take them into the kitchen.

'I suppose it depends,' Tony said in a funny voice.

Eileen looked at him as she ran water into the washing-up bowl. It was important to keep busy at the present time. 'Depends on what?' she asked.

'On whether Nick will be here, too.'

Eileen pursed her lips. 'Nick will be here,' she said, wondering why she sounded so angry.

'In that case, I'd quite like it.' Tony began to kick the ball against the wall.

'Don't do that in here, luv. Do it in the garden.'

'Mam?'

'Yes, luv?' She tried not to sound irritable, knowing she was being unreasonable. She wanted him there, but the thud of the ball was getting on her nerves.

'What's going to happen to me dad?' Tony knew there was something strange going on between his parents, something he didn't understand.

'Oh, luv!' Eileen withdrew her hands from the sink and dried them on the teatowel. 'I suppose it's about time you knew. Come on, let's sit in the garden and I'll try and explain.'

The next day at work, Doris expressed surprise when Eileen joined them in the canteen queue for dinner.

'Have you and Nick had a row?' she asked, grinning broadly.

'No. I didn't tell you, but he's been called up. He's joined the RAF. By now, he should have arrived in Ipswich.' Eileen tried to imagine him in the blue uniform, but it was too much. She burst into tears.

'Eileen! Oh, luv, why didn't you tell us before?'

The women crowded round protectively. Hands reached out to comfort her. Carmel provided a hankie to mop her wet face.

'Here, girl, have a fag.' Theresa thrust the pack under Eileen's nose, whilst Lil stroked her hair.

'I'll get you a cup of tea,' said Pauline, as Eileen was led, sobbing, to an empty table.

At the receiving end of such sincere and heartfelt sympathy, Eileen only cried more. After months spent working together, the girls had become as close as a family and were fiercely loyal to each other. They might say a few words behind another's back, but let someone from outside the workshop utter a word of criticism of one of their mates and they'd receive short shrift. Eileen Costello may well have been rather quiet for their liking and never joined in the often ribald conversation. She was also married yet having a bit on the side, and many a coarse joke was cracked when she waltzed off at dinner time for a quickie with her boyfriend. Even so, she was one of *theirs*! Her tragedy was shared by them all.

In fact Doris, overcome, joined in the weeping. 'It's so romantic,' she sobbed. 'I can't wait to fall in love.'

'I queue jumped,' Pauline said, returning with a mug of tea. 'I told them it was an emergency.'

'I don't know what I'd do without youse lot,' sniffed Eileen. No-one at home knew Nick had gone. Annie was on tenterhooks, expecting the boys to leave any minute, and how could she go crying to Sheila, who bore Cal's absence with such quiet fortitude?

After they'd eaten their meal, the women went outside to enjoy the sunshine, sitting in a row on the edge of the stream where Eileen had first seen Nick. Doris rolled up her overalls and began to apply leg tan with a piece of cotton wool, to a chorus of wolf whistles from the men sitting on the bridge.

'What does it look like?' she asked when she'd finished and her legs were as unnaturally orange as her hair.

'Well,' Lil said dubiously. 'You look like you've got yellow jaundice.'

'Yeh, but does it look all right?' insisted Doris.

Eileen returned to work when the break was over, feeling much better. As someone said, you couldn't cry forever. In no time, the women, who had the knack of turning their own personal misfortunes into jokes against themselves, began to suggest what Eileen could do in her dinner hour, seeing as Nick was no longer there. Most of the suggestions were so outrageous that she got a stitch in her side from laughing. She was glad when Alfie arrived and attention was deflected from her for a while.

Eileen actually felt quite happy when she walked home down Marsh Lane later. The girls had cheered her up no end. Somehow, they'd managed to convince her that Nick would come home, safe and sound. Tonight, she'd begin writing him a letter, though she couldn't post it until he sent a definite address.

She turned into Pearl Street, where four women were standing outside Aggie Donovan's, gossiping, and she waved hello as she crossed over to her side.

'Been having it off with your fancy man, have you, Eileen?' Aggie shouted.

Eileen stopped dead, wondering if she'd heard right. Her heart began to race, as she stammered back, 'I've been to work.'

'Aye, but there's work and work. From what we've heard, they serve a particularly tasty dinner over at Dunnings.'

The women laughed, and Eileen stared at them across the little street, feeling her face grow bright red. Everything that had gone on between her and Nick seemed suddenly sordid. Two of the women weren't from Pearl Street, she only vaguely recognised them, but Ellis Evans was one. Their faces were vivid with excitement, as if they were really enjoying themselves.

'You always thought you were a cut above us, didn't you, Eileen?' Ellis shouted in the lovely Welsh sing-song voice that Eileen had always so admired. 'But you're no better than the rest of us at heart.'

'I never thought I was better than anyone,' Eileen mumbled, though doubted if her tormentors heard.

'She's worse! There's no way a decent woman'd go behind her husband's back when he's away fighting for his country,' one of the other women yelled scornfully.

Eileen felt rooted to the spot, unable to move, wanting to die, as the women shook their fists and continued to scream insults. They hated her!

Then Jess appeared out of Number 5, heavy and cumbersome with child. She'd been treating herself to an afternoon nap of late and the noise had woken her. Looking through the window, she saw Eileen Costello with her back against the wall like a hunted animal, and immediately came to the rescue.

'What's going on?' she called as she made her awkward way towards the stricken Eileen. Sometimes she wondered if, the rate her belly was swelling, she was expecting half a dozen babies, not just one.

'It's nowt to do with you,' Aggie Donovan said rudely.

'Isn't it, now? I'll decide what's to do with me.' Jess's temper was beginning to rise. She put her arm around Eileen and, as if the touch had brought her back to life, Eileen burst into tears for the second time that day.

'Go indoors, love,' Jess urged. 'Put the kettle on and I'll join you in a minute.'

After helping the distraught Eileen with her key, Jess turned on the women, green eyes blazing, 'Are you happy now?' she screamed. 'You've reduced her to tears. Is that what you wanted?' The thirty years away from Pearl Street might never have happened, she thought ruefully. Underneath, she was no different from the rest.

'She deserves more than tears,' Aggie screamed back. 'She deserves horse-whipping. Mrs Casey here's got a cousin at Dunnings, and the whole factory knows what Eileen Costello's been up to.'

The woman beside Aggie nodded virtuously. This, presumed Jess, was the said Mrs Casey. The woman had a thick pink hairnet over her metal curlers and was wielding a yardbrush like Boadicea. 'It's a scandal,' she said disgustedly. 'An absolute scandal.'

'Whatever she's been up to, it's none of your bleeding business,' countered Jess, who was beginning to feel slightly dizzy. She must have got up too quickly. She clutched the door frame for support, adding weakly, 'I'm surprised the factory hasn't got more important things to do.'

'You never knew her husband,' Ellis Evans yelled. 'Francis Costello's a fine chap altogether, a councillor, who deserves better than a bitch who goes with another man the minute his back's turned.'

'That's where you're wrong,' Jess managed to sneer. 'I've met Francis Costello, and he didn't seem much of a fine chap to me, considering he'd just finished trying to strangle Eileen to death . . .'

She felt too dizzy to continue and with some difficulty, managed to lower herself until she was sitting in Eileen's doorway.

The faces of the watching women displayed a quick changing range of emotions; from contempt for Eileen Costello, to shock at Jess Fleming's surprising announcement, then concern as the realisation dawned that this was a pregnant woman they were fighting with, a none-too-young pregnant woman having her first child, a woman who should be treated with kid gloves.

Aggie Donovan darted across the street, ''Ere, are you all right, luv?' she cried solicitously.

'Come on, Mrs Fleming, let's get you inside.' Ellis

Evans helped Jess to her feet.

In Number 16, Eileen Costello blinked in astonishment as Jess was helped into the house by two of the women who'd just been shouting abuse from across the street.

'Fetch a wet cloth,' ordered Aggie, 'and lay it over her forehead. Is the kettle boiled yet? What she really needs is a cup of tea.'

Somehow, Eileen wasn't quite sure how it happened, a few minutes later, all four were sitting in the living room drinking tea and chatting amicably as if the last fifteen minutes had never occurred. Aggie deftly brought the subject round to violent husbands and Ellis confided she and Dai had had a 'right old barney,' the night before, but it had been Dai who'd ended up the worse for wear.

Then Aggie turned her eager gaze on Eileen, who realised Jess must have revealed something outside and it was now her turn to bare her soul. She resisted, easily, as she had no intention of discussing her private affairs with Agnes Donovan, because they'd be public before the day was out, though she was glad in a way that a chink had been made in Francis Costello's armour. It might prove useful in time to come.

That same week, just after midnight, the menacing wail of an air raid siren was heard for the first time in Liverpool.

Eileen, fast asleep, was awoken by the almost un-earthly shrieking noise and felt herself break out in goose pimples as she lay waiting for the sound of enemy aircraft overhead. After a while, the siren faded and there was an ominous, dead silence. She slipped out of bed carefully, so as not to wake Tony who'd kick himself tomorrow when he found out what he'd missed, put on her dressing gown and went out into the street.

There were already several people there, staring upwards. The sharp yellow beams of searchlights criss-crossed the black sky.

'Can you hear anything?' Jacob Singerman came up. 'My ears aren't what they used to be.'

There was a repeated popping sound in the distance, like fireworks going off. 'Yes, I can hear something,' Eileen said, wondering if she should take Tony to the public shelter, or at least bring him down and put him under the stairs. She also felt worried for Sheila, who wasn't at all well and had six little ones to get to safety.

'That's anti-aircraft guns,' Mr Harrison declared. 'I'd better see to Nelson. He doesn't like strange noises.'

Not long afterwards the All Clear sounded, a long high-pitched drone.

'It must have been a false alarm,' someone suggested, and they all went back indoors.

But it wasn't a false alarm when the siren sounded again the following two nights and the drone of aircraft could be heard in the distance. Each time bombs were dropped, and although they landed harmlessly in fields on the outskirts of the city, the raids seemed like a portent of terrible things to come.

The warnings continued throughout the following week. At Dunnings, because the siren couldn't be heard above the noise of the machinery, a klaxon had been fitted, a blaring foghorn, which was a signal for the workers to make their immediate way down to the damp, miserable basement that served as a shelter.

A rumour spread like wildfire throughout the entire country that Hitler intended to invade on 2 July, and every time Alfie or Miss Thomas appeared in the work-shop the women jumped, expecting the worst.

Like millions of people everywhere, Eileen couldn't

sleep that night. She lay, clutching her son, praying that the church bells wouldn't ring to signal the invasion had begun. The night was almost over by the time she dozed off, and she was still asleep when the postman delivered two letters; one from Nick, the other from Francis.

Tony, up first, found the letters on the mat and brought them to her in bed. She was glad when he disappeared, anxious to go to the lavatory, so she could read them alone.

With shaking hands, she opened the one from Francis first. It was brief and to the point. He agreed to a divorce on the grounds described by her father and would like the matter to be over and done with as soon as possible, '*so that I can get on with my own life*'.

Eileen sank back onto the pillow, exhilarated. Tomorrow, she would go and see the solicitor and get the proceedings under way. She was wondering what she would wear when she and Nick were married, when she remembered he'd written and opened the letter eagerly.

She blushed as she read his tender words. He missed her more than he'd ever thought possible. *You never gave me a memento. Send me something, a handkerchief sprayed with that perfume you use, which I can keep under my pillow, and a photograph, definitely a photograph, and one of Tony, too.* He'd spent only a day or so near Ipswich and was now at a base in Kent where he was being trained to fly Spitfires. Spitfires, she read, somewhat incredulously, were 'beautiful', almost as beautiful as she was herself, and he was a little bit in love with them. He demanded a letter 'by return'.

As soon as Tony had left for school, Eileen rushed around to Veronica's, because there wasn't time to go to the Co-op, and bought a new hanky with an 'E' embroidered in the corner, and soaked it liberally with the Chanel perfume which Jess had given her for Christmas. She hunted for the snap of her and Tony taken in New Brighton last summer, and finished off the long letter she'd been writing daily since Nick left. After commenting on his own letter, she added a triumphant postcript. 'I've heard from Francis and he's agreed to a divorce!'

On her way to work, she called on Sheila to tell her the news. 'Will you come to the wedding, Sis?'

'Of course I will! what makes you think I wouldn't?' Sheila looked wretched. For the first time, she was having trouble in the early stages of pregnancy; cramps and stomach ache. She wasn't eating properly either, and instead of blooming, as she usually did, she'd lost weight and her normally rosy cheeks were drawn and waxen.

'Well, it won't be in a church, will it? It'll be a registry office wedding,' Eileen explained. She regarded Sheila worriedly.

'You're me sister, and I'll come no matter where it is.'

'It means I won't be married in the eyes of God!'

'Who knows what God sees,' Sheila said enigmatically, adding anxiously, 'You'll keep going to church, though, won't you, Eil?'

'As long as they'll let me. I'll still be a Catholic, no matter where I get married. No-one can take me religion off me.'

'That's good.' Sheila managed a tired smile.

'Anyway, Sis, I'd better be off now, else I'll miss the bus. Pass the news on to our dad if he calls round later. I reckon he'll be pleased, though hell'd freeze over before he'd admit it.'

As she waited for the bus, Eileen felt guilty at leaving her sister. Although the neighbours helped out, it wasn't the same as family. Perhaps it was time she left Dunnings and stayed at home to see Sheila through the next six months. And it wasn't just Sheila she was worried about. Every time the siren went at work and they were whisked down to the basement, she thought about Tony. What if there was a proper raid? He'd want his mam, not Annie. Even worse, what if the unspeakable happened and he was killed?

She imagined arriving home after a raid, safe and sound and all in one piece, and finding Pearl Street flattened and her son dead. It didn't bear thinking about!

On the other hand, if she left, what would she do for money? She hadn't collected Francis's wages from the Mersey Docks & Harbour Board since she'd begun to earn a wage herself, and under the circumstances she couldn't very well start now! The allowance she got off the Army wasn't nearly enough to live on, and you never know, it might be cancelled once the divorce got under way.

In fact, for all intents and purposes, she was virtually a single woman, with a son to support and a house to keep up. In other words, there was no way she could leave Dunnings. It was another aspect of the war; the worry, the agonising worry of being separated from your loved ones, whether it be a few miles or a few hundred miles and she'd just have to stop moaning, if only to herself, and put up with it!

As for Sheila, perhaps on Saturday they could all go to Melling and spend the day at Nick's house. A day in the country might be just what she needed.

Chapter 15

So far, the summer had been as splendid as the winter had been bleak. Day after never-ending day, the sun shone down relentlessly out of a clear blue sky with an inevitability people began to take for granted.

It was scorching again on Saturday when Eileen took her sister and the children to Melling for the day. Annie, whose sons had gone back the day before, came with them.

The children ran wild once they were released in Nick's big, untidy garden, as if they felt liberated without the confining walls of Pearl Street. They kicked balls, picked what flowers they could find, made daisy chains and did cartwheels on the rough grass. Mary, the baby, sat watching, waving her arms and crowing in delight.

At noon, they picnicked on the lawn where, by now, the grass had become dry and prickly with the heat. Each woman had made an entire loaf of sandwiches to bring, and Annie had baked one of her famous bunloaves.

'It's lovely here,' said Sheila, who'd been put firmly in a deckchair and ordered not to move all day. 'And it all belongs to Nick?'

'It's where we're going to live,' Eileen said shyly. 'You can come every weekend if you like.'

'You won't be able to keep me away,' Sheila warned. 'Least, not in the summer. That sun's a real tonic. It seems bigger than at home and I feel better already. The horrible pain has disappeared from me gut.'

Siobhan came running up with a crown of daisies for her mam. Not to be outdone, Tony brought Eileen an overblown rose, which she threaded through the button-hole of her blouse.

'Take Annie a rose, too,' she whispered, 'so's she won't feel left out – and mind you don't prick your fingers!'

'Who wants more tea?' Annie shouted from the kitchen. 'Make the most of it while you can, tea's going on rations on Monday.'

'We both do,' Eileen shouted back, then added to Sheila, 'I don't know how they expect us to win the war on two ounces of tea a week!'

'I wouldn't care if I never drank another cup,' Sheila said. 'Not when the Merchant Navy have to risk their lives to fetch it.'

'I never thought about it that way before!' The toll of lives lost at sea had reached an all-time high in June.

'People don't,' Sheila said dryly. 'If it weren't for the likes of Cal, the country'd starve to death.'

'Does he know you haven't been so well, luv?'

'Of course not! I only write him cheerful letters, else he'd worry. He'll be home next weekend, and if today's anything to go by, I'll be completely better by then. I feel on top of the world at the moment.'

Annie brought the tea in three cracked cups, the rose tucked behind her ear. With her dark hair and bright red blouse, the yellow flower gave her an exotic look.

'Your Nick doesn't possess a decent piece of crockery,' she said scathingly, 'and his knives and forks need to be seen to be believed. I'll give them a good clean before I go.' Annie had vowed not to mope, but keep a cheerful face on things. She hadn't stopped working since she arrived.

'I don't think he ate much except butties,' Eileen explained. 'I used to let him have me butter ration.'

They all agreed that men were hopeless without women.

'On the other hand,' Annie said thoughtfully, 'women are hopeless without men – men or kids. Women have got to have someone to look after. That's what I miss most, doing me lads' washing and cooking for them. I feel as if I'm a waste of time altogether, having only meself to take care off.'

'Annie! What a terrible thing to say,' cried Eileen. 'What would we do without you?'

Annie decided to prove her usefulness there and then by offering to fetch a jug of lemonade from the pub. 'We should have brought some with us. The kids looked a bit put out when we only gave them water, and I wouldn't mind a glass meself. I'm parched.'

Eileen walked with her to the gate. 'I'd come with you, but I don't like to leave our Sheila on her own in case the kids get out of hand. The pub's only just down the lane and around the corner.'

Annie departed in the shimmering haze, carrying a big earthenware jug in the crook of her arm and with the yellow flower still in her hair, and Eileen returned to the garden.

'Look!' Sheila cried in delight. 'Our Mary's crawling!'

Unable to stand the sight of her brothers and sisters having such a good time without her, the nine-month-old baby, wearing only a white cotton bonnet, was making her way towards them on all fours. The children stopped playing and watched the little figure approaching purposefully and Niall kicked the ball gently in her direction. Mary sat up and clutched the ball and tried to throw it back. Although it landed only inches away, the children applauded.

'My, she's clever,' marvelled Eileen.

'Isn't she?' Sheila was close to tears. 'Jaysus, I love my kids, Eil.'

'I know you do, luv.' Eileen felt as if she could cry herself, the sight of Mary making her first independent way in the world had been really touching. 'Nick and I are going to have lots of babies.'

'Does Nick know?'

'Not yet,' Eileen said fiercely. 'We've got to get through all this haven't we, before we can decide those sort of things? Me and Nick, you and Cal, Annie and her lads.'

'I wonder if we will?' Sheila said in a tight voice. 'I never let meself think the worst, but sometimes, it doesn't seem possible that every single person we know and love will still be alive when it all ends. After all, we've already lost Charlie Gregson and Mary Flaherty.'

As if to remind them that war wasn't very far away, two planes seemed to appear out of nowhere and roared low over the house. The windows of the cottage shook.

The older boys watched intently as the planes zoomed out of sight. 'Did you see them, Mam?' Dominic shouted. 'They were Spitfires.'

'They were Hurricanes,' Tony argued.

'Spitfires!'

'Hurricanes!'

The two boys flung themselves at each other and began to wrestle on the grass.

'I'll see to them.' Eileen laid her hand on Sheila's arm. 'Is it any wonder there's wars, eh? Perhaps it's about time us women got a chance to run the world, then anybody who even mentioned the word "war" would be shot!'

Just then, a flushed and bright-eyed Annie came back,

accompanied by a strange man carrying the earthenware jug.

'This is Chris Parker,' Annie announced in a funny, high-pitched voice. 'The jug turned out to be a bit heavy and he offered to carry it for me. His lad's in the Royal Warwickshires, the same as our Terry and Joe.'

'Did he come through Dunkirk?' Eileen asked as Chris shook hands.

'He did that. Like Annie's lads, he only went back yesterday, so's I understand how she feels right now,' Chris replied in a strong Lancashire accent. He was a comfortable-looking man of about forty-five with a pleasant, open face and thick wavy brown hair. He smiled as he shook hands with the women, showing even white teeth which contrasted sharply with his sunburnt skin.

'Would you like some lemonade while you're here, as a reward, like, for carrying it?' Annie looked very girlish and coy.

'I wouldn't mind a glass, thanks very much.'

'I don't know about a glass,' Annie said darkly. 'It might have to be a cup, and a cracked one to boot. The house belongs to Eileen's feller and the contents of his kitchen would make any decent housewife weep.' With a swing of her narrow hips, she disappeared inside.

It was obvious Annie was rather taken with the visitor. In which case, Eileen had no intention of letting her bury herself in the kitchen. She insisted Chris take a deckchair. 'Our Sheila will keep you amused, while I give Annie a hand.' Having spied the arrival of the drink, the children were clamouring for their share.

Annie was rooting through the kitchen cupboards. 'I'm looking for glasses.'

'He's a bit of all right, isn't he?' Eileen said. 'What does he do?'

'He's not bad,' Annie replied with a too obvious pretence at indifference. 'He's a fireman, and did you notice his teeth? They're all his own.'

'How do you know?'

'I asked him, of course.' Annie slammed the cupboard door and opened another. 'Some of this stuff must have come out of the Ark.'

'That's not very romantic! Where's his wife?'

'I couldn't very well ask him *that*, could I?' Annie snorted. 'Well, bugger me if your Nick hasn't got a whole set of tankards in here.'

'I dunno. It seems a bit less nosy than asking if he had false teeth.' Eileen loved the way Annie kept saying, 'your Nick'.

'I'll just give these a rinse and you can take him his drink.' Annie began to run the glasses under the tap.

'*I'm* not taking it! He'd prefer it from you, and you can ask him if he wears a wig at the same time.'

'Why is this water hot?' Annie demanded.

'Search me!'

'It shouldn't be hot, there's no fire lit. I bet it's one of them immersion heater things and you left it switched on,' Annie said accusingly as she dried the glasses on a rather grubby teatowel.

'*I* left it switched on?'

'Who was last in here?'

'Me, but I didn't know there was an immersion.'

'Anyroad, it means we can give the kids a bath before we go. Would Nick mind?'

''Course he wouldn't. Nick wouldn't mind if we bathed the whole of Melling.'

Annie had begun to scrub the sink. Eileen poured

lemonade into two glasses and took the scrubbing brush out of her hand. 'Stop putting it off, and give these to Chris and our Sheila.'

'Do I look all right?' Annie smoothed her dark hair. 'Does this flower look stupid?'

'Dead stupid, but Chris mustn't think so, else he wouldn't have followed you home.'

'I feel all funny. He'll think I'm a right nana.'

Eileen watched as Chris leapt to his feet when Annie approached. He gave the deckchair a little nudge for her to sit in. She felt convinced there was that little extra tension in his movements, as if he was as smitten with Annie as she was with him.

'Now I suppose I'd better see to youse lot,' she said to the children, who were glaring at her as they waited for their lemonade.

Much to their disappointment, Chris left after about half an hour. 'Me dinner was ready a while ago. I'll get a right earful when I get home.'

'He must have a wife,' Annie said sadly after he'd gone. Later, as the afternoon wore on, she remarked, 'I really liked him. He reminded me of my Tom. He had the same reassuring look.'

'Never mind, Annie!' Eileen gave her friend's knee a squeeze. 'There's plenty more fish in the sea.'

'Aye, but he was salmon, the rest are only cod.' Annie sighed. 'I'm fed up sitting here. I'll bath the children if you like, Sheila?'

'Thanks, Annie. I feel a proper lazybones. I've been waited on hand and foot all day.' Sheila's nose and cheeks had turned pink where she'd caught the sun.

Annie clapped her hands. 'Siobhan, Caitlin! Your Auntie Annie's going to wash you in a proper bath. I hope your Nick's got some clean towels,' she said to Eileen.

'I'll have a look.'

The towels were folded neatly in the airing cupboard, along with several of Nick's shirts, all freshly back from the laundry. Eileen touched the shirts briefly, before taking the towels downstairs.

The girls were already in the big, clawfooted bath in the room which led from the kitchen, both squealing in delight as they splashed water at each other.

'Mind off, you'll have me drenched.' Annie ducked to avoid a cascade of water. 'Perhaps your Sheila'd like a long cool bath later,' she said when Eileen came in. 'In fact, I wouldn't mind one meself if there's enough hot water. It's lovely just running it straight out the tap, 'stead of having to carry it in by hand.'

Annie plucked the girls out and, before she could dress either, they ran screaming into the garden with nothing on.

'Oh, well,' she laughed, 'if that's the way they want it. They can get dressed later, though they won't stay clean for long. Dominic, Niall!' she shouted. 'It's your turn next.'

Before long, all Sheila's children were running naked around the garden. After bathing himself, Tony modestly insisted on putting his underpants back on.

The sun was no longer directly overhead and the three women moved into a welcome triangle of shade. 'Shall we have our tea now?' suggested Annie. 'There's plenty of butties left.'

'Lord preserve us, Annie!' Eileen protested. 'You haven't sat still all day. Go and lie in the bath for half an hour and give us a bit of peace.'

'All right, I know when I'm not wanted!'

'She's only staying busy to keep her mind off the boys,' Sheila said when Annie had flounced into the house.

'I know – and I know how she feels, too.'

Mary crawled over, grabbed her mam's legs and almost pulled herself upright.

'See that! She'll be walking any minute.' Sheila picked the baby up onto her lap, where she promptly fell asleep.

'I'll go and put the kettle on, forestall Annie. We'll have our tea when she comes out.'

When she was inside, Eileen switched the wireless on. Jeanette MacDonald and Nelson Eddy were singing *We'll Gather Lilacs*. She turned the sound up as loud as it would go so Sheila could hear outside. As she busied herself spreading sandwiches on plates, emptying the remains of the tea in the pot, washing the cracked cups, she thought to herself, 'One day soon, I'll be doing this for Nick. This will be *my* kitchen!' She wondered if Nick had enough money to buy one of those stoves like Jess had?

The music changed. Eileen stopped what she was doing as Vera Lynn began to sing *We'll Meet Again* – their song! Suddenly, she was no longer in the shabby little kitchen. Instead, she was with Nick in London, and he was whirling her round and round and round . . .

She came to when a shadow fell over the room. The dark form of a man was standing in the doorway, his back to the sun. Eileen's heart felt as if it was about to burst with happiness.

'*Nick!*'

The man stepped forward. 'It's Chris. I'm looking for Annie.'

'Oh, I'm sorry. I couldn't see you properly. I thought you were someone else.' She was trembling as she turned away to hide her face and began to put the sandwiches back in the bag, then realised they were supposed to be on the plate and spread them out again. 'Annie's in the bath,' she said, hoping her voice sounded relatively normal. 'She should be out any minute.' The water could be heard draining away in the adjoining room.

'That's all right.' Chris folded his sunburnt arms as if he were ready to wait forever for Annie to appear. 'I'm only in Melling for the day visiting me daughter,' he was explaining, just as Annie opened the bathroom door and emerged in her bare feet and petticoat and combing her wet hair.

'That was the gear,' she said. When she saw Chris, she gave a little scream and fled back in, slamming the door behind her.

Chris took a deep breath and rapped on the door. 'Annie?' he said tersely.

'What?' came a muffled voice.

'Have you got a husband?'

'I'm a widow.'

'Well, I'm a widower, and I'd like to see you again.'

There was no reply from the bathroom.

'I think the answer's probably yes,' said Eileen. She shouted. 'That's right, isn't it, Annie?'

There was still no answer. 'Take it from me, it's definitely yes,' Eileen assured him.

'In that case, I want to know if she'll come to the pictures with me on Monday night.'

A garbled response came from the next room.

'What did she say?' demanded Chris.

'She's on late shift Monday. It'll have to be Saturday next.'

'How about tomorrow?'

'How about tomorrow, Annie?' Eileen shouted.

'Tomorrow's all right.'

'Tell her I'll see her at half past seven outside the Odeon in Lime Street.'

Eileen nodded. 'I will.'

Chris seemed to relax. 'In that case, I'll be off. I expect I'll be seeing you again sometime.'

'Aye, I expect you will.'

Eileen watched as Chris said goodbye to Sheila, then disappeared around the side of the house. 'He's gone, Annie,' she called.

The bathroom door opened cautiously and Annie appeared, fully dressed.

'You're a stupid idiot, Annie Poulson,' Eileen cried. 'Didn't it cross your mind to tell him you weren't married?'

Annie burst into tears. 'I feel so bloody lonely nowadays, I always think it must be obvious to everyone.'

'Come here, luv!' Eileen gave Annie a warm hug. 'He's a lovely feller. I really liked him, honest.'

'At least I had me best brassiere on,' said Annie, sniffing. 'The one with the rosebud. I hope he noticed.'

After they'd had their tea and the children were dressed, Eileen began to tidy up their belongings from the garden. Annie found a piece of rope and made a line to peg the towels on.

'I'll take them home with us and give them a proper wash. Anyroad, we need to get them dry a bit for your Sheila. I'll switch that immersion off, we don't need any more water.'

Sheila was at that moment soaking in the bath. Eileen could hear her humming under her breath to the music.

The deckchairs were put away in the tumbledown shed and everyone was lying on the grass, waiting, when Sheila finally emerged, looking the picture of health after her day out in the country.

She came towards them, smiling, then stopped, a

surprised look on her pink face, as she bent over and clutched her stomach.

'Jaysus!' she groaned.

Annie darted across the grass to catch Sheila before she fell, but Eileen couldn't move; she just stared, horrified, at the bright red blood which poured down from between her sister's legs.

'Are you sure she's all right?' Jack Doyle demanded anxiously.

They were in Sheila's house. Eileen had only just arrived back in Pearl Street from the hospital, and having unearthed her dad from the King's Arms, relayed the news about his favourite daughter.

'Honest, Dad, she's fine,' she assured him. 'It was a miscarriage, and she'll be home in a couple of days. Though I'll tell you this much, it gave me the fright of me life at the time.' She'd been convinced her sister was going to die.

'You didn't let her do too much, did you, at this Melling place?'

'Are you trying to tell me it's all my fault?' Eileen asked angrily.

'No, of course I ain't.'

'It was something that *had* to happen, according to the doctor. I was too wrought up to take it in, but apparently the baby was growing in the wrong place, outside the womb or something.'

'As long as she's all right.' He sat down suddenly, relieved. 'Where's the kids?'

'They're upstairs in bed, all seven of them. I'll sleep here till our Sheila's back, and the neighbours will help out while I'm at work. It was Annie who brought the kids home on the bus. I went with Sheila in the ambulance. They were dead good. Apparently, our Tony carried Ryan. He was fast asleep by then.'

'He's a good lad, Tony,' her dad said proudly, 'and Annie Poulson's worth her weight in gold.'

'She is, too,' Eileen agreed fervently. Annie had stayed calm, whilst she herself panicked. She was about to go running to the pub to call for an ambulance, when Annie pointed out a telephone on the hall table which Eileen had never noticed in all the numerous times she'd been there. 'Annie clicked today. She met this lovely feller.'

'Not before time. It's a shame, a good woman like that going to waste.'

'Women aren't exactly wasted just because they haven't got a man,' Eileen said indignantly. 'No-one suggests *you're* going to waste because you haven't got a woman.'

'You're an awkward bugger, our Eileen,' he complained.

'Well, I had a good teacher in you!'

They glared at each other across the room. 'Anyroad,' he said eventually, 'you've room to talk. You've got two men at the moment; a husband and another one on the side.'

'I don't want me husband, do I? All I want is Nick.' There was a catch in Eileen's voice as she spoke the last words. It had been an emotional day, what with Annie, then the terrible thing with her sister. She felt too upset for an argument at the moment.

'Did Sheila tell you about the letter I got from Francis?' she asked.

'Aye. Have you seen the solicitor?'

'Miss Thomas rang up for me and he's on holiday. She said the best thing to do was post the letter to him.'

'Well, let's hope it turns out all right.'

413

Eileen said in a rush, 'I can't wait to marry Nick, Dad!'

Jack Doyle stared at the lovely, flushed face of his eldest daughter. She worried him. The girl was much too highly strung and sensitive, and for all her tough talk she was as soft as a jelly underneath. His other daughter, Sheila, who seemed so pliant, as if butter wouldn't melt in her mouth, was in reality as hard as nails. If anything happened to Cal, Sheila would get over it. It might take time, but Sheila was a stalwart and she'd square her shoulders and carry on. Another thing, there was no way Sheila would have married a man she didn't love just to please her dad. But Eileen had, and not only that, she'd put up with the geezer for five whole years before saying a word. Now this Nick chap she was head over heels in love with had joined the Air Force. Everyone said the next stage of the war would be fought in the air, and Jack wasn't sure if his girl could cope if anything happened to Nick.

He knew he'd always been hard on his eldest child. Perhaps it was because she reminded him of himself, as she struggled to make sense of the world. He'd pushed her away, trying to toughen her up, but he loved her every bit as much as he did Sheila and Sean, perhaps more. He felt a rush of real concern, and tried to think of something cheerful he could say.

'Would you like a window box, luv?'

She'd been so deep in her own thoughts, she looked up in surprise, as if she'd forgotten he was there. 'A what, Dad?'

'A window box for the backyard, to grow things,' he explained. 'We've been told to grow for victory. You could plant a few tomaters or lettuces. I was thinking of knocking one up for meself. I could do one for you at the same time.'

★

414

Calum Reilly came home a few days later to find his wife had lost the baby she was expecting. He made up his mind, there and then, that it was time Sheila had a rest from childbearing. Perhaps they could start again when the lot they had now were at school. He'd bring the subject up later, when they were in bed.

But they hadn't been in bed for more than a few minutes when the air raid siren went, and he leapt out and grabbed his clothes.

'Come on, luv,' he urged, conscious Sheila hadn't moved.

'Where are you off to?' The bed creaked as she sat up.

'The shelter, where else?'

'There's nowt going to happen, Cal,' Sheila said comfortably. 'They only drop bombs on the outskirts. Anyroad, there's no way I'm taking the kids to the shelter. It's worse than a slum in there.'

A warning bell began to ring in Cal's ears. 'What happens if the bombs start dropping nearer?' he asked quietly.

'I've no idea, luv. I just hope they don't, that's all.'

Cal had finished dressing. 'I won't be a minute,' he said.

It was still daylight when he went outside, and several people were in the street staring up into the sky. The drone of aircraft could be heard in the distance, accompanied by the sound of ack ack fire. Cal felt his blood run cold. He hadn't realised things had got this bad at home.

'Jesus Christ!' he muttered in despair. What had the world come to? It was bad enough having to worry about his own safety, without fearing his entire family might be wiped out in his absence.

He walked around to the nearest shelter. Only a

handful of people had taken advantage of its protection, and they were sitting on the narrow benches attached to the walls clutching blankets and their gasmasks. The building stank of urine and was lit by just two fluttering candles, one of which decided to go out as Cal went in. He noticed straight away there was no First Aid box, no facilities to make a hot drink.

'Has someone pinched the door?' he asked of no-one in particular. There was merely an aperture covered with a black curtain.

'Is that Cal Reilly?' a man's voice enquired.

'It is.'

'It's Ernie Cutler, Cal. I used to work on the docks with Jack Doyle until I lost me arm.'

'Hello, Ernie. How are you keeping?' Cal remembered Ernie Cutler well. He'd been a big man once, almost as big and strong as Jack Doyle himself, but since his accident seemed to have shrunk in size, and his face was as wizened as an old man's. The loose sleeve of his threadbare jacket was tucked neatly in the pocket.

'I'm bearing up, Cal, bearing up,' Ernie said cheerfully. 'Course, I didn't get any compensation. They insisted it was me own fault, as if I wanted to lose me arm on purpose. Still,' he shrugged, 'that's another story. As to the door, there's never been one. It was built that way. It'll be bloody freezing in the winter.'

'You mean they're putting shelters up without doors?' Cal said incredulously.

Ernie gave a bitter little laugh. 'The whole thing's a disgrace, Cal. The poorer you are, the less your life is worth – not that we needed a war to tell us that. Better-off folks have got their own Anderson shelters in the garden, but you can't put an Anderson in a backyard. There's actually a posh shelter somewhere in town where you can rent a place for twenty-seven-and-six a week.'

'You're right.' Cal's blood began to boil. 'It's a disgrace.' He was risking his life to put food on the tables of the politicians, and they hadn't the decency to keep his family safe at home. 'I'm not having our Sheila coming here,' he swore. 'It stinks!'

'I only come for the company,' said Ernie. 'The woman next door takes herself and her kids under the stairs.'

'It looks like our Sheila will have to do the same,' Cal said grimly.

First thing next morning, he cleared every single item from out of the understairs cupboard and put them in the washhouse in the yard, then bought a can of distemper and painted the inside of the cupboard white. He spent all weekend fitting shelves for his children to sleep on and built a seat in the corner for his wife. He gave instructions to his family on what bedding to bring down when the siren went. 'Just your piller and a single blanket,' he said. 'No toys, there's no room for toys, except perhaps a book or two and a couple of crayons. Niall, it's your job to see to our Ryan, and Dominic, you take care of the girls. You mam will have her hands full with Mary.'

'How will we see to read, Dad?' asked Niall.

'I forgot about that,' said Cal. He went out immediately and bought a box of nightlights and a supply of matches.

'These are not to be moved,' he told Sheila. 'I don't want you coming out looking for things while there's a raid on.'

'No, Cal,' Sheila said.

'Put a fresh bottle of water inside every morning, case the kids'd like a drink, and a tin of biscuits wouldn't come amiss if there's a few to spare.'

'Yes, Cal.'

Was there anything else, Cal wondered frantically, as he surveyed the little white cocoon which would keep his family safe. There was nothing, he decided, nothing further he could do, except hope and pray he'd be spared and they'd be spared, until the day came when the whole insane bloody business was over.

In the middle of July, Rosie Gregson gave birth to a 3 lb, 6 oz, baby boy in Bootle Hospital. She called him Charlie, after his dad, who she still felt convinced would return to her one day.

Aggie Donovan had scarcely finished going around Pearl Street to collect for a present for Rosie's baby when an item of far more startling news was received, which meant she had to go around all over again.

To everyone's amazement, Gladys Tutty announced that Freda had passed the scholarship and would be going to Bootle Secondary School in Breeze Hill.

'Y'could have knocked me down with a feather when she told me,' said Aggie, as she banged on doors for the second collection. People dug deep into their pockets and their purses and enough was raised to buy Freda Tutty a satchel for her posh new school.

'Thanks,' said Freda carelessly, when Aggie presented the gift. It wasn't a leather satchel, which she would have preferred, but made of canvas, the edges bound with tape. Still, it would do, and would save dipping into Clive's nest egg.

'I bet you never thought you'd see me go to school in a uniform?' she said boastfully.

'I never thought I would and I never thought I wouldn't,' Aggie replied.

'Well, thanks, anyway,' said Freda, slamming the door.

'Stuck-up little bitch,' Aggie Donovan muttered to herself as she walked away.

Not long after Dunkirk, the dinner hour in Dunnings had been cut by half and tea breaks done away with altogether. Although the trolley still came round, the women were expected to take their drink without stopping the machines.

No-one complained, no-one had to be persuaded to work harder in order to produce more planes for the battle that was gradually beginning in the air. According to the newspapers, output rose by two hundred and fifty per cent in factories throughout the land. By the end of the July, the desperately needed Hurricanes and Spitfires were being built in their hundreds.

As July gave way to August, the war reached a new stage of ferocity. But now, instead of the battle taking place out of sight on strange foreign shores, it was being fought right in the British backyard, as wave after wave of German bombers poured in over the south coast, ostensibly to destroy airfields, but destroying the lives and the homes of ordinary civilians in their wake. Not that the Royal Air Force allowed the Jerries to get away with much, and German losses were far greater than the British. In other parts of the country, people could only read about the onslaught in their papers or listen to the commentators on the BBC.

Eileen Costello wasn't the only person to regard the way the whole thing was reported as offensive.

180 FOR 26, ENGLAND STILL BATTING, news vendors scrawled on their placards. To those with a loved one at risk, it was the smaller number that mattered, for it meant twenty-six British aircrft had been lost. Not all pilots managed to land safely once their plane was

damaged. A good proportion of the twenty-six would be dead, and as far as Eileen Costello was concerned, one of them could be Nick!

He said little in his letters. After less than a month's training, Eileen knew he was already taking part in sorties. In fact, he'd sent a snapshot, which she couldn't bring herself to show anyone yet, of him standing beside his plane which had been christened *E for Eileen*. Underneath the name, there was a little black swastika.

'The swastika means I've already got a Messerschmidt under my belt,' he wrote on the back.

Eileen felt she was living on a knife edge – who didn't, when they had a man away doing his bit? For a time, she was worried that, if the worst happened and he was killed, she'd never know. The RAF authorities would inform his next of kin, his mother in America. When she expressed this fear in her next letter, he wrote back straight away.

> As if I hadn't thought of that already! I gave your name and address to the landlady of the local pub. If anything happens, she'll write and let you know. But nothing WILL happen, my dearest girl. I feel as if there's an angel watching over my shoulder when I'm in the air. And don't forget our song! *We'll Meet Again*. If you sing it loud enough and often enough, then we're bound to meet again one sunny day.
>
> So, keep smiling through – Your most loving and adoring, Nick.

Eileen did her utmost to keep smiling, but as each sunny golden August day gave way to the next, men continued to offer up their young lives in increasingly large numbers. Scores took off by day and by night, never to return. Instead, they were burnt alive in the cockpits of their Hurricanes or Spitfires, and the resulting fireball would plunge to earth and explode into smithereens in a Kentish field of swaying yellow corn, or a green Sussex valley or a Suffolk marsh, or it would land with a mighty sizzle in the English Channel, in which so many dead seamen, soldiers and airmen already lay.

Winston Churchill honoured the sacrifice in the House of Commons. *'Never in the field of human conflict was so much owed by so many to so few.'*

It was nothing but sheer carnage, Eileen thought bitterly; a whole generation of young men was being wiped out at the whim of a madman.

And while the slaughter went on, in Pearl Street the children, who were on holiday from school, drew wickets on the railway wall and played a genuine game of cricket, and Mr Singerman had his windows smashed twice in one week. Rosie Gregson did her pathetic best to suckle her sickly baby, but although the women tried to help, the child just wouldn't thrive. A card arrived for Eileen Costello from Helen Brazier, who was in Scotland, 'having a wonderful time', on the same day the Harrisons heard their eldest grandson had been killed in action in North Africa. Chris Parker continued to court Annie Poulson, to the general approval of the street – a firebobby was quite a catch for a woman going on forty. Jack Doyle heard through a friend who had a son in Alexandria that Francis Costello had been injured. The details were vague and when he told his daughter, she'd heard nothing. 'So's it can't be serious, can it?' Eileen said. As for Jess Fleming, she just got bigger and bigger . . .

The air raids over Liverpool began to increase in their intensity. Bombs were no longer dropped on fields, but on built-up areas, and to everybody's horror, five people were killed by high explosive bombs in Wallasey and Prenton, and several seriously injured.

Like Calum Reilly, Eileen had cleared out her under-stairs cupboard and brought down the palliasse off Tony's single bed. The fit was snug and Tony thoroughly enjoyed the time spent waiting for the All Clear to sound. He seemed to consider the whole thing some sort of adventure.

The expression on Annie's face was grim when Eileen arrived home after she'd been on the late shift. 'I've had the wireless on. There's been terrible raids on London and Portsmouth.'

'Jaysus!' Eileen sat down quickly. 'Who was it said this war would be over by last Christmas?'

'Your Francis did, for one.'

'He's not *my* Francis!' Eileen said quickly.

'Sorry, luv. Of course he ain't. I bet he wishes he never joined the Territorials now.'

Eileen shuddered. 'I'm sorry he's been hurt, but even so, I'd sooner forget about Francis. I wish there was something nice we could talk about for a change.'

'Well, actually,' Annie said, 'there is. Chris and me are getting married! He only asked yesterday.'

'Annie! Oh, I'm so pleased, I could cry!' Over-whelmed, Eileen did just that. 'Congratulations, luv,' she sobbed. 'I wish you all the happiness in the world.'

'I would never have guessed!'

'Have you fixed the date?' Eileen asked, still sniffing.

'Not yet,' Annie replied.' We'll leave it till all three lads are home on leave. I've written to Terry and Joe and told them to toss for who'll give me away. Chris's lad, Mark, will be best man. I wondered if you'd consider being me Matron of Honour, Eileen?'

Eileen cried, 'Of course I will, luv. What would you like me to wear?'

'Don't get nothing new,' Annie said dismissively. 'After all, there's a war on. That pink suit you bought for London would be the gear. As for meself, I'll just get something from C & A.'

'What colour?'

Annie smiled shyly. 'Yellow! Chris asked specially if I'd wear yellow, because it was the rose your Tony gave me that first made him notice me in the pub that day.'

'You suit yellow, Annie.'

'Ta!'

There was silence for a moment. Then Eileen said worriedly, 'You don't seem very excited, luv.' Despite the wonderful news, her friend looked remarkably subdued.

Annie began to play with the top button of her blouse, twisting it one way, then the other. She looked at Eileen with a strange expression in her dark eyes.

'I'm so happy, it terrifies me,' she said quietly. 'I'm too scared to be excited, in case it all goes wrong.'

'Chris loves you. He won't let you down.'

Annie gestured impatiently. ''T'ain't that! I've only known him just over a month, but I've as much faith in him as I have in meself. It's all the things outside my control that worry me. A fireman's job is dangerous enough in normal times, but now! Then there's the lads, his and mine . . .'

Eileen looked at her friend helplessly. 'I don't know what to say, Annie, but then I never do.'

Annie shrugged. 'Who does, these days?'

'Is he going to move in with you once you've tied the knot?' Eileen asked, half dreading the answer. Her fears were confirmed when Annie shook her head.

'No, luv. I'm moving in with him.'

'Oh, Annie! How can I live without you just down the street?'

The two women stared at each other, too full of emotion to speak.

'Well, y'see, luv,' Annie said eventually. 'Chris's got this lovely big corporation house in Fazakerley, with a bathroom and two lavs, one upstairs and one down, and one of them sunshine lounges with a window at each end and gardens back and front . . . I'd be mad to give it up and let him move to Pearl Street,' she finished.

'Of course you would. I was just being dead selfish, that's all. Anyroad, I'll be moving meself once me and Nick get married.'

'And Melling and Fazakerley are closer to each other than they are to Bootle, so's we can still see each other regular,' Annie said. 'Mind you, I'll be sad to see the back of the ould street after twenty years, but life moves on, Eileen. Sometimes, you can't make new ties without undoing some of the old ones.'

The air raid siren went a few hours after Annie had gone. Eileen took Tony downstairs to the improvised shelter, and left him there, fast asleep, even after the All Clear sounded half an hour later. During the brief raid, there seemed to be more aircraft than usual overhead.

The early morning news was full of the raids on London and Portsmouth, and the heavy casualties suffered by the RAF the day before. When Eileen arrived in work, Doris was full of excitement. An incendiary bomb had dropped right outside her house.

'Everywhere was lit up with a horrible green light that you could see for miles and bloody miles,' she said with relish. 'Oh, look here's Miss Thomas! I hope you've come to tell us ould Adolf's thrown in the towel?' she called.

Miss Thomas laughed. 'I wish I had!' She came over and put her hand on Eileen's arm. 'I've had a telephone call . . .'

'Oh, no!' Eileen's hands went to her face in alarm. Perhaps Nick had given Dunnings' number to the landlady!

'It's all right!' Miss Thomas said quickly. 'It was your young man. He said he'll ring the cottage at quarter past six.'

'Thank you!' Eileen felt almost dizzy with relief.

'Perhaps this is an appropriate time to ask if there's any further news from the solicitor?' Miss Thomas said.

'He asked me to go in and sign some forms. He's writing to Francis to see if he wants to appoint a solicitor of his own,' Eileen told her. 'At this rate, it's going to take forever.'

'Solicitors like to stretch things out,' Miss Thomas said dryly. 'They seem to think the longer it takes, the more it justifies their horrendous fees. Keep me informed, won't you, Eileen? I feel as if I have a personal interest in your case. If you succeed, I might even have another try myself.'

'I will,' Eileen promised.

The afternoon had never passed more slowly. Eileen could scarcely take her eyes off the clock above the door. She willed the hands to move, to bring nearer the time when she would speak to Nick! It didn't seem possible that, very soon, she would actually hear his voice.

At last, the hooter sounded and she sprinted out the door and down the High Street towards the cottage. Once inside, she sat staring at the telephone, willing it to ring with as much intensity as she'd willed the clock to move.

Quarter past six, twenty past. 'Hurry up, Nick,' she prayed.

It was nearly half past when shrill tones sounded, and despite the fact she was expecting it, Eileen nearly shot through the ceiling. She snatched the receiver up.

'Nick?'

'I'm sorry I'm late. There was a queue for the phone.' He spoke faintly, in a monotone. She could hardly hear for the crackling on the line.

'It doesn't matter. How are you, luv? You sound tired.' If only she could reach out somehow and touch him!

'I'm always tired.' He gave a funny, little dry laugh that didn't sound like Nick at all. 'I'd almost forgotten what a Liverpool accent sounds like. It seems terribly strong over the phone.'

'Is that why you rang? To tell me about my accent?' The conversation wasn't going quite the way she'd imagined. She'd expected to be told how much he missed her, not comments on her voice.

'Of course, not! Look, darling, I've got to ring off now. There's people waiting to use this damned phone.'

'But Nick,' she cried. 'Why did you ring?'

There was a pause. 'Oh, Christ! I forgot. I've got a forty-eight-hour pass. I'll see you in the cottage first thing Sunday morning. Goodbye, darling. Goodbye, I've got to go . . .'

The receiver went dead and she was left to stare at it vacantly until the realisation dawned. Nick was coming home!

Annie insisted on having Tony for the day. 'Chris and I will take him to New Brighton,' she offered. 'You won't have much time with Nick. Put yourself first for once, luv.'

426

'I don't suppose it'd hurt, but he's dying to see Nick almost as much as I am.'

Tony managed to be persuaded that he'd have a far better time in New Brighton than in Melling, by the promise of plentiful ice cream and a visit to the fairground.

Early on Sunday morning, Eileen packed a bag with food and set off in her next-to-best blue dress for the cottage. She arrived just before eight o'clock. There was no sign of Nick. She left a note on the door to say she'd gone to Mass.

It was peaceful in the tiny, surprisingly crowded Catholic church at the end of the High Street. Eileen knelt at the back. Throughout the service, the trees outside rustled gently in the breeze, and as the sun began to creep through the windows, shadows of dancing leaves appeared on the bare cream walls. It was difficult to realise, in such blessed tranquillity, that a war was taking place outside.

When the priest suggested they pray for peace, Eileen bowed her head and prayed, as she had never prayed before, that the conflict would be over soon. 'Please, God. *Please!*'

She'd been back at the cottage only a few minutes when she heard the sound of a motorbike in the distance. A bubble of happiness rose in her throat, and she went outside and stood on the step, waiting.

A few seconds later, Nick drew up. Eileen stood rooted to the spot, unable to move. He was here! She watched him remove his goggles and leather helmet. When he saw her waiting, he flung open his arms.

'Don't I get a kiss?' he called.

She flew down the path. He caught her and hugged her so tightly she could scarcely breathe. Her feet left the

427

ground as they rocked together wordlessly for what seemed like an age.

At last, he released her. 'You're a sight for the sorest eyes.'

Dear God, she thought, he looks dreadful. His mouth was drawn with tiredness, and there were deep lines down his cheeks that hadn't been there before. And his eyes! At first, she thought the dark shadows were dirt from the journey, but when she rubbed them with her fingers, the shadows were real.

'Come in. I've got the kettle on – and the water's hot. I bet you could do with a cup of tea and a wash.'

She took his hand and dragged him indoors and was conscious of his weight, as if he was too weary to walk without her help.

'Sit down,' she urged, as soon as he'd removed his blue greatcoat. 'You don't half look handsome in your uniform.'

'I still haven't had that kiss.'

She kissed the drawn lips softly. They felt dry and hard. 'There!'

Minutes later, when Eileen returned with the tea, Nick was fast asleep in the armchair. She drank both cups and waited for him to wake up naturally. It was mid-day before he opened his eyes.

'Christ!' He glanced at his watch. 'I've wasted three whole hours!'

'They weren't wasted,' she said stoutly. 'Not if you needed the sleep. You must be dead tired.'

'Let's go to bed and you can wake me up!'

Halfway upstairs, he stopped and swayed and Eileen reached and caught him before he fell. Somehow, with her help, he managed to remove his clothes and the minute his head touched the pillow, he was asleep again.

Eileen sat on the chair in the corner of the bedroom and watched him. Although his body was as motionless as a log, nevertheless he seemed restless. His eyes never stopped twitching and he kept making little moaning noises that tore at her heart.

But as she watched, Eileen felt sympathy give way to anger. There was no need for this. He could have stayed safely at home. Today, it could have been *them* going to New Brighton with Tony. Instead, due to his stubborn insistence on behaving like a man, doing his bit, he was lying there, more dead than alive. It was all his own fault, she thought bitterly.

A moan, louder than the others, woke him up. When he came to, he saw her watching from across the room.

'What time is it?'

'I don't know, the clock's downstairs.'

He struggled to sit up. 'I have a feeling I bought you a watch once.'

'I don't like to wear it in case it breaks.'

'Sensible girl!' For the first time, his eyes twinkled at her.

'More sensible than you!'

'Do I detect a hint of irritation in your voice?' he asked flippantly. 'I'm sorry I keep falling asleep.' He glanced at his watch and groaned. 'Another four hours wasted. It's four o'clock.'

'Yes, you do detect irritation,' she snapped. 'And it's nowt to do with you falling asleep. It's to do with you joining up when you didn't need to.'

'Ah!'

'Ah, my foot!'

'Did you just make that up, or is it Shakespeare?'

'Oh, sod off!'

She left the room, went downstairs and made more

tea, half expecting him to follow. After a few minutes, when he hadn't appeared, she thought, 'I bet he's fallen asleep again,' so went back, ready to glare at him from the corner again.

He was still sitting up, wide awake. 'I'd still do it,' he said simply, 'even knowing what I do now.'

'I know you would, because you're a bloody idiot.'

'I have to live with myself for the rest of my life,' he countered.

'If there's a life for you to live the rest of.' She frowned at the rather garbled sentence.

Nick shrugged expressively. 'I'm still here, aren't I?'

'Barely.'

He patted the bed and winked. 'Get in!'

'Nick! I'm sorry, I'm sorry, but I hate seeing you like this.' She threw herself onto the bed and he sank down beside her. She began to stroke his body, but after a while, they both realised it was hopeless.

'I'm sorry, too,' he muttered. 'I'm bone weary. Just let me hold you.'

She lay in his arms for a long time. Inevitably, he fell asleep, his body heavy on hers. Eileen slipped out of bed when she felt herself grow numb from his weight. For something to do, she took his uniform downstairs and pressed it, then cleaned his shoes, brushed his greatcoat and hung it carefully on a hook in the hall.

The nights were drawing in and she left the curtains open and sat by the window as the sun began to set and darkness fell in the little low ceilinged room. The cottage was so quiet, you could have heard a pin drop. At about nine o'clock, there was an air raid over Liverpool and she saw searchlights crisscross the sky like giant swords and the brilliant flash of ack ack fire. She hoped Tony was all right with Annie, who was keeping him all night. Nick was leaving at midnight, and Eileen would sleep in the cottage and go straight to Dunnings for the early shift in the morning.

As she watched the activity in the sky, she was sure she had never felt so lonely in her life. She began to weep, because everything was so tragic. What had they done to her darling Nick? The day, which she had been looking forward to so much, had been a nightmare. All she'd done was look at the clock, whilst he slept and slept and slept. They hadn't even had the opportunity to talk, let alone make . . .

'Eileen?'

She jumped. 'Nick! I didn't hear you come down.'

He was only half dressed and in his bare feet. 'Someone's taken most of my clothes,' he said accusingly. 'It can only be you.'

'I pressed them and cleaned your shoes.'

'You haven't pressed my socks!'

'I straightened them up a bit.'

'Oh, my dearest girl! Are you crying? What are you doing sitting in the dark? Come here!' He pulled her out of the chair, and sat her on his knee. 'There's a raid on!' he remarked in surprise.

'We have them nearly every night now.'

'Do you, now?' He turned Eileen's face towards him. 'Darling,' he said urgently, 'why don't you and Tony move out here?'

When she didn't reply, he went on, 'If you stay in Pearl Street, you'll be doing what you accuse me of, taking risks you don't have to.'

'I don't like to leave me family.'

'Your family are important, Eileen, but it's *us* that matters more than anything in the world; you and me and Tony. Don't you see that?'

'I suppose so.'

His voice rose exultantly. 'Then you'll move?'

'I'll think about it.' Something had to be done about Tony. With Annie leaving as soon as she got married, there was no-one to look after him, particularly when there was a raid. Sheila couldn't have him, not with all six of them already crushed together under the stairs, and her dad was determined to ignore the raids and slept through every one, or so he claimed. Sean was out every night with the Civil Defence Messenger Service. Perhaps coming to Melling, where Dunnings was only a short walk away and she could come to an arrangement with a local woman with children, would be a good idea. She'd tell Pearl Street she was moving to avoid the raids, though she supposed a few tongues would still wag when they heard the news.

'I'd better start getting ready to go back.' Nick gave her a push. 'Did you say there's hot water?'

'The tank's full. Shall I make something to eat? You've not had a bite all day. There's bacon and eggs and a bit of cheese and some cream crackers . . .'

'I'll have the lot. I'm starving.'

'Well, at least you've got an appetite, if nothing else!' she said smiling as she drew the curtains and switched on the light.

'I'll have the "nothing else" next time I come.' He grinned and put his hand over his heart. 'Promise, on my honour.'

'Nick,' she said seriously. 'You mustn't come all this way again, not when you've only got forty-eight hours. You should have stayed on the base and rested. I'd come to you, but what with Tony and me job . . .' Although he looked better than when he arrived, he'd be dead on his feet again after the long drive back to Kent. And tomorrow? What would he be doing tomorrow? She dreaded to think.

'It wasn't a very good idea, was it? It's just that I was longing to see you again.'

'Well, you've seen me.' Eileen tried to sound practical. 'I'll start running the bath. The food'll be ready by the time you're out.'

She busied herself in the kitchen, calling to Nick from time to time in case he fell asleep in the bath. If only he had another day, she thought wistfully.

Suddenly, Nick shouted urgently. 'Hey! Something's happened! Take your clothes off and get in here. Quick!'

Chapter 16

Arthur Fleming stopped the lorry in a lay-by on the crest of the hill so he could take a proper look at the view. The scenery was so spectacular, he was having difficulty keeping his eyes on the road. He leant on the wheel and took in the wild undulant moorland on either side – who would have thought there could be so many shades of green? Olive, emerald, jade – too many to identify. There was one patch almost yellow, another almost blue. The trees had an almost uncivilised look; unlopped and un-pruned, they'd been left to grow as they pleased. In the far distance, a glassy lake sparkled.

It was the first time he'd been to the Lake District, and he was impressed. It was so peaceful. He felt himself drawn towards the natural, almost heartstopping, beauty of the landscape. This was how God had made the world. There were no ugly factories belching smoke, no multi-storey buildings, just little houses here and there, nestling comfortably within a clump of trees, as if they'd grown there.

'Oh, well,' he sighed. 'This won't do. I'd better get a move on.' There was one more load to deliver in Kendal, a few miles away, then he could go home to Jess. He veered the lorry out into the deserted road and drove on.

He found his destination in the small town quite easily – a large grey-stone building at the furthest end of the main road. Arthur alighted from the lorry, went round the back and removed the last remaining item, a wooden crate marked FRAGILE: HANDLE WITH CARE. It was surprisingly light, considering its size.

With the crate hoisted on his shoulder, he rang the bell beside the large double doors of the building and noticed, underneath the bell, a brass plate engraved THE HIGGIN-BOTHAM MUSEUM OF PREHISTORIC EGYPTIAN AND GREEK ART. Arthur felt a stir of excitement as he waited for what seemed like an age. He was about to ring again, when one half of the door was opened by a young man in an open-necked shirt and shorts. He wore spectacles and was surprisingly bald, considering his obvious youth.

'I'm sorry, we're closed Mondays,' he said crisply. 'Oh, I see you've got something for us. Bring it in, won't you?'

Arthur followed, interest rising. He was led through another set of doors into a large room lined with glass cases full of restored objects of ancient Greek art, the sight of which sent the blood pounding through his head. Down the centre of the room were several statues of such disreputable appearance that any decent gardener would have consigned them to the dustbin long ago; earth-stained and crumbling and quite obviously pieced together from their original broken fragments, they were still minus many important anatomical parts.

'Oh, I say!' Arthur breathed reverently, when his eyes fell on this veritable feast of antiquity.

Mistaking his reverence for disdain, the young man said condescendingly, 'I suppose it looks rubbish to the uninitiated, but I can assure you, these items are of enormous historical importance to archaeologists.'

'You can say that again!' said Arthur. He pointed to one of the statues, 'That's Minoan, isn't it?'

'It is.' The young man gaped.

'Rhea, mother of Zeus. I did my thesis on the early

Minoan civilisation.'

The young man gaped again at the lorry driver in his collarless shirt and braces showing underneath his unbuttoned waistcoat. Who would have thought? Well, it took all sorts . . .

'Of course!' Arthur slapped his knee. '*Higginbotham!* Professor Ernest Higginbotham, the Egyptologist. He was one of my heroes.'

'And mine!' the young man said enthusiastically, Arthur's appearance forgotten. 'Did you know he entered Tutankhamen's tomb with Lord Carnarvon in 1922?'

'And died soon afterwards from the curse,' Arthur said knowingly, 'as they all did. But, on the other hand, he was eighty-four!'

They both laughed.

'This is all his stuff, then?' Arthur began to wander around the room.

'It's been added to considerably over the years. Old Ernest's collection came mainly from Egypt, Old and New Kingdom. That's on the first floor.'

'Fascinating! Absolutely fascinating. What's in the crate?'

'It's a bequest, mainly Mycenean tiles, so I'm given to understand.'

'Really? Should be interesting.'

'Yes, but I don't think I shall bother to unpack it.'

'Why not?'

The young man made a face. 'The museum's closing down for the duration. I've been called up. I thought my sight would rule me out, but it appears to be not as bad as I thought.'

'Oh, I say, that's a shame.' Arthur shook his head in sympathy. 'Do you get many visitors?'

'A few tourists drop in now and again, but primarily, our visitors are experts like . . . well, like yourself,' the young man explained. 'They come from all over the world and the correspondence we receive has to be seen to be believed. People wanting photographs, mainly, or just a general chat, as it were, by letter.'

'It sounds like the most interesting job in the world!' Arthur said in awe.

'Actually, there are times when it can get a bit boring. I was beginning to think I'd sooner be in at the deep end, digging things up, not cataloguing and showing them off. But then the war started and put paid to any thoughts of going abroad.'

'I used to think like that when I was young. I managed to get to Crete during my time at university, but that was my one and only visit, I'm afraid. Somehow, life never seems to go as planned.'

'I say, would you like a cup of tea? I'm Marcus Dillon, by the way. In fact, I've a horrible suspicion I left the kettle boiling.'

They shook hands.

'Arthur Fleming, and I'd love a cup of tea.' As they strolled towards a staircase at the end of the room, Arthur asked, 'You actually live on the premises?'

'Yes, there's rather a fine flat at the top, with magnificent views.'

Arthur felt his mouth water as they passed through another floor full of glass cases packed with exhibits. 'Does the place *have* to close down?' he asked. He'd just had an idea, so breathtaking that his voice trembled as he spoke.

'Not really.' Marcus laughed contemptuously. 'It's just that the Trustees are a lazy lot. They can't be bothered to find another curator. They think the war will be over in no time at all, I'll be back, and they won't have had to lift a finger. But, as I said before, I was already toying with the idea of chucking it in.'

'How do you get in touch with these Trustees?'

Marcus glanced at him quickly. 'You're not interested, are you?'

'I'd give my right arm for a job like this!'

'In that case, I'll do my utmost to see you get it — though your right arm can stay where it is, thanks all the same!'

Next morning, Jessica Fleming waddled across the road to Number 16. She badly needed to talk to someone, and Eileen Costello was the obvious person.

But instead of Eileen, it was Annie Poulson who answered the door to her knock.

'Oh, hallo,' Annie said politely. The two women didn't have much to do with each other. 'Eileen's at work. I've just been seeing Tony off to school and giving the place a bit of a tidy up.'

'In that case, I'll come back this afternoon.'

Annie folded her arms and leant on the doorframe. 'How are you feeling?'

'Big!' said Jess.

'You look as if you might be having another lorry for Arthur.'

'I got weighed in Woolworths the other day, and I'm over fourteen stone!' Jess was never quite sure whether to be proud or ashamed of her enormous size.

'I weren't that heavy when I was expecting twins!' exclaimed Annie. 'Look, why don't you pop in a minute for a cuppa?'

'I won't be holding you up, will I?'

'I wouldn't ask if you were! Come in, that's if you can

438

fit through the door. I expect you've had yours widened.'

One of the things that never ceased to amaze Jess was the way the women moved in and out of each other's houses as if they were their own. She went inside and made herself comfortable in the easy chair under the window. There was a cardboard box of odds and ends on the table; books and ornaments and one or two soft toys. Annie disappeared into the kitchen to put the kettle on.

'I understand congratulations are in order,' Jess called. 'Eileen said you're getting married.'

'That's right. Fifteenth of September, that's two weeks on Saturday. The lads are coming from Colchester. They've been given a special twenty-four-hour pass.'

'I hope you'll be very happy,' Jess said sincerely.

'Ta, very much.' Annie appeared in the doorway. 'If you're around on the day, come and have a drink and a piece of wedding cake. The whole street's invited.'

'I'd love to. Where are you going on your honeymoon?'

Annie's dark eyes twinkled. 'Well, I'm not sure if you could call two nights in a Southport hotel a honeymoon. Chris can't take time off, so's the both of us'll be back at work on the Monday.' She vanished again. 'I'll give this a good stir. Y'can't spare an extra spoonful for the pot since tea went on rations, and I hate it weak.' She returned a few minutes later with two cups of pale tea. 'It still looks like gnats' piss,' she remarked.

Jess noticed a framed photograph protruding from the box on the table; a family portrait, the man achingly familiar. Annie saw her looking at it. She removed the photo from the box and passed it over.

'That's Jack Doyle and his wife, Mollie. She died about fifteen years ago. You can see where Sheila gets her looks from can't you, and Eileen's the spitting image of her dad. As for Sean, we used to say Mollie must have had it off with the coalman, he turned out so dark. That was taken at Sean's christening.'

Jess stared hard at the tall figure standing with his hand on the chair on which his pretty wife sat. On her knee, she held a baby dressed in a long white gown. Jack's other hand was on the shoulder of a smiling Sheila. Eileen, who would have been about twelve when the photograph was taken, stood slightly to one side, rather alone, thought Jess, and she was as unsmiling and serious as her father. It occurred to Jess, for the first time, that the baby she carried was related to these children. Perhaps there might even be a resemblance!

Annie said, 'Jack Doyle's a fine upstanding figure of a man, isn't he? It's a shame he never got married again.'

Jess put the photograph back without a word. Annie picked the box up and shoved it under the sideboard. 'Eileen's been packing a few odds and ends to take with her. You know she's moving, don't you?'

'Yes, she said she was going as soon as you got married.' Jess began to twist her cup around and around in the saucer. She *had* to tell someone! 'Actually, I'm moving, too! Arthur's got a good job up in the Lake District.' The old snobbery returned briefly as she corrected herself. 'I suppose you'd call it a position, rather than a job.'

'The Lake District!' said Annie, impressed. 'I've never been there meself, but people say it's very nice.'

'The thing is, I don't want to go,' Jess said passionately. 'I don't want to go more than anything in the world.'

Annie looked taken aback by the obvious strength of feeling. 'You surprise me. I would have thought you couldn't wait to get away from Pearl Street?'

'Oh, don't get me wrong,' Jess said quickly. 'I loathe it here. I was only too glad to escape from Pearl Street the first time, and I was anything but pleased to come back, though I settled in better than expected. I've made some friends, and I've grown very fond of Jacob, next door, but if it was Waterloo or Crosby, I'd go like a shot. The thing is, I've never had the least desire to leave Liverpool. I love the shops and I suppose I love the people, in a way. After all, I'm a city person and a scouse, through and through; the River Mersey probably flows through my veins, like it does us all. Last night, when Arthur was going on about rolling hills and fields, "getting back to nature" he called it, it made me feel physically sick.'

'Oh, lord, Jess! Did you tell him?'

Jess shook her head. 'No, I couldn't. That's why I'm telling *you*! I've never seen him so excited. He looked twenty years younger, just like the man I married all that time ago. He thought I'd be thrilled to bits, him getting a respectable job – not that there's anything wrong with being a lorry driver,' she added hastily, conscious she was talking to a woman about to marry a mere fireman. 'Another thing, Jacob and I intended to begin our concerts again once I had the baby – he was already making plans for Christmas. I was really looking forward to it.'

'There's bound to be a choir you can join,' Annie said comfortably. 'You'll settle in soon enough. They're probably more your type of people up there.'

'I'm not sure if I know what my type is anymore,' Jess said, close to tears. 'I'm all confused.'

Annie patted her arm. 'It's probably the baby,' she said. 'Once you've had it, you'll be your old self again and you'll see things in a different light.'

'Will I?' Jess looked at Annie pathetically. 'I must say, I've enjoyed being pregnant, but what with the heat, and looking like an elephant, I'm beginning to wish it was all over.'

Annie giggled. 'They say elephants take seven years to have a baby!'

'Oh, don't!'

'Anyroad, you're lucky to be getting away from all these air raids. Wasn't that an awful one we had the other night? Mossley Hill church was bombed and three people killed.'

'I suppose I am – lucky, that is,' sniffed Jess.

'Do you love Arthur?' Annie asked sharply.

'Of course I do!'

'Well then, that's all that matters.' Annie squeezed Jess's arm fiercely. 'I'd go to Land's End with Chris, if that's what he wanted. To love a good man and for him to love you back is the most important thing in the whole world – more important even than kids. It don't matter where you live, so long as you're together.'

'You're right!' Jess squared her shoulders. 'I'm glad I came. I already feel better about everything.' The photograph of Jack Doyle and his family stared up at her from underneath the sideboard. Perhaps it would be no bad thing to move away before her child began to grow. What if people, particularly Arthur, noticed a similarity?

'I hope my advice was as good as Eileen would have given.'

'It wasn't advice I needed,' said Jess, managing a smile, 'more a shoulder to cry on. I'd already decided Arthur would never know I'm not as excited as he is – I put on a really good performance last night. He gave up twenty years for me. Now it's my turn to do something for him.'

Eileen stood in the doorway and regarded the living

room of the cottage with satisfaction. The wooden floor, the scratched table and equally shabby sideboard gleamed after the good polishing she'd just given them. Of course the ceiling, which was more grey than white, would be improved by a lick of white distemper, but that was for the future. In the meantime, she'd washed the beams and they'd come up a treat. The long room only caught the sun in the mornings, and it looked cool and fresh, the windows wide open, the flowered curtains billowing outwards. Once there were a few ornaments scattered round and a picture hung over the attractive brick fireplace, it would look like home.

Nick had rented the cottage furnished. The owners must have considered the contents worthless, because they hadn't bothered to remove them once the place was sold, and Eileen thought longingly of the green velvet three-piece in Pearl Street. She was rather fond of that suite, and it was a million times better than Nick's threadbare collection of armchairs that didn't match. But the suite belonged to Francis, and she'd no intention of removing a thing that wasn't hers; she'd just take Tony's stuff and her own personal possessions.

After a last satisfied look, she went into the back kitchen, which looked equally smart, with fresh paper on the shelves of the old dresser and the cheap crockery she'd bought on display.

Jack Doyle shouted across the garden, 'This looks as though it might have been a vegetable patch once.'

Eileen wandered over to the overgrown strip of land behind the hedge at the bottom of the garden which she hadn't even realised was part of the property, until her dad investigated and decided it was.

'See!' he said when she reached him. 'The soil's been dug in furrows for 'taters.'

'Fancy you knowing that!' she said admiringly.

He jerked the cigarette hanging from his bottom lip upwards, took a puff without using his hands and said modestly, 'It's the sort of thing you pick up.'

'You're welcome to use it, Dad,' Eileen said eagerly. 'You could come and tend to it at weekends. It'd be lovely to see you.'

She was overjoyed when he replied, 'It'd be a shame to see it go to waste. We need all the food we can get at the moment. Y'could even have a few hens out here for your own eggs.'

'Eggs!' Eggs were proving more and more difficult to get lately. It seemed little short of bliss to imagine coming out each morning and collecting them fresh for breakfast.

'And you wouldn't be short of a chicken when it comes to Christmas.'

'I couldn't possibly eat the chickens, Dad. I'd grow too fond of them, and Nick could never bring himself to kill one.'

Jack glanced at her, amused. Nick had probably killed quite a few Germans in his time, yet she didn't think he could turn his hand to a chicken. 'You just give their necks a quick twist, that's all,' he said ghoulishly.

'Shut up, Dad! I'll settle for the eggs. Anyroad, I'll go and get on with the bedrooms. Where's our Tony?'

'He's up that apple tree.'

Apparently the apple tree behind the hedge belonged to the cottage, and she espied her son struggling through the leafy branches which were laden with fruit.

'They look like cookers,' she remarked. 'I might take a few home for our Sheila and Annie.'

'I'd leave them a while if I were you. They ain't properly ripe yet, though you can take the rhubarb. I've

444

never seen stalks that big before, they must be a good two inches thick.'

'Okay, Dad,' she said contentedly.

She'd been thrilled to bits when he'd offered to come with her when she announced her intention of spending Sunday cleaning the cottage. 'I'd better take a look at this Melling place where you're going to live,' he said grumpily, though he'd enjoyed himself in the garden. She felt sure he and Nick would get on once they got to know each other.

Once inside, she went upstairs and began to polish the floors which she'd washed earlier. She sang to herself as she worked and made a mental list of things that still had to be bought; a couple of little rattan mats for beside the beds, an alarm clock, because she'd never wake up of her own accord, and some new curtains for Tony's room — the ones already there had faded to holes. One good thing, the previous owners must have provided new bedding when Nick moved in, as there were plenty of new sheets and pillow cases.

Both beds were bare at the moment, rusty springs exposed; the palliasses were airing on the grass outside. The blankets and covers had been washed and were drying on the new line which her dad had put up as soon as he arrived.

'Eileen!'

She went across to the open window and leaned on the sill. 'What, Dad?'

'Did you say there was a pub close by? I'm parched for a pint.'

'It's just down the road.'

Tony must have heard. He came clambering down the tree, shouting, 'Can I come, too, Grandad? We can sit outside, like we did with Nick.'

Jack Doyle looked pleased. 'I reckon so.'

'Go and wash your face and hands first, Tony,' Eileen said. 'They're filthy.'

'Rightio, Mam.'

As Tony scooted into the kitchen, Jack asked, 'Have you got a school sorted out for the lad?'

'The Catholic church acts as a school during the week,' Eileen told him. 'I've already put Tony's name down with the priest. When it comes to after school, Miss Thomas says there's quite a few local women with young kids working at Dunnings. She's going to sort something out for me and promises to turn a blind eye if I disappear at about half past eight when I'm on the morning shift to make sure he has his breakfast. Miss Thomas says if the Government want women to work, they should provide "facilities", I think she called it, for their children.'

'This Miss Thomas sounds like a right old stirrer,' he said approvingly.

'Oh, by the way, Dad,' Eileen hissed. 'If anyone in the pub asks who you are, say you're Nick's father-in-law. They think we're married down there.'

'Oh, they do, do they?' He raised his eyebrows. 'I hope you know what you're doing.'

'All I know is I've never felt so happy in me life,' she sang blithely.

He shrugged. 'That's all right, then.'

Tony emerged from the kitchen, his face shining, and the two of them disappeared round the side of the house, hand in hand. As soon as they'd gone, Eileen sank down on the bed. The springs creaked mightily, and she thought, 'I'd better do something about *that* before Nick comes back.'

The thought of Nick coming back to the cottage, which was now a proper home with a proper family living in it, so overwhelmed her, that she got up and twirled around the room and nearly fell headlong when she slipped on the newly polished floor. She laughed out loud and wondered if you could go mad with happiness.

She'd sobered up somewhat by the time she began on Tony's room. In order to achieve this happiness, she was leaving much behind. She hated the idea of her sister not being just across the road, though Sheila had promised to come to the cottage if the bombing got worse. 'Even if it means you all sleeping on the floor,' Eileen had insisted.

Once here, in this isolated place, there'd be no neighbours to call on if she needed to borrow a cup of sugar or a ciggie, no Jacob Singerman or Paddy O'Hara dropping in for a chat. She reckoned she'd miss Pearl Street more than she thought possible when the time came to leave, but in her heart she knew that even if the worst happened and Nick didn't survive, this was the place she wanted to be; this was where they'd made love and lived together, even though it had only been for a little while. His spirit was everywhere, and that would see her through.

She sighed. On Monday, the country would have been at war a whole year. Winston Churchill had said it might last another two. Two years! It seemed a lifetime away, but if you said it quick, it seemed to take no time at all.

The place wouldn't be so bad, the young medical orderly thought, if it wasn't for the sand. The sand, a fine golden dust, which looked grand in its proper place, in other words, the desert, seemed to get in every orifice, particularly the eyes. Of course, there was also the heat. You hadn't had your shirt on a minute before it was soaked with sweat, and the thought of a long cool bath was little short of paradise. Then there were the insects; flies as big as rabbits, and other unspeakable things he couldn't put a name to, but which made his flesh crawl.

In other words, he thought, grinning, if it weren't for the sand, the heat, and the flies, Alexandria wouldn't be so bad, except he was bored out of his bleeding mind, stuck in this little hospital, miles away from the action in Mersa Metruh, where the lads were really getting stuck into the Eyeties, even though they were outnumbered five to one. He idly drew a picture of a tank on the pad in front of him, though soon threw the pencil down. The little cubicle at the end of the single ward was like an oven, despite the fan whirring away in the corner. He got up, stretching, and went outside. The heat from the midday sun was so oppressive that he realised inside was cool in comparison, and was about to return when a jeep came roaring into the compound, raising clouds of sand in its wake.

It drew to a halt outside the hospital and an officer stepped out of the back. The medical orderly stood to attention and saluted.

'Captain Donnelly, sir!' he barked. The captain was the unit's MO, and had been up at the front for over a month.

'At ease, man.'

The younger man relaxed as Captain Donnelly mounted the wooden steps into the building. 'What's the situation here?' he asked. 'How many spare beds do we have?'

'Two patients, four spare beds, sir,' the orderly replied briskly, adding anxiously, 'I hope this doesn't mean we've had some injuries, sir?'

'Well, there's bound to be *some* injuries, man,' the captain replied patiently. 'There's a battle going on out there, but compared to the Eyeties, our losses are small. No, it's just that I'd like to get the worst cases out of the tents and under a proper roof, where *you* can look after them, can't you, Jones?'

'Oh, yes, sir,' the young man said eagerly. He was longing to do his bit.

'What's wrong with these two men?' Captain Donnelly asked as he entered the ward. A man sitting up in bed, reading a paperback book, hastily laid it down and tried to look ill.

'That's Cooper, sir. He had a fever, pretty bad, but I reckon he could be discharged any minute now.'

'And how do you feel about that, Cooper?' Captain Donnelly asked pleasantly.

'Any minute now would do me fine, sir,' Cooper replied bravely.

'Good man!' The captain pointed to the next bed, where a figure lay prone, eyes closed, and head swathed in bandages. 'And this chap?'

'That's Costello, sir. Normally, he's up and about, but he's just had his injection and it's sent him off to sleep. He had, well, he had an accident.'

'What sort of accident?'

'He went into town one night and got beaten up pretty bad. According to Lieutenant Morgan, he's lost the sight in his left eye.' Lieutenant Morgan was the junior MO.'

Captain Donnelly winced. 'When did this happen?'

'A few weeks ago, sir.'

'I see.' The captain picked up the notes hooked over the foot of the metal bed frame and began to read; 'Costello, Francis, Lance Corporal.' He vaguely remembered the chap from the Paymaster's office; a good-looking fellow, though not young. He searched for the age on the notes – thirty-seven, which meant he'd been a regular or in the Territorials – a courageous man, ready to do his bit for his country. It was a shame, ending up like this. He read further; the man had a wife and child.

'Bloody wogs!' he swore aloud.

'Well, actually, sir,' the orderly said, slightly embarrassed, 'it weren't the wogs what done it. It were two of our own chaps.'

'For Christ's sake, man,' the Captain said angrily. 'We came out to fight the enemy, not each other. What happened? Do you know?'

'Well, sir, I only heard it on the grapevine, like. There weren't no names mentioned, but from what I can gather, Costello made an unseemly suggestion to a couple of young 'uns, who took umbrage and gave him a good going over.'

'He made *what*?'

'An unseemly suggestion, sir.'

Captain Donnelly's face grew so red, the young orderly was worried he was about to explode. Without a word, the older man marched out of the hospital. On the steps outside, he paused and said, 'Have this place ready to receive six wounded men by tomorrow night.'

'But what about Costello, sir?'

Captain Donnelly replied contemptuously, 'Have him sent home on the first available transport!'

As the Saturday before the wedding would be Annie and Eileen's last opportunity to go out together, they thought they should do something special.

'It won't *really* be our last night out,' Annie said, 'but from now on, it'll be entirely different, what with me married and living in Fazakerley, and you in Melling. What shall we do?'

The decision wasn't very hard to make. They decided to go and see *Gone With The Wind*, which was on at the

Odeon in town. 'Most of the women at work have been, and they've raved about it ever since,' said Eileen. 'The thing is, Jess Fleming's dying to go, but Arthur always gets a headache in the pictures.'

'Well, invite her too,' Annie said generously.

'Are you sure you don't mind? After all, it's *our* night out.'

'I'm so happy, I wouldn't care if you asked Aggie Donovan.'

On Saturday, the three women sat near the back of the cinema, Jess on the end seat, as the usherette pointed out they were slightly bigger than the rest. Soon, the glorious music swelled, the dramatic saga of the American Civil War unfolded before them, and the entire audience sat engrossed, eyes glued to the screen. But soon after the interval, Jess began to fidget.

'What's wrong?' whispered Annie.

'I've got a funny pain. I think it's cramp.'

'Stretch your legs out into the aisle,' Annie said un-sympathetically. 'Here, have another chocolate.'

'Thanks. *Bloody hell!*'

'What's wrong?'

'Nothing.'

But Jess continued to shift uncomfortably in her seat. Suddenly, she said in a loud, astonished voice, 'I've wet myself.'

'*Shush!*' a dozen voices hissed.

'But I've wet myself,' Jess said, even louder, 'and the cramp's got worse. It's coming over me in waves.'

'Jaysus!' groaned Eileen. 'Whose idea was it to bring her to see *Gone With The Wind*?'

'It weren't mine,' said Annie.

'Well, I'm sorry if you're embarrassed,' Jess said huffily, 'but I've never wet myself in public before.'

'Will you shut your bleeding gob over there!' a man shouted.

'Shut your own bleeding gob,' Annie shouted back. 'There's a woman here about to have a baby.'

'Where?' asked Jess.

'It's you, you flaming nana. Your waters have broke and you're having labour pains and if you don't get out of this picturehouse in a hurry, you'll have it in the aisle.'

In the early hours of Sunday morning, Jessica Fleming gave birth to a bouncing 10lb 10oz baby girl, whom she called Penelope. By tragic coincidence, it was the same morning that Rosie Gregson found little Charlie, who'd still not reached that weight although he was over two months old, dead in his cot.

A marriage, a birth, and a death, all in the same week, thought Eileen when she was on her way to the cottage the next day. She'd meant to leave earlier, but what with congratulating Arthur and comforting Rosie, it was almost two o'clock by the time she got away. Tony had been left behind to play with Dominic, because Eileen didn't intend staying long. There were just the beds to make, because she'd left the blankets in the airing cupboard, and the new curtains which Mr Singerman had sewn on his machine to put up in Tony's room. Then, a last minute polish and the place would be ready to move into on Sunday, the day after Annie's wedding.

As she went down the path towards the front door, she heard the sound of the telephone ringing and her heart did a cartwheel. It could only be one person!

She dropped everything on the step and fumbled with her key, turning it this way and that before the door would open. As soon as she was inside, she snatched the receiver up.

'Nick!'

'Thank God! I was praying you'd turn up. I've been trying to get through for hours.'

'All sorts of things have been happening which made me late. I'll tell you some other time. Anyroad, how are you? Are you all right? Oh, it's good to hear you!' She nearly dropped the phone in her excitement.

'Actually, I'm in hospital,' he said cheerfully.

She immediately imagined him hideously burnt or minus a limb, but if that was the case, why did he sound so buoyant? 'What happened?'

'I crashed the bike and broke my wrist.'

'You idiot!' But he couldn't fly a plane with a broken wrist, she thought in quick relief. It meant he had to remain safely on the ground for the time being.

'You're not the first one to call me that. Actually, they're rather cross with me. As soon as I'm allowed out of hospital, I've been ordered to get out of sight for a while. Which means . . .' He paused significantly.

'Which means you can come home?' she breathed.

'For a while; a week, perhaps two.'

'Oh, Nick!' She was so overcome, she slid down the wall and sat on the floor clutching the receiver. 'You won't recognise the cottage when you see it,' she told him. 'I've cleaned it from top to bottom.'

'When did you plan on moving in?' he asked.

She'd already told him in a letter of her intention of living in the cottage as he suggested. 'Next Sunday. Annie's getting married on Saturday . . .'

'Darling,' he interrupted, 'if this damn hospital will discharge me in time, I've been offered a lift. There's a chap I know travelling up to Wales on Friday, and he's promised to drop me off.'

'In that case, I'll leave as soon as Annie goes on her honeymoon. Tony and me will see you here . . .'

'No,' he interrupted again, but this time there was a sense of urgency in his voice. 'It's about time we had a honeymoon. Let's meet in town and go to the cottage together like a proper married couple – I'll carry you over the threshold, as all good bridegrooms do.'

'What about your broken wrist?'

'I forgot. In that case, you and Tony will have to carry me!' he said with an attempt at pathos.

She laughed. 'It sounds dead perfect.'

'What time shall we meet?'

'Annie's car's coming at three o'clock. There's a train soon after. I'll see you at Exchange Station about four.'

'I can't wait! I'd better ring off now, darling. I charmed a nurse into letting me use the phone in the doctor's office. She'll give me hell if she comes in and finds me still here.'

Eileen felt briefly jealous of the nurse he'd charmed. 'I love you,' she said fiercely.

'And I love you, my dearest girl, with all my heart.'

The line clicked and he was gone. She sat there for a long time, nursing the receiver. It almost seemed unfair that she should be so happy. Last night, there'd been a horrific raid on London and literally hundreds of people had been killed. But, she supposed, in times like this, you just had to snatch at happiness when it came your way. If you didn't, it might never come again.

The Registry Office ceremony was simple and moving. The only guests were Chris's daughter and her husband, Eileen, and, of course, the three lads, all in their khaki uniforms.

Joe gave his mam away with touching dignity. Annie

454

looked stunning in her canary yellow suit with a little veiled pillbox hat over one eye. She carried a posy of white roses.

'This hat makes me look like an usherette,' she complained to Eileen earlier when they were still in the house. 'Instead of marrying me, the registrar will ask where he's supposed to sit.'

'Annie, you look lovely,' Eileen assured her.

'So do you. Pink's definitely your colour and that hat really suits you.' Eileen had pinned a pink flower to the band on the new white straw boater. She adjusted her short lace gloves. Nick's present, the gold watch, gleamed on her wrist. It was the first occasion on which she could bring herself to wear it.

'I'm meeting Nick like this,' she said shyly. 'I'm going to pretend it's me going away outfit and I'm on me honeymoon, just like you.'

'Oh, Eileen, luv. I hope you'll be very happy.'

'You too, Annie.'

They hugged, just as Terry came in to announce the car had arrived.

A small crowd had gathered to see them off. 'I'll miss the street,' Annie said tearfully, as she waved goodbye through the rear window of the grey limousine.

'I wonder who'll be moving into your house?' Eileen mused as the car turned the corner and they stopped waving.

'I've no idea, luv. What about yours?'

'T'ain't mine, is it?' Eileen said matter-of-factly. 'I'll write and tell Francis I've paid the rent till the end of the month. It's up to him to decide what happens from then on. You'll never guess, but Ellis Evans has got her eye on Jess's place – not that I blame her, what with the electricity and the bath and that lovely stove. I wonder if

Jess'll manage to get back in time,' she mused. 'She's not due out of hospital till Monday, but she feels so well and wanted to see you off. She was having a right old ding-dong with the matron when I went in the other day.'

But Annie wasn't listening. 'Am I doing the right thing?' she burst out frantically. 'After all, I hardly know Chris.'

'Of course you are, Mam,' Joe soothed.

'What happens if he's not there? He might have had second thoughts.'

'Make your mind up,' Terry grinned. 'You're worrying about two opposite things.'

Chris was waiting outside the registry office when they arrived. He couldn't take his eyes off Annie as he helped her out of the car.

They went inside, and within the space of only a few minutes, Annie Poulson became Mrs Christopher Parker.

It was almost as good as the street party people still talked about even though it had taken place more than a year ago. Annie set a table up outside her house to hold the two-tier wedding cake which Mrs Harrison had iced, though she wanted the little well-used bride and groom from on top returned to use another time.

There were sausage rolls and sandwiches and sherry for the women. The men were informed a round of drinks awaited them in the King's Arms, and they all agreed Chris was a really nice feller.

Aggie Donovan presented the newly-weds with a willow pattern teaset, a present from the whole street.

'It's too lovely to use,' Annie said tearfully. 'I'll put it on show, so's I'll be reminded of Pearl Street every time I see it.'

One of Chris's mates from the fire station arrived to take a photograph of the couple cutting the cake, and Annie insisted he take a photo of the whole street. 'I'll frame it and put it by the tea service.'

Freda Tutty emerged in her school uniform, even though it was Saturday, with Dicky and a dazed looking Gladys in tow. Gladys ached for a glass of gin, but Freda ruled the house with a rod of iron nowadays, and she rarely escaped to the pub. She grudgingly accepted a glass of sherry.

'This is what I love,' Sheila said to her sister as they leaned against the window sill watching the proceedings.

'What, Sis?'

'Oh, I dunno; weddings, funerals, christenings, parties. There's always something going on in Pearl Street. It's like living in a great big clock, and you wonder what's going to happen next time it strikes.' Sheila kept a watchful eye on Mary as she made her stiff, unsteady progress along the pavement to where her sisters were playing. 'I don't envy you going to live in that cottage, Eil.'

'Nick will be there!' Eileen said simply. 'I wonder what time it is?'

'You're the one with the watch,' Sheila smiled.

'I forgot!' It was a quarter to three. 'Annie's car'll be here soon, then I'll be off.' At this very minute, Nick would be making his way towards Exchange Station.

'Good luck, Sis. You know you're always welcome at ours if things go wrong, though you'll have to sleep on the settee in the parlour.'

Eileen shook her head adamantly. 'Nothing will go wrong, Sheila.'

'Eileen!' Jacob Singerman drew her to one side.

'Hello, luv! I hadn't forgotten you. I was going to say

457

goodbye before I went.'

'It's not that.' He laid a long gnarled finger on his lips. 'Please say nothing to anyone just yet, but I have had news of my Ruth.'

'Oh, Mr Singerman!' She was so delighted, she kissed him impulsively on the cheek. 'Where is she?'

'She's in Spain, of all places. How she got there no-one knows, but I received a message from a synagogue in London where some sort of refugee centre is run. It was from a rabbi in Madrid that the message came.'

'What about her husband and the children?'

'There was no mention of them.' He spread his arms and shrugged expressively. 'I'll just have to wait and see, but tonight, I shall visit my own synagogue and give thanks to God. Ach!' He screwed up his face in an expression of disgust. 'I am a terrible Jew. I haven't been to the synagogue in many, many years.' Then his rheumy eyes lit up. 'Look, here's Annie's car. The street will be bereft! All the most beautiful young ladies are leaving. Annie, you, and soon Jess will be gone.'

'You always say the nicest things, Mr Singerman,' Eileen laughed. 'Here, have some of my confetti so we can give Annie and Chris a good send off.'

Annie came out of the house in tears after saying goodbye to her lads, who'd soon be returning to Colchester.

Eileen didn't follow the crowd who ran after the car. She caught Annie's eye as she waved through the rear window and blew kisses with both hands until her friend had disappeared. The street was littered with confetti, as if it had been snowing flowers. People began to walk back, laughing and flushed with excitement. Paddy O'Hara started to play *The Wedding March* on his mouth organ, and Mr Singerman linked Sheila's arm and they danced a funny sort of jig to the music. It was a good day to leave, Eileen thought contentedly, with everyone so happy. You'd never guess there was a war on. She glanced around for Tony, but there was no sign of him, so went indoors and washed the last few dishes, dried them, and looked around to see if there was anything else she should do before she closed the door on Number 16 for the final time. There was nothing. She picked up the bag containing her clothes and put it in the hall, ready, then went to look for her son.

'He's playing in the back entry with our Dominic,' Sheila called when she saw her sister glancing up and down the street. 'I'll give him a shout.'

'Ta, Sis. I want to leave soon to catch the train.' She glanced at her watch again. You never know, Nick might already be there.'

As Eileen waited impatiently on the step, Jess and Arthur Fleming appeared at the top of the street, too late to see Annie off. Jess was bursting with pride as she carried her seven-day-old daughter.

Eileen waved, but otherwise made no move towards the newcomers. There wasn't time, and she'd already seen the baby twice in hospital. The two women had arranged to meet before Jess finally left for Kendal. But if there was one thing the rest of Pearl Street was in the mood for at the moment, it was welcoming a new baby.

Jess was swamped with women anxious to get a look at this reportedly magnificent red-haired child whose weight had set a record at the hospital. Eileen noticed Rosie Gregson looking wretched as she stood on the fringe of the crowd, and her heart went out to the girl.

She called, 'Come over here, Rosie, luv.' The child had only buried her own baby on Thursday. She couldn't be left to watch whilst the entire street drooled over another.

Rosie came, dragging her feet disconsolately.

'Stay indoors with me a minute, luv.' She drew the girl inside and took her into the parlour, where she sat wordlessly on the settee. Eileen watched through the window, on tenterhooks, as Jess made her slow and stately progress down to Number 5 with Arthur beaming at her side. Even the men seemed interested in the new baby, Mr Singerman in particular, and Paddy O'Hara was given a chubby finger to shake. She noticed Tony had put in an appearance, and he and Dominic were busy collecting confetti.

By the time Jess reached her front door, Eileen realised she'd missed the train! Nick would wonder what had happened to them.

'Thanks, Mrs Costello,' Rosie muttered. 'I'll be getting back now.'

'I hope things turn out well for you in the future, luv,' Eileen said gently, but Rosie left without saying another word.

Eileen sighed as she picked up the bag, took a final look round, and stepped outside. She had her hand on the knocker, ready to slam the door, when, to her surprise, she saw an ambulance had turned into the street and was being driven slowly down. She paused, she wasn't sure why, because it couldn't possibly be anything to do with her, and was even more surprised when the ambulance stopped right outside and the driver jumped out.

'Mrs Costello?'

'Yes,' she frowned.

'We've brought your husband home to you, missus.' He went round to the back of the vehicle and opened the door.

'Me husband?' They must have got the wrong street. Perhaps there was another Mrs Costello nearby. The crowd fell silent as they began to converge on the ambulance, watching curiously.

'That's right, missus, your husband.' The driver held out a helping hand and a khaki clad figure stepped into the street.

Francis!

'There now!' the driver grinned. 'Isn't that a nice surprise?'

'Hello, Eileen,' Francis said. 'I'm home.'

Eileen felt as if she was falling down a deep, dark hole. He looked more dashing and handsome than ever, with a bandage around his head which was particularly thick over his left eye. His legs seemed a bit unsteady, though he was smiling bravely, every bit the gallant wounded hero. She took a faltering step towards him because that's what everyone would expect her to do, but before she could reach him, he was surrounded by people who began to slap his back and shake his hand and give him the welcome she should have given him herself.

'What's going on?' Paddy O'Hara demanded and Jacob Singerman began to explain.

'It's Francis Costello. He's come home . . .'

'What's the matter, man? What's the bandage for?' she heard Dai Evans ask in a voice full of admiration and awe.

'I've lost me eye. Don't ask how it happened. All I can remember is some sort of explosion.' Francis looked more proud than upset, as if he'd come home with a medal. Eileen thought as she watched dazedly. No-one seemed to notice she hadn't gone near.

A small hand took hers and she looked down. Tony! 'What's going to happen now, Mam?' He looked frightened. 'Are we still going to Melling?'

Through the blur in her head she realised there was

something very important that had to be done. She sat down on the step and pulled Tony down beside her. 'Listen, luv, you're a big boy now, and I want you to go on a big message for me. I want you to catch the train into town. Nick'll be waiting and you must tell him what's happened. Tell him I can't come. I can't come *ever*! He'll put you on the next train back. Here's the money for your fare.'

'Is me Dad home for good, like?'

'I don't know, luv.' Her voice broke. 'I don't know anything.'

'Oh, Mam!' His little face contorted. He was about to cry, when she gave him a gentle shove. 'Go on, luv, before your Dad notices you. Nick'll be worried about where we are.'

'He's a brave chap altogether,' Paddy was saying emotionally to Mr Singerman. 'He'd still be waiting for his call up papers, a man of his age, if he hadn't joined the Territorials. Francis!' he called. 'Where are you? I want to shake you by the hand.'

'In a minute, Paddy,' Francis said jovially. 'I've been home all of a minute and I still haven't kissed me wife.'

Eileen froze as he came towards her. She turned her head when he clasped her by the shoulders so that his lips merely brushed her cheek.

'Where's Tony?'

'He's on a message,' she said stiffly. 'He'll be back shortly.'

'Eileen, luv,' he murmured softly so no-one could hear, 'they're discharging me from the army. I'm sorry about the way things have gone in the past, particularly last Christmas. But I promise I'll be a good husband from now on. You have my word on that, luv.'

Eileen didn't answer. *This wasn't happening!* The whole

462

world seemed to have turned itself inside out in the space of a few seconds and her brain was numb with the shock. Fortunately, Francis was dragged away by eager hands as the fact that he was home began to flash like wildfire throughout the neighbouring streets. Someone had even brought out a chair for him to sit on.

'Will you still be moving to this Melling place, Eileen?' Aggie Donovan asked. 'It'll be nice for Francis. He'll get better more quickly out in the country.'

The question brought Eileen to her senses. '*No!*'

'Well, in that case, girl, you can always count on a hand from me and the other women if he needs looking after. You mustn't think of giving up your job, now.'

'Thanks, Aggie.' She knew the neighbours would always be there to stretch out a helping hand.

Eileen was about to go back into the house which she thought she'd left forever, when her sister came running up.

'I was indoors,' Sheila panted. 'I've only just heard . . .'

'If you don't mind, Sheil, I'd like to be by meself awhile.'

'Anything you say, luv. I'll go and look for our Dad.'

Eileen went inside. With a sigh that came from her very roots of her being, she curled herself up in a chair and sat there for a long, long time, completely unaware of the commotion outside as more people turned up to welcome Francis Costello home. She prayed no-one would knock or come in, because she didn't want to be disturbed whilst she was with Nick.

He was twirling her around and around to *their* song and the music swelled, so loud, it filled the room. Eileen smiled. They were making love on the grass outside the cottage; then he was coming towards her down a sunny

London street with that funny loping walk, his lovely dark eyes smiling . . .

Tony's thoughts were also with Nick as he sat on the train making its way into town. He felt very small all by himself – it was the first time he'd travelled so far alone – but also rather important. It was a responsible thing Mam had asked him to do, but what did she mean, she couldn't come *ever*?

More than anything in the world, Tony had been looking forward to moving to the cottage in Melling, to the room with the white walls and the flowered curtains Mr Singerman had sewn specially for him. He couldn't wait to play football in the big garden, even though it meant playing by himself until he made friends at his new school, but most of all, he was looking forward to having Nick for a dad.

It was difficult to imagine there'd been a time he hadn't liked Nick, when nowadays he loved him almost as much as he did Mam. Nick was brave and handsome and had fought the Battle of Britain almost single-handed. But now, Tony thought fearfully, his real dad was home and what did that mean? His real dad never asked his opinion on things and seemed genuinely interested in the answer, or chucked him under the chin and called him 'son', the way Nick did. When he remembered the things his real dad did, Tony felt a ball of something unpleasant rise up and gather at the back of his throat, which made him shiver.

An old man sitting opposite noticed the shiver. 'Are you cold, lad?' he asked in a concerned voice.

'A bit,' said Tony. He wasn't cold at all, but how else could he explain the shiver to a stranger?

'I'll close the window.' The old man stood up and

began to struggle with the window without much success. Tony climbed onto the seat to help and between them they got it closed.

'Better now?' The man had a loose, drooping fold of flesh between his chin and his throat which wobbled when he spoke.

Tony nodded. He had a horrible feeling he was going to cry and kept blinking his eyes furiously to hold back the tears. He would sooner die than cry in public, and felt almost glad when the old man began to chatter on about football and how there'd never be another player like Dixie Dean, because it meant he had to be polite and concentrate and supply suitable answers from time to time. Anyroad, it was quite interesting and stopped him thinking about Mam and Nick and his dad for most of the journey.

When the train drew into Exchange Station, the old man said kindly, 'Keep your pecker up, lad. Things are never quite as bad as they seem,' and Tony realised he hadn't hidden his feelings after all.

As soon as he got off the train, he saw Nick. He was wearing one of those shabby suits Mam always made fun of, clutching the barrier with both hands as he strained his head to see the passengers making their way towards the exit. He didn't notice the little boy darting in and out of the crowds because his anxious gaze was set too high. He was looking for the smooth blonde head of Mam. Tony had handed over his return ticket and had it clipped and was tugging at Nick's sleeve before he realised he was there.

It was only then the tears which had been threatening for so long refused to be held back another minute, and Tony began to cry.

He and Nick stared at each other for quite a while,

neither speaking. There seemed no need for words. Then Nick picked him up and hugged him very tightly and Tony slid his arms around the neck of the man he'd so wanted to be his dad. After a while, Nick gave a long shuddering sigh and said in a strangely patient voice, 'What's happened, son?'

Jack Doyle thought his heart would break when he saw the frozen, tragic expression on the face of his girl.

They stood in the living room, facing each other. Jack shuffled his feet awkwardly. 'It ain't the end, luv,' he said gruffly. 'Y'can still see Nick.'

She shook her head. When she spoke, her voice was flat and tired, as if something had died inside her. 'No, Dad. I'll never see Nick again. It wouldn't be proper, not now.'

'But, luv . . .' he began, but she shook her head again.

'It wouldn't be fair, Dad, either. Nick's only young and he'd have no future with me. When could we get married? Under the circumstances, I can't leave Francis, can I?' Francis had been disfigured fighting for his country. For all his many faults, he was entitled to something from her, his wife.

'Nick'll find a way round things,' Jack said desperately. 'You'll see.'

'Oh, he'll try, but there's no way I'll let him.' There wasn't a shadow of doubt in her mind that he'd be waiting outside Dunnings on Monday, but she wouldn't go. She'd stay in the canteen with the girls and they'd laugh and joke and she'd join in, although she'd be tearing apart inside.

'If only I hadn't missed the train, Dad.' They'd all be in Melling by now, and Francis would have returned to an empty house. Would she have come back, she wondered, once she was ensconced with Nick and she discovered Francis was home? It was something she'd never know.

'My poor, dear girl!'

For the first time Eileen could remember, her dad took her in his strong arms and held her close. 'P'raps, once this bloody war's over . . .' he muttered, leaving the sentence hanging in mid-air.

'Aye, Dad, p'raps then, but I've a feeling it's only just begun,' she said hopelessly.

The entire thing was his fault, Jack thought guiltily. If Eileen hadn't been so daft, she wouldn't have been hooked up to Francis Costello in the first place.

'Mam!' Tony came in, panting. He'd run all the way from Marsh Lane Station. The knife twisted even further in Jack Doyle's heart when he noticed his grandson's eyes were red with weeping.

'Did you see him, luv? Oh, what did he say?' Eileen grabbed him, patting his clothes as if she could still feel traces of Nick there.

'He didn't say much, Mam,' the little boy said breathlessly. 'But he bought a card and wrote something on it. I've got it in me pocket.'

He handed Eileen a postcard. It was a sepia photograph of St George's Hall, with a few words written on the back in the familiar untidy scrawl. Eileen knew, before she read it, what the message would say, and despite everything, she wanted to believe it more than anything on earth.

We'll Meet Again, Nick!

If you have enjoyed
Lights Out Liverpool
don't miss

THE HOUSE BY PRINCES PARK
by Maureen Lee

available in Orion paperback

Price £6.99
ISBN: 0 7528 4835 6

Chapter 1
1918–1919

Olivia had only been to London once before, on her way to France, and she'd liked the busy, bustling atmosphere. But now, she hated it. She hated everyone looking happy because the war was over. Surely there must be people around who'd had relatives killed? And women who felt as empty and desolate as she did.

There might even be women, single women, single *pregnant* women, who could advise her, tell her what to do, how to cope, where to go.

Because Olivia didn't know. She didn't know anything except that she couldn't look for work in her condition. She'd always planned on going straight from France to Cardiff when the fighting ended. Matron had promised to take her back at the hospital where she'd been a nurse. But she'd got off the train in London and there seemed no point in going further. Matron wouldn't want her now. She was ashamed of feeling so helpless when, since leaving home, she'd thought of herself as strong.

Never before had she had to think about money or somewhere to live or where the next meal would come from. The small amount of money she'd earned was more than enough to buy occasional clothes and over the years she'd managed to save a few pounds. Now, the savings had almost gone on accommodation in a small hotel in Islington. She was eking it out, eating only breakfast which, as a nurse, she knew wasn't enough for a pregnant woman.

Despite this, she felt well and had never had a moment's sickness. It was one of the reasons she hadn't suspected she was pregnant when she missed her August period. She'd thought it was because she was upset over Tom. It could happen to women; their periods ceased when they were faced with tragedy. For the same reason, she wasn't bothered when there was still no period in September, but by October, she had started to feel thick around the waist, and the terrifying realisation dawned that she was expecting a child. At that point, her brain seemed to freeze. She became incapable of thought.

With November came the Armistice. Olivia was glad, of course, but instead of rejoicing, she felt only despair.

She still despaired, weeks later. New clothes were needed because she could hardly fasten the ones she had. Soon, she wouldn't be able to go out, and the proprietor of the hotel, a woman, was looking at her oddly because she was in her fifth month and seemed to be growing bigger by the day.

It was strange, but she rarely thought about Tom. If it hadn't been for the baby squirming lazily in her womb, she wondered if she would have thought of him at all. The ring he'd given her that had belonged to his grandfather was in her suitcase. It wasn't that the memory of him hurt, but it was impossible to believe the night had actually happened. It seemed more like a dream. She couldn't remember what he looked like or the words he'd said or the things they'd done.

Mrs Thomas O'Hagan! She recalled whispering the words to herself the day he'd left.

'What was that?'

Olivia was eating breakfast in the dingy dining room of the hotel. She looked up to find the proprietor glaring down at her. 'Sorry, I must have been talking to myself.'

'I've been meaning to have a word with you, Miss Jones,' the woman said officiously. 'I'll be needing your room from Saturday on. I've got regulars coming, salesmen.'

'I see. Thank you for telling me. I'll find somewhere else.'

'Not in a respectable place you won't,' the woman sniffed as she went away.

It had been bound to happen; either she'd run out of money or be asked to leave. Olivia's thoughts were like a knot in her head as she walked towards the city centre. She preferred the noise of the traffic to the quiet streets, even if the West End clatter was horrendous. There were homes for women in her condition. They were terrible places, so she'd heard, but better than wandering the streets, penniless. But how did you find where they were? Who did you ask?

If only she didn't feel so cold! Specks of ice were being blown crazily about by the bitter wind. She turned up the collar of her thin coat, pulled her felt hat further down on her head, but felt no warmer.

On Oxford Street, one of Selfridge's windows had a display of warm, tweed coats, very smart. Olivia stopped and eyed them longingly. Even if she'd been working, they would have been way beyond her means, but she hadn't enough to buy a coat for a quarter of the price from a cheaper shop.

She could, however, afford a cup of tea. She made her way towards Lyons' Corner House, noting all the shops were decorated for Christmas – only a few weeks away – and trying not to think where she would be when it came.

A large black car driven by a man in uniform drew alongside the pavement in front of her. Two young women got out the back, wrapped in furs, silk stockings gleaming. Their matching handbags, gloves and shoes were black suede. They swept across the pavement into a jeweller's shop in a cloud of fragrant scent.

Olivia had always been perfectly content to be a nurse,

earning a pittance. She'd never envied other women their clothes or their position in life. But now, standing shivering outside the jeweller's, watching the two expensively-dressed women seat themselves in front of a counter, the assistant bow obsequiously, a feeling of hot, raw jealousy seared through her body. At the same moment, the baby inside her decided to deliver its first lusty kick.

'Are you all right, darlin'?'

A man had stopped and was looking at her with concern as she bent double clutching her stomach with both arms.

'I'm all right, thanks.' She forced herself upright.

He nodded at her bulging stomach. 'You'd be best at home in a nice warm bed.'

'You're right.' She appreciated his kindness. Perhaps he wouldn't be so kind if he knew that beneath her summer gloves she wasn't wearing a wedding ring.

She recovered enough to make her way to Lyons. As she drank the tea, Olivia realised with a sinking heart that there was only one way out of her predicament. She would have to ask her parents for help.

She couldn't just turn up, not in her condition. Mr and Mrs Daffydd Jones could never hold up their heads in public again if it got out that their unmarried daughter was having a baby. Her father was a town councillor, her mother given to good works which she carried out with a stern, disapproving expression on her cold features. Olivia, an only child, was already in disgrace. There'd been a row when she gave up her job in the local library to take up nursing in Cardiff, and an even bigger one when she announced her decision to nurse in France. She daren't go near the place where she was born, let alone the house in which she'd lived.

A letter would have to be sent, throwing herself on their

4

mercy, and it would have to be sent today, so there would be time for a reply before Saturday when she left the hotel.

The tea finished, she searched the side streets for a shop that sold inexpensive stationery, then went to the Post Office and wrote to her mother and father, explaining her plight. She didn't plead or try to invoke their sympathy. She knew her parents well. They would either help, or they wouldn't, no matter how the letter was framed.

The reply came on Friday morning. She recognised her father's writing on the envelope. Although he wrote neatly, he had managed to make the 'Miss' look as if it might be 'Mrs' – or the other way round. The proprietor didn't look impressed when she handed the letter over. It crossed Olivia's mind that she could have bought a brass wedding ring and signed the register as Mrs O'Hagan, claiming to be a widow if anyone asked, but she'd been so confused it hadn't crossed her mind. Still, all it would have avoided was the indignity of, in effect, being thrown out. She would have had to leave in another few days when she came to the end of her savings.

The envelope contained a rail ticket and a curt note.

'Catch the 6.30 train from Paddington Station to Bristol on Saturday night. I will meet you. Father.'

Bristol wasn't far from where she'd lived in Wales. Relief was mixed with a sense of sadness as she re-read her father's note. No 'Dear Olivia.' He hadn't signed 'Love, Father'.

At least now she was leaving she could treat herself to a decent meal with what was left of the money.

Her father was waiting under the clock at Temple Meads station, legs apart, hands clasped behind his back, glowering. He was rocking back and forth on his heels, a big, broad-shouldered man, in an ankle-length tweed overcoat and a wide-brimmed hat that made him look rather

5

louche, though he would have been horrified had he realised. His coat hung open, revealing a pinstriped waistcoat and a gold watch and chain.

There was something forbidding about the way he waited, as if his thoughts were very dark. Olivia had always been frightened of him, although he'd never laid a hand on her, either in anger or affection.

He nodded grimly at her approach and had the grace to take her suitcase. He made no attempt to kiss the daughter he hadn't seen for two and a half years. Even if she hadn't been returning home under a cloud, Olivia wouldn't have found this surprising.

She followed him outside and he stowed the case in the boot of the little Ford Eight car that was the only thing she'd known him show fondness for. He would pat it lovingly when it had completed a journey and murmur, 'Clever little thing!'

'Where's Mother?' Olivia asked as they drove out of the station.

'Home,' he said brusquely.

There was a long silence. The gaslit streets of Bristol were mainly deserted at such a late hour. They passed a few pubs that had recently emptied and where customers still hung noisily around outside.

'Where are we going?' Olivia asked when the silence began to grate. She wondered if she was being taken to a home for fallen women. It would be horrid, but she'd put herself in a position where she had no choice.

'A Mrs Cookson, who lives near the docks, will look after you until . . . until your time comes.' His voice was grudging. 'It's most unlikely anyone we know will visit the area, but I would be obliged if you would stay indoors during daylight hours in case you're recognised. Mrs Cookson has been given money to buy you the appropriate garments. You'll be comfortable there. When everything is over, you will leave. I'll make arrangements for the child to be taken care of, if that is your wish. If you decide to keep it, don't expect your mother and me to help. We never want to see you again.'

Although she'd had no wish to see them, either, the bluntness of his words upset her. They made her feel dirty. She opened her mouth to tell him about Tom, but before she could say a word, her father said tonelessly, 'You're disgusting.'

She didn't speak to him again, nor he to her. Shortly afterwards, he turned into a little street of terraced houses, and stopped outside the end one. He got out, leaving the engine running, and knocked on the door.

It was opened by a gaunt woman in her fifties with hennaed hair and a vivid crimson mouth. She had on a scarlet satin dress and a black stole. Long jet earrings dangled on to her shoulders and she wore a three-strand necklace to match. Her long fingers were full of rings – if the stones were real, she must be worth a fortune, Olivia thought.

Her father grunted an introduction, almost threw his daughter's suitcase into the hall, and left. The Ford was already in motion by the time Mrs Cookson closed the door. She folded her arms and looked Olivia up and down.

'Well, who's been a naughty girl?' she said archly.

Olivia couldn't remember the last time she'd smiled. She'd been expecting to be treated like a wanton woman over the next few months and, although Mrs Cookson wasn't quite her cup of tea, it was a pleasant surprise to be greeted with a joke.

'Come along, dearie,' the woman seized her arm, winking lewdly. 'Come and tell us all about it. Would you like a cuppa? Or something stronger? I've got some nice cherry wine. I'm about to have a bottle of milk stout, myself. Oh, and by the way, call me Madge.'

available from
THE ORION PUBLISHING GROUP

___

☐ **Stepping Stones** £6.99
MAUREEN LEE
978-0-7528-1726-2

☐ **Lights Out Liverpool** £6.99
MAUREEN LEE
978-0-7528-0402-6

☐ **Put Out the Fires** £6.99
MAUREEN LEE
978-0-7528-2759-9

☐ **Through the Storm** £6.99
MAUREEN LEE
978-0-7528-1628-9

☐ **Liverpool Annie** £6.99
MAUREEN LEE
978-0-7528-1698-2

☐ **Dancing in the Dark** £6.99
MAUREEN LEE
978-0-7528-3443-6

☐ **The Girl from Barefoot House** £6.99
MAUREEN LEE
978-0-7528-3714-7

☐ **Laceys of Liverpool** £6.99
MAUREEN LEE
978-0-7528-4403-9

☐ **The House by Princes Park** £6.99
MAUREEN LEE
978-0-7528-4835-8

☐ **Lime Street Blues** £5.99
MAUREEN LEE
978-0-7528-4961-4

☐ **Queen of the Mersey** £6.99
MAUREEN LEE
978-0-7528-5891-3

☐ **The Old House on the Corner** £6.99
MAUREEN LEE
978-0-7528-6575-1

☐ **The September Girls** £6.99
MAUREEN LEE
978-0-7528-6532-4

☐ **Kitty and Her Sisters** £6.99
MAUREEN LEE
978-0-7528-7818-8

All Orion/Phoenix titles are available at your local bookshop or from the following address:

Mail Order Department
Littlehampton Book Services
FREEPOST BR535
Worthing, West Sussex, BN13 3BR
telephone 01903 828503, *facsimile* 01903 828802
e-mail MailOrders@lbsltd.co.uk
(Please ensure that you include full postal address details)

Payment can be made either by credit/debit card (Visa, Mastercard, Access and Switch accepted) or by sending a £ Sterling cheque or postal order made payable to *Littlehampton Book Services*.
DO NOT SEND CASH OR CURRENCY.

Please add the following to cover postage and packing

UK and BFPO:
£1.50 for the first book, and 50p for each additional book to a maximum of £3.50

Overseas and Eire:
£2.50 for the first book plus £1.00 for the second book and 50p for each additional book ordered

---

BLOCK CAPITALS PLEASE

name of cardholder ....

address of cardholder ....

delivery address
(if different from cardholder)
....
....
....
....
....
....

postcode ....   *postcode* ....

☐ I enclose my remittance for £ ....

☐ please debit my Mastercard/Visa/Access/Switch (delete as appropriate)

card number ☐☐☐☐☐☐☐☐☐☐☐☐☐☐☐☐☐☐

expiry date ☐☐☐☐   Switch issue no. ☐☐

signature ....

prices and availability are subject to change without notice